THE DISPOSABLE

D1598971

This book is a work of fiction. The characters, incidents, and dialogue are drawn from the author's imagination and are not to be construed as real. Any resemblance to actual events or persons, living or dead, is entirely coincidental.

THE DISPOSABLE
Copyright © 2020 by Katherine Vick.

Cover design by Nada Orlic.

Thinklings Books
1400 Lloyd Rd. #279
Wickliffe, OH 44092
thinklingsbooks.com

The Plot Bandits, Book 1

THE DISPOSABLE

by

Katherine Vick

Thinklings

Thinklings Books, LLC
Wickliffe, OH

PART ONE

No, hang on, that's already done with.

PART TWO

Nope, that one's over too.

Ah, here we are....

PART THREE

A piece of paper.

That's what it was, when all was said and done. A simple, straightforward piece of paper, the words upon it written in the familiar, authoritative, unnaturally regular lettering that signified instructions from the Taskmaster. It spelled out a sequence of events that had to be ruthlessly prepared for by every living thing in the Realm, and it was to be obeyed without thought and without question. That was merely the way it was, and to disobey would be unthinkable.

Wouldn't it?

Because there were days, sometimes, when he couldn't help but wonder if the world would really come to an end if he just chucked the paper away and went back to bed.

Probably not. After all, he was only a Disposable. Who would notice? Who would care? For if there was one word that could be used to describe Fodder of Humble Village, it was *ordinary*.

His nose was neither hooked nor pointed, neither snub nor aquiline, neither especially big nor noticeably small. His hair was brown— no fiery reds or midnight blacks for him—and his eyes, also brown, did not glow or flash or compellingly catch the gaze in any way whatsoever. He was neither fat nor particularly thin, no weakling but hardly of godlike physique, no towering giant but not notably on the short side. He was an ordinary man on an ordinary day, dressed in ordinary, rusty, badly fitting armour and waiting on a lonely road.

For what felt like the hundredth time since Preen had thrust the paper into his hand and frogmarched the four Disposables of Humble Village over to the barn to get changed that morning, Fodder lifted his now rather dog-eared instructions and skimmed through them.

Official Taskmaster Summary:
The Ring of Anthiphion:
Part Three

Elder and the band agree to follow the trail of the
stolen Ring and Erik finds that for some reason, he
can intuit which way it went. As they follow the
trail, local guards attempt to apprehend them but
are tossed aside.
While crossing a mountain pass late at night, the
companions hear screams and ride up to find men in
the livery of Sleiss attempting to abduct Princess
Islaine, who is riding to Mond for her wedding. With
the princess rescued but her guard dead, Sir Roderick feels he must see her back to the palace.
Since the Ring trail goes in a similar direction and
they need to speak to the king about shoring up the
borders against the possible return of Craxis, Elder
agrees to the detour. The princess and Erik argue
incessantly as she tries to push him around, and by
the time they reach the palace, they hate each
other.

Local guards attempt to apprehend them but are tossed aside....
Fodder sighed.

"Well, isn't that just the story of my life?" he muttered.

"What was that, mate?"

Fodder glanced up to find Shoulders standing just to his right,
shifting his shoulders awkwardly as he adjusted something in front of
his neck. Something that looked like it had started life as half a beer
tankard. Shoulders's left hand, as always in this matter detached from
the reasoning centres of his brain, rubbed reflexively against the skin
beneath his badly cut, scraggly dark blond hair and scruffy attempt at a
beard. There was something a tiny bit maniacal about his smile.

Fodder just succeeded in turning his grimace into a grin in time. He
was starting to worry about Shoulders.

"Nothing," he managed, rather proud of the cheery unconcern he
managed to instil into that single word. *Don't ask about the tankard.
You don't want to ask. You don't want to know. It will only hurt your
brain.* "I was talking to myself. Well, thinking about the fight and talking and...oh, it's no bloody good. Shoulders, what is half a tankard

doing tucked under your chin?"

Shoulders's smile spread as he rapped his knuckles against it with a hollow clunk. "Good, isn't it?" he exclaimed with, in Fodder's opinion, inexplicable enthusiasm. "I nipped into the pub before we left and got it off Flirt. She even cut it in two for me and knocked the bottom out, bless her."

"That's nice." Maintaining the smile was starting to hurt. *"Why?"*

Shoulders grinned. "Clank-proofing."

And there it is. I told you that you didn't want to know.

Fodder's smile slipped into pity. "You do know it won't work, don't you? He'll get you, mate. He always does."

But Shoulders was shaking his head, his eyes bright with the fervour of desperate hope. "Not this time. Not again. This'll thwart the bastard, I know it! Bloody Clank and his bloody broadsword, poncing about in his bloody armour on his bloody horse and thinking he can make sport of people's necks! Well, let's see what Mr All-Steel-And-No-Brain-Cells makes of this!"

Pieces, Fodder thought to himself, battling a near-overwhelming urge to drop his head into his hands. *That's what.*

"It's not in the Local Guard uniform code, you know," he offered wearily. "The Narrative might notice. If Preen spots it, you'll have to take it off."

Shoulders glanced back down the muddy road to where officious little Preen, in his gold-trimmed purple doublet and prissy, curly-toed shoes, was haranguing the burly Thump and stick-thin Clunny about some aspect or other of their artfully badly arranged armour.

"Preen." Shoulders snorted. "He's a little *oik.* How much time does he spend out there on the front lines, hmm? What does he ever do apart from strut about in the background, pushing people around and giving out bits of paper? One of these days I'm going to tell him where to stick his—"

"Places, everybody! The Narrative is on its way!"

Fodder winced. There was something about the way that Preen clapped his hands. The fingertips tapping delicately against the palm, elbows raised so that his connecting hands were framed by an entirely insincere smile—a smile that told the observant watcher that there were blasted heaths and barren wastelands that would be more appealing to him than this place. It also whispered of the universe's profound need for someone to give the man a damn good kicking. It would be for the good of humanity; Fodder just knew it....

But now was not the time for such thoughts. Through the screen of trees marking out the Rambling Woods, he could see the glow of the strange, brilliant, impossibly vivid light that signified the approach of The Narrative, and the dust rising from the track to show the galloping horses of the Merry Band as they wound their way towards another episodic encounter. Adjusting his neck tankard with an odd mixture of determination and resignation and palming his rusty short sword, Shoulders dropped into place beside Fodder. To their left, Thump fingered the pet cudgel that, for reasons no one had ever mustered the courage to ask about, he'd named Ronald; and beyond him, Clunny, with his perennial fidget and inexplicable odour of beans, wrapped his fingers around his crossbow and clicked a bolt into place. Behind them, Dunny and Midlin from Fertile Fields and Donk and Tumble of Provincial Town, who'd arrived that morning to Bulk Up their numbers, exchanged glances.

None of them spoke. Since this was Fodder's territory—and since Preen had dismissively labelled Fodder Lead Guard for this particular encounter—the spare Disposables would stay silent and follow his lead.

Poor blighters. Work was work, but Bulking Up was just plain drudgery. You didn't even get a description.

"Now, remember!" Preen's voice, it had to be said, perfectly suited the impression given by the way he clapped. "Follow the lead of the Merry Band and don't draw it out too much. This is only a time-filling skirmish, gentlemen, so let's make it quick and easy for them! I've got to be going; important things to do and all!"

Preen's voice was already fading into the distance as Fodder's lip twisted sardonically. Important things indeed. Every man and his dog in the Realm knew that Preen hated the sight of blood and guts and severed limbs and always found *important things to do* whenever the men he was supposed to be supervising went into battle.

Although he'd never yet let it stop him from doing his job, Fodder wasn't that fond of blood and guts and severed limbs himself.

Especially since they were always his own.

Just part of the job. And somebody had to do it. The instructions said so.

Though there was one tiny part of Fodder's brain that wondered what would happen if the instructions declared and nobody showed up.

The light approached the corner of the trail ahead, spreading rapidly towards them like a flood of glimmering water.

Grasping his spear, Fodder sighed. "Well, lads," he said with a simple shrug. "Here we go again."

Light...

"...following the instincts of a mere boy! This is folly! Surely—"

Zahora's irritable tirade cut off without warning as they rounded the corner of the quagmire-like wooded trail, and for a moment Erik was nonplussed at her sudden silence. But as he glanced at Elder, he saw the old man rein in his horse, his eyes narrowed. Following his steely-eyed gaze, Erik felt his eyes widen. Eight soldiers dressed in the tattered, ill-cared-for armour of local guardsmen had spread out to block their trail.

"Why, those impudent—!" Halheid reared, bear-like, in his saddle, his huge beard bristling as he reached over his shoulder for his fearsome axe. "What do they mean by this?"

"Hold, my impulsive friend." Sir Roderick had raised his visor, and though he fingered his broadsword thoughtfully, he did not draw it. "Leap not to violence so rapidly. Perchance they mean nothing by it, and this may yet be resolved without the spilling of blood."

"That seems unlikely," Gort retorted. The dwarf scratched his beard thoughtfully. "They look like money-grubbers to me; and I, for one, have no intention of paying up."

"Perhaps they know of our mission." Zahora's sharply drawn features were fierce. "Perhaps they seek to thwart our quest for the Ring."

"Them?" Slynder's voice was rich with silent laughter as he leaned back in his saddle, surreptitiously loosening his throwing knives. "Our enemy has already proven he has better troops to throw in our path than this motley gang. I'll bet half the money I won off Friend Halheid last night that all they want is enough coinage to fund an oblivious night in an alehouse."

"Whatever they want, we will not learn it sitting here." Elder's rich voice commanded instant silence. "Come, but be wary. Sir Roderick, stay with young Erik. The boy is not much used to combat, but his instincts are valuable. Keep him safe."

Erik felt a surge of resentment. He was sixteen, not some child to be brushed aside! But the armoured bulk of Sir Roderick had already pulled alongside him, his eyes stern as he lowered his visor; and reluctantly, Erik was forced to drop safely into his shadow.

"Eldrigon commands it, my young friend," the knight said firmly. "You are not yet skilled enough to mount your own defence."

"My good fellows!" Elder's voice hailed the guardsmen as they reined their horses to a halt before the eight dishevelled men. "Why do you block our trail?"

The lead guard tipped his head in a show of mocking respect as he sauntered forwards, holding his spear loosely but with intent. Three of his friends grouped behind him, leaving the other four to fan out across the road.

"This is our trail, my rich friends," the first man said with a sneer. "My Lord Khactas, baron of this fief, demands payment of all who use the roads that he so carefully maintains. For but a simple payment, you can be about your business and shall be troubled here no more."

"And if we do not pay?" Slynder retorted. "If we refuse to pay for passage through this mud bath of a track he reputedly maintains with such care?"

"Then we shall have no choice but to escort you good people to tell my lord of your reasons for shirking your debt in person." The guard leered. "You have already travelled a good league on his road and owe us for every hoofbeat. And my lord is not...kind to debtors."

Elder sighed wearily. "Fellows, we have no quarrel with you. But we are on a matter of some urgency and cannot afford to be delayed."

"Then just pay, why don't you, and stop with your jabbering!" One of the other guards—a scruffy, unshaven wretch dressed in armour that fitted strangely around his shoulders and neck—darted forwards, waving his sword. "This is our road!"

Sir Roderick drew himself up. "This is the kingdom of my noble King Cyrus, and I know without question or doubt that he would not permit the accosting of innocent citizens, were it known to him. We are on important business, you wretches, and you will stand aside!"

"No, you will pay!" the smallest of the guards, a weasel-faced little man hefting a crossbow, said threateningly. His companion, a burly thug, hulked menacingly. "Or you will face our lord!"

Slynder laughed. "I think you'll find we shall do neither!"

The unshaven man gave an indignant screech. "You will pay or you will die!"

"Or both." The lead guard's face was avaricious. "For your impertinence, we shall have every piece of coin and jewellery from you, my friends. And we shall take them from your corpses! Get them!"

The weasel-faced guard had already hefted his crossbow but staggered backwards screaming and clawing at his throat as one of Slynder's knives buried into it up to the hilt. Halheid had palmed his axe and spurred his horse forwards, slicing away the right arm of the burly guard in one clean motion before wheeling around and felling two of his fellows with the same awesome swing. Gort's hammer crashed down upon the skull of the flailing one-armed guard, felling him for good, even as Zahora's bow sang out, her arrows striking one guard through the eye and another in the shoulder. The latter, a giant of a man, still stumbled forwards with sword raised, but Sir Roderick's broadsword cut him quickly and cleanly in half.

"You swine!" The lead guard was roaring in impotent rage as he leaned back and flung his spear with deadly force at Elder, but the old wizard raised his hand and, with a violent flash, the spear spun back and, with cruel irony, buried itself through the chest of its owner. The guard stared down at it, goggle-eyed and shocked, before slowly keeling over backwards.

Now only one guard remained: the unshaven soldier, who stared about in sudden fear at the bodies of his colleagues before turning on his heels to flee.

"Stop him!" Elder commanded. "He'll bring others!"

Instantly obedient, Sir Roderick turned and spurred his horse after the unfortunate man, broadsword raised and ready. His first blow sliced his belly open, hurling purple entrails high into the air. The second, with a screech of yielding metal, sliced through his strange makeshift armour and sent his head flying from his shoulders.

Elder shook his head in despair as he stared down at the wreckage of human remains that lay strewn across the road around them.

"Poor fools," he said in soft regret. "Too foolish and greedy for their

own good. Come, let us leave this awful place. Erik, does the trail
continue down this road?"

Erik closed his eyes, reaching out with his mind. He felt for the
strange, tingling sensation that told him that the Ring had passed this
way.

"Yes, Elder," he replied. "Straight ahead."

"Then let us make good time."

Spurring his horse, Elder led them forward, mud splattering beneath
their hooves as they...

...passes

For a moment, there was only silence, greyness, and that gentle
sensation of *settling* that fell across the land when The Narrative had
passed: colours dulling, light fading as everything slipped quietly back
to simple, straightforward normality. Leaves rustled in the gentle wind;
birds previously unheeded began to sing again; and in the mud of the
forest trail, the various components of eight bodies lay scattered and
broken and—

"Sod it. Right through me bleeding liver."

"Could be worse. I think my liver's somewhere over there."

"Gagh! Gugai! Gurgh!"

"Clunny, if you want to say something, you'll have to take the
dagger out of your windpipe."

"Can anyone else hear something gurgling?"

Fodder opened his eyes. A long wooden spear shaft cut a line
through his vision towards the grey sky overhead. His chest tingled
uncomfortably as he carefully worked his shoulders and arms, the eight
inches of steel spear blade imbedded in his heart shifting with a nasty
squelch as he moved his muscles. Elbows sliding slightly in the inch-
deep mud, he struggled to right himself, pushing first onto his lower
arms and then up onto his hands, trying to ignore the unpleasant way
that the vibrating spear shaft threw his balance off and sent shudders
all through his body. Freeing one hand from the mud, he stilled its shiv-
ers quickly and fought back an urge to moan. *Bloody spears, bloody
pikes, bloody halberds. At least with swords and axes they take the
weapons away with them! And even arrows are so light that you can*

just leave them be and get on with things. But bloody spears, especially ones driven in by magic...

It could have been worse, he told himself sharply. And he'd had the ironic death. It had been Narratively memorable and nothing to be ashamed of. It had been a while since he'd died ironically. He supposed he must have been due.

And it hadn't been a bad skirmish: fairly standard and run-of-the-mill for a Disposable on duty. Limbs had flown, though luckily not his, since hunting for limbs after a skirmish wasn't the most interesting way to pass the time. They had impeded the Merry Band briefly but in a lively manner, just as they had been told. He'd gotten to leer and everything. There wasn't anything to moan about.

So why did he feel so...so *Shoulders-y* about it all?

Because it was always the same. Every time. A lonely road, a pass, a gatehouse—they'd stand there, make threats for a bit, and then start the fight because it was inconceivable that the Merry Band would spill blood without provocation. And then they'd get chopped to pieces, wait for Squick to show up and fix them, and head off to the pub.

That was his life. It had been his life ever since he'd been old enough to graduate from Village Urchin, and it would be his life until he either achieved Garrulous Old Man status and got to hang out in the pub for the rest of his days or retired to being a simple Background Villager.

He remembered the day that, back when he was an Urchin, he'd asked his father if he could join the Merry Band and ride around on Quests In Narrative when he grew up. And his father had looked him straight in the eye and said *no.*

Patting his little arm, his father had sat him down and explained once and for all how the world worked and why he'd never be anything but Fodder of Humble Village. Members of the Merry Band came from specific families, specially bred and trained. The many branches of the Royal Family provided all Kings, Queens, more mature Heroes and Heroines, and any spare Princes who happened to be required for the Quest. The even vaster Noble Family offered up Knights required for the Merry Band, as well as the Swooning Ladies, Noble Generals and Significant Nobles, and the occasional injection of breeding stock that prevented the Royal Family from producing eight-toed Princes and

Princesses with three-and-a-half noses. The Mage Family dealt with Sorcerers, Sorceresses, Crones, and Boys of Destiny. The latter had two career choices on passing out of adolescence: either to join the Royal Family and wait to mature into a King or to grow a grey beard to the right kind of length to become a Sorcerer. The Dark Family dealt with Dark Lords, Dark Generals, Dark Henchmen, and Evil Enchantresses. There were clans who bred Barbarians, Warrior Women and Noble Mercenaries, Thieves and Courtesans, Gods and Deities, Dwarves and Elves, and Assorted Freakish Creatures. There was a whole Family of Officious Courtiers, Scholars and Priests and Priestesses who, out of Narrative, were responsible for ensuring that the Taskmaster's every instruction was distributed and obeyed.

And then, there was everyone else. Some families provided Interchangeables—Minstrels, Assassins, Seadogs, Merchants, Innkeepers and Barmaids, Doomed Relatives, Servants and Maids, Trappers, and other small but regular Narrative Roles. The remaining people were Ordinary; background noise in busy scenes, having maybe one line, a brief description or an exclamation, if they were lucky. And there was always plenty of demand for young men to be guards, ruffians, soldiers, and bandits in the Disposables, provided you didn't mind picking up your own limbs afterwards. Why, his father had declared proudly, Fodder's great-grandfather, after whom he'd been named, had been disposed of sixteen times in the Quest in which the current Sorcerer had been the Boy of Destiny.

Since dying had seemed like the most excitement he was going to get, Fodder had applied to join the Disposables as soon as he was old enough. It had seemed like a good idea, at the time. He'd always taken pride in his work. Even Preen respected him in his own pretentious way, making sure that, more often than not, the role of Lead Guard for skirmishes scheduled in the regions of Humble Village and Rambling Woods was handed to him. Fodder had always made sure that the one line of regular writing that made up his lethal instructions was executed with efficiency and interest. The Narrative guided him in the right direction, of course, flowing around him like honey, suggestions for words and actions popping unbidden into his head; but whereas some Disposables grunted their lines and acted as wooden as blocks In Narrative, Fodder prided himself on instilling just that little bit of *character*.

But deep inside, something had always nagged at him. Those brief minutes of character had never quite been enough. The voice of the Urchin he had been, sitting on his father's knee, still echoed with a single question:

"But why not me?"

And his father's answer reverberated in reply:

"Because that's just the way it is."

And so, here he was, sitting in the mud with a spear in his chest and surrounded by the assorted remains of his comrades while the likes of Thud the Barbarian, Swipe the Thief, Clank the Knight, Harridan the Warrior Woman, Gruffly the Dwarf, Bumpkin the Boy of Destiny, and Magus the Sorcerer rode off merrily unscratched In Narrative.

Fodder allowed himself one brief sigh and then, as practicality set in, he let it go, just as he always did, every time. He was only a Disposable. And as things stood, that was all he'd ever be.

Glancing around, Fodder called out to his friends. "Everyone else all right?"

It was a daft question and they all knew it, but they always felt better somehow for knowing someone had asked. There was a chorus of shouts, mutters, and gargled spitting. To his left, Clunny had wrapped his hands around Swipe's dagger and was slowly drawing it out of his throat, whilst Thump rubbed the fingers of his remaining arm against the substantial hole in the side of his head. To his right, Dunny was amusing himself by making the arrow sunk deep into his right eye waggle up and down, whilst Midlin and Tumble compared torso slices. Donk was wearily reaching for his legs, which lay alongside his head, and squinting into the mud in search of missing organs. And Shoulders...

Lying in the mud, half a tankard had been split cleanly into quarters. One half of its owner lay beyond. And as for the other...

A protracted and indignant gurgling came from the muddy puddle that Fodder knew, with grim certainty, had filled the bottom of the ditch that ran by the road. Well, at least it wasn't up a tree. It had taken them two hours of poking with their halberds to dislodge him from that branch the last time, and Shoulders had used up so many swearwords that he'd had to start inventing his own.

With a muddy slurp, the headless body of Shoulders lurched

unsteadily to its feet. Clumsily reeling in the way that only a body separated from the part of it giving instructions can, it lurched towards the ditch, slipping and sliding but fortunately remaining upright. It reached down and groped uncertainly around for a moment. And then, awkwardly, its hands lifted something out of the puddle and into breathable air.

The hitherto unintelligible gurgling all at once became *extremely* clear.

"Bloody Clank! Bloody, bloody, *bloody Clank!*"

Shoulders's fingers were making some effort to wipe the worst of the mud away from his face, but the inevitable loss of motor control that came from having one's head cut off resulted in him mostly poking himself in the eye. With an irate huff, Shoulders abandoned that task and instead lifted his head by his bedraggled hair and twisted his hands to wring it out. His dangling face continued its tirade unbroken.

"Every time! Every bloody time! He doesn't have to hurl it so damned far; he does it on purpose, I swear he does! If he had a sense of humour, I'd think he was trying to be funny!"

Fodder sighed. Generally, he preferred those days when Clank sliced his friend's head off above the voice-box. Then the moaning was deferred until they were all on their way to the pub.

His hair wrung out, Shoulders lifted his head to a more normal vantage height.

"Six Quests! Six Quests and in every bloody skirmish, he's cut my head off! Ever since he took over Knight duties from old Gallant…oh, now, *he* was a gentleman, if he took your head off, he always made sure it landed somewhere soft and dry! But oh no, not Clank, not Mr Heads-Are-My-Signature-Move! This is a vendetta, it's personal, I know it is!"

"Well, you did go up to him after the third time it happened and call him a pillock," Thump remarked fairly. "But there's no point in moaning about Clank. He's in the Merry Band; he's not going to change to convenience a Disposable. He's doing his job, same as the rest of us."

The raspberry sound that Shoulders retorted with was made doubly unpleasant by the fact it came out of both ends of his throat. "Doing his job? Right. Of course… Because it's not like he hadn't already done me in with that belly swipe, was it? No, he had to go for the head as well! Just for the show of it! Utterly unnecessary! He'd already cut me open, and…oh, speaking of which…"

Carefully tilting his wrists, Shoulders angled his head so that his eyes were pointing down the length of his body. His face fell as he sighed with plaintive irritation.

"Perfect," he muttered mordantly. "Has anyone seen my entrails?"

Donk gestured from his prone position. "There's some over there."

"Nah, those are mine." Tumble scrambled to his feet, grasping his open belly protectively as he hurried over to retrieve them. "They got caught on Thud's axe."

"Gup gat gree?" Clutching his damaged throat, Clunny pointed to the branches of a nearby oak where something purple was dangling and swaying slowly in the breeze. "Gook gike gengrails gu gee."

Shoulders gave a gusty sigh. "They'll be full of splinters! My guts will be woody for days." He pulled a muddy face. "Where's Squick? That bloody pixie should be here by now!"

Grasping the shaft firmly in both hands, Fodder slowly pulled the spear out of his chest, trying to ignore the tingling itchy sensation that he'd come to associate with Narrative damage. Dropping the spear on the muddy ground with a splat, he pulled himself up and wandered over towards his friend.

"Don't start on Squick or he'll put your head on backwards again," Fodder remarked as he leaned down to pick up Thump's arm, tossing it over to him as he passed. "And we'd better have all our bits and pieces to hand when he gets here or he might decide he can't be bothered."

Shoulders was still staring forlornly up at his entrails. "How am I supposed to get those down?" he asked plaintively. "If I yank them, they'll get torn, and you know that Squick gets sniffy about fixing the damage if it didn't happen In Narrative!"

Rubbing the tingling, gaping wound in his chest, Fodder halted beside his headless friend. "I think that's more to do with being a clumsy oaf by falling downstairs and breaking your leg out of Narrative than fishing your entrails out of a tree after a Narrative battle," he pointed out reasonably. "If it happens in the course of the Quest, I'm sure he won't mind."

"If he ever turns up." Shoulders rolled his eyes. "Grumpy little—"

"You want those entrails back in your belly, laddie, you'd do best not to finish that sentence!"

Fodder's eyes snapped up. Hovering about a yard above their heads was a little man perhaps a foot tall, his face gnarled and twisted like an excitable fungus beneath his loose green hat, his legs crossed and arms folded as the nearly transparent silvery-purple wings that sprouted from his back worked at impossible speed to keep him hovering in midair. Contrary to what one might expect of someone who was, in point of truth, a pixie, he was wearing a tiny leather jerkin, canvas workman's trousers, and worn but practical boots. A glittering needle, a spindle of dusty purple thread, and two small pouches hung at his waist.

Fodder smiled in genuine relief. "Hi, Squick. What kept you?"

The potato-like face of the Senior Duty Pixie in charge of Human and Animal Repairs scrunched as his shoulders gave a wild approximation of a shrug that pitched his hovering position about a foot off to the right. "I was at Humble Village, putting the haunches back on Bessie." He huffed loudly. "I told Stout, I said, that ain't a job for a Senior Duty Pixie on his way to a skirmish, not when there're limbs hanging off in the Rambling Woods, but would he have it? He would not! *Fix my cow back up*, he says; *I need another helping of good stewing steak or the veg I've cooked will spoil!* I ask you!"

"Beef stew tonight, is it?" Thump looked happy as he wandered over, cradling his loose arm. "Great! And Bessie's haunch is always the best; old Daisy's getting a bit stringy."

Fodder grinned to himself. He remembered the time, a couple of Quests ago, when a Princess named Sweetness had stopped the night off Narrative with the Merry Band at the Archetypal Inn and had refused to eat the roast on the grounds it had once been a living thing. He could vividly recall the look on her porcelain face when Stout the Innkeeper had respectfully pointed out, in deference to the fact that the Royal Family clearly had people to deal with butchery for them and obviously had no idea how real life worked, that actually the cow *still was* a living thing. All the beef in the village came from the same four cows, which were knocked out, butchered, and then fixed up with their bits replaced by the Duty Pixies on a regular basis. In fact, he'd told her, he was pretty certain that the cows had no idea that they were eaten once a week.

"Can we not talk about food?" Donk requested. "It's really disconcerting to feel your stomach rumble from three feet to your left."

Squick had apparently forgotten his Bessie-related grump as he surveyed the scene before him with a professional eye. "Quite a skirmish you lads had," he remarked thoughtfully, jerking the silvery needle out of his belt and deftly threading it. "An arm, a pair of legs, and...hah, of course, a head needing reattachment. A few organs to patch up and put back in place, one skull, one windpipe, an eye and a heart in need of reassembling, and three torsos to close up. Anyone reckon they need any replacements?"

"I think my entrails might have had it," Shoulders remarked, gesturing to the tree with a kind of doleful hopefulness. "I wouldn't mind trading them in."

"Hmmm..." Squick sucked thoughtfully at his teeth. "I think we may be lacking a bit in entrails—we ain't finished restocking after the Final Battle for *The Sword of Grul.* Hold up, I'll check."

Pulling open the first of his two pouches, Squick shoved his arm inside up to the shoulder and rooted around. "Hmmm," he said again. "I've got some, laddie, but I don't think they're your size. Young Offle's doing his best to whip up some more supplies, but it ain't quick or easy to conjure up a decent organ out of nowt. I could put an order down for next time, get Thud or Clank to do the honours In Narrative when the new entrails are ready...?"

Shoulders's sigh could have blown down a small village. "No, it's fine," he said wearily. "Just do your best with the ones in the tree."

Squick gave an earthy chuckle as he opened his second pouch. Purplish pixie dust glittered as he dipped his needle into the pouch and withdrew it shimmering. "Well, if it makes you feel better, my best is better than most. Get your bits together, lads. I'll have you good as new in no time."

* * *

In spite of having lived in Humble Village all his life, Fodder often had trouble finding his way to the Archetypal Inn. It had a tendency to wander.

The layout of Humble Village was very rarely mentioned In Narrative and was, as a result, relatively stable. The Archetypal Inn was the one feature that most often merited a description and hence,

Fodder had, over the course of the last few Quests, drunk in the Lion Inn, a sturdy, stone-built building at the foot of the hills leading to the Bandit Pass; the Rose and Crown, a friendly wooden building next to the fishing pond with a broad veranda and a stable yard to the rear; the Slaughtered Lord, a rather creepy two-storey construction made of dark, tarred wood half hidden at the edge of the trees; and even in the Hunter's Horn, a lonely inn on a remote hillside with a squalid fireplace and a broken sign, a good mile up the road towards Bandit Pass and almost beyond the village's designated limits altogether. The latter had not gone down well with the village's drinking population.

But luck was with the Disposables today. As they arrived at the small, scrubby village green, they found the Archetypal Inn parked up not off towards the cattle pen where they'd left it, but on the opposite side of the green. Today, it was a wood-and-stone construction all under the name of the Good Shepherd. The slight greenish twinkle settling across the neatly carved eaves implied that Higgle, the Duty Pixie in charge of Landscape and Architecture Alterations, had only just finished work.

"So, are you lads sticking around for the night?" Shoulders had cheered up a great deal now that his head had been efficiently re-attached, although he remained apparently oblivious to the fact that his left hand, as it had done for most of the time since Clank had joined the Merry Band on a regular basis, was rubbing along the line of his neck rather rabidly. "Or are you hopping a cart back to Fertile Fields and Provincial Town?"

Donk smiled down at him. Shoulders was by no means short, at least with his head attached, but Donk was one of those enormous, friendly gentle giants who simply towered over everyone. He was vast enough that he generally got described In Narrative as such, in a passing word or two, even when on Bulking Up duty. "Preen's asked us to stick around for a day or so," he replied cheerfully. "On the instructions it says there'll be a bandit ambush up in Bandit Pass tonight, and it'll probably be more than Lurk, Pounce, and Twister can handle on their own. I think we'll be Bulking Up."

"Tonight?" Shoulders sighed wearily as they pushed open today's dark wooden creaky door and stepped into the long, low-beamed room with a flickering fire and broad counter that would be this evening's local. "I've barely got my head back on!"

The inn was quite busy, as it generally was when it was conveniently placed for the villagers, but a table by the fire with eight foaming tankards of ale had been left empty for them. A steaming stew pot was just being lifted from the fire by a woman dressed in a familiar white blouse and a long red skirt topped by a brown apron. Her hair, which changed as often as the inn she worked at, was dark and curly today, rather than the blonde or bright red The Narrative more often demanded, but as ever, there was no mistaking her.

Fodder smiled. Good old Flirt. She knew what Disposables needed after a hard day of being slaughtered.

The Barmaid of the Archetypal Inn grinned as the men filed over, professing various degrees of undying love for her as they took vast swigs of ale and savoured the stewy aroma. Fodder could see from the slight hint of glimmery pink around her cleavage that she had recently reduced the size of her chest back to normal—although The Narrative required that a Barmaid should be busty, Flirt had not been so endowed by nature and had to employ the services of Urk, the Duty Pixie in charge of Cosmetic Adjustment, for her hair and chest whenever the Quest required it of her. Thump had once dared to ask her, with a hint of a leer that certainly hadn't helped, why it was that she didn't leave her chest inflated between Quests and have done with it. The lengthy and irate lecture he had received on issues of weight, comfort, and balance had insured that the subject had not been raised again.

"All right, boys," she said cheerfully. "How far did Shoulders's head go this time?"

Thump rumbled a chuckle. "I think it was the record, actually. And it landed in a puddle."

Ignoring Shoulders's irritable huff at the reminder of the indignity, Flirt started spooning stew into the bowls. "Any good swordplay, was there? Double reverses or half-moon crescents?"

At the flurry of blank looks she received, Flirt sighed and deposited the stew pot on the floor. "You know!" she exclaimed, hauling the poker out of its cast iron support and flourishing it back and forth in what Fodder had noticed many times before was an alarmingly professional manner. "Like this!" She swept the poker back and forth in a complicated manoeuvre that Fodder was reasonably certain he couldn't have achieved at his best. "Or this!" The curving sweep that followed nearly sent Midlin fleeing, albeit unnecessarily, under the table. "I know Clank's been studying them both; I heard him telling Harridan so last night when they stopped here for an overnight paragraph. He said he was looking for a chance to use them."

"Sorry, Flirt." Fodder smiled sympathetically as he took another swig from his tankard. "We were a bit busy getting chopped up to watch the swordplay."

Flirt gave a gusty sigh. "I wish I could come along," she declared with palpable frustration. "If I was in full armour and just Bulking Up at the back, I know it wouldn't affect The Narrative. And nobody would spot me, would they…"

"Preen would never allow it." Fodder felt himself squirm at the dying of the brief surge of light within her eyes. "You know what he's like. Besides, if you went into battle against the Merry Band, you'd probably *win*."

There were guffaws around the table but the gratitude in Flirt's smile was far more rewarding. Carefully, she lifted the pot back up and resumed her dishing out.

"You lads are properly fixed, aren't you?" she said as she watched Thump shovelling Stout's best Bessie stew down his gullet with unseemly haste. "Only, I remember what happened last week with the vegetable soup…"

"It was one little stab wound!" Clunny protested, his spoon halfway to his lips. "I didn't notice, I swear, and I helped clean up the floor-boards, didn't I?"

Flirt's single raised eyebrow spoke volumes, but she chose not to comment on the previous week's memorably messy evening meal. "I think I should warn you," she said instead as she took Thump's already-emptied tankard and gestured to Stout's ever-growing adolescent son Lank for a refill. "I saw Preen outside talking with Bard the Minstrel. We may be in for a performance of *the story so far* again tonight."

A chorus of groans sounded around the table, and Fodder enthusiastically added his own. "Again?" he declared wearily. "What is it with Preen and this *story so far* business anyway? We've read the instructions. We spent half of them getting chopped up! It's hardly as though we don't know what's been happening."

"Not to mention that Bard's voice makes me want to smack him," Tumble added matter-of-factly. "I think it's all the unnecessary flourish. And the pose. There's definitely something about the pose."

His companions nodded in sage agreement. No man who stood with one hand on his belt and the other extended flat towards the ceiling as he melodramatically recited things that they already knew did not deserve to have some manner of violence inflicted upon him.

"We could pelt him," Dunny suggested, waving his fork in an offhand manner that considerately splattered his companions with little bits of stew. "It worked over at the Farmstead during *The Sword of Grul*. Old Bumble—you know, the plump chap who always plays Doomed Uncles and the like? Well, he took offence at being described as rotund and foolish and threw a cabbage at Bard's head. When we all joined in, Bard left in a huff."

"He is just doing his job." It was Midlin who piped in. The Disposable from Fertile Fields was a quiet, bland, unremarkable man who spoke so rarely that Fodder, to his own acute embarrassment, often forgot he was there. If anyone had been born to be Ordinary, it was Midlin. "We shouldn't grumble, really."

Clunny gave an undignified snort. "Wouldn't that just take all the fun out of life? Not to mention that we'd never hear Shoulders speak again."

Shoulders's mouth gaped indignantly, but, fortuitously or not—for Fodder couldn't quite decide whether the grumbling would have been worse than the interruption—the creak of the door being opened and the audible groans of his companions at the sight of the foppish figure framed dramatically in the doorway cut him off.

Bard the Minstrel was a relatively young man with shoulder-length blond hair that could only be described as flowing and a tiny blond beard clinging to his chin that could only be described as daft. His eyes, inevitably, were blue. His floppy scarlet hat, equally inevitably, was crowned by a plume of blue feathers. His doublet was a painfully fashionable mass of patched colours, and his hose were striped in purple and white. The toes of his shoes curled up so far that they touched the top of his feet. He had a green cape that whipped dramatically in the breeze. His hands rested upon his hips. His chin was raised. The smile on his face succeeded in being both facile and condescending.

Fodder shook his head. One look at the man really did tell you everything you needed to know. Add the fact that he was a good friend of Preen, and you could virtually write his biography.

"Good morrow, gentle village folk!" Bard strutted gamely inside, cheerfully allowing the door to slam in the face of Crook the Shepherd, who had been waiting impatiently for him to move aside so he could get inside for a quiet sit down and an ale. "A glass of your finest mead to wet my whistle, if you please, good wench! I will have much need of a well-lubricated voice before this night is done!"

Once again, Flirt's eyebrows did the talking for her. *Wench* had never been a term that sat particularly well on her shoulders, but she knew better than to offend a friend of Preen. With an expression that would have required whole pages of Narrative to do justice to, she left the resigned-looking Disposables and headed over to the counter. Her fists were powerfully clenched.

"Told you," Tumble remarked under his breath. "It's the voice. Makes me want to smack his chops every time."

"Maybe we could chop his head off and get Squick to take his voice box out?" Dunny suggested, with a gesture that sent ale slopping down his tunic. Fodder had always liked Dunny well enough, but he'd never been all that fond of his shocking table manners. "He probably would. I heard him say he thinks he's a pillock."

"It wouldn't stop him," Donk remarked morosely. "He'd just write it down and get Preen to read it out for him."

"The trouble is, he thinks he's The Narrative," Fodder chimed in sourly, watching the pompous twerp with barely concealed dislike. "He doesn't even know what half the words he uses mean. I mean, good *morrow?* It's almost evening!"

Tumble pulled a face. "It was probably the best he could come up with. I'm not sure there is a pompous, outmoded term for greeting someone after midday."

"Good affow?" Clunny offered with a hint of a grin.

Several tankards of ale were snorted.

Over by the counter, Bard finished wiping and smacking his lips with melodramatic pleasure, and placed down his barely touched mead with a thud. "Ah!" he proclaimed. "A fine and hearty brew indeed! I feel fortified, alive, and ready to entertain these good people with tall tales of faraway derring-do!"

"Not that far away," Thump muttered under his breath. "They're only out in the Woods."

"And so!" His cape flaring, Bard proceeded forth with what Fodder could only assume was his best attempt at *striding manfully* across the room, to stand, head lifted and expression lofty, in the very centre of the floor. One hand, he rested firmly against his belt. The other, he raised towards the rafters—open to the heavens as though pleading for inspiration. Fodder always clung to a vain hope he'd be inspired to bugger off, but such had yet to come to pass.

"Settle ye down, good people, and hearken well!" Bard's fingers flared intently at the empty air. "For I shall tell you a tale—unfinished yet, but already teeming and riddled with emotion and adventure. For I am here to tell you of the Quest for *The Ring of Anthiphion!*"

Like the air release from a punctured bladder, a great sigh of resignation settled across the inn. The men and women of Humble Village sagged wearily back in their seats and stared into their drinks as one, quietly trying to tune out a too-familiar horror.

"The Ring of Anphithion! The mark of power of the greatest king the world had ever known! Legendary! Powerful!"

"Pronounced *Anthiphion*," Flirt added sardonically as she wandered over to rejoin the Disposables by the fire. "Even *I* know that."

With all due respect to him—which wasn't that much, Fodder had to admit—Bard didn't miss a beat. "But our hero, young Erik, an ordinary stable boy at his Uncle Alwin's remote and lonely inn, knew nothing of such ancient folly. He lived an ordinary—such an ordinary—life in the peaceful farming kingdom of Doss, knowing nothing of the ancient legends and a magic ring that would cast his world asunder!"

"What's this Quest's Boy of Destiny called?" Shoulders queried absently, paying scant attention to Bard's performance. "I can never tell one from another."

"Bumpkin," Thump submitted as he drained his second tankard of ale with barely a blink. "He's old Magus the Sorcerer's great-nephew. He's not too bad—over-angsts a bit, but then don't they all?"

Clunny grinned suddenly. "You know how up himself old Magus

is? Well, my grandpa says he was the Boy of Destiny back in *Timoni's Firebird*. Back then he was known as Yokel, and he got dumped in a horse trough by a feisty princess. Sort of adds a new dimension to the wise-and-noble-guardian act, doesn't it?"

"...lonely and lacking in companions, Erik's only true friend was the eccentric, mysterious but friendly old man known as Elder, who lived in his crumbling tower..."

"It's always a tower, have you noticed?" Tumble remarked clinically. "And a crumbling one at that. These mysterious, eccentric old men pretending not to be wizards always hang out in crumbling towers. You'd think they'd have enough time on their hands waiting for those Boys of Destiny to grow up to make a few repairs or move into a nice cottage somewhere."

"...these mysterious strangers, who seemed known to Elder and held him in strange regard. The first was introduced as Sir Roderick, first knight of the Kingdom of Nyolesse and legendary for both his skill and for his tragic love of a mysterious woman he could never have..."

"Skill!" Shoulders all but spat the word, almost succeeding in drowning out the melodramatic monologue behind him. "Where's the skill in chopping someone's head off, hey? What's legendary about that? That Clank is nothing more than a sword-wielding bully boy!"

Bard was soldiering on, although his expression, Fodder noted with no little satisfaction, had become somewhat strained.

"...Slynder, a thief renowned and resented for his skill throughout the Six Kingdoms..."

"Swipe," Clunny noted. "I had a drink with him once and he's not so bad. He's just a bit of a smug bastard. And he never shuts up."

"Wandering fingers, too," Flirt inserted grimly.

"...Gort, a dwarf miner, with a mysterious resentment of Slynder..."

Donk chuckled slightly. "Gruffly," he said. "Did you know he's scared of enclosed spaces?"

"...Halheid, a gruff barbarian from the northern reaches, brutish, uncivilised, and quick to anger..."

"Thud." Flirt's expression was icily irritable. "Thick as two short planks, isn't he? And he can't hold his drink—I have to put cold tea in his tankard when he drinks In Narrative so he doesn't fall off his chair and mess up the flow of the story." She sniffed sourly. "He always pulls me onto his lap and gives me a chummy slap on my thigh and bloody hell, *it bruises*. And his beard smells like a badger's backside when you kiss him."

Fodder felt a momentary surge of something he couldn't quite define. Not exactly guilt, not exactly resentment, not exactly pity either but…something or other. He was no Minstrel, chucking a convenient word into a hole it barely fitted, but he did know that, as much as he had found himself resenting his lot as he'd sat in the mud with a spear through his chest, he'd never really considered before that it was as bad, if not worse, to have no choice about having your thigh slapped until it bruised and kissing someone with a beard that smelled like the hind end of a badger.

"…and Zahora, a quick-tempered warrior woman who disliked Halheid the barbarian for his attitude that only men should fight…"

"Harridan." Flirt's voice was vaguely wistful. "She gets to beat Thud up and anyone else who touches her. If The Narrative hadn't decided she has to fall in love with the groping git, I'd love to have her job, wouldn't I? I'd show the next sod who pinched my bum a thing or two…"

And she deserves it too. She should have it, if life were fair. The thought popped into Fodder's head almost before he realised it was there; and sternly, he told it to push off. It was stupid to have such thoughts, thoughts he had made himself abandon as an Urchin, thoughts about a different life and how things just weren't quite right. There was no point to thinking like that. After all, there wasn't exactly anything he could do about it.

"…though he was banished from the room, Erik could not resist listening at the door. But the words were muffled by the sturdy wood, and he could make out only that something had been stolen and that someone called Myhessia was pleading for his aid, for the age-old prophecy of the Seeress Mydrella was finally coming to pass…"

"There's always a prophecy, have you noticed?" Dunny remarked with a casual chuckle. "These Narrative folk don't seem to be able to cope without one. What do you reckon they'd do if it wasn't there to shove them kicking and screaming in the right direction?"

Fodder hadn't meant to say anything. But Dunny's simple observation struck an alarming chord, and the words popped out of his mouth almost before he'd had a chance to think about them. "Probably the same thing we'd do without instructions from the Taskmaster. Find out the future for ourselves."

"…in spite of the objections of his comrades, Elder smiled in benediction at Erik and told him that he admired his spirit and that he could indeed be a part of their noble quest…"

Except for the drone of Bard's voice in the background, there was a sudden silence at Fodder's table. The seven other Disposables stared as one, regarding Fodder with expressions that ranged from confusion to discomfort.

"You *what?*" Clunny declared at length, his features twisted into an expression of outright incredulity. "Mate, you do realise what you just said is *rubbish*, right?"

"Yeah, don't be stupid." Tumble gave a slightly edgy laugh. "A prophecy's just a prophecy, a convenient shortcut for The Narrative. The instructions are *life*. You can't find a future without them because there isn't one."

"But what's the difference?" To Fodder's surprise, it was Flirt's voice that softly intervened. "They both dictate our future, don't they? Map it out? And if Dunny's saying following prophecies is foolish…"

"But it isn't, though." Once again, the quiet, unexpected voice was Midlin's. "I've been in enough stories to know that bad things happen if a prophecy isn't followed. It has to come true."

"But how do you know?" Flirt's eyes were strangely intense. "How do you know that what'll happen when a prophecy's not fulfilled is bad when they *always are?*"

"…found his uncle Alwin's inn ablaze and there, nailed cruelly to the crumbling wall, his uncle's brutally mutilated body! The strange, warped creatures surrounded them, teeth gnashing, eyes blazing like the fire that had engulfed all Erik ever knew…"

"The good old AFCs." Clunny's overly cheerful intervention was more to break the uncomfortable moment, Fodder suspected, than out of any real desire to speak, and a part of him felt a profound relief at his friend's change of subject. He didn't want to consider the part that was feeling *disappointment*. "Bless them. I was talking to Fang and Gibber from the AFC camp a few days ago, and they were telling me about the

Assorted Freakish Creature look that Urk came up with for this Narrative's Quest. They've got these big bat-like ears, leathery grey skin and claws, not to mention two rows of teeth! Can you imagine having so many teeth that you have to take them out to eat?"

Thump forced a grin. "I've always thought if I hadn't been born human, it might have been fun to be an AFC, with all that leaping and wailing and tooth-gnashing they get to do. Minions of Darkness get all the fun. It'd make a nice change from standing around in rusty armour getting slaughtered just to break up The Narrative a bit."

"...and Erik felt a fury well within him as he faced the killers of his uncle, a power deep inside that he'd never truly touched before, never known that he was capable of..."

Fodder wasn't entirely sure why he couldn't fight the strange urge to stir up a subject his friends clearly did not find comfortable, but something was itching at his soul and nothing but speaking out could scratch it. "A nice change. Yeah." He took a deep breath, wondering if he really had the nerve to say the words out loud, to articulate these secret, private thoughts. "But don't you lads ever wonder... *why?*"

"...as we move into *The Ring of Anthiphion* Part Two! Approaching the mountains..."

Thump pulled a face at him as he wiped an ale-foam beard from his chin. "Why what?"

Fodder frowned. *Go on. Just say it. Just do it.* "Why we have to do this? Getting chopped up and left in bits in ditches? Why does it have to be us?"

"...told Sir Roderick that he must return to Nyolesse, for the wedding of Princess Islaine to Prince Tretaptus of Mond was fast approaching, and with the threats made against the princess by her rejected, embittered ex-suitor, the evil High Lord of Sleiss..."

Dunny shrugged, shaking loose various pieces of half-adhered beef stew that had until then clung tentatively to the front of his tunic. "We volunteered, didn't we? Better than being a Background Villager or a Farmhand."

Why was it so hard to say? Why was it so hard to explain? "But why is that the only choice we've got?"

His friends were glancing at each other—and the looks they exchanged seemed to be of one solid opinion.

It was Tumble who cleared his throat gruffly and voiced it. "Mate," he said quietly. "How many tankards have you had?"

"...barren wastes where legend had it that an evil warlord had reigned supreme thousands of years before, and where the ancient prophecy proclaimed great evil would rise again..."

"We're Ordinary." Donk's gentle voice rumbled out. "That's what being Ordinary *is.*"

Fodder found himself grimacing. They were right. Everything he had been taught, every part of the world in which he lived was telling him not to be so stupid, to sit back, enjoy his ale, and let this foolishness drop into nothing. But that truculent corner of his mind, the one that was tired of waking up in the mud in several different pieces—the part of him that couldn't help but feel that Shoulders had a point about his constant humiliating decapitations—the part of him that whispered that however hard he tried, however much character he tried to instil, his contributions to The Narrative would never actually amount to anything worth remembering...that part refused to let him back down.

"But don't you ever feel that what we do is just a bit...pointless?" he asked softly.

"...arrived at the Temple of Athiphnion, which had been carved out of a mountain in honour of a great king who united the Six Kingdoms against a vicious enemy from across the seas by using a magical ring fashioned for him by the great and ancient sorcerer Eldrigon and tied to his blood and his alone..."

Once again, his friends exchanged a flurry of glances. These ones implied opinions had shifted from assuming the damning influence of alcohol into wondering if good old Fodder, the reliable Disposable, was actually quite right in the head.

Tumble was the first to venture into the murky waters of this new turn of conversation. "We play our part In Narrative. Just as the instructions tell us. We do what has to be done. And that's important."

"But why is it important?"

Clunny stepped in. "Because the Taskmaster says so."

"But why does the Taskmaster say so?"

Clunny blinked in disbelief. "Because it's the Taskmaster! The one who runs The Narrative? Honestly, mate, what kind of question is that?"

"The kind we ought to be asking?" Fodder had no idea where that had come from, and the looks of shock that rippled over his friends' faces implied that *not right in the head* was venturing in the direction of *in need of medical help*. "I mean it, though. We do everything we do because the Taskmaster says so, but we've got no idea *why*." It was like someone had lit a fire inside of him—the effort to speak of moments before tossed away, words tumbling out, before he'd even had time to think them through. "Yes, it's life, it's the way it's meant to be. But *why* is it life and *why* is it meant to be this way? Why does the Taskmaster decide that some of us get to ride around on horseback and have a great Quest while others get chopped up and left in the mud? Why do the instructions give all the character to those from the families that supply the Merry Band and never to anyone who's really Ordinary? Why them? *Why not us?*"

Until that moment, Flirt had remained silent, simply listening to the debate with her familiar eyebrow raised. But abruptly, she inserted a thunderbolt phrase:

"Why do we have to obey the Taskmaster at all?"

"...elder son Craxis was consumed by jealousy and smote his brother Avikhelion in an attempt to steal their father's Ring..."

Slowly, almost absently, Fodder found his eyes drifting around the table, drinking in the faces of his companions as they absorbed this brazen statement: Shoulders, his expression incredulous as his left hand continued its reflexive journey along his neck; Dunny, with his fork frozen halfway to his lips and dripping gravy down his front, stared at Flirt in openmouthed astonishment; Tumble, his solid, good-natured features locked in shocked horror; Midlin, his bland face closed, shut down, withdrawing from words he could not stand to hear. Clunny's thin face was riddled with disconcertion, Thump's with outright discomfort, and Donk was staring at her with the quiet but undeniable stare of someone who has decided a good friend has gone stark staring mad.

And, leaning back against the edge of the fireplace, was Flirt, one eyebrow raised, her eyes almost surprised at her own nerve. But...there was something, just something, glittering there. A kind of awakening. A kind of...hope?

"...Craxis had discovered evil, life-prolonging magicks and, hidden in the Northern Wastes, he vowed revenge on Eldrigon and his daughter Myhessia…"

It was the final step. The final step along this impossible, runaway train of thought. *Why do we have to obey the Taskmaster at all?* Fodder wasn't sure if he would have taken it.

But Flirt had. She'd thrown it out into the world like a net, and Fodder found himself thoroughly caught.

"She's right." He was barely aware he had spoken aloud until he felt the incredulous eyes of his friends swinging as one in his direction. "Why do we?"

Clunny swallowed hard. "You've both gone bonkers. Stark staring bloody bonkers!"

"It's the *Taskmaster*." Thump stressed the latter as if he was addressing an imbecile. "The one who runs The Narrative? You can't ignore it! It's…it's life!"

"Why not?" Fodder was feeling vaguely as though he were In Narrative himself, as though some other force had hijacked his lips and taken him over completely. But a thousand days on lonely roads being chopped to pieces and pulled back together rode up inside him and screamed with frustration.

"Why not?!" Clunny's admonishment was sharp enough that Bard faltered slightly in his description of the stone temple where Myhessia the sorceress had guarded the Ring of Power. "Because it's the bloody Taskmaster! It's the reason we're here!"

"…they parted company, Myhessia to protect the Ring and Eldrigon to watch over the descendants of Craxis's murdered brother, whom they knew they must now protect, for their blood was the only other that could wield the great Ring and one of that line, so it was prophesied, would defeat Craxis and reunite the Six Kingdoms under one benevolent rule…"

"But why is the Taskmaster the one who gets to decide? Why is this the way we live?" Fodder could see from the horrified looks that accompanied this heresy that he wasn't making many allies with this re-emphasised line of thought, but he struggled to articulate the nagging in his soul all the same. "We go out, we get chopped up, we get fixed, we go to the pub, while people born to the right families get to ride around with swords and magic, having adventures, having *character*. Whereas us—it's so…futile."

Midlin's voice, when it came, was low but profoundly audible. "It's not futile. It's life. Just life. And it isn't going to change."

"But having character." Yet again, Flirt stepped in, her eyes suddenly bright. "A description and a voice! Imagine it, will you? We only get a glimpse, right, but isn't that glimpse wonderful? All Urk ever has to change about me is the colour of my hair and the size of my chest, because what else about a Barmaid does The Narrative need to know? I giggle on some sod's lap and get my arse slapped as I walk by. That's not me, is it? I can't contribute anything to that! And you boys— you never have to change a thing, do you, because you're there to die, so how you look doesn't even matter. Wouldn't it be nice to have more than one scene and a couple of lines? Wouldn't it be nice to have a say?"

"…Erik learned that it was the Ring that had been stolen and was astonished when the sorceress Myhessia addressed his old friend Elder as *father*, for he was indeed the Eldrigon of legend!"

"Not getting my head chopped off." Shoulders's voice was so quiet that for a moment Fodder almost didn't recognise it. His friend's left hand dug into his neck almost violently. "I'd like a say in that."

Fodder stared at Shoulders for a long moment. In the quiet of his own mind, he had admitted a worry about his friend's growing obses- sion with Clank and his repeated decapitations but, given Shoulders's tendency towards high-decibel grouching, it had always been a bit of a joke, a laugh that could sweep away any real concerns. But for a moment, that look in his eye…

"And, of course"—the slightest curl of a manic smile tugged at the corners of Shoulders's lips—"if I had a say, I could line him up in a fair fight and cut *his* bloody head off! The vindictive, steel-clad—"

"See?" Clunny intervened abruptly. "Nice one! Now you've set Shoulders off again!"

Fodder sighed. "I was just trying—"

"Well, just try something else!" Clunny's snapped riposte cut away the rest of his sentence. "You're talking nonsense, both of you. I'm tired, mate, and we're likely to be up until late. I just want a quiet drink."

"I just want to be described as something other than a hair colour and a bust!" Flirt retorted abruptly. "I just want to not be slapped on the arse and called *darling* by sweaty Barbarians and *wench* by stupid Minstrels! We don't always get what we want, Clunny. And that's the point. We ought to have a *choice*."

Donk's soft tone restored a rather strained element of calm. "Whether we ought to have one or not," he said quietly, "we aren't going to get one."

"Because there isn't one," Dunny inserted with a glare. "Because the Taskmaster says so!"

Donk continued in the same calm voice, as though Dunny had not spoken. "And more to the point, if Preen comes in and hears us talking like this, we'll be bumped down to Background Villagers before we can blink."

"...Zahora was chief of the Temple guards and Gort one of the dwarf stonemasons who maintained it. Slynder stole the Ring once for a challenge, although he returned it afterwards. Halheid was in charge of patrolling the Northern Wastes and watching for any sign that Craxis was rising..."

"Preen!" Flirt snorted in a distinctly unladylike fashion. "That putrid weasel! Why should we have to listen to him?"

"Because he's the one with the instructions from the Taskmaster," Clunny retorted. He raised one finger as Fodder and Flirt both opened their mouths. "No, not a word! Either of you! If this doesn't stop right now, you can both bugger off somewhere else! Understand?"

"...that Myhessia was Sir Roderick's forlorn love, though they were torn from each other's arms by their duties to the world. And now, as we move into Part Three, the noble questors have begun to follow the trail of the Ring, guided by Erik, who can mysteriously intuit its passing..."

They don't understand. The words played through Fodder's mind unbidden. *I don't think they can.*

I'm not even sure if I *understand.*

But I think I'd like to.

Slowly, almost tentatively, he met Flirt's gaze. And that same lingering thought was mirrored in her eyes.

"...And after a brief skirmish with some brutish local soldiers, they rode towards a mountain pass, unaware of the danger and excitement that awaited them there! And that, dear gentles all, is the *story so far!"*

As the patter of half-hearted, vaguely sarcastic applause smattered its way across the common room, Fodder couldn't help but note, with no small lashing of irony, that in Bard's great, pompous recitation, Fodder's part had been dismissed in seven words at the very end.

It isn't fair. It really isn't.

But there's nothing we can do about it.

"Bravo! Bravo! Excellent!"

In the final flourish of Bard's recital, Fodder had missed the sound of the door opening once more, but there was no mistaking the sound of Preen's voice as he pretentiously applauded his friend.

"There, you see?" he heard the Officious Courtier declare. "I told you he was talented!"

Oh no. And there, I thought things couldn't get any worse.

"If you say so. Though, of course, he has nothing on the professional storyteller at the Palace." The reply was spoken by a voice to be reckoned with. A voice that had condescension engrained deeply into every syllable. A voice that carried echoing overtones of a large nose and a distinctively chinless profile. A voice that had superiority written in neat calligraphy into every rolling phrase.

It was a voice that would have said: "Sod the throne, the Nobles, and the Merry Band; I'm the one who really runs things down here." That was, if it had a single grain within it that could possibly be persuaded to be so uncouth.

It was the voice of the ultimate in Officious Courtiers. The voice of a Taskmaster's taskmaster. It was the voice of Strut.

Strut did the same job for the Merry Band that Preen, reluctantly, fulfilled for the Disposables—he made sure that they were in the right place at the right time in the right clothes and with the right equipment for when The Narrative passed by. It was no secret that, like most of his family, Strut considered himself a cut above what his fairly minimal Narrative time would usually define as his social position. It was even less of a secret that his cousin Preen coveted his job and the circles it enabled him to move in with an almost insatiable passion. While Preen was picking his way down muddy roads to remote guard posts and bandit ambushes or rounding up his charges in a humble inn, Strut was sat in state in castles and palaces, attending balls and parties, eating carefully stuffed delicacies, and holding his wine glass *just so*. He lorded it over his fellow Courtiers with shameless superiority, and it was always just a little bit amusing to see the strained mixture of fawning and loathing that danced a jig on Preen's face whenever his cousin dropped by to patronise him.

"Are these your...men?" Lost in his moment of introspection, Fodder had missed the fact that Strut's stiff-necked gaze had shifted in the direction of their suddenly quietened table. "For the ambush?"

"Yes, that's right." Preen's voice curled anxiously around the words. "They'll be Bulking Up, though. The ambush will be run by the Disposables we met earlier."

"Ah. Yes." Fodder wasn't entirely sure how Strut's voice could so effectively drip so much disdain into two simple words. "That funny little fellow with the uneven face—what was his name?"

"His name is Lurk. He's been Lead Bandit of Bandit Pass for eleven Quests now, a very reliable—"

"Yes. Lurk." Strut sniffed as though the very odour of the name offended him. "He will be in charge of the ambush? And these men will assist him?"

Preen's face was distorted as he waged a private internal war between the urge to fawn to a superior and his jealous resentment of him. "That's right, yes."

Strut's eyes roamed over the eight Disposables as though he had found something particularly unappetising on his shoe. "I've assigned the Disposables from the Palace to provide the guard for the princess, of course, given the vital importance of this incident to The Narrative. I was considering handing the task of the attack over to Primp and his Minions of Darkness, just to be certain of a suitable outcome. But given the uncouth nature of the men of Sleiss, I suppose these men will be... *adequate.*" He turned to his cousin, one immaculate eyebrow pointedly raised. "You'll find their livery in the cart outside. See to it."

"Yes, absolutely! I know how busy you are. Let me show you to the door...."

Fodder watched, strangely detached, as Preen scurried along, trying to keep up with the tall, rake-thin Strut's long, ramrod-straight strides.

Adequate.

He'd been a Disposable for so many Quests now, taking part in countless skirmishes and battles throughout numerous Narrative tales. They all had. They had done every fight and confrontation that The Narrative had asked of them to the very best of their abilities. They spilled their guts into the foliage on a near-daily basis in the name of the Quest. He had earned, if not the respect, then the acknowledgement of Preen that he was someone capable of seeing that a skirmish went ahead with a little bit of character behind it. But all that effort, all that work—what did it amount to in the end?

Seven words of summation in Bard's recital and a dismissive *adequate* from the Taskmaster's taskmaster.

And it was never going to get any better.

This is it. This is my life.

Seven words. And adequate.

"Bloody, pompous, stuck-up... Swanning around, ordering me about as though I can't do my job! Who does he think he is?"

Fodder jumped violently as Preen unceremoniously thumped down a coat of chain mail, topped by a blue-and-red surcoat, against their table.

"Finish up and wipe that foam off your chins!" the Courtier ordered harshly. "You gentlemen have a job to do, and I'm here to see that it's done right!"

* * *

The chain mail was bright and heavy, not the half rusty, badly tended stock to which Fodder had become so accustomed. The helmet, emblazoned with the crest of this Quest's Dark General, Sleiss, weighed down against his skull as his fingers twitched uncomfortably along the edge of the fine weave that made up the belted surcoat. It was well made and well cared for, lacking the artful decay that had become his standard work clothes. Even the sword belted to his waist was brightly polished.

Normally, the chance for a slightly different costume and a different part to play, even when merely Bulking Up, would have left him excited and cheerful. But it was not the thrill of new equipment that was ringing through his head as he sat, rocking with the motion of the familiar cart that carried them slowly but steadily up the variable and treacherous turns of Bandit Pass, but the last, dismissive words that Preen had tossed over his shoulder as he mounted his primly manicured horse and set off up the pass ahead of them.

"I know this is better kit than you generally get, but it's on loan from the Palace Disposables, so take good care to return it in the condition it was received. And *don't* get used to this."

Don't get used to this. Well, didn't that just sum everything up? Even amongst the ranks of the Disposables, he and his friends were considered second class, not to be allowed to play with anything shiny or good for more than a couple of scenes. A life of loyal service, of obedience to The Narrative, and he wasn't even trusted to hand back a piece of armour intact.

Seven words. Adequate.

Nobody really noticed what they did. Nobody really cared. They were told from birth how important they were, how every person was a link in The Narrative chain and how vital it was that they play their part as designated, be it Boy of Destiny or Background Villager. But the truth of it was that certain big shiny links were far more important than the little rusty ones in the corner. Would anyone even notice if they rusted right through? What would happen to their precious chain then?

Lost in his musings, Fodder failed to notice that the cart had shuddered to a halt until he heard the clatter of chain mail and felt the wagon bed jerk as his companions dismounted one by one. Glancing up, he caught a glimpse of Shoulders squinting at him quizzically, but his friend's eyes darted away on being caught, and Shoulders hurriedly flung himself, jingling, out onto the rocky ground. With a sigh, Fodder pulled himself up and followed.

Around him, Bandit Pass loomed, grey and imposing against the darkening twilight sky. Bandit Pass had been born to loom, a narrow cut through the gap between two vicious-looking mountains, ringed by towering cliffs and long, scattered slopes of fallen scree. Its proliferation of boulders, caves, and rocky up-thrusts made it ideal ambush territory. Lurk, Pounce, and Twister, the three scruffy Disposables who made their home up here in this remote spot, knew every crouching point, dramatic leaping post, and cunning hidey-hole by heart. They were an odd trio. Bulky Pounce, who was Thump's brother, had been born in Humble Village and often wandered down to the pub for an ale and a chat. But the twins Lurk and Twister, both of whom had originated in the strange, ever-so-slightly creepy environment of the mountain Trapping Station, were a bit more of a mystery and rarely left the hidden but surprisingly comfortable cave in which the three Bandit Disposables slept, ate, and practiced for their work. But Fodder respected professionalism when he saw it, and he knew with absolute certainty that there was no one better at the art of the sudden, sneak attack than Lurk of Bandit Pass.

But tonight's attack was not to be Lurk's usual wares, and Fodder couldn't help but notice as he followed his companions over to where Lurk, Pounce, and Twister were conversing with Sentinel, one of the Palace Disposables, how utterly uncomfortable the threesome looked. More accustomed to leaping out from behind rocks in scruffy tunics, wearing eye-patches and waving cudgels, the lean, leathery faces of Lurk and Twister in particular looked bizarrely out of place crammed into polished armour and a liveried surcoat. But the demands of Narrative were king.

They wouldn't be dressed up like this, not if they had their way. Pounce is always saying how much Lurk and Twister hate being made to wear armour. Doesn't matter, though, does it? We do as we're told and what do we get in return?

Seven words. Adequate.

One man who did look comfortable, however, was Sentinel. The Palace Disposable's armour shone by the gleam of the torches his men were lighting around the perimeter of the ornately decorated carriage that was drawn up at the edge of the road nearby with one wheel artfully broken.

"Good evening," he greeted the arriving Disposables formally, nodding to them in a precise and professional manner. *Precise* and *professional* were the two words that most thoroughly summed Sentinel up—Fodder had known him for four Quests and had yet to detect the slightest hint of personality about him. "I presume you gentlemen are aware that you are here to Bulk Up for an ambush of some significance?"

"We are?" Shoulders muttered sardonically under his breath. "And there, I thought we were here to trip the light fantastic."

If Sentinel heard Shoulders's remark, he singularly failed to react to it. "Your instructions are as follows: to ambush the carriage of the princess as it traverses the pass and make a spirited attempt at her kidnap. You will already be locked in battle with us, her loyal body-guard, although the last of us, myself, will be felled within moments of engagement with The Narrative. On the arrival of the Merry Band from the south, you are to offer lively resistance and attempt to drag the princess away north-westwards. You shall, however, be beaten back by their skill and strength, leaving many of your number dead or mortally wounded on the floor, although at least three of you, one of which is to be Lurk, are instructed to slink away like cowards in order to report back to your master. One of those survivors will be felled by an arrow as you spew curses, but the other two will vanish into the darkness, leaving the now unprotected princess to be taken into the care of the Merry Band. Lurk will act as Lead Guard, and you will take instruction from him as necessary. Is that understood?"

Fodder nodded along with his companions, adding his grunt of assertion to the mix without any real emotion. For all they were wear-ing posh armour and standing in a dark, windswept pass rather than on a country road, it was pretty standard fare. He was certain that he hadn't missed the flash of disappointment on Lurk's face at the news that The Narrative would enter halfway through the fight—leaping howling from behind rocky outcrops was easily the most enjoyable part of any ambush and for tonight, it had been denied them.

Not that it was up to them anyway.

Seven words. Adequate.

"Are we ready here?"

Fodder suppressed an internal groan as Preen fussed busily over to join them, his tight smile a strong indicator that he had just been forced to abandon a significant fawning session with someone he considered of far greater import than they in order to make sure his charges were doing his job for him. He clapped his hands together in a brief and irri-tating staccato.

"Now, I've been conferring with Princess Pleasance, who will be taking the role of the Princess Islaine for the course of this Quest…" *Aha. That explains it, then.* "And she has insisted upon approving any Disposable who will be required to manhandle her in the course of the ambush. She has requested that I assign our most"—his eyes wandered over the ranks of his Disposables with a vaguely unenthusiastic air— *"hygienic* specimens." He smiled with utter insincerity. "So, perhaps you, Fodder? And your...friend there? Although..." His gaze fixed upon Shoulders, whose expression, on being fingered for kidnap duty on the basis of being questionably more hygienic than his comrades, was hardly one of goodwill and gratitude. "Perhaps he could...wash his hands first?"

Fodder hadn't believed it possible that his thoughts about his job could sour much further that evening, but as he followed Preen over to a nearby water barrel, ignoring the sound of Shoulders muttering ill-temperedly under his breath a step behind, he found himself amending his mental litany.

Seven words. Adequate. And hygienic.

Not because I'm good. Not because I'm reliable. Not because I'm worthy of meeting his precious princess. No. Because I'm cleaner than a man who magnetically attracts food and his friend who smells of beans. There's a tale to tell the grandchildren. Yes, young Urchin, I got to manhandle the princess in **The Ring of Anthiphion** *because I remembered to scrub my ears! Let that be a lesson for life!*

This is not fair. It's not fair.

He splashed himself half-heartedly from the icy water in the barrel, trying to tune out Preen's fussing about whether there was time to send down to the village for some soap. As Preen reluctantly approved their efforts as *having to do for now* and turned to bustle them in the direction of the carriage, Fodder found himself wondering if there was time before the ambush to track down a good mud puddle to roll in.

He knew he shouldn't be this moody, this angry, about his job, about the way things were. But the dark thoughts refused to go away and he was unable to banish them. He felt as though he was suddenly seeing the world he'd always taken for granted with new eyes, and he didn't like what—

"Bloody hell!"

At his side, Shoulders jumped at least a foot. Fodder started violently himself as a vivid scream rang out, echoing with potent power against the cliffs, battering against itself until it broke into a thousand pieces and finally faded away. A tumble of loose scree nearby flopped downwards in a dusty little flurry, driven to flee from the sound.

"No, no, no!" From behind the carriage, a figure strode imperiously into the ball of light cast by the blazing torches: slender, elegant, her face delicate and beautifully crafted to catch the light *just so;* her long blue gown, golden tiara, and artfully draped velvet travelling cloak sweeping behind in a manner that left one in no doubt that royalty stood before them. Her hair was blonde and curly, with a hint of red about it, although Fodder was quite certain that such a whisper of colour would become a glint of shining fire given the right light and Narrative conditions. One milk-white hand rested carefully against her bodice as her bosom heaved with graceful artifice.

"This scream has to be perfect!" As Pleasance of the Royal Family, soon to be known as the Princess Islaine of Nyolesse, wheeled back the way she'd come with one precise whisk of her heel, it took Fodder a moment to realise that she was addressing the mousey little figure in a plain coif who waited, head bowed, in the shadows behind her. "Don't you understand, Menial? It's my first moment of Narrative! My introduction! This is the scream that draws my true love to ride to my rescue! It has to be of the best quality! It must inspire a glorious description! Otherwise, what's the point?"

Every word the princess spoke was punctuated by an artful gesture, every exclamation emphasised by a perfectly arranged expression. Every motion she made, every feature she had, was keyed up, controlled, and released in a fit of pure high drama. There was really only one conclusion that Fodder could possibly draw.

Oh good grief. It's Bard in a dress.

A pair of ruby red lips pursed carefully. "Perhaps if I varied the cadence a little, inserted some rise and fall? Hmmm, maybe…"

Fodder just found the wherewithal to cover his ears in time. The dusty trickle of scree rapidly transformed into half an avalanche.

The rise and fall was very impressive, though. He gave her that.

Shoulders's eyes were bulging in their sockets as Fodder tentatively lowered his hands from his ears and glanced over at his friend. Shoulders returned his gaze with mute horror for a moment, his lips working in silent misery before finally alighting on a sentence.

"She's a screamer," he whispered hoarsely.

Fodder could only nod. "Yeah. I noticed."

"We have to grab her."

"Got that part too."

"Our heads will be right next to hers."

"At least until Clank arrives."

"And she will be screaming like that *the whole time.*"

Fodder sighed grimly. "We'll just have to hope that Squick's got a good stock of spare eardrums. But on the plus side, if she deafens us, we won't have to listen to Bard."

Shoulders was quietly shaking his head. "I hate screamers," he muttered, his expression harrowed. "If I'd have known it meant working with a screamer, I would have left my head in that muddy ditch and my entrails up that tree...."

But there was no time to belabour the point further. A pair of striking blue-violet eyes had alighted upon them, beneath the suddenly creased perfection of a porcelain brow.

Princess Pleasance was staring at them, and her expression was hardly one of respectful satisfaction.

"Are these my kidnappers?" she drawled, her rich voice dripping with disdain. Her eyes swept briskly over their shining armour before lingering with rather more disgust upon their faces. In one sweeping turn, she wheeled on Preen. "Is this the best you could do?"

Preen bobbed his head in a sickeningly servile manner. "I'm terribly sorry, my lady. But the choice is very limited. These were the best I had available."

Pleasance's lips pursed as she regarded the cringing Preen with the closest she could manage to sympathy.

"You poor man," she declared, her voice throbbing with passion as only a princess's could. "I pity you having to work with such *torrid* material."

Fodder could actually feel his jaw hardening. Even the mud puddle suddenly didn't seem like enough.

Seven words. Adequate. Hygienic.

That *is not worth* this.

Don't they realise we're people too? Don't they think we have feelings? Doesn't that bloody woman care that we are standing right here?

"Well, needs must, I suppose." With an air of tragedy, the princess laid one delicate hand against her cheek. "In the name of The Narrative, we must all make sacrifices. So." With a snap like a general, she swung round to face Fodder and Shoulders, her eyes narrowing as she regarded them with sudden icy coolness. "Ground rules, gentlemen. I am not to be manhandled. You will take utmost care to ensure that while you appear to be vicious brutes treating me abominably, you will not grab me, haul me, yank me, bruise me, scratch me, or damage me in any way whatsoever. You will not touch my skin under any circumstances and you will also cause no damage to my clothes. You will not mess up my hair. One of you has to brutally stab my Maid, but you are not to get any of her blood on my dress or cloak." She gestured casually over her shoulder at the mousey young woman, whose expression, unnoticed by her mistress, was one of quiet, mute terror at the prospect of a stabbing, even a Narrative one. Fodder had become accustomed to the daily brutality of his job, but the poor young Maid had probably never been killed before and had no idea what to expect. And it didn't seem like anyone around her had considered her worth reassuring.

Her mistress was ploughing on. "And of course, you will allow me full latitude to put up the kind of spirited fight that is appropriate to my character. You will push your helmets back so that I will have free rein to scratch at your faces with my fingernails. You will insure that certain parts of your anatomy are kept within my range to kick. You will, however, acquire mail gauntlets. Those hands don't look nearly clean enough to me." Drawing herself up, Pleasance regarded them with the full force of her regal training. "Make me look good, gentlemen. That's what you're here for. Now, off you go. And make sure you remember what I told you. Any deviation, and I will instruct Strut to make certain that you spend your next ten Quests shovelling dung. Understood?"

A smile. It spread slowly, almost grimly over Fodder's face as he stared at blonde, pale Princess Pleasance glaring at them with such disdain, detached completely from any reasoning centre of his brain.

"Yes," he said softly. "I understand completely."

And he did.

We don't matter. We're replaceable.

Disposable.

Seven words.

Adequate.

Hy-bloody-gienic.

And why?

Because it says so on a piece of paper.

Somewhere far away, Fodder could hear Preen hurrying them to their places, could see the faces of his friends as they dropped into position around the carriage ready to launch on command into a half-finished fight. He saw Pleasance bustling into her carriage, arranging her face into an expression of horror as she braced to deliver her big introductory scream with just the right amount of rise and fall. He saw Strut appear like a phantom at the edge of the road into the Bandit Pass, one hand raised imperiously in signal as the darkness and moonlight behind him deepened and sharpened with The Narrative's approach.

He could feel his sword grasped in his hand. He could see Shoulders at his side, bracing himself for the inevitable vocal assault as he rested his hand upon the carriage door and prepared to batter it open. He knew it was happening. He knew The Narrative was coming.

But it all seemed so far away.

It says so on a piece of paper.

Who *says so?*

Why should we?

Why should I?

Like a beam of vivid moonlight, a single thread of Narrative alighted on the carriage.

And Princess Pleasance screamed her lungs out.

Scream...

...as the last echoes of the vivid scream curled and shattered against the rock around them, seeming to reach out with desperate fingers to plead for their aid, the companions crested the rise to behold a scene of horror. An ornately decorated carriage lay crippled at the narrowest part of the draw, cast in moonlight and shadow beneath the towering cliffs, its horses fled, one wheel efficiently snapped. The coachman had been pinned against his seat by the length of a spear through his body, his eyes wide with gaping terror as he lay spread-eagled in the moonlight. Around him, guards dressed in the familiar, bright livery of the Kingdom of Nyolesse lay in bloody, slaughtered heaps upon the rocky earth. Soldiers swarmed everywhere, their livery an

unknown pattern of blood red and midnight blue, battering at the
carriage as they charged, bellowing at the last Nyolesse guard still
standing—a tall, solid figure desperately outnumbered as he battled to
fend off the attackers surging at the carriage door. Even as Erik stared,
his eyes wide at the sight of the unexpected carnage, the final bold
guardsman was hacked down with a vicious blow and his body cast
aside. The way to the carriage was clear.

"My lady! My princess! Stand away, you dogs of Sleiss!" Sir
Roderick's sword whistled from its sheath, a steely song of death as he
drove his heels into the sides of his horse and charged ruthlessly
forwards, Halheid, Slynder, Zahora, and Gort hot upon his hoofbeats.
Erik started forwards too, eager to dive into battle, but Elder's harsh
hand upon his arm stayed his charge.

"No!" the old man ordered harshly. "Stay back!"

Alerted to these unexpected foes by Sir Roderick's bellow, the
majority of the soldiers had fanned out into the road to meet their
charge, leaving only two of their companions to continue their assault
upon the carriage door. Even as Erik watched in helpless horror, the door
cracked, broke open, and was yanked aside to reveal two pale, female
faces washed with moonlight. One of the soldiers' hands lashed out,
catching hold of a mousey little figure and dragging her out into the
road, her wide, terrified eyes evoking no sympathy from her attackers. A
sword lashed out, arcing viciously towards her, but to Erik's astonishment, not to mention the girl's, the blow fell inexplicably wide. Erik was
certain the blow would come again, that no such luck could befall the
poor creature a second time, but the soldier did not raise his weapon to
strike that mortal blow—instead, with a heartless shove, he hurled the
bewildered girl aside. His companion stared for a moment as she staggered to her feet, clearly torn as to whether he should finish the job his
associate had failed to complete, but it was already too late; with a flash
that Erik could almost have taken for gratitude, the girl turned and fled
safely into the night.

The fight was going much as Erik had come to expect—Sir Roderick
and Halheid were cutting wide swaths through their opponents with
their swinging blows as Slynder hung back behind them, picking off any
who escaped their wrath with the pinpoint accuracy of his dagger
throws. Zahora had abandoned her bow and drawn her slender swords,

sweeping men aside with graceful swipes that sent arcs of bright blood curling through the night air. Gort's hammer blows lacked her finesse, but equalled her efficiency, splattering brains and skull fragments wherever it happened to land. But three fighters, hard faced and vicious looking, were putting up a valiant resistance and their delay was keeping Sir Roderick from reaching his prize.

No such problems assailed the two soldiers at the carriage.

That same vivid scream that seemed to call to Erik's blood rang once more throughout the mountains—one of the soldiers staggered back as a foot lashed out at him from the carriage, his companion recoiling as fingernails scraped viciously across his face. Erik caught a tantalising glimpse of a pale face and a flash of blonde hair that glinted with a hint of moonlight-ignited fire as the girl, presumably the princess of Nyolesse, fought back frantically against her would-be kidnappers, screaming at the top of her voice. One of the soldiers winced and staggered back from a second and then a third fervent kick and his eyes seemed to flash with sudden, irrational rage.

"Shut up!" Erik heard him screech. "Shut up and stop kicking me!"

But the princess paid no heed to this demand, continuing her resistance with bright spirit as the first soldier surged forwards past his companion, grasping her pale, white arm and hauling her sharply into the entrance of the carriage.

"Get your hands off me!" she screamed desperately. "Unhand me at once, you foul, stinking, worthless wretch! You have no right to touch me! How dare you think yourselves worthy to lay a single finger…"

But the soldier laid more than a finger. His hand lashed out almost of its own volition, smacking against her mouth and shoving her head back against the wooden frame of the carriage. The princess's eyes widened in sudden shock at the impact for an instant, but then her eyes rolled and fluttered closed, her slender body collapsing against the soldier and his companion helplessly.

To Erik's surprise, the second soldier's expression at this turn of events was one of mild horror.

"We weren't supposed to knock her out!" Erik heard his hiss even over the slash and roar of battle. "That wasn't in the plan!"

The first soldier was staring at the princess's slumped body almost blankly, his expression strange and unreadable. He seemed to stare down at his own hands for a moment as though shocked to find them there. He stared at his companion, who had hoisted the unconscious princess onto one shoulder instinctively but apparently lacked any further impetus to act, instead gaping at his colleague in bewilderment. And then the first soldier turned and stared for a moment into the darkness where, just a minute before, he had allowed the servant girl to flee.

The fingers around his sword flexed. Slowly, his head rose. His eyes seemed faraway and almost mad. It was as though he were staring at a different world.

But his distraction looked likely to prove fatal. With a roar of fury, Halheid had broken free of his battle, leaping from his horse as he hefted his axe and charged towards the motionless soldier with an epic cry for blood.

The soldier's eyes snapped up at the sudden assault, his features suddenly hardening. But it was too late. Halheid brought his axe around in an arcing, deadly curve, inevitable, unstoppable, towards the soldier's exposed neck, its blade slicing painfully through the air as it was deflected by the soldier's upswinging sword. With one simple, ruthless thrust, the Sleiss soldier lunged forwards and ran him through.

And the very world seemed to shudder in pain.

For a frozen instant, Halheid gaped, his mouth wide as he stared down at the blade that had just pierced his heart. His eyes drifted painfully upwards towards the soldier's face, as the man stared at him, his expression one of dawning astonishment, of disbelief, of release, as though his own audacity in such a blow had astounded even him. Slowly, almost gently, the soldier stepped back, pulling his sword carefully free of the barbarian's body. For an eternal moment, it seemed as though Halheid wouldn't, couldn't fall, but then bright blood erupted from his bearded lips as he staggered, stumbled, slumped to his knees.

"You…" he whispered harshly. "You…"

But he could manage no more. Slowly, like the toppling of a mighty oak tree, Halheid slammed to the earth and lay still.

The battle, raging around them moments before, had staggered to a bizarre halt as even the soldiers of Sleiss stopped and stared in disbelief at the body of this fallen giant. Even Sir Roderick, who had charged forwards, sword raised, to smite the head of the impudent wretch who had laid hands on the princess, stopped dead in mid-swing. Only

Halheid's slayer seemed able to retain some skill at motion; turning sharply on his heel, he wheeled back on his companion and grabbed him by the arm, hauling both him and the unconscious princess sharply away from Sir Roderick's frozen blade, ducking behind the carriage and vanishing from sight in the scattering of rocks that...

...fades

The old escape tunnel that Pounce had told Fodder about one night in the pub gaped before them; grabbing the wide-eyed and bewildered Shoulders by the arm, Fodder shoved both him and his Royal burden hurriedly under the ground. Beneath the vivid darkness of Narrative behind them, Fodder could hear the Merry Band stuttering and stammering their way through disbelieving mourning as they struggled to improvise around the gaping hole that he, a simple Disposable, had torn in their nice neat plot.

I did it.

I can't believe it.

I changed The Narrative.

He had barely realised he was doing it until it had happened. The frustration and rage that had bubbled within him after his conversation with Pleasance had failed to disperse when the smooth, honey-like warmth of The Narrative had wrapped around him, taking over his body and guiding his actions. He had felt it driving him forwards, ushering him to the door of the carriage, just as he was supposed to; but when he had reached inside himself to find that touch of character he always called on, he had found only the whirling thoughts and rampant feelings that had consumed him ever since he'd left the pub. He'd stared at the young Maid's face, her terror unfeigned as she braced for a death no one had ever prepared her for, and he'd felt himself twist his wrist, deflect the blow that The Narrative had prompted, and cast her free.

He'd barely realised what he'd done, as the warmth of The Narrative engulfed him more strongly, dragging him back down to obedience. Perhaps that single moment of defiance would have been the end of it.

Until Pleasance had kicked him in the face.

And the anger he had felt as she'd belittled him and scolded him and commanded him like a worthless servant had exploded right back to the surface.

He'd felt himself yell at her as she'd battered them, her stupid little instructions leaping into his brain and enraging him all the more. He didn't deserve to have some spoiled brat kicking him and screaming in his ear! She didn't deserve the Narrative attention she was about to receive! He just wanted her to bloody well shut up!

Whacking her one really had been phenomenally satisfying.

He'd felt The Narrative surge again, curling around him, battling desperately to draw him back into the fold of the plot. He'd heard Shoulders's cry of disbelief at his sudden, unscripted action. But it had been too late. He'd felt the hold of Narrative, once warm and all-consuming, thin suddenly around him. He'd moved his hands and stared down at them as The Narrative's resistance shuddered, fought, and utterly failed to contain him. Realisation had swamped him as he'd stared at Shoulders, at the unconscious princess, and off into the darkness where Menial the Maid had fled. And then, with glorious terror, he'd known:

He could do anything. Anything he wanted.

But by now the Taskmaster, the faraway guide of The Narrative, had, it seemed, registered the rogue element lurking in its midst and stealing the limelight. Fodder had felt the sudden vivid concentration of Narrative energy that surrounded Thud, capturing him, driving him forwards to wipe out this interference before any more harm could be done.

And Fodder had known right then, right there, that he didn't have to let it.

He'd killed Thud. In Narrative. In the Quest. He'd killed a character that every instruction they had received had stated quite clearly was due to survive heroically and live happily ever after. And then he'd grabbed Shoulders, preventing his ritual beheading by Clank in the process, and hauled both him and the not-supposed-to-actually-get-kidnapped princess out of The Narrative and away before the Merry Band had had time to blink.

He'd broken with Narrative. And to top it off, he'd quite severely buggered up the entire plotline of this Quest.

And it was glorious.

He had never felt so alive.

I did that. I did it!

I made a difference!

It should have been all about the battle and the princess. Instead, it had been all about him. An unnamed soldier of Sleiss.

Why do we have to obey the Taskmaster? Flirt had asked.

The answer was that they didn't.

A part of him was screaming, asking what he'd done. He'd broken everything, disobeyed that which must be obeyed, done the impossible, shattered every natural law of their world. He should go back, let them capture and kill him, return the princess and help them get back on Narrative track, and then maybe he wouldn't spend the rest of his life as a nameless dung shoveller or a torture chamber victim.

But the rest of him knew that he couldn't.

He couldn't go back.

He didn't know exactly what he'd done, what he'd started. But whatever it was, he was damned well going to *finish* it.

The far end of the tunnel loomed. Side by side, he and Shoulders stumbled out onto the winding road that led from Humble Village up to the pass, breathing hard, staggering slightly as they stared back up the road in disbelief. Fodder had feared a Narrative pursuit, but his actions had apparently thrown the Merry Band into too much confusion, and the vividness of Narrative stayed firmly fixed in the pass high above them.

I did that. Me! Fodder of Humble Village!

I bet I get a few more than seven words now!

And he could keep going. He had to keep going.

Going with what, he wasn't sure. But he was certain he'd figure it out.

By the pale moonlight, Fodder sought out the face of his friend, his fellow Disposable, the man he'd saved from the Clank-inflicted neck severance. He found him, still shouldering his burden, his eyes wide.

Shoulders stared at Fodder.

Fodder grinned.

Shoulders did not.

"We won." Shoulders's voice was quiet, shocked, as though the truth were suddenly dawning, trickling into his brain and making itself known. "We kidnapped the princess. We won."

Fodder's grin broadened. "I know."

Two hands lashed out, slapping down on Fodder's shoulders as his friend stared at him with wild eyes and began to shake him madly.

"But we *weren't supposed to win, Fodder!* We won! We weren't supposed to win! What have you done? What have you dragged me into?"

Shoulders looked scared. Actually scared. But it would come, he would learn, once he felt the exhilaration of defying The Narrative for himself.

"I'm not sure," Fodder admitted softly. "But I like it."

Shoulders's jaw gaped. "What the hell are you—"

"What have you done? What have you done?"

For the second time, a sweeping, heeled foot caught Fodder hard in the face. Even as he staggered back, he saw Shoulders writhing as his velvet-cloaked burden, now free from the Narrative-forced obligation to reflect any damage caused there, woke sharply and made her feelings very plain indeed. Fingernails raked, feet flailed, and ruby lips parted to release what Fodder was certain would have been an almighty scream had Shoulders not acted faster, flinging the furious Pleasance to the ground and slapping his hand quite firmly over her face.

"No more *screaming!*" he screamed.

Pleasance's regal and ever-so-sophisticated response was to bite him.

Shoulders gave an unmanly screech and staggered back, wringing his fingers in pain at the unexpected onset of non-Narrative damage. Pleasance scrambled to her feet, her skirts tangling around her legs, her pale face unflatteringly flushed as she stared at the two Disposables with unrestrained horror.

"You hit me!" she shrieked, jabbing one manicured finger viciously into the air before her. "You *hit* me!"

Fodder couldn't help but feel that the matter of his blow was the least of the issues at hand. "It was In Narrative!" he retorted incredulously. "It's not like it hurt you!"

Pleasance drew herself up, mustering what dignity she could manage on a dark road when faced with two men whom she quite clearly regarded as dangerous lunatics. "That is not the point!" she proclaimed furiously, one slender hand punctuating her proclamation for dramatic effect as she swirled her cloak around her body. "Nobody, absolutely nobody, ever hits a princess! How dare you! I am a member of the Royal Family! You can't treat me this way!" She took two stumbling steps back onto the road, the sharp heel of her shoe spearing the velvet hem of her cloak with pinpoint accuracy. "You filthy, degenerate fiends! You've ruined my moment! This is my Quest, my romance, my *glory!* I will not have my story ruined by a pair of pointless nothing Disposables who don't even have character names!"

She staggered again, heel lodged in and tearing her cloak.

Irritated though her speech was making him, Fodder felt obliged to point this matter out. "Erm…your foot, it's—"

"Shut up!" The words were a violent screech. "Just you wait! Just you wait until I get back up that hill! When I tell Strut what you've done, you'll be locked away as dungeon victims for every Quest from now until you wither into nothing! You've dragged me away from my moment, you've touched my skin, you've messed up my dress and my hair! How dare you!"

"No, really, your foot—"

"Just you wait!"

"Only it's really rather caught up down there…"

"I'll make you pay!"

"And if you do that heel turny thing you did earlier—"

"You'll wish you'd never been born!"

"You're really going to—"

"And I'm going to get the others right now!"

And with that, the Princess Pleasance whisked furiously around on her heel.

The resulting fall was suitably spectacular.

As her heel swivelled, the snagged velvet cloak twisted like a serpent up the princess's leg, snaring her skirts and clamping her legs together into a sudden, cloth-bound vice. With a shriek that probably shattered the snowcaps of the distant Savage Mountains, Pleasance went tumbling wildly downwards, arms flailing uselessly. Her head collided with a nearby roadside rock, jolting her into silence.

"…go flying," Fodder concluded over the resulting quietude. He shrugged. "Well, I did try to warn her. And at least she's quiet."

"Yeah, but for how long? How long, huh?" The manic note that shivered through Shoulders's voice caught Fodder's attention. His scruffy friend had yanked off his helmet and was grasping it fiercely in his right hand as he paced across the road and then sharply back again, staccato steps punctuated by abrupt and violent turning. His left hand scrubbed so frantically at the exposed skin of his neck that Fodder was surprised he wasn't drawing blood. "Non-Narrative damage like that'll be healed clean in a couple of hours and what then? She wakes up and what do we do? *What do we do then?*"

Shoulders's eyes were wild, wilder than Fodder had ever seen. Even a Clank decapitation had never fostered such manic terror within his friend. His unshaven jaw was working madly as his hand rubbed against his neck, harder, faster, more intensely, his footsteps doubling in speed, his breath coming in short, violent gasps that attacked the very air into which they were expelled. As he spoke again, his helmet-clasping hand gesticulating madly, Fodder realised that his fellow Disposable's voice had risen by at least an octave.

"She'll wake up and she'll go running back to Strut and then we'll be finished, you hear me, we'll be finished! What am I talking about? We're already finished; Preen knows who we are! We'll never see daylight again! Oh sod it, oh sod, what have you done, Fodder? What the bloody hell have you *done?*"

Fodder hesitated. The euphoria that had been driving him along like a runaway cart fizzled and drained slightly at the sight of his friend's pale, frozen, *terrified* features. Oh, Shoulders had piped up for him in theory down at the pub, when offered the prospect of no more undignified beheadings at the hands of an iron-clad moron, but here, now, facing the absolute reality of a broken Quest, a kidnapped princess, and an actual In Narrative rebellion, his fears seemed to have consumed him.

Fodder felt a sudden wash of guilt. Shoulders hadn't asked for this—Fodder had taken advantage of his friend's shock and dragged him along for the ride. He'd never actually asked him if he wanted to be a rebel.

The look on Shoulders's face strongly suggested the answer would have been *no.*

In all honesty, Fodder had never asked *himself* if he wanted to be a rebel. But, now he was one, he didn't plan on going back. He wasn't quite sure where forward was, but back was not an option.

But what was he supposed to do next? What could he do that didn't involve a lifetime of punishment for breaking the fundamental purpose of their lives?

And then, he heard the hoofbeats.

He didn't stop to think. Diving forwards, Fodder scooped up the unconscious princess and hurtled back into the hidden mouth of the escape tunnel. Dumping his burden unceremoniously out of sight, he hurled himself back out, grabbed his friend's arm, and hauled him hurriedly into the shadows of the entrance.

"But what about my plot?"

Thud. The Barbarian of the Merry Band was mounted on a fairly miserable-looking pony as he rounded the corner of the mountain road, riding as rapidly as was safe on a winding trail by darkness. His bearskin tunic was a tangle of blood and earth and his beard was black with dirt—strong indicators that The Narrative had given him an impromptu and rapid burial up on the mountainside. Squick hovered beside him, dabbing at the stab wound in his chest with his purplish pixie dust, although the big man's gesticulations and the jolting of his pony weren't making the job any easier. The pixie's potato-like face was scrunched and irritable as he struggled to complete the fix-up.

"For the moment, I'm afraid you have no plot."

Fodder shrank back even more deeply into the shadows as Strut, the Taskmaster's taskmaster, rounded the bend on his elegant stallion. Preen, his head bowed, his face a cocktail of humiliation, mortification, and fury, rode at his side, deferentially carrying a lantern. "Halheid is dead."

"But I *can't* be dead!" Thud burst out, slamming one meaty fist against his own thigh and sending Squick reeling through the air like a drunken seadog in an effort to avoid having to repair himself. "What about my heroic battle feats? I save the day! I marry Zahora and become regent of one of the Six Kingdoms! That's what the schedule says! I can't be dead!"

Squick stowed his needle and thread neatly away, and wiped off his hands with a purple glitter as he rose back into the air on frantically pumping wings. "You were stabbed through the chest In Narrative, laddie. I assure you, you are."

Thud shot Squick a venomous look, but Strut's pointed intervention put pay to any prospect of a pixie-Barbarian showdown.

"The actions of that pair of rogue Disposables have severely disrupted the plot." Preen sank down more painfully in his saddle as his cousin fixed him with a steely glare. "Their attention-seeking has damaged everything. I have received word from the Taskmaster that new schedules are being prepared in an attempt to mitigate the damage that has been done so as to get this Quest back on course as neatly as is possible. Halheid's burial was conducted magically, and the rest of the Merry Band have settled into a paragraph of searching for the princess's trail whilst we wait for further instructions."

"Burial!" Thud gave a vile snort. "Two rushed paragraphs of dumping me in the earth with magic so they could bugger off after the precious love interest! I was supposed to be a lynchpin of this plot! Where's the mourning, the rending of garments, my companions manfully sobbing, Zahora throwing herself on my grave? It's *not fair!*"

Not fair? Fodder ground his teeth as the three horses passed the concealed entrance to their tunnel. *You got a funeral, mate. I never have done! I always end up rotting in a ditch!*

"Stop complaining." Strut's stark declaration proved who was really running the Quests at ground level. "We need to...ah!"

It was like a tinkle of distant bells. A golden glow rose like pixie dust from both the tapestry pouch perched on Strut's waist and the more familiar pink satin pouch belonging to Preen. Both Officious Courtiers reined in their horses a dozen yards down the road from Fodder's concealment and rooted in their bags, Preen rather more awkwardly by virtue of still holding the lantern in one hand. Each drew out a small, elegantly bound book that glowed a gentle gold around the edges. Strut's was silver, overlaid with a vivid gold binding that twinkled in the unsteadily held lantern light. Preen's was a more prosaic muddy brown.

From his concealment in the shadows, Fodder saw Strut smile with something approaching relief as he fanned through the pages of his book. "A new schedule," he declared. "I knew the Taskmaster could fix this mess."

"That was quick," Squick observed, one knobbly eyebrow raised.

"Even for up yonder."

"What does it say?" Thud leaned half out of the saddle, peering over Strut's shoulder in a manner that the latter clearly found to be highly uncouth. "Will I be resurrected? What about my romantic subplot? My battle glories?"

In spite of his clear irritation with Thud's invasion of his personal space, Strut was smiling at his book with a hint of respect. "Both salvaged. You are to return some chapters from now as Halheid's twin brother, Torsheid, out to avenge his brother's death by taking up his charge. You will pick up your plot strands from there."

"Yes!" Fodder's heart plummeted as Thud emphatically punched the air. "Take that, you stinking little Disposable!"

Well, that was it. Fodder's head drooped as Strut's words sank in. He'd failed. He'd thought he'd impacted on the plot, made a difference, made himself stand out, made people take notice. But in less than a quarter of an hour, the Taskmaster had fixed the precious plot and worked around him.

Had he been a fool in thinking he could defy the Taskmaster and The Narrative? Had he thrown away a sufficient if not satisfying career for the sake of a few paragraphs in a fight that would soon be forgotten?

The stinking little Disposable had taken it. And defeat tasted very sour indeed.

Powerless and nothing. That's all he was. That's all he would ever...

"Pardon me." Preen was squinting down at his book with one manicured eyebrow raised. "But if I'm reading this right, all of this plot salvage depends upon us finding the princess quickly."

Fodder's ears pricked up, as sudden hope leapt in his heart. Leaning forwards, he peered over into the ball of lantern light to get a closer look at Strut's expression.

And there it was, just for an instant. *Concern.*

The euphoria was back, bubbling in his brain. *Oh, this isn't over yet. And I see now. I see what it is I have to do.*

"I don't see why that should be a problem." The steel in Strut's voice denied the hint of worry that lingered in his eyes. "They are only Disposables, and they will soon realise how foolish they've been. I'm sure they shall be found before the night is out and the princess reinserted into The Narrative nice and smoothly. In fact…" Strut twisted in his saddle to face Thud. "Since you have a few chapters' grace before you are due to return, why don't you take my cousin and his remaining Disposables and comb the area? When the malfeasants are found, summon me immediately and I will see to it that The Narrative and the Merry Band arrive promptly to slaughter them and retrieve the princess. And then I will make certain that the pair of them spend the rest of their days as resident prisoners in the Dark General's dungeons. They can howl in the background until their throats are raw as far as I'm concerned."

Preen was staring at Strut with sudden horror. For a brief, impossible instant, Fodder wondered if their Officious Courtier was actually planning to stand up for them. But of course, their punishment was not what was bothering Preen's mind.

"Wait a minute," he stammered. "The Disposables are *my* responsibility. And you're sending *Thud* to—"

Strut fixed his cousin with the most utterly superior gaze that Fodder had ever seen. It could have stripped the bark off the mightiest of trees and sent the noblest of kings and knights into a cringing huddle in a corner. "You've done a less-than-magnificent job up until now," Strut drawled coolly. "I thought perhaps a fresh pair of hands at the helm might actually see the job gets done."

Preen shuddered, torn desperately between cringing and fury. "But he knows nothing of doing such work!" he protested, more fiercely. "You need those with knowledge, Strut! What if this is the start of another incident like *Quickening* and—"

One look. One look of utter, silent fury from Strut was all it took to clamp Preen's jaws closed. A moment later, the Taskmaster's taskmaster turned to face the road once more as though nothing had happened, tucking his book neatly away and gathering his reins. "Off you go, the pair of you, and start the search. I need to spread the word of what has happened here. We must make certain these Disposables have no place to hide."

With a whip of his reins, Strut vanished down the road, leaving Preen and Thud to stare at each other with wary resentment. After several moments more of eyeballing, the duo turned their horses and set off back up the road to Bandit Pass.

And that left only Squick, hovering quietly in the darkness.

The pixie gave a gusty sigh as he swivelled in midair. And then his beady eyes fixed straight on Fodder's.

Fodder jumped a good foot at the unexpected stare, but the pixie made no move to raise the alarm. His brow knotted as he regarded the Disposable he had fixed up on countless lonely roads with something akin to concern.

"I don't know what you're playing at, laddie," he said softly. "But it's a dangerous game, and you'd best watch your back. Because the way things are rolling out, they ain't likely to let me fix it."

"Squick..." Fodder started to rise, but the pixie had already banked sharply in the air, surging away into the night.

And then there was silence.

In the darkness of the tunnel, Fodder could hear the shrill whistle of Shoulders's frantic breathing, could see the still, slumped form of the unconscious princess propped up against the wall. But none of that mattered, not with the conversation he had eavesdropped on echoing vividly through his mind.

Because it held the answer.

He knew. He knew now exactly what to do.

His mind worked madly, fizzling with a euphoric hysteria fuelled by realisation. He'd broken The Narrative, yes, but it was fixable. If the others got the princess back quickly, the story could be guided back on course. Thud's death had been worked around already, his romantic subplot and his battle glories passed on to his soon-to-be-introduced twin brother. Fodder of Humble Village would be caught, killed In Narrative, and then banished to scream in the background in the Dark General's Grim Fortress for every Quest until he shrivelled up and died. Nothing had really changed. The whole world would go on as it always had before.

He couldn't let that happen. Not now.

He'd come too far.

He'd broken the Quest. Now he had to see that it stayed broken.

He had to keep going—keep sabotaging, ruining subplots, making what remained of the Taskmaster's instructions unsalvageable. He had to show that he could change the world, that he had that power, that he deserved to be listened to. He had to prove that it wasn't just the members of the Merry Band who were important anymore.

If he was caught while things could still be made the way the original plan dictated, nothing would change. He had to make *The Ring of Anthiphion* unfixable.

Then they'd see. They'd listen. They'd have to.

They had to stop the Taskmaster's precious Narrative cold. It was the only way.

But he was also honest enough to admit he didn't want to do it alone.

There was Shoulders. But he was hardly the most willing of allies.

Fodder found his eyes drifting down the hillside, towards the distant twinkle of Humble Village and the Archetypal Inn.

Flirt. He needed Flirt. She'd understood all this, that forever-ago over supper. She'd grasped what had to be done before it'd even crossed his mind. If she'd been allowed to play, she would have been clobbering princesses right alongside him.

And perhaps she still could be....

The pub. They needed to get to the pub.

"We need to get to the pub."

Fodder hadn't even realised he'd said the words out loud until Shoulders grabbed him by the arms and swung him round.

"The pub?" he half-screeched, his voice more than a little on the hysterical side. "The pub?! I never thought I'd hear myself say this, but this is no time for ale!"

Fodder tried to grasp his friend's arms, only to find that they were shaking too badly to be stilled. "Shoulders, listen..."

"No!" It was a high-pitched shriek. "No, no, no! You did hear that conversation, didn't you? You did hear Strut say that we are going to be banished to the bloody dungeons! I didn't ask for this! I didn't want to do this! But do you think they'll believe that? Oh no, of course they won't! If you had to go stark staring mad, couldn't you have dragged *someone else* down with you?"

Fodder finally managed to get a grip on his friend's arms. "But don't you see? It can be better!"

"The dungeons are *better?*"

Fodder fought valiantly not to roll his eyes. "Forget the dungeons!"

"Forget the dungeons? Forget the bloody dungeons?" Shoulders's eyes were all but popping from their sockets. "How the hell am I supposed to forget the bloody dungeons when I'll be spending the rest of my bloody life in their bloody cells?"

The urge for wit was probably one that Fodder should have resisted. "Actually, they probably clean up the blood when the dungeons aren't In Narrative...."

The thump to the shoulder, Fodder had to concede, was probably deserved. "You've condemned us both to life in prison! And you're trying to be *funny?*"

Fodder sighed. "Mate, please, just calm down and listen to me. If you'll just let me explain..."

"Explain? *Explain?*" Shoulders was, Fodder felt, growing somewhat repetitive. "I don't care about you trying to explain! I care about not getting locked up!" With a rough shove, he yanked himself free of his friend's hold and staggered towards the tunnel's entrance. "Maybe it's not too late!" he gasped hoarsely. "Maybe if I take the princess back up the hill and tell Preen that you dragged me along against my will, I'll get off with a demotion to stable hand! Even dung's got to be better than dungeons, right? Yeah, if I take her back..."

"No!" Fodder darted between his friend and the princess's supine form. "No, we can't take her back."

Shoulders's jaw dropped. "Okay, now I know you've gone barmy. Not take her back? What else are we supposed to do with the gnashing cow?"

Fodder found himself wishing sublimely that he could make his idea sound as good out loud as it was in his head. He rather doubted he could, though.

"We have to keep her away from The Narrative. It's important."

Shoulders stared at him incredulously. "I know I'm going to regret asking this. But never mind, here goes nothing. *Why?*"

Fodder took a deep breath. "Because if we can keep her out of The Narrative, it'll bugger up the plot."

Shoulders's features settled into a kind of resigned horror. "And why in the name of anything at all would we want to do that?"

Fodder risked a tentative quarter of a smile. "Because if we bugger up their plot beyond repair, it proves that we don't have to follow the Taskmaster's instructions. And if the instructions are no longer sacred…" The smile hoisted to half-mast. "No more heads in ditches. No more entrails up trees. If we don't want to play, we don't have to. We can demand character. We can demand to be the heroes or just to be left alone. We finally get a *say.*"

Shoulders was staring at him blankly. "Not from a dungeon."

Fodder gently rested his hands on his friend's shoulders. "If we can make them listen, there won't be a dungeon. If we can spread the word, make everyone realise that The Narrative isn't untouchable, they won't have any choice. But that can only happen if the schedule gets mangled. If the Taskmaster can still get things back on track, they can still lock us away. But if we can sabotage The Narrative, make it run to our instructions rather than the Taskmaster's, everyone will *have* to take notice. I'm sure of it."

Shoulders was still regarding him, but some of his manic edge had slipped away into sudden solemnity. "You really believe this, don't you?" he said softly.

Fodder gave a quiet nod. "I really do. Do you?"

Shoulders gave him a frank stare. "Not really. I think you've gone crazy. Because if you're saying what I think you're saying…you want to take on the *Taskmaster?*"

It was a mind-boggling idea, but Fodder had to admit that Shoulders had seen right to the heart of it. "That's who's pulling the strings. That's who's made it unfair. So pretty much, yeah."

"Insane." Shoulders drew the word out, spilling it slowly and vividly into the air. "We're two Disposables, Fodder. We don't stand a chance."

Fodder returned a stare of equal frankness. "It's this chance or the dungeon. And imagine if we could make it work. No more being slaughtered on lonely roads. And Clank would never be allowed to cut your head off again. Not if you didn't want him to."

One hand twitched briefly and awkwardly along Shoulders's neck. "Stop trying to make me hope," he retorted sharply. "We both know that isn't going to happen."

Fodder leaned forwards, meeting his friend's eyes intensely. "But what if it *could?*"

Shoulders closed his eyes, slowly shaking his head. "I can't believe I'm even listening to you. Taking on the Taskmaster? This is loony! I'm going to wake up back home in bed any minute and laugh at the stupid dream I just had!"

Fodder shrugged slightly. "But while you're dreaming away, what do you reckon? Will you help me?"

Shoulders gave a long and weary sigh. "Fodder, it's either follow a nutter like you or get locked in a dungeon. What choice have I got?" He rolled his eyes. "It's nutter all the way, heaven help me." He turned sharply and jabbed one finger into the night air. "But you'd better have a bloody good plan! Something better than just dragging the princess around with us and keeping her out of The Narrative, anyway!"

One look at Fodder's expression was apparently enough. Shoulders slumped against the wall, running one hand across his unshaven face. "We're doomed," he muttered darkly. "Just hand me that rope Preen gave you, will you? And there had better be a gag, or I'm taking my chances with the dungeon!"

Fodder handed over the rope without comment and set to work ripping a broad strip of cloth off his surcoat as Shoulders knelt, plonked the slumped princess's wrists unceremoniously onto his lap, and set to work binding them.

"She's going to go ballistic when she wakes up," Shoulders commented matter-of-factly. "You do know our regal pain in the arse here is going to be far more trouble than she's worth, don't you?"

Fodder sighed. He could picture the histrionics that they would be in for in the days to come, and it wasn't a prospect that filled him with joy and contentment. But what choice had they got?

"She's too important to the plot," he replied wearily, kneeling carefully as he hauled her head forwards and shoved her mass of coiffured ringlets messily aside so that he could secure the gag in place. "Without her, they'll have to change almost everything. We'll just have to live with her." He shook his head. "And I was thinking. If we can get to the pub, I'm sure we could get Flirt on our side. And she'd definitely sort her out."

With little decorum, he deposited Pleasance's head back against the rock wall, her elegantly arranged curls reduced to a frizzy mess by his indelicate handling. Picturing the look on her porcelain face as she'd scolded them about her hairdo, Fodder found himself unable to resist the urge to reach forward and ruffle her hair a touch more, locking his fingers into the few remaining orderly blonde ringlets that hung beneath the small, neat tiara and pulling them every which way until the resulting mess more closely resembled a hedge in a hurricane than a human head of hair. It was surprisingly satisfying.

Shoulders grinned at him tightly but made no comment on his actions. "Flirt? You may be—"

"—worth checking, I reckon. I'm sure I told Fodder about this tunnel in the pub once, and Preen's frothing at the mouth. If we don't find them soon, he'll have a seizure."

"Don't know what those two idiots were playing at back there. All this trouble and Preen screaming like a banshee. I'm tempted to whack them one myself when we track them down."

It was Pounce and Lurk. And neither sounded particularly in the mood to listen to Fodder's glorious revolution.

The Humble Village Disposables exchanged a brief, horrified glance as footsteps echoed in the tunnel behind them. Snatching up their Royal pain once more, Shoulders bolted for the entrance with Fodder sharp on his heels. A quick glance told them that the road was clear and, with the lights of Humble Village glistening in the woods below, the two men launched themselves out into the dark unknown.

It was definitely time to head for the pub.

* * *

"...to be brought to me immediately upon their discovery. Is that clearly understood?"

Through the crack in the narrow doorway that, in its current form, led from behind the counter of the Archetypal Inn through to its kitchen, Flirt the Barmaid watched the thin, brittle form of Strut the Officious Courtier. He was carefully eyeballing the recently roused and decidedly dozy-looking residents of Humble Village whom he had so firmly had Sentinel and the Palace Guard round up and shepherd into the common room. Of those who looked conscious enough to understand the enormity of what they had just been told, most seemed able to do little but blink and stare, their jaws hanging open, no hint of the true meaning behind his words dawning in their eyes.

But Flirt had understood everything.

Closing her eyes for an instant, she allowed herself to lean back against the wall, breathing hard, brain reeling and circling. And then, slowly, she felt herself begin to smile.

He did it. He actually did it.

Fodder defied The Narrative.

She couldn't believe it. Of all people, that it would be Fodder—sensible, reliable, down-to-earth Fodder—who would find a way to do what she'd always dreamed could happen! She'd had no idea that he or anyone else had even considered the inherent unfairness of the world in which they lived until that extraordinary conversation over beer and stew and *the story so far.* She watched them potter contently along with their humdrum lives and wondered if she could really be the only one who fought the urge to scream every time The Narrative rolled into the village and stripped away everything that made her *her.* There was no part of her that took pleasure from thrusting around a chest that wasn't hers, from having her bottom smacked and pinched until it was black and blue, and from perching on the lap of smelly Barbarians whilst they slobbered and slurped their way over her face. She loathed every coy smile, every raucous laugh, every bumptious hip-wiggle that The Narrative prompted her to make and despised the way that so many of those with whom she cavorted In Narrative honestly expected her to cavort with them out of it too.

All she wanted was to be allowed to be herself. Why should anyone, even the Taskmaster, have the right to say she couldn't?

She'd always dreamed of adventure, of something to challenge her, a leap into the unknown. She adored the idea of being allowed to fight back. A slap for a smack, a punch for a pinch, knowing she could turn around and kick the pasty backsides of anyone who so much as leered in her direction. That'd put an end to Swipe's wandering fingers and Thud's bruising squeezes! But adventure was out of the question for those to whom it was not assigned, and The Narrative had always melted her anger into a syrupy haze until she emerged from its grasp once more, sore and dishevelled and hopelessly frustrated. She'd never tried to fight it. She'd thought fighting to be impossible.

But for Fodder, apparently, it wasn't.

She had to know how he'd managed it. She *needed* to know.

She had to find him. She had to find out what he'd done and how she could do it herself. And then, at last, she would be able to prove to every smug, self-satisfied groping bastard who'd ever pinched her backside, slobbered on her cleavage, and called her *wench* or *darling* that she was more than a pushed-up bosom in a corset! And if the chance arose to repay a few of the *affectionate* bruises she'd accrued over the Quests, so much the better!

But first, she had to find Fodder. And that meant gathering what she needed and getting out unspotted.

It didn't take her long to slip up the back stairs to her room and even less time to toss a handful of practical clothes and some light blankets into an old pack she generally used to hoist around the laundry. Then, with quiet efficiency, she ransacked the kitchen, grabbing food and water, flints and candles, a coil of rope, and, in lieu of proper weaponry, a sturdy kitchen knife and the poker from the fireplace. As an afterthought, she also grabbed a pot of ale. If Shoulders really was out there with Fodder, as Strut's descriptions had implied, she strongly suspected he'd need it.

Finding them wouldn't be easy, of course. That thought alone was enough to sober her enthusiasm. They could have headed in any direction from the pass, hidden anywhere, decided anything. She had no idea if they'd had any plan in mind when they'd defied The Narrative or if it had been a spontaneous act that had forced them to desperately improvise. Even as she pulled open the back door, she knew her search was certainly not going to be...

Oh.

Two very familiar faces and a velvet-cloaked backside blocked her path.

Fodder gave a tentative grin. Shoulders was far more preoccupied trying to deal with the wriggling mass of velvet and blonde curls hoisted over his right shoulder.

For an instant, Flirt could only stare, trying to slap her mind back from probably-futile-search mode into the less well explored region of what to do when she found them. Fortunately, common sense was quick to kick in.

"What do you think you're doing, you pair of idiots?" she hissed fiercely. "Strut is right there in the common room baying for your blood, and you walk straight back to the pub? What kind of rebels *are* you?"

Grabbing the fronts of their surcoats in each hand, the Barmaid propelled her two Disposable friends rapidly backwards across the cobbled stable yard and through the door into the dusty, hay-riddled stable. Several horses glanced up and fixed the new arrivals with curious looks as Flirt bundled her companions into the nearest empty stall and firmly slammed the gate shut.

There was a long moment of silence, damaged only by the muffled squeaks emanating from beneath the gagged, dishevelled blonde whom Flirt knew could only be the missing princess. With a weary huff, Shoulders shot the backside of his twitching bundle a filthy look and then tipped her unceremoniously off his shoulder into a pile of nearby hay. Constrained by rope and blue velvet, the fuzzy-headed princess flailed and kicked helplessly on her side, her blue-violet eyes wild with fury as she struggled to find a more royally appropriate stance. Through much undignified wriggling, she managed to haul herself into a sitting position. From there, she glared up at her kidnappers with a look that would not only have killed, if it were possible, but flayed the two Disposables alive and whacked them round the legs with wet towels for good measure.

Flirt could tell at once that she was going to make simply wonderful company.

But for now, a kidnapped princess was not the issue. The Barmaid's eyes raked over the two men before her: first Shoulders, battered, fraught, and weary looking, his face a potent cocktail of desperation, resignation, and irritability; and then Fodder, who...

Who...

Looked *alive*. So very, very alive. Alive in a way that Flirt hadn't realised it was possible to be.

His smile was vibrant. She couldn't help but smile back.

"Come on then," she said softly. "Tell me everything."

They did. Fodder watched her face carefully as he recounted their strange tale. Within her expression, he was thrilled to find the understanding and excitement that had been so lacking from Shoulders's. She nodded and smiled and gasped in all the right places, even wordlessly handing Shoulders a pot of ale as he worked himself up at the recounting of his horrific night thus far. True, the fact that he viciously downed it in one meant it did not stem the tide of muttering for long, but it was a thoughtful gesture, and that was enough.

Fodder'd known she'd be an asset. Flirt was always prepared, and a quick glance at her pack proved tonight was no exception. That she had already been coming to find them was gratifying; that she could understand and accept his rough outline of a plan, even more so. And also as expected, it didn't take her long to whip it into shape.

"We'll need more people, won't we?" Flirt's gaze roamed the ceiling thoughtfully as she broke the brief silence that had followed Fodder's none-too-detailed explanation of what he intended to do. "The three of us aren't much of a rebellion, and more people means more fuss."

"What's good about fuss?" Shoulders grumbled irritably. "Fuss means being chased by men with spears and having holes poked in your gullet. Fuss means dungeons."

"But it also means attention, doesn't it?" Flirt grinned broadly. "The more people who know what we're doing, the more likely it is we'll find the ones who'll listen. And the more people who listen, the more likely it is we'll find the ones who like what they hear. And once we have enough of those, we can't be ignored anymore. They can't lock us up after that, can they? If the people who've listened outnumber the dungeons, what are they going to do then?"

Shoulders looked slightly mollified. "I suppose," he conceded rather grudgingly. "But where do you propose we find these magic listening people who'll keep me out of prison?"

Flirt frowned thoughtfully. "Not round here," she admitted. "Not if the lads last night are anything to go by. Maybe we could try the mountain Trappers or the folk up at the Grim Fortress? They might be more up for a change of scenery...."

"But what are we going to do about her?" Shoulders gestured violently with one thumb to where Pleasance's glare had, if anything, intensified. "We can't keep dragging her around kicking and screaming indefinitely. Aside from anything else, she's going to do my back in!"

The slight smile that touched the corners of Flirt's lips was exactly what Fodder had hoped to see. "Oh, you leave madam to me," she said conspiratorially, bending over and rummaging around in her makeshift pack. "Now where...aha! Here we are!"

The look that crossed Pleasance's face defied description. For what Flirt was flourishing so cheerfully appeared to be nothing more than a pair of sewing scissors and a small box of cosmetics.

"I'm sure you recognise these, don't you?" she asked the furious Pleasance cheerfully. "And that being said, us being girls together and given that we are about to spend pity-knows-how-long in each other's company, I thought we might be able to talk looks. Specifically, *your* looks. And what's going to happen to your looks if you don't calm down, stop kicking my friends, and start doing exactly as you're told." She glanced up at Fodder and Shoulders, her smile cheery and matter-of-fact. "What do you reckon would look better In Narrative, boys?" she remarked thoughtfully. "A bowl cut or no hair at all? Or maybe a bit of turquoise eyeliner in a check pattern to highlight her cheekbones?"

Rage was gone in a flash. A pair of blue-violet eyes filled with instant, flat-out horror.

"Lime green." Fodder barely managed to hold back the grin that was threatening to wash away his faux-thoughtful expression. "Definitely."

Flirt's lips twisted thoughtfully. "Really? I was thinking puce."

"Both." The beatific interruption came from Shoulders. "Stripes. Or better still, you could shave her bald and draw pictures of goats on her head..."

"Or maybe hedgehogs," Fodder offered.

"Paint her nose red with nail polish." Shoulders was gaining momentum.

"Shave her head down one side."

"Write *dunce* on her forehead."

"Glue some spare hair to her chin as a beard."

"Paint her arse..."

"Yes, thank you, Shoulders." Flirt fixed the Disposable with a brief, irritable look. "There is a limit, isn't there; and well done, you've found it." But her expression remained one of reasonable friendliness as she turned back to face the saucer-eyed princess. "But that doesn't matter, does it? We've got more than enough," she said, her tone a picture of explanatory helpfulness. "Our imagination is infinite. Our patience isn't. Okay?"

For a moment, Pleasance barely seemed capable of moving. Fodder was fairly certain that nobody in the whole of her life had ever spoken to her in such a way before. But then slowly, but distinctly, she nodded.

"Good." Reaching out, Flirt tucked the box and scissors neatly back into her pack before rising, her expression abruptly practical. "So, what do you reckon?" she said. "Lie low in the woods and then make a run for the mountains? Because—"

But she got no further. For it was then, with a creak, that the stable door opened.

A hand slapped down sharply against Fodder's head, and he found himself thrust to the floor next to a shocked-looking Shoulders and Flirt's abruptly abandoned pack. One glance at Pleasance was enough to tell that she was drawing breath to muster the loudest muffled scream she was capable of. With the barest of shared looks, he and Shoulders pounced, clamping her mouth and flailing limbs as quietly as they could. Flirt had turned sharply the moment she had finished shoving her companions to the ground, pulling open the stall and stepping out into the stable, wearing an admirably arranged expression of curiosity.

"Oh, hello, Midlin!" she exclaimed. "What are you doing here?"

Midlin. Fodder cursed fluently under his breath as he struggled to keep a silent grip on their thrashing captive. Of all of his Disposable compatriots, why did it have to be the one who was so emphatically Ordinary?

"Thud and Preen sent me and Donk down to search the village." Midlin's bland voice drifted from just a few yards away. "Have you heard what's happened?"

"Who hasn't?" Flirt's tone was impressively grave. "I came out here myself to check the outbuildings for them, but I haven't found a trace, have I? It doesn't surprise me, though. I'd imagine Fodder would have more sense than to blunder back home."

Fodder considered that remark entirely uncalled-for as he tried to ignore the gyrations of the fuzzy-haired princess he was desperately trying to keep silent. But Flirt was already ploughing on.

"So have they got you all scouring the countryside then?" she asked conversationally. "I imagine Preen's spitting blood, isn't he?"

"He's not happy." From anyone other than Midlin, such a remark would have contained more than a hint of sarcasm, but Midlin's dull voice offered it up as simple fact. "Especially since Strut put Thud in charge of the search. He sent Thump and Clunny off into the woods and set Dunny and Tumble to patrol the roads. Sentinel and his guards are out in force as well."

"Sounds serious, doesn't it?" How the hell was Flirt managing to stay so cool? "Are they sure it's not a mistake? Some misunderstanding with the instructions?"

"I wondered that too," Midlin admitted solemnly. "But after what Fodder was saying at dinner, I've started to doubt it. I've already passed the awful things he said to Preen."

Fodder fought to keep his blood from boiling, and the look on Shoulders's face strongly implied that he too considered violence to be in the air. Midlin had told *Preen* about their conversation? Whatever happened to friendship, to Disposable loyalty, of all being in it together?

It seemed, however, that that was exactly what Midlin's loyalty was. Disposable.

He'd hated the conversation at dinner. Fodder had gotten the impression that Midlin not only didn't understand, but couldn't. And here was the proof. He'd broken the unwritten rule. You *did not* tattle to Preen about your mates.

"You passed it on?" Flirt sounded as shocked as Fodder felt.

"It was the right thing to do." Midlin actually sounded surprised by her question. "I don't know where he got those unnatural ideas from, but he needs to be stopped as soon as possible. He's trying to destroy our way of life, and we can't let that happen. I know you spoke up for him earlier, but now this has happened, you must be able to see that."

Pleasance's wriggling had not ceased. Fodder had been hoping the prospect of Flirt's cosmetic improvements would be enough to calm her, but apparently with the prospect of rescue a few yards away, her fear of goat-decorated skin and shaved-off hair had gone out of the window.

"Of course I can!" Just beyond the stall, Flirt was bluffing wildly. "I can't believe what I was thinking! In fact, why don't I help you search? I've done this stable, but if you head out to the cowshed, I'll go and check the yard...."

It was worth a try, but Fodder knew the moment the words passed her lips what the result would be. Midlin was too set in his ways, too obedient to instructions.

"I was told to do it myself. I have to check the stable."

Footsteps, moving through the hay, Midlin starting forwards, Flirt ferociously back-pedalling.

"But there's really no need, is there? I've searched it from end to end!"

"I was told to do it myself."

"Don't you trust me?"

"It's not about trust. I was told to do it myself."

A hand, Midlin's hand, on the stall gate, as Flirt's curly head thrust forwards to block his view. Fodder shouldered Flirt's pack as quietly as he dared even as Shoulders took a firmer grip on the horrified princess, ready for an abrupt hoist.

"Honestly, there's no need!"

"I was told to do it."

"But you'll be wasting your time! They could be out there right now, getting further away with the princess!"

"But I was told to—"

"Midlin!"

"Yes?"

Midlin had already half opened their stall. And so it was that Fodder got to witness an uppercut punch straight out of the Narrative textbook.

"Leg it!" Shoulders was up and running before Midlin hit the floor—Pleasance hurled over one shoulder, leaving Fodder and Flirt little choice but to follow. Even as they skidded out of the doors into the stable yard, Flirt wringing her right hand, they could hear Midlin—alas, still conscious—yelling at the top of his voice and, oh sod it, there were the villagers pouring out of the inn, looking bewildered and tired.

"Woods!" Flirt bellowed commandingly, and Fodder didn't bother to argue with her as she belted off towards the dark trees on the far side of the village. Torches were flaring behind them. Strut's strident tones echoed through the cluster of houses, trying to muster Fodder's sleepy community into some manner of pursuit. Shoulders was stumbling and staggering under the weight of his Royal burden, Pleasance's head bumping and bobbing unceremoniously against his back. Fodder could feel the pack bouncing, the inexplicable poker that Flirt had packed digging painfully into his right kidney as he pumped his legs into the kind of exertion unfamiliar out of Narrative. In the shadows to his left, he caught a glimpse of Donk's massive frame lumbering out of Shoulders's tatty cottage and, further back, he could see Tumble and Dunny belting down the woodland road towards them. And—oh bugger—away over his shoulder, perhaps a mile back up the trail, he could almost taste the advance of the vivid blackness of The Narrative.

They want to capture us In Narrative. They want to make it plot, have the Merry Band do it. Well, let them try! I defied it before; I can do it again!

Probably…

Now was not the time for doubt. Hot on the heels of his companions, Fodder plunged into the darkened woods.

Fodder knew these woods. Most former Humble Village Urchins did. All of them had played amongst the trees in their youth, found their own special spots and secret places. Most amongst their number, including Fodder himself, had at one time or another claimed that they could traverse the woods blindfolded.

This was proven immediately to be a lie as Fodder ran into a low-hanging branch, stumbled upright to reel into a patch of brambles, and then promptly stuck his foot down a badger hole.

Somewhere to his right, Fodder heard a loud thump and the sound of Shoulders's voice cursing with enthusiasm. To his left, he heard Flirt sigh.

"You two are *bloody useless*," he heard her mutter.

A hand grasped his arm, hauling him out of the badger hole and away into the darkness. A brief stop also retrieved Shoulders and the bound Pleasance, who had been dropped rather indelicately, if accidentally, into the mud puddle that had earned Shoulders's wrath. And then they were off, moving through the trees in a manner which strongly implied that, while other claims at moving blindfolded through the woods had been exaggerated, Flirt's had not. How she managed to avoid the brambles, briars, roots, mud, and low branches that thwacked, tore at, and generally tormented Fodder and, to judge by his swearing, Shoulders too, he genuinely didn't know. It was entirely possible that she simply handled herself with more panache. But whatever the cause, by the time Flirt led them down a sharp slope into a narrow gully and into a low, round opening concealed in the roots of a tree, Fodder was fairly certain that he was bleeding from more places than he wasn't.

After a brief crawl on their hands and knees through a tight tunnel, they emerged into a low-ceilinged grotto. Fodder added a bruised head to his ever-growing list of wounds.

As Flirt lit the small lantern concealed in an alcove out of sight of the entrance, their hidey hole flickered into view. It appeared to have started life as a badger's set, judging by the even narrower tunnels that vanished between the curling roots into the earth behind, but it had clearly been adopted more recently by something more human-shaped. A ratty old rug had been spread on the uneven floor, and three broken-down boxes had been placed about, apparently as makeshift chairs. A tiny wooden chest, a bottle, a stone pendant on a string, and a sad, damp, mouldy piece of ribbon lay scattered about on the floor.

"It's my childhood den." Flirt answered the unasked question as she dropped onto one of the rickety boxes with a sigh. "My sisters and I used to play here as girls. Only the three of us ever knew about it."

"Are you sure?" Shoulders propped the surprisingly unresisting princess up against the nearest wall, then dropped onto the rug, rubbing at a long bramble cut running down his cheek.

"Did you know it was here?" Flirt countered. "It was our secret place. We never told anyone." She smiled slightly. "We didn't want any noisy boys sticking their noses in."

"I trust you," Fodder stated frankly. "But what about Levity and Lass?"

"It was mostly me and Levity really," Flirt replied with a shrug. "And I doubt they'll go all the way to Provincial Town tonight to ask her where in the woods I might go to hide, will they? Lass only came here about twice—she didn't like getting her dresses dirty."

"But she has been spending an awful lot of time with Clunny lately," Shoulders pointed out somewhat dubiously. Fodder was relieved that his friend had shown enough good sense not to go into the kind of detail that Clunny had when he'd gleefully described their latest evening together whilst waiting on the road a few days before. "If she does remember…"

"I doubt she'll see him before morning, what with all this fuss."

Flirt dismissed the concern with a wave of her hand as she reached into her pack and dragged out the blankets. "And by then we'll be well and truly gone, won't we? You two should try and get some sleep—I reckon it'll be in short supply for a while. I'll stand watch." Her eyes raked over Shoulders's muddy armour and Fodder's bloodstained face, not to mention the filthy state of Princess Pleasance's precious hair. "Those wounds will most likely be healed by morning, but there's a stream just outside if you need to wash."

"Yeah, I know," Shoulders muttered bad-temperedly. "I bloody *trod* in it."

"Use this." Flirt handed Shoulders the battered old bottle from the floor. "Clean it, then bring some water inside, will you? And be careful. We know Clunny and Thump are out there and probably half the village by now too."

Muttering about how he was hardly an idiot and how he had been there when they'd been chased, Shoulders crouched down and crawled out of the narrow entryway.

There was a moment of blessed silence. Fodder glanced over to where Flirt had settled herself, her expression thoughtful as she rummaged through their pack once more. How lucky they were that she'd so easily taken their side. Without her, Fodder was certain that they'd have been captured already.

Ordinary she might have been born, but ordinary Flirt of Humble Village most certainly was not.

"Thanks for this." The words slipped out almost unconsciously. "You know, for taking charge. Sorting us out."

Flirt glanced up, and Fodder was surprised to see a hint of consternation on her face.

"You don't mind, do you?" she asked, her voice suddenly filled with concern. "I mean, I've been bossing you around, and this is your plan after all...."

"No, no!" Fodder stuck his hands up in the air with a smile that he hoped portrayed his outright relief that she had come along. "We needed it, and you're much better at this than I'd ever be. I'm more than happy to be the ideas man. You keep bossing us as much as you like." His smile spread. "You're bloody good at it, you know."

Flirt grinned broadly. "I always said I was more than a hair colour and a bosom, didn't I? I've been waiting for a chance like this all my life!"

Fodder gave a short laugh, meeting her eyes quietly. "You know what?" he said softly. "I think I have too. I just didn't know it."

"I dreamed of it." Flirt's eyes drifted far away. "I've always wanted to show every leery bugger who ever pinched my bottom or called me *darling* that I'm made of sterner stuff than they are. Well, let me tell you!" she exclaimed with sudden fervour. "No man's going to call me *wench* again! Not unless he wants his guts yanked out and roasted over a slow fire! I'll show them what they're made of!"

Fodder frowned slightly. "Shouldn't that be you'll show them what *you're* made of?"

The glint in Flirt's eye was just slightly alarming. "Not if they call me *wench*! The next man to do that'll be seeing what he's made of spread all over the road at his feet...."

"Trod in the bloody stream again, didn't I?"

Fodder had never been so thankful to hear that grouching tone. Accustomed as he was to senseless brutality, the mental imagery that had accompanied Flirt's words had not sat well in his brain. He liked her very much, but there were times when she could be deeply, deeply scary.

With a shuffle and a thud, Shoulders's distinctly cleaner head appeared suddenly through the hole. Abruptly, he thrust the icy cold bottle of water into Fodder's hands.

"It's bloody freezing, that water!" he declared. "But there's no one about. I think there was a hint of The Narrative over the trees somewhere north, but I didn't get close enough to tell. It wasn't very close, anyway. Are you going to use that or what?"

Startled out of his surprise at the intrusion, Fodder busied himself in tearing a fresh rag from his already ripped surcoat and damping it down with the water.

"Yeah, thanks," he managed inarticulately. His eyes strayed over to the grubby, tangled, and subdued princess, looking over her pale face and wide, miserable eyes. In spite of his ongoing irritation with her, Fodder couldn't help but feel a little twinge of guilt.

"What about her?" He gestured with less-than-considerable enthusiasm. "Do you think we should clean her up a bit too? She did behave when we were running."

"I suppose there's no harm in rewarding good behaviour, is there?" At Flirt's gesture, Fodder tore yet another rag from his now-belt-length surcoat and handed over the bottle. "You see?" she told the princess with a smile. "Misbehave and creative things happen involving scissors and skin illustrations. But if you behave, we'll make sure you're comfortable. Okay?"

At Pleasance's reluctant nod, Flirt settled down with the rag and bottle to clear away the worst of the grime from the porcelain features. Fodder and Shoulders, stooped to avoid collision with the low roof, set about laying the blankets in the limited available space. Fodder shook his head quietly as he settled down. It had been a strange few hours. He could only hope the night would be more restful.

What am I doing? What have I gotten myself into?

But that was a question for mornings, for the cold light of day. For now, he needed sleep.

* * *

It was not the most blissful night's sleep that Fodder had ever had. The aches and pains of the non-Narrative damage he had suffered faded away overnight, but the ground was hard and slightly damp and several times, he was woken by the distant sound of voices and tromping feet somewhere in the woods beyond the grotto's entrance. Flirt had kept the early watch, but she had apologetically woken Fodder a few hours later, explaining that she'd decided the grumbling if she'd roused Shoulders for such an unpleasant watch would have lasted several eternities. And so Fodder had yawned his way through several hours of nervous listening before he had braced himself and woken Shoulders. But the sleep he dropped into after his watch was thin and unsatisfying, and he was already half-awake when Flirt roused him. The pale, dusty light trickling down the tunnel from the gully implied that it was about dawn.

"I've had a scout round the woods," Flirt informed her companions thoughtfully as they packed up and readied themselves for their first official day of rebellion. "And it's teeming with people out there. Mostly it's the villagers, and they really aren't trying that hard to find anything, but Thud's been striding about bellowing like a lunatic and The Narrative's been circling the woods like a vulture with the Merry Band, so I think we'll have to be careful."

"Jolly good," Shoulders muttered without much enthusiasm as he inspected the thin scars that were all that remained of the non-Narrative damage he'd suffered the night before. "But how the hell are we supposed to get up Bandit Pass and into the mountains in broad daylight without being spotted?"

"I have had one thought." Flirt pursed her lips as she clinched the pack closed. "I snuck up to the edge of the woods and took a quick peek into the village. It's almost completely empty—just a couple of Urchins knocking about and Tumble and Dunny guarding the edge of the trees. Sneaking past them shouldn't be too much of a challenge, and if we can get back to the inn, they've parked up the princess's ambush carriage in the stable yard. That'd get us up into the mountains fairly sharpish."

"Flirt." Shoulders spoke slowly and with a distinct hint of irritation. "I've seen that carriage. It's got a broken wheel."

"They've fixed it, haven't they, you prat!" The insult was matter-of-fact. "They had to, to get it down off the pass. They're waiting for Sentinel and his team to come back before it gets returned to the Magnificent City. Nobody's watching it—Strut's dragged the poor coachman out into the woods to search for us."

Shoulders was still glowering slightly in the wake of newly acquired prat-hood. "And we can't just take the horses and ride them because…?"

"Horses are easier for The Narrative to mess with, aren't they?" Flirt pulled a face. "One touch and you'd be thrown or tossed in a ditch or sent off in another direction. But a whole team of horses should be much harder to interfere with. It'll take more time to turn them all or make them veer off, and that time could make the difference between us getting caught and escaping." The look she gave Shoulders was slightly reproachful. "I did think this through, you know!"

But Fodder could see one major drawback immediately. "That coach is very distinctive. They'll spot it a mile off."

"Not in the mountains, they won't, will they?" Flirt, it seemed, had made up her mind. "We'll dump it off a cliff once we get near to the Trapper Station and let the horses go. It's just a means to an end. A way to get out of the area in a hurry." She glanced at Shoulders with a sudden smile. "Plus, it means Shoulders won't have to hoist her Royal Wriggliness around for a while."

Faced with an instant two-against-one, Fodder had little choice but to concede the argument. "All right." He backed down gracefully. "We'll take the carriage. But that is a good point about the princess. Shoulders can't keep carrying her around forever."

Shoulders seconded him with enthusiasm. "Damn bloody right I can't! She's doing my back in! Either you two take a turn, or she can walk!"

Flirt turned to where the princess was slumped up against the dirt wall. In deference to her recent good behaviour, Pleasance had been cleaned up, the blood and grime wiped from her skin, her battered clothes straightened, her previously perfectly coiffured hair scraped into some semblance of order. A strong hint of a pout was visible beneath her gag and her violet eyes stared mournfully out across the room. But there was just a hint, just a glitter behind those sorrowful eyes that the furious rage they had witnessed in her on the mountain-side was waiting for its moment to strike.

"Okay, little madam." Flirt addressed the princess with her usual cheeriness. "If I take this gag off, I don't want to hear any screaming from you. Not if you want to be sparkling and pretty for your Boy of Destiny if you ever do find your way back into Narrative. Are we all clear?"

With palpable reluctance, the princess nodded.

"And you promise to behave?"

Again came the painful nod.

"Good girl." With a flick of her wrist, Flirt unknotted the gag.

For an instant, it seemed to Fodder as though Flirt's words had been pointless, that the princess was drawing in air for a scream in spite of the warnings. But Flirt's fingers darted towards the cosmetic box with the speed of lightning, and their captive immediately thought better of it and aborted to a lower volume.

"You won't get away with this!" The dramatic tone had lost a little of its verve overnight, but the melodrama of her voice still ran rampant. "Thieves! Brigands! You shall be found and brought to justice, and I shall visit you in the dungeons and laugh in your faces until my lungs are raw! Laugh, I tell you! *Laugh!*"

Shoulders glanced over at Fodder with the first hint of a grin he had displayed for quite some time. "Do you think she's going to laugh, mate?"

Fodder couldn't help but grin back. "Think she might, yeah."

Violet eyes glared furiously. "Common peasants! You mock me while you can!"

"Yep, we will, ta."

"But you won't be laughing soon!" Pleasance ploughed on, thoroughly ignoring the interruption from Shoulders as she hit her rhythm with her tirade. "Soon you will be the ones chained and gagged and mocked and I will have my vengeance upon you! You will rue the day you ever... *mmph!*"

Flirt glanced back over her shoulder from where she had just thrust a whole apple into Pleasance's delicate mouth.

"Either of you ever *mmphed?*" she enquired cheerfully.

"Nope."

"Can't say that I have."

"Me neither. So I doubt I'll ever rue the day I did it." Flirt smiled sweetly at the indignant princess. "Eat up."

Once this rudimentary breakfast had been completed, Flirt prudently restored the gag but not before eliciting a promise that, if Pleasance were allowed to walk, she would go where directed and not make a fuss. Since the Barmaid had tied the sewing scissors prudently within reach against her apron, grudging agreement had been given and Shoulders, rather than carrying his Royal burden, was put in charge of shepherding her.

Carefully, cautiously, they moved out into the gully and set off into the Rambling Woods.

Flirt had been right when she'd said the woods were teeming. Tired, sleepy villagers were shambling in small packs through the trees, half-heartedly searching but mostly dreaming of bed and sleep and being just about anywhere but where they were. They were evaded by the simple measure of ducking behind the nearest tree and waiting. The first hint of more serious opposition came as Fodder and his companions neared the edge of the woods and found a troop of Sentinel's shiny, professional Disposables sweeping their search area in an alarmingly proficient manner—batting at bushes with their swords and actually looking behind trees as they walked past them. But these men were Palace Guards, used to standing still and staring straight ahead and, tricky as it was to force Pleasance into climbing a tree, Flirt's theory that they would not even think to look up was proved accurate.

Their leafy vantage point offered another advantage: Fodder spotted The Narrative.

It was close, over near the rough track where they'd staged their ambush what felt like forever ago, its vivid, unreal light gleaming like a sunbeam down from the grey sky. As he strained his ears, Fodder could hear the strident voices of the Merry Band drifting on the breeze, proclaiming in grand tones that these impudent swine who stole the princess would be brought to justice. Somewhere off to his left, he also heard a brief bout of Thud yelling at somebody or another to pay more attention and sort themselves out.

And every single one of these people was out there after him. Hunting for him. Because of what he'd done.

It was terrifyingly exhilarating.

The exhilaration wore off in something of a hurry when he was forced to manoeuvre Pleasance's velvet-clad backside down out of the tree. There was nothing more likely to restore cold, hard reality than having a whole princess dropped on you from several feet above.

But finally, thankfully, they reached the edge of the woods. As Flirt had said, Tumble and Dunny were indeed patrolling the village border, but they were doing so without much enthusiasm. It was no great chore to wait until they'd wandered past and dive into the cluster of deserted cottages. Carefully skirting their way past the various buildings, Fodder, his friends, and the princess headed for the village green.

Thankfully, the Archetypal Inn was exactly where and how they'd left it: perched on the edge of the green under the name of the Good Shepherd and looking unnaturally peaceful in the quiet of the abandoned village. It was alarmingly easy to slip around the edge of the green, ushering the grouchy princess before them, and duck into the stable yard, where, as Flirt had promised, the Royal carriage had been left idling. It was a clunky great thing, carved of dark wood. It bore a vast array of intricate carvings ranged along its eaves and corners and the coat of arms that, for the purposes of this Quest, belonged to the Kingdom of Nyolesse engraved or painted in on almost every available panel. The word *ostentatious* might have been invented for it.

Along with the word *hideous*.

"Subtle," Shoulders commented blandly. "Not trying to get noticed at all, is it?"

Fodder grinned. "You've never met the Artisans down in the Magnificent City, have you? I ran into them when I Bulked Up for a chase scene down there a couple of Quests back. Since they almost never get more than a passing sentence of Narrative time themselves, they throw everything they've got into making their props as loud and noticeable as possible. To them, a decent description of their handiwork is as good as having a decent character."

"Weird bunch."

Fodder had to admit that Shoulders's assessment did sum up the slightly odd cluster of men he'd chatted to while waiting for The Narrative that morning rather nicely.

"And not much taste either."

"Gaudy is the way to go if you want to get described, isn't it?" Flirt appeared from the stables, leading a couple of uncertain-looking horses and wearing an expression almost as grouchy as the princess's. "It doesn't matter if you're a shiny prop or a shiny princess. Brown and ordinary doesn't get you into Narrative." One of the horses she was leading whickered and bucked slightly against her hold. "Give me a hand, will you?" she called out. "I've never hitched a horse to a carriage before."

As Fodder hurried over to lend a hand, Shoulders glanced at the princess, who was sat slumped in a sulky heap against one of the carriage wheels.

"What shall I do with her ladyship?" he asked curiously. "Do you want me to guard her or give you a hand?"

"Just truss up her legs and find somewhere safe to leave her," Flirt called back. "We can deal with her when we're done."

* * *

When all matters were considered, weighed, and taken to account, it had to be said that Princess Pleasance of the Royal Family was not having a good start to her first Quest.

The ropes around her wrists were tight—not so tight as to make her profoundly uncomfortable but tight enough to insure there would be no wriggling free. The gag was secured around her mouth with equal firmness, and the scraggly Disposable who had been hauling her around in so disrespectful a manner had bound her feet before dumping her in an empty horse trough between the wall and the carriage—her carriage!—that they were trying to steal and rushing off to help with the horses. She had fidgeted experimentally for a moment when their backs were turned, but it quickly became clear that she wasn't going anywhere.

Not away from this nightmare. Not back to her story where she belonged.

It was happening without her, her legend, her Quest, her chance of a lifetime, fluttering by while she sat gagged and bound in a horse trough that smelled very strongly of things she did not want to consider. It was winding away, disappearing from her grasp while she sat and watched three common brigands stealing her royal coach so they could kidnap her more comfortably.

And it *wasn't fair.*

She had waited so long for it to be her turn. She'd seen her older sister Sweetness swept off her feet in *The Vile Rose,* her brave defiance of dark magic allowing just enough time for her noble, knightly hero to save the day. She'd watched as her cousin Vanity rode out not once, but twice, defending the city against the Rachsis horde in *The Tide of Crimson* and rallying the people just in time to ride to the rescue of her beleaguered love in *The Sword of Grul.* And of course, she had heard, many times, the stories of her mother, once Princess and now *Queen* Eminence, shouldering the burden of magic herself to save the kingdom in *The Seed of Darkness.* And Pleasance had waited and waited, impatient and desperate to reach the right kind of maturity to be up for selection, knowing that with her heritage and her lineage—Princesses for generations down one side, Kings and Heroes and Boys of Destiny right down the other—it would surely only be a matter of time before her turn came.

And then, at last, it had.

The Sword of Grul had tumbled into epilogue and Happily Ever After, the quiet lull time between the end of one Quest and the launch of another. After starring in two impressive sagas, a stroke of good fortune enabled by a slightly more mature Hero and Heroine in the latter, Vanity had been retired and, as had become firmly expected, she'd finally gotten around to accepting one of the two marriage proposals she had received out of Narrative from her romantic counterparts. She had chosen Valiant, the second of her two Heroes—the first, she had confided to Pleasance, was very handsome but had a terrible tendency to mess up her hair when he kissed her—and was comfortably maturing as an attractive Duchess at court until she was old enough to take her place as a Queen. And so Pleasance had waited, her patience strained almost to the breaking point as new instructions and preparations for a new Quest with characters, countries, and an ever-evolving plot outline laid themselves out in the impressive new Golden Tome that had appeared to replace its *Sword of Grul* counterpart in the never-visited-In-Narrative rear of the city's Grand Temple. Slowly, painfully, ideas solidified, characters were nailed down, and the Priests and Scholars handed out the interactive *Ring of Anthiphion* Quest books to the Officious Courtiers and sent them on their way.

And so it was that Strut had gathered the Principal families, as always, in the grand throne room of the Royal Palace and set about distributing the roles.

The squeals she had emitted when he had announced her as Princess Islaine had nearly shattered the rafters. At last! She was to be a Heroine! At last!

Her enthusiasm for the Quest had waned only slightly when she'd discovered it would be Bumpkin she would be playing opposite. He wasn't so bad looking, of course, and she knew he would grow into a muscular, pixie dust-enhanced maturity as the Quest progressed, but she'd known him for a while and found him just a bit childish. She'd been hoping for this to be a Quest for a more mature Hero than the coming of age of a Boy of Destiny—a handsome King or noble Knight who'd sweep her off her feet, not some gauche adolescent love story. And her consternation had grown more than a little when Bumpkin had taken her aside before setting out for Fertile Fields and his humble beginnings and asked to get in some kissing practice.

Pleasance had indulged in a degree of practice herself, ably assisted by the handsome young Knight that Clank was training up as his apprentice. And she knew full well that kisses such as Bumpkin bestowed were definitely at the slobbery end of the spectrum.

And if she wasn't chosen as Heroine again for the next Quest, it was expected that she marry the Hero of this one. That was the way it was done. It was right and proper that way. Because even though it was usually simply implied behind closed doors, concealed by billowy curtains or in a secret, sparkling pool that required no actual *doing*, every so often, certain romantic deeds betwixt Hero and Heroine did prove to be necessary In Narrative. And once the deed was done...

Maybe he'd improve with practice. She'd have to give him proper instruction.

If she could endure the constant drool dripping down her chin until he learned...

But right now, Pleasance would have taken a thousand slobbery kisses from Bumpkin to be riding with the Merry Band to fulfil her rightful destiny.

It was her turn! And they'd ruined it.

Her ire refocused once more upon her three kidnappers: the bland, unremarkable one who'd started it; his scruffy, whiney companion who continued to toss her about like an object; and the chirpy harpy they'd recruited to boss them around. How dare they treat her this way? She'd done nothing to deserve it, nothing at all! A pair of rough, common Disposables and their bitchy Interchangeable Barmaid, dragging her out of her own story before she'd had the chance to get started, hurling her around, messing up her hair and clothes, mocking her, making her dirty, hauling her up trees and down holes in the ground like she was nothing more than a velvet-clad sack! And that was not to mention threatening her, ordering her around, and gagging her! How dare they?

And why? So they could usurp her and her family and obtain themselves a starring role! It was the most ridiculous thing that Pleasance had ever heard. For goodness' sake, how could they possibly believe that anyone would be interested in a Quest about *them?*

And for this pointlessness, they'd disrupted the pinnacle of her life and threatened her with humiliation and ridicule.

She shuddered slightly at the memory of that awful threat, at the thought of an impromptu haircut with sewing scissors or childish tattoos made of eyeliner. If they were unscrupulous enough to do that to an innocent prisoner, what else might they do? The thought of what might be her only lead role in a Quest being turned into a joke as she staggered into Narrative with a shaved head and dancing hedgehogs on her cheeks… The thought of being *comic relief*…

Occasionally, it happened. A princess would be mocked or made fun of In Narrative, but it was always as character development, as plot, never just because a stupid Barmaid and her loutish friends felt like it. And Pleasance had vowed that Islaine would be a princess of dignity, that she would be admired and respected and part of the fun, never the butt of it. But who could admire and respect her if she was seen In Narrative with half her hair hacked off and her skin used as a place to doodle?

No. She couldn't let it happen. For the time being, she was in their power. She had to—her teeth gritted behind her gag—*behave*.

She would have her revenge. Of that much she was certain. When Strut and the others got hold of them, she would make sure that every insult and indignity that she'd suffered was repaid a hundredfold. None of them would ever see the light of freedom again! She was going to make them suffer!

The swift neighing of an irritable horse turned her attention back to her captors and their awkward efforts to manoeuvre a team of horses into the cradle of the carriage. Beneath her gag, Pleasance sneered silently at their incompetence at completing a simple job that the Palace stable hands could do in mere seconds. In the face of such uselessness, her revenge would come sooner than she'd thought.

"Come on then! Nice horsey!"

"Nice horsey? You really think it'll respond to that?"

"You never know until you try, do you? Here, hold these reins a sec, Shoulders…"

"No, I don't want them! Fodder, here!"

"I'm already holding one!"

"Then you won't mind holding two!"

"I bloody will!"

"Oh for the love of… You two, just… Here, I'll hold it! And keep it down, will you? If someone hears us, we're done for!"

"You were the one shouting about nice horseys!"

The bickering dropped to a lower, more discreet level but continued nonetheless as the reins were dragged into place over the poor beasts' faces. The horses continued to whicker uncomfortably, her captors' muttered arguments doing nothing to stem their nervousness. Honestly, they had to be the most pointless…

"Clunny, do you think anyone will notice we've gone?"

Pleasance froze.

This was not a voice she knew. And it was coming from the other side of the stable wall.

Someone else was coming. Someone was right outside.

She wanted to bellow, scream out *I'm here, I'm here, save me!* but her gag gave no leeway. She glanced frantically at her kidnappers, but one look was enough to see that they were too distracted by their horse wrangling to hear these new arrivals approaching. And Pleasance knew at once that her only chance was not to alert them until it was too late.

"I doubt it." A second voice, weaselly and as common as the other, bit down a yawn as it joined the first. "They're too busy having their backsides whipped by that sadist Thud. But I've been up a whole day and night now and if I don't get a sit-down and an ale, I'm going to go insane."

"Do you reckon Stout will mind?" Footsteps, a pair of them, were getting closer and closer to the still-wide-open stable gate, a position from which only a blind man could fail to see what was going on inside. *Oh let this be it, let me be rescued! Please!*

"Thump, mate, he'll cheer us on. Now come on. I need a serious amount of drink before going out into those woods again."

Closer, closer, closer, come on, come on, come on…

"And after all," the voice continued, rounding the corner, so close to the gate, *see them, come on, see them, save me!* "They'll be long gone by now. The odds of us just blundering across them are—"

The corner was rounded. The voice faded away. Two figures dressed in unexpectedly shiny armour wandered into view, stared, faltered, and froze. And behind her gag, Pleasance screamed with joy.

I'm going to be saved! Vengeance is mine!

But vengeance, it seemed, was slow off the mark. Why was no one *moving?*

* * *

Fodder stared at Thump and Clunny.

Thump and Clunny stared back.

And then Clunny's shoulders dropped wearily. "Oh bloody hell," he muttered fervently. "You couldn't have hidden or something?"

Fodder blinked. "Pardon?"

"I just wanted a sit-down and a break." Clunny gritted his teeth as he fingered the short sword he'd been carrying loosely in one hand. "And now I've got to arrest my mates instead." He groaned out loud, his tone irritably plaintive. "I didn't want to be the one who had to do this."

"Well then, don't." Shoulders was not one for beating around the bush. "Go and have your pint, and we won't tell if you don't!"

Thump's expression was resigned as he hefted his axe. "We can't do that, can we?" he muttered wearily. "They'll drag us off to the Grim Fortress right along with you." He shook his head. "Come on, lads...Flirt. Just toss us the princess and come quietly, yeah? We don't want to get into a fight with you."

Flirt moved slowly away from where Fodder had secured the final clinch in the horses' reins, her eyes fixed warily upon the two new arrivals.

"Shoulders, get the princess," she instructed quietly.

"What?" Fodder could feel a wellspring of alarm threatening to bubble up his throat. Surely Flirt wasn't giving up so easily. She couldn't. "But we can't just..."

"And put her in the carriage." Flirt finished the sentence very deliberately. "We're leaving. And they're not going to stop us."

"Hey, now hold on." As if by magic, the alarm that had been building in Fodder transferred instantly onto the faces of Clunny and Thump. Thump moved one step away from his friend, his features suddenly nervous as he watched Shoulders hoist the wild-eyed and incredulously infuriated princess and haul her to the waiting carriage door. "You've had your moment of madness, but it's over. If you turn yourselves in, admit you made a mistake, they might even go easy on you."

"What mistake?" Fodder decided it was time to get to the point. "We didn't make a mistake. We made a *beginning.*"

Clunny's narrow face hardened sharply. "This is last night again, isn't it?" he snapped abruptly. "All that rubbish you were spouting over supper about defying the Taskmaster! Well, fine, Fodder, you've proved your stupid little point! You've managed to upset everything and every-one, bully for you, aren't you clever? But enough is enough. It's time to stop."

Over his shoulder, Fodder caught a glimpse of Shoulders peering through the carriage window with the incandescently furious princess at his side. Behind him, he heard rather than saw Flirt climbing into place on the coachman's seat with a rustle of leather as she grasped the reins.

"This isn't about proving a point," he retorted softly. "I don't want to make some statement that they'll brush under the carpet and ignore. I want to make people see from our point of view. I want to be treated with respect and given an equal chance in life." He cringed over the words he was about to say, but they really were the only ones he could come up with to summarise his hopes. "Don't you see? I want things to be different. I want to *change the world.*"

Clunny snorted. "Don't want much, do you?" His fellow Disposa-ble had always been a fidgeter but now his limbs were twitching so hard that Fodder wondered if his friend was about to have a seizure. "Change the world? There's nothing wrong with it!"

Fodder grimaced. "So you enjoy getting chopped up and left in a ditch then?"

Clunny's shrug was a tiny bit too quick. "It's a better living than some. It's better than being background."

"But what if you had the chance to be foreground?"

Clunny gritted his teeth. "What chance? We're Ordinary."

"Only because the Taskmaster says so!"

"And who'll say so if the Taskmaster doesn't? Huh?" Clunny's narrow face thrust forwards angrily, the veins on his neck standing out in an alarming manner. "So we do ignore the Taskmaster, what then? What do we do with ourselves? What's the point?"

Fodder found himself slightly at a loss in the face of his friend's sudden insight. But he ploughed on regardless. "The point's whatever we want it to be!"

"You mean whatever *you* want it to be!" Clunny stabbed his sword viciously into the air as though to emphasise his point. "You want to write the world to your tune, do you? You bang on about the Task-master bossing us around, but if you want to make our world over without our say-so, how does that make you any different?"

Fodder actually found himself floundering. "We just want a choice...."

"We have a choice! Like it or lump it!"

"But if things were different..."

"What makes you think we want them different? Some of us are quite happy to have the world the way it is! And if it's a choice between trusting the all-powerful Taskmaster who's looked after us for generations or relying on you to run the world, I know where my money's going!"

Thump was glancing from one Disposable to the other with an expression of outright confusion on his face. It was clear that he wasn't really following what was being said. But Clunny's eyes were all too clear.

Fodder knew at once that this was an argument he wasn't going to win.

He tried to ignore the cold, nagging doubt that Clunny's words had lodged in the back of his mind. But he knew he'd have to face it later.

There was a hint of bewildered desperation in Thump's eyes now. "Look, why don't you give us the princess?" he suggested, his fingers twisting nervously around the axe shaft. It was clear he was longing for Ronald the cudgel—his solid, reassuring weapon of choice, something familiar in a sea of strange confusion. "You can go. We don't want to arrest our mates. But we need you to hand the princess over."

Clunny didn't look so certain about this compromise, but it seemed he was fairly willing to take any option that would make this no longer his problem. "I'll go with that. You can wander off and go barmy in private, all three of you. It's not like you're going to get anywhere. But you have to give the princess back."

It was a genuine option, Fodder had to admit. If they were able to evade capture, they could most likely remain incognito in a new and distant corner of the map.

No. Events had come too far. That was never going to happen.

Thump and Clunny were still blocking the entrance to the stable yard as Fodder backed away past the horses, groping for the coachman's ledge. Flirt's hand caught his and helped haul him upwards. He gave his friends a thin smile.

"Sorry, lads," he said, quite sincerely, knowing the trouble they were likely to get into over this. "But we're leaving. All four of us." His eyes met Clunny's. "Like it or lump it."

Thump squared himself off unconvincingly. "You'll have to get past us first!" he blustered loudly.

"Through you, actually," Flirt noted clinically. "I reckon the kind of non-Narrative damage you'll pick up from being run over by a carriage will take a few days to heal. But you'll get your rest that way, won't you?"

Fodder could see in their eyes doubt waging war with incredulity. Was Flirt bluffing? Was she really as bold as she'd always claimed? Would she really charge straight at them and run down two long-time customers and part-time friends?

One whip of the reins proved the answer to be *yes*.

"This is for every time you two have leered at my fake chest! *Yah!*"

It took every ounce of strength Fodder possessed to cling on to the ornately decorated carriage seat as the surge of abrupt motion sent his head ricocheting painfully off the wooden panels behind him. The horses, already spooked and distinctly irritated by the cack-handed attempts to hitch them, took off with considerable gusto, pounding towards the open gate where Clunny and Thump were still standing, with hooves mashing the dirt floor into pulp. In spite of the relative evenness of the surface, the carriage bounced impossibly, wheels jerking and hurling Fodder from side to side like a rag doll as he dug his fingernails into the wood and prayed with all his might.

He managed not to close his eyes, though it was a close-run thing. It took an astonishingly short amount of time to close down on the wide-eyed, horrified faces of Clunny and Thump. With mere inches between them and a mangled week in bed, both leapt out of their path and dived for cover.

Flirt yanked sharply on the reins as they plunged through the gate and out onto the road. They took the resulting corner on two wheels.

Closing his eyes was no longer an option. It was a necessity.

Over the pounding of the horses' hooves, the rattle of wheels, and the clatter of wood—not to mention the frantic, insane pounding of his own heartbeat—there was no mistaking Clunny's voice bellowing into the morning.

"Over here! They're over here! In the village! They've taken the carriage!"

In spite of himself, Fodder risked a glance to his right. Over the top of the smear of green that was all he could make out of the Rambling Woods, he saw a patch of too-vivid light wheel and lurch in their direction.

"The Narrative!" he bellowed though gritted teeth. "It's coming!"

He heard the reins whip once more. "Hold on!" Flirt shouted.

"To what?"

He could hear voices now, see more streaks of colour surging out of the woods as the searchers converged upon Clunny's yell as the carriage lurched and careered even more madly up the trail. A cluster of Palace Guards in shiny armour surged out onto the road mere yards ahead—Fodder ducked barely in time as the hurriedly swung axe of one of them embedded itself in the wooden panel where his head had been moments before.

This time, there was no avoiding a collision. The carriage pounded a shiny figure into the mud with a sickening crunch and a bounce that sent Fodder flying, his precarious grip finally torn free. Ironically, it was the axe that saved him, its protruding haft deflecting his tumble towards the road and providing a last precious handhold. His feet scrabbled for a moment in wild air but his grip held firm. Grasping the seat once more, he pulled himself back on board.

But for how long?

He could almost smell The Narrative, stalking them from behind, limited only by the speed of those whose exploits it dictated, a taper of bright light tugging at the rear end of the carriage as it sought to drag it into its hold. Fodder could feel the sick, syrupy feeling of it lapping at them, and he knew that the moment the Merry Band caught a glimpse of them, they would be caught, held, drawn in...

Further up this trail lay the lower reaches of the Tumbling River, where, Fodder knew, the road divided three ways: left up to the Bandit Pass and the Trapper Station; straight on towards the dusty devastation of the Battle Ground, the Stinking Marsh, and various bastions of darkness; and right to the Magnificent City and the Noble Plains. And the junction was on the edge of the Rambling Woods that had so far protected them from being caught in a Narrative sightline. Their cover was running out.

He was certain that Flirt was planning to turn left, up into the Least Savage Mountains to seek out the surly Trappers and plead for their support. But she didn't know The Narrative as he did, for she'd never been under its command in open space before, never seen the way it could reach out and envelop anything within eyeshot—and the hairpin bends of the Bandit Pass were clearly visible from below. The Narrative would have them, and though Fodder was certain that Flirt would have the strength to fight it, he was forced to admit an equal certainty that Shoulders wouldn't. And Shoulders had the princess right now. One glimpse would be enough.

But where else could they go? Straight on into the wide open plains that hosted a regular succession of Final Battles? No, they'd be visible for miles that way. And right, over the narrow stone bridge, would only hurry them out into more open country, past the thinning edge of the woods and out towards the Magnificent City, straight into enemy hands.

Unless...

All they had to do was stay out of sight. If The Narrative didn't see them, it couldn't catch them. If they could reach the bridge before the Merry Band turned the corner, then...

Touch...

"I see them!"

Erik felt a surge of triumphant glee. Elder had been right! It had just been a glimpse in between the trees, a hint of dark wood and a fleeting sight of two figures crouched on the driver's seat, one wearing the somewhat tattered livery of a Sleiss soldier, but...

...slips

Flirt gasped and lurched, clutching at her chest as her grip on the reins faltered. Grabbing them more firmly, her face set into a stubborn mask, she whipped the faltering horses back up to speed. She'd been caught unawares. Fodder was sure she had also felt the powerful, insidious urge to slow down, pull back, allow the Merry Band to catch up.

Time was running out.

The trees were thinning. Ahead, Fodder caught a distant glimpse of the old crossroad gallows and the open country beyond. It was closing faster than he'd like.

"Turn right!" he bellowed. "At the crossroads! We have to turn right!"

One glance at Flirt's pale, incredulous face was enough to show that she had yet to follow his reasoning.

"Towards the city? Are you barking? We need to hide! The mountains—"

"They'd see us on the pass! We'd have to wade through The Narrative!"

"But the city—"

"Not the city! The river!" He was struggling out of his mail coat, a perilous course in such an unstable position. "On the bridge! We have to jump before they see us and hide under the bridge!"

"What?" The exclamation was dual—Fodder hadn't even seen that Shoulders had pulled open the sliding hatch between driver and passengers, clinging to the rim by his fingertips until his voice rose up to join Flirt's.

There was no more time to explain. "Trust me! Shoulders, you have to bring the princess! Flirt, we have to jump!"

Neither of his friends' faces was filled with joy and happiness at this prospect. But there was just enough resignation to tell Fodder that they'd do it.

Which was just as well, since they hadn't got any other plan ready and waiting.

The mail coat was off, along with the livery. Pulling off his helmet, Fodder draped it awkwardly over the protruding axe haft and used his headgear to jam it in place. It wouldn't hold for long, he was sure, but as long as there were enough glimpses of Sleiss livery to satisfy The Narrative until the horses ran out of puff...

Here came the junction....

At least this time Fodder had the axe to cling to as two wheels left the ground. The edge of the woods dropped away from them as the road arched out into green fields strewn with distant castles, quiet villages, and the sparkling mass of the Magnificent City out on the horizon...

Glimpse...

...flash of the carriage and its Sleiss driver as it plunged around the corner of the junction that had just appeared ahead...

Lost...

Fodder gasped, the wind knocked half out of him as the carriage righted itself once more. The touch of Narrative had been slight, but it had been enough to tell him that the Merry Band were close, within sight of the junction and closing fast. They wouldn't have much time to get out of view once they bailed....

Ahead, the Tumbling River sparkled as it cut the road in two, though whether the sparkle was with invitation or menace, Fodder couldn't be sure. The narrow stone bridge arched across it pointedly. Closer, closer, closer...

"Get ready!" he screamed.

He heard the door latch release, heard the carriage door slam back as Shoulders braced to leap for it with the muffled-shrieking princess in tow. After one last determined yank intended to aim the horses squarely at the bridge, Flirt abandoned the reins and grabbed hold of the opposite corner of the driver's seat. Fodder grasped his sword belt and scabbard desperately as he braced himself for the coming impact.

Blue water rippled as it surged beneath the stone, carrying with it a wooden prow...

Wait, was that a *boat?*

Sod it. Too late now.

"JUMP!!!!!"

And then everything was swirling.

Air buffeted him viciously as he hurled himself outwards with all his strength, flipping over and over as he tumbled, stone, sky, water, stone, sky, water, stone, sky...

Water.

The impact hurt far more than it reasonably should have. Water surged around him, filling his nose and mouth as a solid weight bore down on top of him, sending him hurtling ever deeper. It took him a moment to realise that the impact he had felt had not been the water alone, that something heavy and metallic had slammed down on top of him as he'd hit the river surface.

That moment of realisation was all he had time for before the rocky river bottom hurtled up to meet him and knocked him into darkness.

* * *

Clunny's voice, cutting through the darkness with ruthless precision, rolling over the words he had hurled across the stable yard, over and over again: *You've managed to upset everything and everyone, bully for you, aren't you clever? Change the world? There's nothing wrong with it! So we do ignore the Taskmaster, what then? What do we do with ourselves? What's the point? You want to write the world to your tune, do you? You bang on about the Taskmaster bossing us around, but if you want to make our world over without our say-so, how does that make you any different? Some of us are quite happy to have the world the way it is! And if it's a choice between trusting the all-powerful Taskmaster who's looked after us for generations or relying on you to run the world, I know where my money's going....*

Enough is enough. It's time to stop.

Fodder opened his eyes.

"...how many times do I have to apologise? I didn't land on him on purpose!"

Ah. That explained the headache then.

Groaning softly, he reached up and fingered his forehead gently, probing at the diminishing scar that marked the site of what had apparently been a very nasty head wound. He'd obviously been out for a while for it to have healed so well.

The facts that it was dark and he was dry were also strong indications that a fair amount of time had passed. But how much time? Enough time to be captured and dragged off to a cell? Enough time for it all to be ruined?

And would that be for the best?

"Oh! Fodder!" Flirt's pale face, framed by her tangle of dark curls, filled his vision, slightly fuzzy-edged as she blocked out the pale light of the moon overhead.

The moon. He was outdoors, then. No torture chamber, no prison cell. The relief at that and at having seen Flirt's face and heard Shoulders's voice was profound. They hadn't been spotted; they hadn't been caught.

"How's your head?"

"Tender," Fodder admitted as his sight stabilised. It was difficult to see clearly in the darkness, but he could make out rocky walls stretching up towards the narrow crack of stars that arched across the sky above. "What happened? Is everyone all right?"

Flirt's brow creased, a shadow against her skin. "Oh, it worked like a charm, your plan. Right up until Shoulders sat on your head and cracked your skull."

"I couldn't help it!" Shoulders's scraggly face thrust into his line of sight. "I was still wearing chain mail! I just sank! And because I leaped right after you, you happened to be underneath me! I'm sorry, mate, but I had the princess in one hand, and I was trying to get out of my armour with the other. I couldn't exactly steer!"

"Don't worry about it. No harm done." Fodder smiled slightly as he pushed himself up onto his elbows. "It's healing quickly. The headache'll be gone by morning." He squinted against the darkness. "Where are we?"

An odd, disconcerted expression flickered across Flirt's face. "It's sort of a crevice," she hedged awkwardly. "It's off the Traversable Gorge. It's well hidden."

The Traversable Gorge. Fodder blinked. Of course he knew it, the low, rocky gorge that spat out the Tumbling River onto the Noble Plains. But that was upstream by more than a mile, back up into the foothills of the Least Savage Mountains and in plain view of the road all the way.

There was no logical conclusion. But Fodder groped towards one the best he could. "You swam upstream?" he managed. "Dragging me and the princess? How?"

Flirt pursed her lips. "We didn't swim, exactly...."

Fodder couldn't help but frown. "Then how...?"

"I gave them a lift."

In a Narrative situation, Fodder was sure, the sudden shock of a new voice in a perilous situation would have had him leap to his feet in a smooth, fluid instant, his sword whipping out of its scabbard as he wheeled to face the potential threat. As it was, however, his feet and hands scrabbled in the loose gravel that lay scattered over the rocky surface, skidded away from him, and sent him tumbling down onto his backside before he'd got halfway to his knees.

"It's all right!" Flirt's face thrust into his line of sight once more, her hands gentle on his shoulders as she eased him up to a more stable sitting position. "If he was going to dump us in it, he'd have done it by now, wouldn't he? He was hiding under the bridge in his boat, keeping out of the way of The Narrative when he saw us dive for it. But he didn't shout out; he waited until everyone had barrelled past after the carriage and then helped us into his boat. He hid us under his kit and took us upstream."

"But…"

That was all the coherence that Fodder could manage. He could see the new arrival now, washed in the glow of the small taper he had struck to light his pipe.

The familiar figure matched the familiar nasal voice, his lank, dark hair as greasy as ever, and his sharp, sallow features cast strangely in the pale light as he lounged against the nearby rock wall. Pleasance was propped up beside him, her tiara apparently lost to the river, her eyes glaring as her nose registered the vaguely offensive aroma from the strong mash of lit tobacco. He grinned at her expression, his teeth ever crooked as he took a cheery puff and leaned out to rest his elbow firmly on her head. The look of utter outrage that washed over her face could have shattered glass at thirty paces.

Fodder knew him. He'd lurked in his posse of brutes on more than one occasion.

It was Cringe. The Dark Henchman. The Narrative's hands-on doer of evil, facilitator of his boss's dark deeds, a thorn in the side of the Merry Band, and one of the most consistently longstanding Principals in the history of their world. Twelve Quests and twelve ironic deaths later, he was a man who was ever in demand for his ability to lurk with feeling, spit insults at the good guys, and run like a coward as the situation required of him. He was well-respected, well-liked, and well-admired throughout the land as a thoroughgoing professional and a safe pair of hands.

He had nothing to gain from Fodder's plans. Indeed, he had an awful lot to lose.

As did others. Fodder hadn't thought of that. Why hadn't he thought?

Because he was selfish. Just like Clunny had said. And his selfishness had dragged Flirt and Shoulders along in this impossible, ridiculous…

There was nowhere to run to. Nowhere to hide. No way to succeed. All this disruption, all this pain for nothing.…

A small, deep-sunk pair of eyes fixed upon him. Cringe's gaze was speculative as he looked the Disposable over. "You all right then, Fodder?" he asked, his voice the casual lilt he used when he wasn't required to spit, snarl, or swear in every other breath. "It's been a while. Got to be two, three Quests since we worked together?"

"*The Vile Rose*," Fodder acknowledged. "I was in your brute squad when you ambushed the Merry Band in the Rambling Woods."

"Oh, yeah. Urk gave you a ginger beard."

"Yep. It itched like a bugger."

"And it smelled too," Cringe pointed out. "I always wondered whether Urk grew it fresh or whether he borrowed it from someone else."

"I think it was borrowed. I don't think a fresh one would have had fleas." His chin had been sore for weeks after that particular mission. Fodder had vowed from that moment on never to don a fake beard again if he could help it.

"Got you a description, though." Cringe shrugged as he chewed pensively on his pipe. His stare remained uncomfortably thoughtful. "Can't argue with that."

That was all Fodder'd wanted back then. A description. He'd been so happy to make it into Narrative in that small, distinctive way, set apart from his fellows by a feature that wasn't even his.

And he had been happy, in those days, for those times. When had that stopped being enough? Why had it?

And why the heck was he dancing around with this faux-casual conversation when all he wanted to say was, *What the hell are you doing helping us out? Where did you come from? Why are you here?*

The words lurked at the edge of his lips, a can of worms pleading to be opened. But then he'd have to explain their...cause.

Some cause. Selfishness was more like it. Selfish personal obsession...

Cringe's grin reappeared somewhat abruptly as he blew a series of pale smoke rings out into the quiet of the night. "Fodder, are you going to argue with that or what? I haven't got all night, you know."

Fodder blinked sharply. "Pardon?"

"You!" Cringe waved his pipe absently through the dark air, leaving a faint trail of glowing light against the blackness as he nestled his arm more comfortably onto the princess's nest of curls. "The whole time since I dragged you out of the river with your head split open, your friends have been telling me about this great and glorious crusade that you started by defying The Narrative—and that as soon as you were awake, you'd make me see that it's the best thing for everyone if I help you out rather than washing my hands of you and tossing you back to Strut and Thud." His lips twisted humorously as he grinned again—his grin abrupt, unexpected, unnatural on a face handpicked to be sinister. "I've rather been looking forward to it. And what do I get? Ponderings on the ginger-bearded brute. I've never been so let down."

Great. That was all he needed, his friends building him up. Fodder was certain that they'd meant well, but with doubts cascading through his mind like a spring melt waterfall, now was not the time for preaching to converts. Not when he was starting to wonder if he should be converting at all...

Something Cringe had said tagged abruptly against his thoughts. "Wait. You pulled me out of the river?"

"I did indeed." The grin was back again, a flash of yellowed teeth in the darkness. "There I am, pottering along in my boat under that bridge, and suddenly I find myself surrounded by damp rebels and a soggy princess." His expression was gleeful. "It was the funniest sight I've seen in Quests."

Fodder did not feel greatly enlightened. "Why were you under the bridge in the first place?"

Cringe gave an easy shrug. "Easiest way downstream, isn't it? I'm due a big confrontation down in Salty Port...or I was." He winked with a level of cheer that Fodder found astonishing. "I'd rather cruise down the river than walk, and I reckoned The Narrative would be heading for the Magnificent City by now and the way'd be clear. That is, until I got a message from Hauteur. You know him?"

Fodder shook his head. He'd never had any direct dealings with the Officious Courtier in charge of the senior figures of Darkness, although he had on occasion seen him around.

Cringe shrugged again. "No matter. Well, Hauteur told me that there were these crazy Disposables down near Humble Village who'd made a mess of the plot and that I was to hang around at the Gallows junction and await further instructions. I think they were hoping I'd be able to get involved in incompetently losing the princess to the Merry Band. After all, you two were dressed up as men of Sleiss when you decided to play with The Narrative, and I am supposed to be Lord Sleiss's illegitimate brother." He chuckled, a surprisingly friendly sound out of a voice designed to be unpleasantly creepy. "And so there I was, just fishing and minding my own business, when I realised that The Narrative was coming at me at speed from the Rambling Woods. Since the bridge was the only cover, I paddled my boat underneath and hoped I wouldn't get noticed. And then all of a sudden, it's raining Disposables." He laughed again, more loudly. "Oh, you should have seen your friends' faces when they saw me!"

"You should have seen them when he didn't turn us in!" Flirt added fervently as she absentmindedly handed Fodder a flask of water. He took a sizable swig and handed it back, wishing in the quiet of his mind that she had thought to pack more ale. "We were waiting for him to draw in The Narrative, but he let it pass without a word. And then, when Strut and Thud rode over in pursuit a couple of minutes later, we were dreading it all over again, but he just sat there, smoking his pipe and grinning at us! We didn't know what to think, did we? And when he reached out, casual as you like, and offered us a lift…"

"It was only polite." Cringe tapped his pipe cheerfully against the rock wall beside his head, scattering drifts of ash down over Pleasance's tangled curls. "You were bobbing there with your head cracked open and your friends were floundering around looking like drowned puppies trying to keep you afloat and stop this sodden little nuisance from kicking up a noisy splash." He patted the glowering Pleasance on the head in a phenomenally patronising manner. "Leaving you there would have been like kicking a basket of kittens. Unnecessary cruelty."

"So that's why you hauled us all the way upstream to a hiding place? Because you felt sorry for us?" Fodder wasn't entirely certain whether he should feel grateful or insulted.

"I wouldn't put it like that." Cringe squinted thoughtfully towards the sky. "It's more…" He frowned. "I've been in this game for a while, and the one thing I know for sure is that this life can be damnably repetitive. It's all lurk, spit, sneer, die, lurk, spit, sneer, die—and, to be frank, after twelve Quests of more of the same, I'm getting bloody bored. I like it better when things are interesting, and you lot are the most interesting thing that's happened around here for a long time. I've never seen a Quest wander this far off plan before, and no one has the faintest idea what's going to happen next. This world's never seen anything like it. And that's fantastic." He laughed again. "And that's why I don't want to see you get kicked down before you've really got started. I want to watch where this thing goes." His gaze narrowed once more, his deep-sunk eyes boring with startling sharpness into Fodder's face. "That's why it's so annoying that the Taskmaster is *cheating.* Planting in a Disposable! Damned underhanded if you ask me."

Fodder felt a strange jolt of shock, as though Cringe's boring eyes had clubbed him from behind. "Planting? What do you mean by that?"

Cringe's eyes widened in surprise. "You haven't heard of it?"

"I've heard it mentioned." Flirt ventured into the resulting silence. "The last time the Merry Band stopped over at the Archetypal Inn, I listened in on Harridan telling Clank about something The Narrative had *planted* in her backstory that they needed to set up. But I didn't have a clue what they were talking about."

Cringe shook his head, his dark expression almost matching the kind he wore In Narrative. "Cheating," he reiterated irritably. "I was sure you wouldn't have experienced it, but I didn't know you'd never heard of it." He pulled a face. "Have any of you ever appeared in The Narrative as the same character twice? Gone out and come back in again as the same person?"

Fodder and Shoulders shook their heads as one. It was rare that they survived their scenes, let alone came around for a repeat performance. Flirt pursed her lips. "Just once, I think. I served the Merry Band one night and let them out again in the morning. It was hardly much of a character, though. I don't think I said much more than *yes sire, no sire, can I get you a drink, my lords?"*

Cringe gazed at her thoughtfully. "Was it easier the second time? In the morning?"

Flirt shrugged. "All I did was bob a curtsey and unlock the door. Can't say that I noticed."

"Ah, well." Cringe pulled a face as he patted the princess on the head once more. Pleasance had apparently run out of steam with her non-stop fury and was wearing an expression of martyred resignation. *"She'll* have been told about this. Anyone who plays a character with any regularity will have. For those who spend most of the Quest immersed in The Narrative, it's practically a way of life. You see, if you've got a recurring character, The Narrative doesn't just affect you when you're up to your eyeballs in it. It gets in your head in between scenes as well." One thin eyebrow arched upwards. "I'm guessing The Narrative got a touch on you while you were running from it?"

Fodder nodded, his mind whirling, his mouth hanging open with blank horror. Surely, that couldn't be right! It wasn't fair!

Cringe grimaced. "Thought so. You had that faraway look about you, that look you see in recurring Principals when they're mulling over their character before The Narrative arrives. You see, The Narrative has a way of dropping what it wants you to do into your head—you'll know about that. But if you're likely to pop up again, it also drops the knowledge of that character into your head as well for you to study and utilise later. It plants it there so it can grow. It helps make the character you're playing automatic, effortless, and consistent; and the more you appear, the easier it gets. And it can do that to you now, Fodder. You've appeared in The Narrative twice as the same soldier. You're fair game."

Cringe pulled his pipe from the corner of his mouth and emptied it irritably onto the floor. "Most first-time Principals are warned about this, told that it'll happen so they don't mix up their character thoughts with their own. But for someone who didn't know what was happening…well, it'd be easy to let a character work itself into your brain and take control of your behaviour. And I'm assuming from the lack of persuasion you've thrown at me thus far that your new character isn't in favour of what you're doing." He shook his head yet again. "It's just cheating," he exclaimed for the third time. "It's not on, not at all. You people deserve a fair chance."

Fodder stared at Cringe, his words resonating with horrible clarity. Could it be? He'd been doubting so much, considering giving up, believing the cause to be lost and his actions to be selfish, but had they really been his thoughts at all or what the Taskmaster *wanted* him to think? Clunny's words had lodged like a festering sore, itching at him, whispering, assailing him in the darkness of unconsciousness—*who am I to make such a decision for everyone else? Am I being selfish by running around trying to change the entire world without asking the rest of the people who have to live in it what they think? Why should the whole world listen to the ideas of someone so* Ordinary?

But that was the point, wasn't it? He was only ordinary because that was all he'd ever been allowed to be. He'd never had the chance to show he could be anything else.

And now the Taskmaster and The Narrative were trying to steal away his will—his choice—by planting a character riddled with self-doubt into his head.

It was everything he'd started this to get away from.

Clunny was wrong. And he'd been wrong too. He didn't want to change the world. He just wanted to tweak it a bit. He wanted to make things *optional.*

He dreaded to think what would have happened if he'd stepped into Narrative with this character still in his head. No doubt he would have given them up in despair, his will to fight drained by a planted personality that had no place in his life. But Cringe's explanation had sent that spectre packing, loaded it off into the back of his mind and locked it firmly away like the invading force it was. He was not going to dance to the Taskmaster's tune again! He was not going to dance to any tune but his own!

And that was what mattered: getting people to accept that things could be seen differently. Cringe's attitude boded well for that: the idea that change could be more interesting. And in a strange way, so did Clunny's attitude, for all that it was negative, for it told Fodder something very significant.

Clunny had got it.

Last night, it had been clear that most of his friends hadn't even been able to comprehend what he was saying, couldn't grasp the idea of speaking out against the Taskmaster, couldn't consider that the world could be any other way. But Fodder had seen in Clunny's eyes that his friend had been *thinking* about it. He'd seen what had happened last night and realised it was possible that the Taskmaster's way was not the only one. That he didn't like it, and didn't have the nerve to stand up against the status quo over it, was obvious. But he'd understood. He'd understood enough for it to scare him.

And that was a big first step.

Perhaps there was some hope for them yet. If they could sow the seeds of the idea, put it into people's heads, make them look at the world that little bit differently...

"Feeling reinvigorated, are we?" At some point while Fodder had been lost to his musings, Cringe had refilled and relit his pipe. "That often happens. Once you put down a clear line between yourself and what's been planted, things tend to clarify. So." He filled the air with smoke in one easy exhalation that set the weary-looking princess coughing beneath her gag. "Are you going to try and convert me now?"

Fodder tried his best. He ran through his thoughts and arguments, explaining everything that had happened since last night—*was it only this time yesterday that this had all begun? It felt like forever!*—solidifying it all in his head as much for his own sake as for Cringe's. He didn't want to risk it being taken away from him again. It was just as well, since, in spite of his assistance to their cause, Cringe remained so firmly perched on the fence that Fodder was tempted to offer him a cushion.

"I respect the nerve of what you're doing, and I respect your right to do it." The Dark Henchman was on his fourth helping of tobacco, whilst both Shoulders and the princess had long ago fallen asleep. Even Flirt's eyelids were looking a little droopy. "But to be honest, I'm not fussed as to whether you get your way or not. My life doesn't thrill me, but I can live with it. Given the choice, I'd probably give up lurking for a living, but it won't be the end of the world if I don't. I'm no rebel, and if it's all the same to you, I'd much rather keep my nose clean." He grinned cheerfully. "I don't want to be in the thick of the chaos. I'd much sooner sit back and watch." He raised his pipe in a mock salute. "Must be the influence of all the cowards I've played. I wish you the best of luck, though."

In spite of the yawn she was battling, Flirt stepped in. "Do you reckon any of the other Principals might be interested in helping us? Much as I hate to say it, more people would probably listen to them than to us."

"You mean you haven't tried to convert the princess yet?" Cringe snorted at the looks on their faces. "You're probably right. Every princess I've ever worked with has been a brat from start to finish. I swear they must breed them that way." He grinned slightly. "I can't even begin to tell you how good it feels to see one gagged. Marvellous! And as for the other Principals..." He sucked his teeth thoughtfully. "Trouble is, I don't socialise with many of the others outside of a professional capacity. Mostly I just hang out with Doom and...hmmm." He paused, his face pensive, tapping his pipe against his nose absently. "That's a thought. I could take you to see Grim."

"The Dark General?" Fodder had never met him personally, although he had seen him from a distance during numerous Final Battles. "You think he'd listen?"

Cringe waved one hand in an uncertain see-saw. "He might. He was bitching to me only last week about how tired he was of hanging around the Grim Fortress being hearsay. He's grumpy about the fact he's always name-checked much more than he's featured. Our Grim's a bit of a glory hound, and he never gets as much of it as he feels he deserves."

"Surely it's the same for Doom the Dark Lord too," Flirt piped in suddenly. "He's never anything but hearsay for more than the last few chapters, is he? Maybe we could persuade them both?"

Cringe laughed out loud. "Grim's a maybe," he conceded. "But Doom doesn't give a steaming monkey's about his lack of Narrative time. It gives him more time for his hobbies. Do you know he's learning macramé?"

Fodder's mind deliberately shied away from the idea of the enormous armoured figure he'd seen striding through The Narrative crushing innocents by the horde sitting down in the Dark Citadel to play with yarn. It was just too disconcerting.

"Doom's content with his lot," Cringe continued, "but Grim isn't. He wants more." His smile widened crookedly. "Tell you what," he offered suddenly. "You could kill two birds with one stone. What if the High Lord of Sleiss *actually got* to marry the Princess Islaine? Would that mess up the Taskmaster's plan enough for you?"

Flirt and Fodder exchanged a long, thoughtful glance before looking over at the sleeping princess. The High Lord of Sleiss, played by Grim the Dark General, was the threat: the dark suitor lurking, threatening to steal away a precious rose from the humble Hero but never, ever meant to succeed. What if he did? How would the Taskmaster marry the Hero to someone who was married already?

Easy. By making her a widow. She'll even have a nice, tortured aspect after her terrible ordeal as the forced bride of pure evil....

Fodder shook his head wearily. Perhaps it was because The Narrative had gotten into his head so recently, but he was starting to get a better idea of the kind of mind he was up against. "It's a nice idea, but I've seen how The Narrative works around these problems. It'd just have Bumpkin or Clank kill Grim off and rescue her nobly for an angst-riddled recovery in the arms of her true love." He sighed profoundly. "There has to be something we can do that it can't wriggle out of."

"I have an idea."

Fodder started. He hadn't even realised that Shoulders had woken up until his friend's voice cut into their conversation. The dim, moonlight-washed glimpse he caught of his fellow Disposable's face as he pulled himself closer showed the faintest trace of the too-familiar maniacal grin.

Oh, no.... Was it because I mentioned Clank? Am I going to want to hear this? It'll be another half-tankard idea, I swear....

"Do you?" Flirt's voice echoed the wariness that Fodder was feeling to the bone.

"Oh, *yes.*" The grin was spreading; not a good sign. "You see, I've been hoisting brat-features over there around for a whole day, with her kicking and scratching and screaming in my ears, and that's done wonders for my imagination. Because I was having a glorious dream about how I pushed her off a cliff and listened to the scream just fade away...." His eyes drifted off dreamily for a moment before he snapped back to reality. "But when I woke up and heard you lot pondering what we could do to mess The Narrative up, it occurred to me. Why can't we do that?"

"Throw the princess off a cliff?" Flirt retorted sceptically. "Shoulders, for goodness' sake, she'd just bounce. The non-Narrative damage would heal or Strut would have Squick fix her right up and they'd insert her straight back into Narrative. It'd do nothing but make you feel better."

Shoulders actually rolled his eyes. "I'm not talking about picking a cliff at random for the fun of it. I mean, what if we killed the princess off? *In Narrative?*"

Fodder paused, his mind seizing upon the suggestion and running it through in his head. *Hmmm.... That's not so half tankard after all....*

"You see what I mean, don't you?" Shoulders was gesticulating wildly, his face lit with enthusiasm in the pale moonlight. "Think what it would do to the story. Bumpkin's inevitable romantic subplot would be shot! Only killing Bumpkin himself would make more of a mess! And it's been a while since I read the full set of instructions for this Quest, but doesn't the princess make the decisive difference in the Final Battle again this time round?"

Cringe was grinning too—in spite of his refusal to become openly involved in their endeavours, his fence appeared to be wobbling slightly. "She disguises herself as a man and rallies the troops, I think. But she's the only heir to her kingdom, and it's that kingdom the Hero needs to marry into."

Fodder mulled it over. It was an idea with definite possibilities. But...Thud's Halheid had been important to the Final Battle and romantically entangled too, and now he was coming back as his own twin brother. It would stretch Narrative believability to pull the same trick twice, but would that stop the Taskmaster from trying?

But wait a minute. Hadn't Cringe just said...?

"She's the only heir? No siblings?" he asked with sudden intensity. "Is that Narratively set?"

Cringe nodded cheerfully. "In stone. They established it in her backstory through discussion amongst the Merry Band before she was introduced. That's why Sleiss is so keen to marry her. He wants her kingdom. No brothers, no sisters, not even any close cousins. The absolute, very last descendant of a long and ancient line."

"So no magic twins this time." Flirt was smiling with sudden grimness. "We'd have to do the thing properly," she stated firmly. "We'd have to make absolutely sure—give her a death that there's no wriggling out of with last-minute rescues or magical resurrection. And it'll be tricky to do it In Narrative, with it doing everything in its power to keep her alive. But such a huge change to the Quest..." The smile slipped to a grin. "Everyone would notice, wouldn't they? They wouldn't be able to just bundle us away and write off what we've done. They'd have to listen to us after that."

The idea was solidifying, becoming possible, becoming real. And it could work, it really could. Flirt was right; such a massive change to the plot could not be overlooked or brushed aside as random chance by Strut and his ilk.

In the space of a day, their actions had made a few people understand that the world was not as set in stone as they believed. If they could make even more people realise that what they did could make a difference, there would be no hushing this up. Seeds planted, ideas dropped into Ordinary minds. The Taskmaster wasn't the only one capable of that anymore. Even if they threw them in the dungeons, it would be too late to stop the idea.

"We'd need to find The Narrative." The thoughts tripped off Fodder's tongue. "It'd need to be somewhere we could hide, somewhere it couldn't see us until we wanted it to."

"With an escape route," Shoulders added fervently. "I want a way out if this all goes wrong."

"We'd need to be quick too," Flirt chimed in. "To make sure The Narrative has less time to stop us. Quick, decisive, and unavoidably dead."

"I know exactly what to do." The mad gleam in Shoulders's eyes showed Fodder the direction of his thoughts. "We *chop her head off.*"

Flirt had seen it coming too, and it alarmed Fodder slightly that, just for an instant, she seemed to pick up the slightest edge of Shoulders's gleam. "Yes! On a cliff! If the head went off a cliff but the body stayed at the top, there'll be no undoing that."

Cringe tapped his pipe thoughtfully against his nose. "You know, I heard Strut saying when he rode past that if they didn't catch the carriage, they'd be sending the Merry Band to besiege Lord Sleiss's castle to kill time whilst they hunted you down. They're probably on their way as we speak. And if you want a cliff, the Grim Fortress is on a pretty decent outcropping this time around. There's a thousand-foot plunge into the Tumbling River from the walls. What if you put the two ideas together? You take the princess to Grim and have it declared that he's married her. But since they're married, he's got his claim to her kingdom and so he doesn't need her anymore. So what does he do? Kill her in front of her would-be saviours."

Flirt pulled a face. "Would Grim be able to defy The Narrative well enough to pull that off?"

Cringe shrugged. "As long as Fodder is the executioner, what does it matter? If Grim falters, all you'd have to do is swing an axe. And if it does go wrong, the Grim Fortress has plenty of secret passages you could scarper down. If the worst comes to the worst, you could even jump into the river again." He grinned once more. "It's only a thousand-foot drop. No trouble."

Fodder nodded, ignoring Shoulders's look of downright horror at the escape plan as his own grin matched those of his companions. "You know," he said thoughtfully, "this might just be worth a try."

* * *

The Grim Fortress was truly grim. There really was no better word for it.

Like the Archetypal Inn, Fodder knew that the Grim Fortress wandered between a few strategic locations in its chosen corner of the Least Savage Mountains, sometimes perched on top of the towering peak off to their left, at other times balanced on the narrow ledge that broke the otherwise sheer face of a massive cliff in the neighbouring valley, and occasionally lingering on the terrifying overhang that plunged down over the swirling white mass of the Wild Waterfall. The Grim Fortress could block off a whole valley mouth or loom over a gorge—it was versatile that way. On this particular occasion, as Cringe had said, it lurked on top of a jutting outcrop of sheer-sided cliffs that thrust out from the mountainside and pushed the turbulent white waters that gave the Tumbling River its name out and around it in a dramatic and highly describable curve. Say what you would about the Grim Fortress, it did a wonderful line in imposing.

But as ever, the Fortress itself was unchanged. Heavy walls of dark, harsh stone were roughly hewn into giant blocks that seemed to grow out of the very rock upon which it happened on this occasion to be perched. The windows were high and narrow, the battlements blocky and solid, and the gatehouse, with its vicious-looking portcullis, gaped like a yawning maw exactly as it should. And finally, towering to exactly the right height to make a climb up its outer edge just terrifying enough, one enormous tower loomed over the walls, brooding with perfectly managed menace.

It really was a masterpiece. It was a shame that it wasn't used more often. Usually, it only showed up for a small siege, a raid and skirmish, or an early capture and flee, with the glories of the final confrontation inevitably going to the even-more-imposing Dark Citadel in the Barren Wastelands to the north. Judging by the scuffle of figures Fodder could see silhouetted on the battlements, hanging out the blue-and-red Sleiss livery and preparing to look threatening with pikes, the Grim Fortress had not been expecting to see action in this Quest and was being hurried into place. Fodder had Bulked Up here once or twice and was familiar with the Disposables who plied their trade inside. Dodge, Slump, Gurgle, and Thrash were renowned amongst their fellows for the ability to be snuck up behind and have their throats cut by the Merry Band with just the right level of dramatic thrashing. It wasn't as easy as it sounded and, rebel or not, Fodder had to admire artistry when he saw it.

It did make one aspect of Fodder's mission somewhat easier, though. The Grim Fortress Disposables were so used to being snuck past that getting inside unspotted via one of the numerous secret passages that honeycombed whatever bedrock the Fortress happened to be on probably wouldn't prove particularly challenging.

That prospect was something of a relief to Fodder. It had been a long morning.

The most trying aspect of it had been just before they'd set out, when Pleasance had overheard them hammering down their plans to get her killed In Narrative and had gone up like the Brooding Volcano during a final confrontation. Since this had also coincided with feeding time, she had been unfettered in the venting of her spleen, and the aftershocks of her epic fury were still echoing in Fodder's ears.

"Kill me? *Kill me?* In Narrative??? You can't kill a princess In Narrative! No one has *ever* killed a princess In Narrative! It's unheard of! It's wrong! I will not let you ruin my Quest and make me a laughing-stock! I will not be the first princess ever to die! It's vile! It's crass! It's undignified! Princesses *don't die!*"

Fortunately, further elucidation on the subject had been halted when Flirt had shoved the gag back in place, but Pleasance's icy gaze had followed Fodder like a glacial stab for the rest of the walk upriver. Fodder was certain that she was plotting something.

The second problem had been Shoulders's sudden attack of paranoia, apparently stemming from the fact that they were headed to exactly the place that they had been trying to avoid. The Grim Fortress was, after all, the home of the dungeons and torture chambers, and the idea of walking right into his own potential life sentence was not sitting well with Shoulders.

"Couldn't I just wait outside?" he queried for the fifteenth time as he, Fodder, Flirt, and the princess lurked behind a rocky outcropping waiting for Cringe to return from checking whether the path ahead to his secret passageway was clear. "If this Grim doesn't go for it, all he needs to do is have us bundled down a few flights of stairs, and it's hello torture chambers! I don't want to spend the rest of my life lying on a rack being bored out of my brain just because we trusted a stranger! Why do we have to go in there anyway? Why can't Cringe bring Grim to do the execution out here?"

Flirt fixed him with her best intimidating glare. Fodder had to admit she did a fine line in them, and this was most definitely one of the good ones. "Because the Merry Band are coming this way, aren't they?" she retorted impatiently. A morning of listening to Shoulders grumbling over the same complaints had not done wonders for her mood. "And if we're standing out here when The Narrative comes, they'll slaughter us and reclaim the princess before you can so much as swear at Clank. We have to behead her on the battlements where they won't have time to get to us, and for that, we need to be inside. Unless you want it to be your head that goes flying off the cliff?"

Shoulders jutted his chin out stubbornly but his left hand jerked reflexively in the direction of his neck. "No, but…"

"Must you?" Flirt exclaimed with sheer exasperation. "I've been patient, Shoulders, I really have, but we're going inside and that's final. Okay?"

Shoulders scowled slightly. "I was just saying I have a bad feeling about this. That's all. I wanted you to know so when it all goes horribly wrong, you can't say I didn't warn—"

"Shoulders, please!"

The second intimidating look did the trick. Glowering at Flirt with as much irritation as he had the nerve left to muster, Shoulders damped his moaning down to muttering under his breath.

Loath as he was to admit it, Shoulders's grumblings had sparked a bit of worry inside Fodder's head. "Flirt," he said quietly. "Much as I hate to say it, I think Shoulders might have a point. Cringe has made it pretty clear that he'll help us to a point, but if trouble starts, we'll be on our own. What if Grim does decide to turn us in? We'll be in a pretty nasty situation in there."

Flirt stared at him briefly before she sighed wearily. "It had crossed my mind...."

"Hah!" Shoulders's indignant exclamation forestalled the remainder of her sentence. "So when I'm worried, it's all glares of death and *must you*, but when Fodder says he's concerned, suddenly it's crossed your mind? That is so—"

"Shoulders!"

The dual exclamation put an end to Shoulders's diatribe. With an angry huff, he returned to muttering under his breath as Flirt picked up the thread of her broken sentence.

"I've thought of it, but we don't have much choice anymore, do we? We can't still be out here when *that* arrives." She gestured over her shoulder to the distant horizon where the familiar, vivid glow of The Narrative was edging closer through the winding valleys of the mountains. "And I know we could just do this ourselves, but, much as I hate to say so, it'll make more impact if a Principal's involved. We can be written off as malicious discontents and locked up out of sight without much fuss being made. But if a Principal sabotaged the plot in our name, far more people would notice." She sighed again, deeply. "And if we don't get noticed, we're doomed, aren't we?" A frown creased her forehead. "And speaking of Principals, where's Cringe? He's certainly taking his time in there."

It was true. Cringe had insisted it wouldn't take more than a few minutes for him to nip up and check the way was clear, but time was slipping by and there was still no sign of him. Surely it didn't take that long to check a tunnel....

"Okay there?"

Fodder jumped a good foot, and the startled look on Flirt's face and the hyperventilation coming from Shoulders's direction implied that he hadn't been the only one caught by surprise. Cringe grinned wickedly as he slipped out from behind a nearby rock and slunk over to join them. A large, heavy-looking cloth-wrapped bundle was slung over his shoulders, weighing them down. He dumped it with a heave and a sigh of relief.

"King of stealth, that's me," he told them cheerfully. "Even while hoisting that monster around. All part of the job description."

"You took your time in there, didn't you?" From the breathless edge to Flirt's tone, she didn't enjoy being taken by surprise any more than Fodder did. "What the bloody hell happened?"

Cringe raised an eyebrow carefully. "No need to get brusque with me," he told her pointedly. "I *am* doing you a serious favour here, you know. Entirely at my personal risk, I might add."

Flirt bit her lip, suitably chastened. "Sorry," she apologised, more gently. "It's been a long couple of days, and you said you'd only be a few minutes."

"I was only going to be." Cringe had put his pipe away since they had set out that morning, but the odd twitchiness of his fingers implied a certain need to have it back. "But I remembered when I went into the passage that it comes out not far from the armoury—and since you gentlemen lost your armour to the river, I thought a replacement set might be in order." He kicked the cloth-wrapped bundle, which gave a metallic jangle. "Three sets of chain mail and Sleiss livery for you. It should make it easy to move around inside, as long as no one gets too good a look at your faces. And while I was in there, I had another piece of luck. Grim showed up to have his torso plates taken out." He shrugged slightly. "He's put a bit of weight on lately. And since the chance came up, I decided it was probably better for me to take the liberty of testing the waters for you rather than you lot walking blindly inside to an entirely unknown reception. So I told him what was going on."

"And?" Fodder couldn't quite conceal the note of eagerness to his voice. "Did he agree to do it?"

Cringe grinned again. "He took a little persuading, but yes. He likes the idea of a bit of Narrative upstaging." He positively beamed at the pale-faced and sullen-looking princess, who was slumped against the rock nearby. "So, if you three would care to kit yourselves out, we have an execution to attend to."

* * *

Now this was more like it.

The chain mail was heavy, there was no denying it. It chafed madly in unexpected places, it had an odour that was most kindly described as distinctly its own, and it pressed uncomfortably down on the parts of her anatomy that most wearers of chain mail did not possess. But compared to the breath-stealing horrors of a too-tight corset filled almost to overflowing with a highly inflated bosom, it might as well have been light as a feather and lined with goose down. Flirt wouldn't have traded it for the world.

The sword wasn't too bad either. It was traditional fare for a Disposable—short, sturdy, and utilitarian—but although it was no Merry Band-esque ornate broadsword that danced through the air as though weightless, it was a damned sight better than a fireplace poker. The scabbard bounced unexpectedly against her leg, but that was another discomfort that could be lived with if it meant that she was armed.

Armed and dangerous. She'd waited half her life for this day. The chance to stand up for herself, the chance to show what she was made of and to prove that she had the mettle to be more than just a pair of fake breasts that provided tankards of beer. One chance, one fight and she'd show them all!

But she knew that a fight was probably not meant to be. They were unlikely to cross paths with anyone, according to Cringe, for the inhabitants of the Grim Fortress weren't as numerous in comparison to its size as they had once been. Formerly, the Grim Fortress had been home to the entire of the Dark Family, responsible for breeding and training up generations of villains, evil witches, and henchmen; but the family had grown so tired of living in ever-changing remote, rocky corners of the kingdom that they had upped sticks as one around fourteen Quests back and moved down to the Magnificent City. They had a nice set of warm, cosy houses in a part of the city not used In Narrative and only dispatched those of their number currently employed by Narrative necessity back to their old stomping grounds. That meant that the inhabitants of this once-great bastion of darkness now numbered one Dark General, one Dark Henchman, four Disposables, five Servants who also doubled as prisoners and torture victims as the situation required, one large black guard dog without a vicious bone in its body, an armourer who often doubled as a jailor in between knocking up or repairing overstated suits of armour for the Dark General, and two professional torturers for the dungeons who spent most of their professional lives doing absolutely sod all.

There were no full-time prisoners at present. Genuine criminals were all but unheard of, and only a genuine criminal would be given that most boring and tedious of lifestyles, left lying permanently on an unattended rack or in a prison cell waiting in a location that was visited In Narrative once every couple of Quests at the most. Nobody was ever actually tortured, except in a harmless Narrative context. It was dullness that formed the ultimate punishment.

Dullness and being ignored.

She wasn't going to let that happen. Not after all this…

But now was not the time for such musings. They were walking into the heart of potential danger. She needed to concentrate.

The passageway into which Cringe had led them was dark, long, and windy, ascending awkwardly up uneven, rough-hewn stairs through the rock. It was narrow, which was fortunate, as the total lack of light meant that it was necessary to feel the way up the walls, stumbling on the invisible steps and praying for the top. Cringe was apparently unbothered by the darkness—he told them with irritating cheer that he had spent so much of his professional life skulking around in the shadows that he barely even noticed it anymore—but the same could not be said of Fodder, who tumbled frequently against her back, or Shoulders, who tripped even more frequently on top of the equally ill-equipped princess. By the time they reached the dungeon corridor where the passage emerged, the four of them were black and blue from head to foot and seriously considering ganging up on Cringe and throwing him over the battlements for picking such an awkward and painful route.

At Shoulders's strident insistence, they did not linger near the dungeons, but hurried up another, better-lit staircase towards the Fortress walls. Cringe had arranged for them to meet Grim in his private turret, one of a couple of sturdy but unassuming towers wrapped around a corner of the battlements that were so rarely visited In Narrative that the inhabitants of the Fortress had been able to set them up in an unexpectedly homely fashion. It was, Flirt had to admit, an odd experience to glance out at the harsh stone courtyard, with its leering, battered gargoyles dangling from the epic central tower and a bloodstained execution block lurking in the shadows from the window of the warm, friendly little kitchen that Cringe had led them into. The fireplace was clean and cheery; the counters gleamed; the cupboard doors were painted in bright, bold colours; and even the kettle had a floral pattern painted on its metal surface. The large black guard dog, with sharp, crooked teeth and shaggy, matted fur that slavered and snapped for the flesh of anyone who came near it In Narrative, was curled up by the fire on a yellow blanket with a greasy-looking bone clamped in his jaws. His tail was wagging.

Fortunately, other than the dog, the tower was deserted. As Cringe had said, the rest of the inhabitants were still out uglifying the more commonly used parts of the Fortress ahead of the Merry Band's arrival. It did not take long to hurry as inconspicuously as possible along the fifteen-foot span of battlement between the larger tower and the small turret beyond, but one brief look at it was enough to tell Flirt exactly what she needed to know. Of all the towers, it was the furthest from any potential action, perched, almost dangling, over the very edge of the thousand-foot drop. It was half-roofed: a small curl of dark tile topped a narrow doorway that presumably marked the top of the stairs, but the rest of the top was flat and open, ringed in by crenulations. Thanks to the curve of the jut on which the Fortress was positioned, it was clearly visible from the gatehouse and the road leading up to the Fortress, but it was out of natural bowshot range and would be tricky to get at quickly, even with The Narrative's aid, without chucking any hint of realism entirely out of the window.

In other words, it was the perfect spot to stage a princess's execution.

Flirt smiled to herself. Brilliant.

Ahead, Cringe opened the small door to the turret and ushered them inside. Flirt obeyed, glancing back over her shoulder quickly to scan the courtyard, but it was still deserted, the Ordinary residents of the Fortress caught up in set-dressing in the gatehouse and largest tower. And even if any of them did happen to look out of the window, they'd probably just assume that the three figures in Sleiss armour were here to Bulk Up the numbers.

Satisfied, Flirt turned her head as she walked into the dim chamber.

And screamed.

Armoured figures. Everywhere.

She hit the door with a mail-clad clatter, her eyes darting everywhere as she struggled to drink in the scene. Her fingers had already half-groped for her sword before her mind actually managed to register what her eyes were telling her. They still weren't moving, not one, still motionless, still silent. Surely, nobody waiting to spring a terrible trap would have so much self-control....

And then her eyes adjusted to the shadowy light and showed her the truth.

Well. Now I feel just stupid....

The walls of the shadowy room were lined with suits of armour. They stood silent, unmoving, empty, and lifeless: vast, ornate visors of burnished, lacquered black metal that concealed nothing but shadows; gauntleted fists clenched beneath enormous, curving breastplates that covered no vulnerable flesh. Some were covered in engravings, images of horror and pain, of torture and brutality, fire and blood tattooed across their metal skin. Others lurked as a mass of corners and curves, demonic horns, dragon jaws—a helmet here like the head of a furious bear, another capped by the figures of two fighting wolves writhing together, eternally frozen in mortal combat. Each one was a horror to behold as it hovered in terrible silence as though waiting for her to collapse and die in terror of her own accord.

Well, she wasn't doing that. Not for a load of empty metal.

But that was what they'd been designed for. These were the work suits of Grim and Doom, stored away for future recycling in later Quests. And because she'd been distracted and hadn't paid attention, she'd made a complete prat of herself by assuming it was an ambush.

She was going to get mocked for this. She could just smell it.

The chuckle came from Cringe. That was disappointing. If it had been Shoulders or Fodder, she'd have felt more able to clout them one.

"Sorry," he said with irritating cheer. "I should have warned you. We keep Grim and Doom's armour down here—the air up at the Dark Citadel makes it rust up more." He grinned in a manner that took the possibility of a slapping one step closer. "That'd be a thing to behold, though—being ambushed by thirty Quests' worth of Lords of Darkness."

"Cringe?" The unexpected voice echoed down the stairs as, from somewhere above, a door slammed with hurried force. "Is that you?"

Cringe sauntered forwards, peering vaguely through the archway that led onto the spiral stairs. Metallic footsteps were clattering downwards against the rough stone.

"Obviously," he called back. "Were you expecting someone else?"

"No, no!" The reply was quick-fire. "You were just faster than I thought you'd be!"

A pair of black-lacquered metal feet, followed rapidly by armoured legs and then an intricately decorated torso—that did indeed show signs of a recent, necessary panel-beating—appeared around the curl of the steps. A moment later, two padded arms dropped into view, cradling an armful of shaped black metal, followed by a helmet that had clearly been thrust into place somewhat hurriedly, given that it was tilted at a very challenging angle that made its wearer appear to be perpetually staring off to his left. He looked, in short, like a refugee from a fight between two dodgy ironmongers.

Flirt's lips twitched. She couldn't help it. Fortunately, the wild angle of Grim's helmet and the rapidity with which he turned to face Cringe made her almost certain that one of the major faces of Narrative evil hadn't even noticed they were there.

Cringe's grin never left his face. "Sorry, Grim, old chum," he said casually, stepping forward to meet his fellow doer of foul deeds. "Were you still dressing?"

Grim gave his long-time collaborator a pointed look. "No, I like looking like a pillock for fun. Of course I bloody was. Help me out with this, will you?" With a decidedly Shoulders-like huff, the tall, admittedly nicely broad-shouldered, if slightly pot-bellied figure dumped his armful of arm plates into Cringe's reluctant grasp so that he could pull off the badly positioned helmet. Grim the Dark General was, as was typical of the men of his family, possessed of thick black hair, pale skin, and angular features. His nose was large and imposing and his eyebrows thick and sharp-edged. His eyes, with equal inevitability, were deep-sunk and dark. He had been born, bred, and raised to cast an imposing shadow over a Quest and provide a more genuine threat than a creepy henchman without being quite so scary as the root of evil that the Merry Band would have to confront at the end.

It was a difficult line to walk, between the sublime and the ridiculous. But Flirt had to admit that, in spite of his height and his musculature and a face that was born to exude dark and profound menace, Grim wasn't exactly casting much of a shadow. Specifically, he was hopping awkwardly on one foot as he adjusted a leg plate to a more comfortable angle.

"By the Taskmaster, today is a mess!" he exclaimed, punctuating his sentence with a small but well-executed selection of swearwords as he teetered and rocked in search of an elusive hint of balance. "Emergency instructions, last-minute changes of plan, The Narrative on its way, and then you show up babbling on about this rebellion! I'd better get some proper recognition out of this, I'm telling you right now!" He righted himself with an awkward huff, straightening his breastplate and reaching for the arm pieces that Cringe was still cradling. "And it had better be done well; I've quite enough of being made to look a fool. Where did you leave those Disposables of yours anyway? You said you were bringing them with you."

Cringe cocked an eyebrow. "Grim, I did."

Grim glanced up at him with a distinct hint of irritation as he scrambled away at his left shoulder plate. He had still not at any point actually turned to face the room. "You what?"

"I said I did." Cringe jerked his head deliberately towards the doorway where Flirt, Fodder, Shoulders, and the gagged and bound princess were lingering patiently. "They're standing right behind you."

"What?" Finally Grim's head jerked up, his eyes darting across the room and widening in shock as he fixed upon the three armoured figures that weren't a part of his collection. He started visibly. "Oh!

They're…but!" He wheeled on Cringe with an almighty glare. "Why didn't you say that *first?* Letting me blather on!" He allowed himself a stuttering moment to regain his composure, fiddling about as he arranged his armour into a more usable formation. And then, with a shake of his shoulders, he turned and noisily crossed the room.

"So, you're the rebels?" he said, squinting curiously as he tapped one thumb against his bottom lip. "Hmmm. You don't look much. Shouldn't you all be taller?"

Flirt could see Fodder's expression. It would have defied even The Narrative's best efforts at description.

"Taller?" he ventured. "Why?"

Grim pulled a slightly incredulous face. "Well, that's how it's done, isn't it? Rebels are always tall with flowing hair, and they hang around up trees with horns and longbows and ambush the henchmen of evil authority. Your comely wench isn't too bad, and there's a diverse band of you, so at least you're doing that part of the thing properly." He shook his head. "But just this isn't going to cut it. You're going to have to attract yourself a handsome and charismatic leader soon or, frankly, it'll just look silly."

But Flirt had stopped listening. Two words had blotted out the entire of the rest of the world.

Comely wench?

Did he call me a comely bloody wench?

I'm not having it. I AM NOT HAVING IT!

Her hand had whipped down to her sword hilt almost before the words had finished passing his lips, but fortunately for Grim's ongoing good health, Fodder had seen the danger. One hand lashed out, catching Flirt's arm, and spinning her round on the spot, he bundled her and her half-drawn sword viciously into a corner.

"Don't kill him!" he hissed sharply under his breath. "We need his help!"

The glare Flirt offered in return could have burned through granite. "Did you hear what he called me?" she hissed back. "Comely wench, he said! *Comely bloody wench!*"

"I know, but we need his help! Do you think he'll give it if you've brained him?"

"How about gutting? I could just gut him a little bit.…"

"No gutting! No splicing, dicing, chopping, or slashing either! We need his help!"

"But…"

"We need his help! If he says no, you can kill him as much as you like! But not if he agrees!"

"Promise?" Flirt's anger was draining away but the sound of those two words burned against her brain. She'd promised herself, she'd *promised* when she'd joined Fodder that she would never allow anyone to subject her to such indignities again. Letting a man call her *wench* and keep his guts seemed like killing the dream.

Fodder gave a wan smile. "I promise. But please, Flirt…"

"I know." With an angry huff, Flirt released her partly drawn sword and shoved it back into its scabbard. "We need his help."

"Everything all right?" Flirt ground her teeth as Grim's voice drifted over from behind them. "Was it something I said?"

Fodder turned back to the Dark General, his expression carefully arranged in neutral. "No, it's fine," he said carefully. "Just a small difference of opinion."

Grim's slightly patronising smile made Flirt want to thump him. That wasn't much of an achievement at the moment, though. With *comely wench* ringing in her ears unpunished, Flirt suspected even his toenails would make her want to thump him.

"There, you see?" he said chummily. "I told you. That's why you need a tall, handsome, and charismatic leader. No one ever argues with *them.*" He tapped his nose slyly. "These things do need to be done by the proper people, you know. Otherwise, how's anyone supposed to know what's going on?"

Fodder's eyebrows rose so violently that Flirt was surprised they didn't rupture his forehead. "So…you're saying you can only rebel if you're tall, handsome, and charismatic?"

"Well, of course not!" Grim chuckled irritatingly. "Not the underlings, anyway! But how's anyone supposed to know you're a rebel if you go around not looking like one? That's hardly sporting, is it?"

Fodder's eyebrows dropped to half-mast, but Flirt suspected that was only in deference to the effort it was taking to keep them there. "I didn't know rebellions were supposed to be *sporting,*" he offered, unable to conceal the hint of cynicism troubling his tone.

Grim crossed his arms, still grinning in what he seemed to think was a helpful manner. "Well, it's a good thing you've come to me then. I mean, how do you expect to be taken seriously if you don't even do the thing properly?"

Flirt could see Fodder's face quite clearly. It told her plainly that she was probably only a few exchanges away from permission to gut.

"Do you really believe that?" Fodder asked with well-controlled curiosity, his eyebrows sinking from their former heights to crease his forehead into a frown. "Do you really think a rebellion can't succeed if it doesn't look the part?"

Grim returned his frown measure for measure. "I don't see how else it can *be* a rebellion," he responded frankly. "You can't make a stew without the right ingredients."

"But you might be able to make a nicer stew with different ones," Cringe interjected suddenly, his face strangely thoughtful. "I think that's what he's saying, Grim. You did say you liked the sound of it earlier."

"But I thought it would be done properly! That it would look good." Grim's expression was abruptly disconcerted. It was much the same look that Flirt had pictured might cross his face as her sword slid into his gullet. "It's one thing to stand up and get some proclaiming time out front backed up by some proper, impressive rebels—the right kind. You know! Feathered hats! Longbows! Green tunics!" His voice turned sour. "It's another to be told it's...*this*." The wave of his hand spoke a dictionary full of dismissal. "I didn't expect it to be so"—he waved one hand raggedly in Fodder's direction—*"ordinary."*

"But that's the point of it." As Flirt had half-expected, Fodder leapt onto the opening. "That's what our rebellion is about. You're the Dark General because you look like a Dark General should. You have to stomp around in armour because people expect that to be what a Dark General does. But if you want to lead the forces of evil, or even the forces of good, from a treetop lair wearing a green tunic and a feathered hat, why shouldn't you be allowed to? We're fighting for the choice. We want the chance to be what we want to be rather than what people expect us to be." He smiled slightly. "I mean, take this scene you've got coming up. Wouldn't you like to come out on top for once? Wouldn't you like to see the Merry Band thwarted instead of you?"

Grim's face contorted into several strange configurations. Flirt suspected her imaginary sword in his gullet had just been wiggled about. "You mean... *win?*"

Fodder's smile spread. "Exactly!"

"Hang on." Grim looked worried all of a sudden. "Cringe said *rebel.* More time front and centre. A change of pace. Upstaging bloody Doom. He never said *win.*"

It must have been so hard for Fodder not to roll his eyes. Flirt didn't even bother to try not rolling hers. How thick was Grim?

Fodder's voice was astonishingly patient. "The point of rebelling is to win," he said very slowly. "Why else do it?"

"It looks good. It gets attention. And that's fine." Grim's head was shaking slightly from side to side. "But I don't *win.* I'm the Dark General."

"Well, this is your chance to." Flirt wasn't convinced that Fodder was onto a winner. Mr Comely Wench didn't seem to be able to comprehend the idea with alacrity and speed.

"But I have dark hair. Angular features. Deep-sunk eyes." Grim's tone was incredulous. "That's not a winning face."

"That's the point." Fodder shrugged slightly. "There's no reason why it shouldn't be. You can win if you really want to. Why not?"

Grim was staring at him. It was not a happy stare. "But..." he managed, his voice as contorted as his face. "That's not...how it works."

Fodder grinned. "Not yet. But if we play this right, it could be. For example—how would you like to marry the Princess Islaine?"

Grim wrinkled his nose. "That's not supposed to happen."

"Neither is a rebellion. Or you getting more noticed. Making things happen that aren't supposed to means we don't have to do what's expected anymore. We can do anything and be anyone." Fodder opened his hands expansively. "And imagine how much recognition you'd get as the husband of Princess Islaine. You'd be slap bang front and centre of The Narrative; everyone would see you. Doom would be nothing. No one would *ever* forget you."

"Ever?" There was a hint, just the tiniest brush of distant light glimmering at the back of Grim's eyes.

"Yes!" Damn Fodder for looking so pleased about it! Now she might never get to gut Grim! "The great evil force of The Narrative.

Leader of the rebel horde. And you can dump the armour and head out and sit in as many trees as you like, if that's what you want. Because it'll be up to you."

Grim's frown was back. "Hold on, though. How would anyone know I was a Dark General without the imposing armour?"

Fodder shrugged. "You could just tell them. Or you wouldn't even have to be a Dark General if you didn't want to." He grinned slightly. "You could be a rebel and sit in a tree."

Grim sighed irritably. "But we've been through this. I can't be a rebel if I don't have the right look. Which I don't. Neither do you."

Flirt could feel her sword hand twitching. No, it wasn't her imagination. He either wasn't very bright or he really wasn't listening properly.

Maybe the gutting might be back on?

Fodder appeared to be losing the fight not to roll his eyes towards the ceiling. Shoulders was slowly shaking his head back and forth. Cringe was rubbing one hand against the bridge of his nose with a weary expression. Even Pleasance seemed incredulous at Grim's failure to grasp Fodder's meaning.

"That doesn't matter." Fodder stressed each syllable with scarcely restrained impatience. "You wouldn't even have to be a Dark General anymore if you didn't want to."

"Not a Dark General?" Grim was still frowning in disbelief. "But what else would I do?"

Fodder glanced once in Flirt's direction. She could tell at once he was considering releasing her promise.

"You can be...whatever you like," he drawled wearily.

"Grim, you never stop moaning about how much being the Dark General sidelines you," Cringe intervened sharply. "About how no one respects you and how Doom gets all the glory. So why not try something new?"

"Or if that's too much for now, be a different Dark General," Fodder added, with far more hope than Flirt felt was warranted. "Like we said, be the Dark General that beats the Merry Band. Be the one to win."

"Win." Grim expelled the word carefully. "And people would remember that. People would notice."

"Everyone would notice!" Fodder's face was a wash of relief as Flirt forced herself to stifle disappointment. *Damn, I think he's getting there....* "It'll be glorious. Look, why don't we go and sit down, and I'll explain it to you properly. Then maybe you might be able to help us out?"

But Grim's frown was still creasing his features. "My study is on the second floor," he said absently. "But I need to sort my armour out first, and I hate doing that with an audience. Cringe, why don't you show them up? I'll be along once my gauntlets are straightened. I need to think this through. *Winning.*" He whirled the word round in his mouth as though trying it on for size. He glanced up uncertainly. "That might take some getting used to."

Fodder's smile was encouraging. "But imagine how nice it'll feel when everyone's looking at you."

Flirt wasn't personally convinced that Grim was endowed with any great imagination. He seemed very much a man of fixed ideas, and it would probably take a stonemason and heavy moving equipment to dislodge them. But grudgingly, she was forced to admit that he did look distinctly thoughtful as they left him to wrestle with his breastplate and headed after Cringe up the stairs.

"So I can't gut him then?" she muttered irritably to Fodder as they passed the sturdy-looking door on the small first floor of the spiral staircase.

Fodder shrugged. "Sorry. But I think he's coming round. And..."

"We need his blasted help, I know." Flirt gave a gusty sigh. "I promised no one would ever call me *wench* again without suffering the consequences. Bugger."

"Maybe it's better to make him see the error of his ways?" Fodder offered thoughtfully.

Flirt gave him a long, hard look. "For you, maybe. But personally, I'd rather have seen his guts."

* * *

It was almost time.

The turret roof was windy. Whether that was a Narrative conceit or plain coincidence, Fodder wasn't sure, but it couldn't be said it was helping matters. Given the low, vaguely ornamental nature of the crenulations that ringed the small, weathered, uneven expanse of stone and the vast drop off into the Tumbling River that lay beyond, it was possible that one good gust of Narrative wind would be enough to send any one of them plunging.

Fodder was willing to bet just which of them it would be.

Squinting into the wind, he could see the glow of The Narrative, hovering just below the horizon of the final rise at the end of the valley. He knew with icy certainty that the moment it topped that final ridge, the castle would become vulnerable to Narrative and battle would commence.

It wasn't a battle he was greatly looking forward to.

It was hard to imagine any situation with more things that had the opportunity to go wrong. The feeling of mild optimism he'd briefly indulged in when Grim had eventually arrived fully armoured up the stairs, taken a deep breath, and declared that he was in had lasted only the few seconds that it had taken Shoulders to begin listing every potential disaster he could foresee. By the time he was done, Fodder found himself three-quarters tempted to jack the whole business in and run like a rabbit for the hills.

If only they didn't have to rely so much on Grim. Once they'd gradually eased the man past his initial misgivings and bolstered him into agreement at the prospect of a win, he had given Fodder no particular reason to doubt him, but having to rely so much on anyone he barely knew for something so important was never going to be comfortable. Fodder had insisted that the Dark General wait out of sight at the head of the narrow stairs. Though he appeared to have been swayed over to the cause, Fodder could tell that Grim had not dispelled all his doubts. Besides, there was simply no way to tell how he would cope when the syrupy smoothness of Narrative consumed him.

When the moment came, would he do his part? Would the prospect of feeding his mountainous ego be strong enough to overcome the habits of a lifetime?

They'd have to wait and see.

It had been a straightforward enough plan, when it came down to it: Fodder would play the Sleiss executioner while Grim proclaimed the marriage and death of his bride. Cringe would keep a lookout at the foot of the turret, standing ready to block any sneaky Narrative attempts to break in, whilst Flirt and Shoulders waited, as Sleiss guards, in Grim's study, ready to defend against any convenient, magical plot devices the Taskmaster might use to deposit a Merry Band member inside the tower. The princess would be bound using chains, to forestall any Narrative-induced fraying of rope or leather bindings, and Fodder would keep the axe to her neck at all times. At the slightest hint that Grim was faltering, he would chop.

Before him, the princess was bound and thoroughly gagged, her legs clamped together like a steel-wrapped caterpillar, her arms pressed to her back by heavy chains so thick and numerous that even the most determined rusty link would have trouble freeing her. Her head lay facedown in the gap between crenulations, lodged as best possible to deter her wriggling out of the axe's path. Her blonde hair had been scraped roughly by Flirt into a bun, so that her porcelain neck stood out clearly, her chin propped over the edge to hold her in place.

He glanced down at her face, buffeted by the wind, pale and wind-swept; her blue eyes, forced by her indelicate position to stare down the thousand-foot drop where, if all went to plan, her head would soon be descending, were wide with both fury and fear.

Fodder allowed himself a moment to feel a touch sorry for her. She was just a girl, really. In all fairness, she had been at the wrong place at the wrong time; she certainly hadn't asked for this....

Other than when she'd kicked him in the face. And screamed in his ear. And called him torrid. And threatened to demote him if he messed up her hair. And treated him and his fellow Disposables like dirt. And...

But still...

He'd always prided himself on being a nice bloke. And even though she was a screaming little brat who'd spoken to him like something she'd scraped off a dung heap, now was probably the time to be magnanimous.

"I know it's hard to believe," he told Pleasance conversationally, trying to ignore the venom that pooled in her blue eyes as she glanced up at him. "But this really won't hurt a bit. I've been killed more times than you've had hot dinners. Think of it as a new experience." In a move he suspected he'd live to regret, but nonetheless felt obliged towards, he reached down and loosened her gag slightly. "And you'll go down in history too. The first princess ever to be killed In Narrative. No one will ever forget you...."

"I don't want to be remembered like this!" The wail was slightly muffled but distinct enough to make out. "Not as a laughingstock! Not as a failure!"

Fodder shrugged slightly. "At least you'll *be* remembered, Your Highness. That's the difference between you and me. I appear a hundred times In Narrative and get killed and it's never mentioned again. But if you appear once In Narrative and die, it changes the whole story. And that's why I'm doing this." He leaned closer, searching in her pale eyes for some hint of understanding. "Because I don't see why it should be you and not me."

There was a muffled snort. "You want to be a princess? The dress wouldn't suit you!"

Fodder ignored the sarcasm. "But why is it always princesses and knights and secret kings who ride off on these Quests? That's what you need to understand. Why is it never someone Ordinary?"

This time the snort was joined by a muffled laugh of disdain. "Because Ordinary is boring! Honestly, you stupid Disposable! Who'd want to hear about *you?*"

The moment of pity dissolved in her acidic retort. Hefting his axe, Fodder rested it squarely against the narrow neck pressed to the parapet.

"When I'm done," he told her, his voice rich with determination, "everyone."

Propping the axe briefly against his knees, he reached down to secure the gag once more.

"No! No, you can't do this to me! The Narrative won't let you! The Narrative will protect me! You won't *gegemmphmmph!*"

The gag restored, Fodder rested the axe back against her neck once more, holding the wriggling, chained-up Royal caterpillar in place by planting his foot firmly against her velvet-clad buttocks. But in one respect, he was forced to admit, the blonde brat did have a point.

For their biggest problem remained The Narrative.

The trouble was that The Narrative had the whole world at its command. Fodder knew, as they all did, that there had to be some limitation, that the ability to do anything in a character was pretty much shooting any hope of creating an atmosphere of peril and danger in the future in the foot. But how far could The Narrative be stretched in order to bring them back into line? How far would the Taskmaster actually go if it meant a return to the plan?

And would Fodder still be able to resist it?

He always assumed that since he'd broken with The Narrative once, he'd have no trouble doing so again. But the planting incident had shaken him badly. The way the Taskmaster had pushed into his head, twisted his thoughts, even out of Narrative… It hadn't been ready for him that first time. It hadn't been prepared. Now it was.

Was he?

He wasn't sure. But he was going to try. He had to.

The vivid light of Narrative was pounding its way towards the ridge top. Any second now and he would be in view.

He needed to keep the princess out of Narrative for as long as possible. Pleasance was right: It would protect her with all it had, and the longer it had to work out ways to free her from her restraints…

That meant he'd have to do more In Narrative manoeuvring. But he could do it. He was sure he could.

Grabbing the princess, he hauled her backwards and dumped her unceremoniously below the line of the crenulations. And then, with scant regard for her dignity, he sat on her.

The muffled squeal was oddly satisfying.

Ducking his head carefully to stay below the line of the battlements, Fodder glanced over to the entrance, where sounds of metallic clanking implied the Dark General was adjusting his armour.

"Grim," he called out. "Are you ready?"

There was a clatter of armour from the top of the stairwell. "I suppose so."

Fodder shook his head. Why couldn't he have spoken with a bit more confidence?

"You remember what you have to do?" he called back one last time.

"Marry her, pose a bit, order the kill. I've got it."

Fodder squared his shoulders. Well, at least he had it firmly in mind.…

I need this to work. It has to work. I can't let The Narrative beat me. I can't let the Taskmaster win.

Please, please, please...

Any second now and...

Vivid light washed over the battlements above his head as Fodder pulled himself deeper into the protective lee of the wall, watching as The Narrative engulfed the visible parts of the Grim Fortress in what Fodder was certain was a most evocative description. But after a few moments of descriptive attention, the light paled and waned a little, a cursory-glance kind of light as the Merry Band observed what lay before them. There was no pinpoint of attention, no flat-out assault, but Fodder knew without question that any movement into that light would nonetheless catch a Principal's attention. Someone's hawklike eyes would spot him. That was just the way it worked.

He had to time this perfectly. He had to wait until they were close enough to clearly see what was happening but not give them enough time to sneak inside by a secret passage that someone of their number was bound to find. If they got inside, all bets were off.

He had to get them to stand before the gates. Somehow.

And maybe...

Oh please, let this be the right thing. You can do this, Fodder. You can do it. You can do it....

Twisting round, Fodder pushed himself off his Royal cushion and...

Light...

"There!" Zahora's finger snapped out, pinpointing a remote turret as her hawklike eyes fixed upon a shadowy figure that had just appeared, silhouetted against the battlements. "A guard!"

"Has he seen us?" Slynder slipped back deeper behind the rocks amongst which they had concealed themselves. "That tunnel I know of won't be much use if they see us coming!"

"I am not certain." Sir Roderick was peering round the edge of the rocky outcrop as carefully as he dared as he observed the Sleiss guardsman lingering before them. "He does indeed seem disconcertingly focussed upon our..."

"We know you're there!" The voice was a bellow, distant from the faraway tower but magnified by the bouncing echoes that rode from mountain to mountain in the towering gorge before them. "The High Lord of Sleiss would speak with you, bold adventurers! He invites you to ride and stand before his gates! He wishes you to join him as he celebrates his marriage to the Princess Islaine! Come willingly or we shall have to fetch you! Or would you rather we just threw you her head?"

"Infamy!" Sir Roderick's voice was a snarl. "The black dog! I shall rend…

…shade

The princess gave a muted shriek as Fodder dropped heavily back on top of her once more, pressing his back against the battlements as he breathed rapidly. It'd worked! He'd done it! Oh, he'd felt The Narrative pulling at him, encouraging him to turn away and allow the Merry Band to sneak inside unhindered, but he'd fought it off, said his piece, drawn the lines. Surely they'd have no choice but to do as he'd goaded....

He hoped they wouldn't.

But for now, until they reached the gates, all he could do was wait.

* * *

"I just think we'd be better off waiting downstairs, that's all! I mean, if the Merry Band does sneak in here with The Narrative, we'll get butchered anyway, and what's our only escape route? A thousand-foot leap out of a window that's probably too narrow for us anyway! But if we went down and waited in that room full of armour, at least we'd stand a chance of making it to one of those secret passages before they clapped us in irons and dragged us off to Grim's dungeons to sit strapped to a rack for the rest of our days...."

Shoulders tailed off, slowing from his frantic circling of Grim's ornately carved desk and eyeing Flirt with abrupt suspicion. "Are you listening to me?"

In point of fact, Flirt hadn't been. Like most of the Humble Villagers, she'd long ago raised tuning out Shoulders's grumblings to a fine art. But she also had enough common sense not to admit it.

"You want to be downstairs." She'd caught that part, at least. "I heard you, didn't I?"

Shoulders folded his arms, regarding her with one eyebrow firmly raised. "You're thinking about gutting Grim again, aren't you?"

"No." It was a lie, but Flirt wasn't about to admit it.

"Fodder told you to forget about it."

"Fodder's not the one he called"—Flirt ground her teeth, refusing to let the hated moniker pass her lips— *"that name*, is he? I was stood there, dressed in armour, and he still…"

"Called you a we—"

"Don't say it."

Much to her irritation, Shoulders chuckled. "You've never got this worked up about it before. What is it about Grim popping it out that's rattled your chain so hard?"

"It was part of the job before." Flirt fingered her sword soothingly. *I am not a Barmaid anymore. I am a fully armed warrior. I should get some respect.* "I had to put up with it; I had no choice, did I? Now I don't have to."

There was something distinctly irksome about the amusement on Shoulders's face. "So you're going to gut everyone who uses it? Wouldn't it at least be fair to warn them first?"

Flirt indulged herself with a brief grin. "Would you warn Clank?"

The arms uncrossed in an instant. The left hand flew instinctively to the side of his neck. "Would I bollocks!"

"Exactly!" Flirt punctuated the exclamation with a jabbing finger. "I know you don't want to be here, Shoulders, but for me, this is what it's all about. While the Taskmaster is in charge of everything, I've got no choice but to be slapped on the bum and called… *that*, any more than you can make Clank stop slicing your head off. But if this works…" She smiled beatifically. "I can say no. So can you. We can get some respect at last from all the smug bastards who take advantage of the fact we get no say." The smile hardened slightly. "And maybe as we go along, we can even get our own back."

The smile that slid over Shoulders's face was remarkably similar to her own. "I like the sound of that."

"I thought you might." Grinning slightly, Flirt glanced at the window, at the vivid light lapping at the glass. Fodder was up there In Narrative. There was so much at stake….

It was no good. If she sat here pondering, she'd only worry.

"Why don't we check downstairs like you said?" she offered, pulling herself to her feet as she slid out from behind the overgrown desk. "I think you had a point earlier."

That she had no idea what that point might have been didn't matter. Shoulders was at the door in seconds, dragging it open and vanishing down with what Flirt considered to be unseemly haste. Whatever his point had been, he'd clearly been quite anxious about it. Drawing a deep breath, Flirt hurried after him.

She could hear the jangling of his mail a moment before her own footsteps drowned it out. The spiral steps flashed before her as she gained momentum, but then as she rounded the final turn before the first floor landing, she barrelled round the corner and crashed straight into Shoulders's immobile back.

She staggered as he did, both clinging for an instant to the walls to prevent an undignified double tumble. Flirt half-opened her mouth to inquire exactly why in the heck he had chosen such an inauspicious spot to grind to a halt, but to her astonishment, one gauntleted hand flashed out and slapped across her mouth. At her indignant expression, he pulled a face, but the anxiety writ large and vibrant in his features stilled the retorts she had been mustering. With a jerk of his head, he gestured downwards.

Flirt followed his gaze and gasped. The door to the first floor room was standing slightly ajar.

And from within came a very familiar voice.

* * *

It was time.

Narrative light had engulfed the top of the turret utterly. Fodder could hear the Merry Band below, calling up their lyrical defiance, demanding they show themselves, demanding answers. The unexpected and glorious triumph of the High Lord of Sleiss was finally nigh.

As was the death of Princess Islaine.

He was going to show them. The Narrative would not command him. Whatever it wanted was exactly what he wasn't going to do. He knew he could just kill her the moment he came into view. But somehow, that wasn't enough. One small act of defiance was one thing. But if he could show them that he could take their plot and twist it his way, take the Taskmaster's intentions and make them his own...

No. He was determined. He wasn't going to fear The Narrative. He was going to defeat it. And he was going to do it with *character*. Not the character the Taskmaster had tried to plant either. It would be a character of his choosing.

And so, with a deep breath, Fodder grasped the bound and gagged form of the princess and thrust himself up into view.

* * *

"I was coming to tell you. Honestly! I was on my way to find you when you collared me on the stairs!"

It was Cringe. And though there was no hint of vivid light from the gap in the door below, he did sound quite alarmingly in character.

"I can't believe you could think any differently. You know me, Hauteur. Since when do I want any trouble?"

Hauteur! Flirt didn't need Shoulders's horrified mouthing of the name to feel her stomach drop like a stone. An Officious Courtier, here in the turret!

"Well, you *have* trouble." The low, unfamiliar voice was unmistakably Courtier-ish. No one could insert a sneer into a sentence in quite the way that they could. "Grim has told me everything. Indeed, thanks to his diligence, I was able to overhear your deliberations for myself from this very room and pass them to the Taskmaster. Your little coup is ready to be crushed, Cringe."

Flirt's stomach stopped plummeting in favour of quietly imploding. *They know. Oh bloody hell, we're doomed....*

"*My* coup?" Cringe's voice was rife with indignation. "This has nothing to do with me! I was only trying to help the Taskmaster sort this mess out!"

Hauteur gave an imperious snort. "And you expect me to believe that? When I met Grim an hour ago and he confessed it all, it wasn't hard to persuade him his best interests lay in loyalty. He then also imparted to me that you had made some effort on behalf of the transgressors to sway him to their side. Fortunately, he had the wherewithal to inform me immediately of what was afoot and the fortitude to play along with them as I, on behalf of the Taskmaster, required him to. He will be appropriately rewarded with an expanded role—mostly, I imagine, taken from tasks that would have been yours. Whereas your fellow conspirators are *doomed*. Once they are In Narrative, the matter will be swiftly resolved."

Fodder. Shrapnel from the implosion tore violently at her guts. *Oh no, he's up there alone with no idea we've been betrayed....*

"I was testing him out!" Cringe insisted fervently. "He's forever whining on about how little glory he gets, and I had to make sure he wasn't likely to blow this for me by developing sympathies!" He gave a gusty sigh. "I've been working on this ever since I got my hands on them. I could have left them be, you know, or called the guards and made a big messy scene of it where all those Ordinary folks were watching! But you'd already told me how desperate Strut is to keep this thing under wraps, so I thought, when they fell in my lap, how can I keep this quiet the best? And then it occurred to me. All I had to do was get them to come here!"

Flirt met Shoulders's eyes, her expression filled with horrified rage and his with a distinct hint of *I-told-you-so*. Cringe the Dark Henchman had, it seemed, decided to live up to his weaselly Narrative reputation.

"And if you had failed?" Hauteur's tone was icy. "What if we had faced another Quickening incident because of your selfishness?"

"Another what?" For an instant, Cringe spoke for Flirt.

"Nothing you need concern yourself with." Hauteur's retort was swift and stern, although Flirt did detect a tiny hint of alarm behind his words that she didn't quite understand. "I asked that you explain yourself. Continue."

"I knew if I could get them to trust me, I could do it." There was a vaguely boastful tone to Cringe's voice. "If I could persuade them to come with me to the Grim Fortress, how much trouble would it be to clap them quietly in irons and hustle them down to the dungeons? No fuss, no mess, no outcry, no one asking awkward questions about why they've been arrested as you drag them kicking and screaming through the countryside. But I couldn't blow my cover until I was sure we had them cornered, so I foisted them off on Grim so I'd have time to come and find you, only to find he'd beaten me to it. If Grim told you I tried to persuade him, surely he also told what I said about what we could do if he *didn't* want to play."

There was a moment of ominous silence, finally broken by a rather grudging Hauteur. "He did mention you suggested they could be quietly locked up if he chose not to participate," the Officious Courtier conceded. "Very well then. I will admit you did appear to be acting in the interests of the Taskmaster. But don't think I won't be watching you from now on."

Flirt barely heard Cringe's release of breath over the thundering of her own heartbeat. "I wouldn't expect anything less."

* * *

And then, from the top of the silent, brooding tower came a sudden flurry of movement. From beneath the shadow of the parapet, the same Sleiss guard who had hailed them rose abruptly into view, his mail gleaming, his vicious, hook-pointed axe gripped firmly in one hand. Even from their distance and beneath the pall of his heavy helmet, Erik saw his cold smile.

"My lords and ladies," he sneered condescendingly, "welcome to this grim fortress."

His armoured shoulders hunched and tense, Sir Roderick drove his horse hurriedly to the fore of their party. "Where is the High Lord of Sleiss?" he roared, fury dripping from his every word. "I would speak with the master, not his yapping dog."

"You'll speak with whomever we decide you speak with." There was a cool air of defiance, almost of triumph, to this simple guardsman as he lingered atop the safety of his tower. Erik could see Zahora edging for her bow, longing to take a shot, but Elder's quiet gesture forestalled her. The old sorcerer clearly had some other plan in mind.

"But first," declared the insolent guard on the parapet, "perhaps you would care to see the High Lady of Sleiss? I know she's very keen to see you."

Sir Roderick actually snarled. "Give us the princess, you foul canker! Stop with these absurd games!"

"You want the princess?" came the offhand retort. "Fine. Here she is."

And then she was there.

The beautiful, perfect face that Erik remembered so vividly was thrust abruptly into view, her golden, fire-tinted hair scraped back into an undignified mess, her ruby lips lost behind a viciously tied gag. Her body had been bound cruelly from top to toe in chains.

Her eyes were desperate.

With scant regard for his poor victim, the guardsman thrust the princess helplessly facedown against the parapet. With the same cold smile, he rested his axe harshly but carefully against her delicate, snow-white neck.

Erik could feel the rage coursing through his body like white fire even as Sir Roderick bellowed with anger.

"And now, my lords and ladies," the guardsman declared. "You shall get your wish. I give you the High Lord of Sleiss."

* * *

"Aha!" There was a low, musical tinkling like distant bells, followed by a pale glow and the ruffling of pages. Shoulders was frowning, his expression thoughtful. It seemed he at least had heard that sound before.

"Confirmation of the final instructions from the Taskmaster." Hauteur's voice sounded sickeningly smug. "The players have entered The Narrative and banter has begun. The High Lord of Sleiss is declaring his marriage and his intention to kill the bride as those rogue Disposables planned, but after drawing his agonies out, he will find himself unable to bear to kill his love and will fall upon the executioner instead. In the confusion, the Merry Band will invade the castle and the transgressors will be felled, ready to be removed to the dungeons. The High Lord will escape, and the princess will be much distressed by the fact she is married to him as she falls for Erik. But she will slay Sleiss in the Final Battle, and all will be well."

"What if the transgressors escape?" There was an odd note to Cringe's tone as he ventured the question.

Flirt could almost smell Hauteur's haughty shrug. "They can't. The windows are too narrow to climb through, and the doors below are already being guarded ahead of the Merry Band's arrival. They will be locked up as soon as you and I depart. There is no way out for them."

Flirt knew that the utter horror on Shoulders's face was mirrored in her own. They were trapped!

"Why don't you let me deal with them?" The casual way Cringe posed the question set Flirt's teeth on edge. "They still trust me. I could nip up, knock them both out, and lock them in a cupboard so they can't interfere when The Narrative arrives."

Hauteur gave a thoughtful little huff. "A sensible plan. I approve it. Now, if you'll excuse me, I intend to get out of the way."

Suddenly Shoulders was hustling Flirt back up the stairs as the door below flung further open. The pair of them barely managed to fling themselves out of view before distinctively prissy footsteps emerged and faded away down the stairs below them.

Flirt heard a sigh. "Oh *bloody hell*," Cringe's voice muttered with feeling. "There goes my reputation."

And then, with startling abruptness, Shoulders was gone.

* * *

As Erik stared at the swaggering, armour-clad figure that had just emerged from the secluded doorway at the rear of the turret, he knew that in all of his short life so far, he had never felt such hatred for any man.

But was he even a man? Vast, imposing armour coated the High Lord of Sleiss from head to foot, his face concealed beneath the visored helmet upon which engraved flames and raging battles seemed almost to writhe in the dim light. The sword that dangled from his waist was cruelly hook-pointed, its blade serrated in such a manner that implied it was intended to do far greater damage upon removal than on entry. The dark fur cape that hung loosely from his shoulders proved, upon a second glance, to be made from the skin of a whole wolf.

And this was the beast who had stolen the innocent princess away. What horrors had he inflicted upon the poor girl in the time she had been his prisoner? Of one thing Erik was absolutely certain: He would be made to pay for every one.

The princess's eyes gazed down towards him. He could sense their mute appeal.

I have to help her, he thought frantically. *There must be something I can do!*

"Sir Roderick." The dark, cold baritone rolled out of the metallic face that towered above them like an echoing peal of thunder. "Welcome to my humble home."

"You rancid mongrel!" Sir Roderick, it seemed, was in no mood to mince his words. "How dare you lay a hand upon the maid of Nyolesse!"

The laughter echoed down, dancing through the hills around them in a mocking, spiteful spiral. "I have laid no hands upon the maid of Nyolesse, my noble knight. Only upon the Lady of Sleiss! Your precious princess is now my wife!"

"No!" Sir Roderick's jaws crashed together in fury. "You cannot!"

"Too late!" was the sharp retort. "The deed is done, signed and witnessed by three priests. It is a matter of record. The Princess Islaine of Nyolesse is mine!"

"It is forbidden!" Erik had never before heard such a frantic note to Sir Roderick's voice. "It is invalid! She may not marry without her father's consent!"

The laughter snaked around them once more, a venomous serpent's sting. "In Nyolesse, perhaps. But we are in Sleiss, and here my word is law! I may marry whomever I see fit, and I have seen fit to marry Islaine! And in that marriage..." Cruelty dripped from every syllable. "By the laws of Sleiss, all that was hers is mine. Including her claim to your precious king's throne."

Sir Roderick's sword whistled from its sheath. "Nyolesse will never accept you!"

"It does not need to." The High Lord slowly, deliberately drew his own blade out. There were dark brownish stains along the length of its pitted steel that sent icy chills through Erik's stomach. "I have my claim to the Nyolesse throne. The only claim left but hers. And given that..." Coldness seemed to flow in waves from the armoured figure high above. "I hardly need my bride anymore."

* * *

Flirt was so shocked by the speed with which Shoulders vanished down the stairs that she barely managed to rouse herself to follow him before she heard a horrified gasp and the sound of something fleshy being slammed very hard against stone.

"You lying, filthy, deceitful little weasel!" Shoulders's voice hissed viciously. "I knew it! I knew this was too good to be true!"

The scene as she turned the corner was much as she'd expected. A furious and red-faced Shoulders had apparently caught Cringe completely unawares, pinning him against the wall of the steps with both hands wrapped around his throat. His left knee was already positioned for a highly indelicate strike.

"No, wait, no!" The words were rasped and badly garbled but the look of desperate alarm on Cringe's face was most emphatically not feigned. "I was *playing* him, I swear! I lied to him so I wouldn't get into trouble for helping you!"

His eyes turned to Flirt in mute appeal, but if he was looking for an ally, he failed to find one.

"Really? Excuses? Just be honest!" Flirt thrust her face in next to Shoulders, her sword singularly failing to whistle from its sheath as she yanked it awkwardly free. *Damn, that's harder than it looks.* "You sold us out!"

"*Grim* sold you out!" Cringe was rapidly turning purple as Shoulders's grip tightened, his fingers scrabbling at the hands that gripped his throat. "I never said a word!"

Shoulders snorted wildly. "But you suggested it to him, didn't you? All that time you were being friendly with us, all *here's an idea*, and *follow me to the place where the dungeons are*, you and your clanking mate were setting us up!"

"He wasn't biting!" Cringe's voice was a squeal as his pipe tumbled with a violent clatter to the stone floor. "He wanted to tell Hauteur, get some glory through reward—he couldn't see what was in it for him! I wanted to give him the reassurance of an out! I didn't think he'd *take* it!"

"You expect us to believe that?" The fury was dancing wildly with the fear swamping Flirt's thoughts. She could barely focus herself, shocked that she had been right, that everything was crashing down so quickly, that they were trapped, that Fodder was in danger. The one thing she did know was that it was all Cringe's fault.

"I don't *care* if you believe it!" was the frank, if strangled, retort. "But while you're wasting time throttling me, you're not stopping them setting up Fodder! He's already In Narrative! How much time do you think we have?"

It was as though he'd slapped them both across the face. Shoulders's death grip loosened as Flirt took a step back, breathing hard, fighting against the sudden swamp of desperate despair that threatened to drag her down.

"But we're trapped," she gasped out. "What can we do?"

"You're not trapped." Cringe slumped like a rag doll against the wall as Shoulders's hands finally released their furious grasp upon him. "Narrative or not, there's still the top of the turret. Get up there, get Fodder and the princess, and *jump*. Even if they've killed him already, you can take the corpse and beat the Merry Band out of here! It's the only chance you've got!"

The long, high plunge through empty air down to vicious, swirling water flashed across Flirt's mind. Her stomach lurched. At her side, Shoulders's face had drained from red to white in seconds.

But Cringe was right, lying bastard though it seemed he was. It was the only way out.

* * *

"If you so much as lay a finger upon her..." Sir Roderick's face was utterly incandescent with rage, and similar fury was flashing across the faces of Erik's companions. Elder was already muttering under his breath, and with a start, Erik recognised the incantation he was forming, the action he soon planned to take.

But would it be too late?

The guardsman—or executioner as Erik could now see he truly was—was poised over the princess, his axe lingering lovingly over her neck. The man himself, the monster, seemed twitchy, anxious, impatient to spill the princess's blood. It seemed that the High Lord of Sleiss turned to men as cruel and vicious as he was in such matters. How could any man be so keen to murder such beauty? How could he not be assailed by fear, regret, or doubt?

And then to Erik's astonishment, the axeman caught his gaze. And with a tiny, curving hint of a smile, he shrugged.

Erik could feel fury fill him. Why, that vile...

"It pains me to do so." To Erik's surprise, he did indeed detect the first note of genuine regret behind the High Lord's words. "She is a thing of great beauty, great spirit, and I admire—nay, adore—that. It would make me the happiest man alive to keep her at my side." But with icy abruptness, the coldness returned. "But I know she will not stay here with me. She will never be my willing bride. And I cannot risk any other claimant arising at her side. She is my wife. And she will die as such."

Moving slowly forwards, his blade gripped harshly in one hand, he came to stand just yards from his executioner.

"My loyal servant," he commanded, his voice suddenly shaky. "Prepare your blow."

* * *

Flirt stared at the Dark Henchman, his still rather purple face breathing hard as his deep-sunk eyes raked them over. Slowly, she shook her head.

"Cringe," she said softly. "Whose side are you on?"

The tiniest hint of a smirk sprang to the corners of his lips. "Mine," he replied sardonically. "Obviously." He gave a quiet laugh. "But, heaven help me, my side does have a lot of respect for what your side is up to." He closed his eyes for a moment and sighed before reaching down to rummage in his belt pouch. "In fact…I'm probably going to regret this, but…*here.*" Sharply, he thrust a small velvety purse into Flirt's hands. "Take this, hide it away, and don't let them have it back. Even if you lose the princess, that'll mess things up for them just as badly."

Flirt stared at the heavily knotted drawstrings in bewilderment. "What…"

"Not now!" Cringe was shaking his head frantically. "You two keep on wasting time! Now hit me over the head and go!"

"*Hit* you?"

Cringe actually rolled his eyes. "Oh for the love of… I have a reputation to salvage here! I want them to think I at least put up a fight! Now bloody hit me and bugger off!"

It was Shoulders who obliged. His fist swung round in a raging arc that slammed Cringe's head back against the stone with a sickening thud. The Dark Henchman slumped to the ground, leaving a bloody smear down the wall, and lay still.

Flirt pursed her lips as she shoved Cringe's inexplicable purse down the front of her chain mail. "Nice shot."

Shoulders shrugged slightly. "I liked it."

There was a brief, eternal pause.

"Into Narrative?" she said softly.

Shoulders grimaced. "Not much choice, have we? Good luck, Flirt."

Flirt nodded. "You too, Shoulders."

And then, their respective swords grasped firmly in their hands, the Barmaid and the Disposable turned and flung themselves back up the stairs.

* * *

It was as though the very world itself had slipped into slow motion.

Erik heard his own voice cry out, saw Zahora grope for an arrow, saw Sir Roderick wielding his sword as he screamed at Slynder to open the hidden tunnel, to hurry, to move, to get them inside. Elder's hand was outstretched, the incantation that would summon a raging wind already half leaving his lips, but all too ponderous, too hopeless, too late. Sleiss's executioner had already raised his axe, blade held high, ready to strike with all the force that he could muster to send the head of the Princess Islaine flying from her body.

Even from so far away, Erik felt the eyes of the princess meet his. Her gaze was one of utmost terror.

Help her! He heard himself scream in the silence of his mind. *Somebody, please help her!*

And then, to his utter astonishment, somebody did.

"No!" The High Lord of Sleiss barrelled suddenly forwards, his terrible sword abruptly raised not at the princess but his own servant. "No, I cannot bear to see it done! My wife!"

The axeman had half-turned to gape, but his eyes never lost their steely resolve. Even as the sword swung, the axe started to descend, but the High Lord of Sleiss was faster, his blade connecting with the axe and sending it tumbling over the parapet into empty air.

"Dog!" he screamed at the hapless executioner, who'd staggered back, wringing his hand and staring at his lord with a strange mixture of resignation, irritation, and surprise. "You shall not harm her!"

The sword was raised again, high and lethal, a deadly overhand blow that slashed and screamed through the very air as it—

"NO!"

The turret door slammed open. The action seemed to surprise the High Lord as much as it did Erik—he staggered, half-turned, hesitating in his violence, as two soldiers of his own guard hurled themselves clumsily out onto the flat turret roof. Both seemed for an instant bewildered, confused, half-staggering, half-drunk as though fighting against some mysterious, unseen force, but then the jaw of the smaller visibly hardened and he hurled himself forward with an oddly high-pitched war cry.

"Lying bastard!" the high-voiced guardsman screamed inexplicably. "I'll give you comely wench!"

The High Lord of Sleiss seemed frozen in spite of himself, seemingly unable to keep up with or respond to the desperate nudging that must have been passing through his mind to defend himself, fight back, lay waste to these insane intruders. But from behind, the suddenly regalvanised executioner dived forward and snatched the terrible sword out of the High Lord's grasp. A moment later, the newly arrived guardsman's sword plunged forwards and pierced the High Lord cleanly through the gap in his visor. With a horrid gasp, he staggered backwards and then slumped in a clattering heap onto the stone. He did not rise again.

Even as Erik and his companions gaped in outright shock at this inexplicable turn of events, the second of the guardsmen flung himself forwards, stumbling, staggering over his own feet as though wading through some viscous fluid rather than clean air, his sword shaking as he waved it over his head in a strange and awkward circle.

"Off with her head!" he bellowed frantically.

Erik gasped with horror. The princess! Surely they wouldn't still...

"Evra-dal Alain!" With a slash of his fingers, Elder unleashed the spell he had been brewing—a violent, screaming wind rammed out of nothingness and hurled itself full force into the turret above. Even as the guardsman's sword plummeted down towards the princess, the wind caught his body, jerked him sideways into the parapet with a thump, and the blow fell wide, slicing not the tender flesh of his victim, but the padlock that sealed her chains. It shattered under the force of the impact and the chain slipped, suddenly freeing her.

"Oh no you don't!" The executioner was clinging to the stone by his fingertips, his feet all but dragged from the ground by the force of Elder's hurricane. Somehow, he managed to lash out one hand to grab the tattered velvet of Islaine's dress as she shrugged the chain away and started to dive for the stairs. The material ripped in his grasp but still he refused to give in, his hand lashing out again to bury itself with ruthless efficiency into the very depths of her hair. She jerked and writhed in his grasp, the gag she still wore muting her screams into muffled gasping.

"Break that!" he snapped, irrationally aiming the words towards the sky.

Erik could barely believe what he was seeing. His companions were already moving, pouring down the tunnel that Slynder had opened, hurling themselves inside to ensure that there would be no escape for these insane, pinned-down soldiers. Only Elder remained, still slashing at the turret with raw, elemental force, desperate to keep them in place until the others were able to reach them. But why did those soldiers not simply surrender themselves? They were trapped, with nowhere to run to and nowhere to hide, and their deaths would be swift the moment Sir Roderick made it to join them. Could they not simply let the princess go?

But then, Erik's stomach plunged. What were they doing?

"We have to jump!" The high-pitched, almost feminine voice of Sleiss's killer was almost snatched away by the howling wind, but somehow Erik just managed to catch the words. "This side! If they can't see us, his wind can't lift us back up!"

Elder started forwards, his eyes filled with horror, but it was already too late. Grabbing the princess in one hand and the still reeling guard in the other, the executioner of Sleiss hurled himself over to his other fellow's side and, grabbing hold of him as well, launched himself and his three companions with a cry off the other side of the parapet. Erik jerked himself up in his saddle, desperate to keep them in sight, but it was no use—the curve of the jutting promontory on which the fortress had been built concealed them immediately from...

...drop

The Narrative was gone. But that was the least of Fodder's concerns.

"Gaaaahhhhh!" he shrieked.

Wind, entirely unaided by any magical conceits, battered at his plummeting body, twisting him, slapping him, rattling his armour. His stomach had already been left far behind as he blinked through streaming eyes at the rapidly approaching swirl of the Tumbling River below them. He could still feel the hair of the writhing princess gripped in his left hand; the arm of a keening, whimpering, plunging Shoulders in his right; and Flirt's hands gripping at the back of his belt frantically as they fell together in one big, messy ball of limbs and armour.

"Keep together!" he screamed. "We have to stay attached!"

He could feel that Flirt had already locked one of her arms through his sword belt and he saw the second lash out to drag Shoulders into their huddle as well. With very little concession to delicacy, Fodder yanked the now free, thrashing, and, in spite of the muffling effect of the gag, really rather impressively screaming princess into his arms as best he could and prayed she would be washed along with them. They would sink like a stone when they hit the water, but a bit of drowning they could survive as long as they weren't separated.

The water rocketed up to meet them.

Fodder gritted his teeth. This was going to hurt.

He was right.

He managed one foggy half-second of damp consciousness as the water closed over him, but then the combined weight of three armoured bodies dragged all four of them downwards. A moment later, darkness engulfed him and dragged him into silence.

* * *

"Fodder! Fodder, bloody wake up, will you? Damn, you're heavy! If we ever get home, you're laying off the Daisy stew!"

In Narrative, Fodder knew, an unconscious person often awoke to birdsong, to soft sheets, to an attentive nun tending his wounds in a quiet convent. It was rarer, he suspected, for a poor beleaguered victim to be brought round facedown and half in a puddle as his nose was dragged roughly along on a distinctly sharp bed of pebbles while a Barmaid friend swore like a trooper and yanked indelicately at his mail-clad armpits.

Typical, really…

"All right, I'm awake!" He offered a half-hearted swipe, and Flirt retaliated by letting him drop with a crunch onto the rock. His nose screeched in protest, and he obliged it by vocalising.

"Ow!" he protested. "Bloody hell, Flirt!"

"You have to get up!" A foot pushed with not inconsiderable force against his shoulder. "We have a problem, Fodder! A *big* problem!"

"What else is new?" Groaning in a manner he considered highly appropriate to reflect the achiness of his body and the soreness of his lungs, Fodder pulled himself to his knees and blinked heartily. "Everyone okay?"

The question had popped out automatically. He glanced up in time to see Flirt grimace.

"I'm fine, just bruised and a bit drowned. But Shoulders..." Flirt gestured to one side and Fodder followed her gaze to find his fellow Disposable slumped against a nearby rock, groaning with even more fervour than Fodder had. One whole side of his helmetless head was swathed in blood. His bloodshot eyes rose groggily and met Fodder's.

"I tried to stop her, mate," he stammered weakly. "I really did, but I was only half-conscious, and she'd already picked up this great pointy rock...."

A very nasty feeling fluttered into Fodder's chest and lodged itself in place there.

"What do you mean?" he managed, blinking the last of the water out of his eyes, but he knew, deep down, what Shoulders and Flirt were about to tell him. A moment later, his eyes had scanned the narrow beach onto which they had apparently been washed and solidified his fears. "Where's the princess gone?"

Flirt was chewing on her lip. "It looks like she woke up first, Fodder, and since that chain broke, she wasn't restrained anymore. Shoulders woke up and saw her about to leave and he reached out and caught her leg but..." She sighed. "The princess grabbed a rock and...well. You can see what happened." She pulled a face. "By the time I came to, she'd already disappeared. I left you two for a minute to see if I could catch up with her but..." She shook her head. "She was out of sight, and I couldn't go on without you two, could I?"

Oh bugger. We need the princess. They can fix the plot so easily if they get her back, and all this will have been for nothing....

"We have to go after her." The words came out more resolutely than even Fodder had expected. "We have to get her back. No matter where she's gone to. No matter who she's with."

"No matter what a sodding pain she is," Shoulders injected

mordantly. "Wonderful."

"I know but…" Flirt sighed again, gustily. "But, Fodder, I followed her tracks and it's not going to be easy. In fact, it's going to be a nightmare. We'll be going right into the heart of big trouble." She met his eyes and her gaze was filled with disquiet. "She's headed straight for the Magnificent City."

Official Taskmaster Summary:
The Ring of Anthiphion:
Part Four

At the palace, they are greeted royally by the King
and Queen and then by Prince Tretaptus, who has
ridden in from Mond and agrees to have the wedding
here. Islaine hates Tretaptus, who is pompous and
arrogant, and when the band leave, she hides away in
their party. They leave quickly at news that the
Northern Wastes are crawling with creatures who
claim that Craxis is coming just as the prophecy of
Mydrella foresaw and that they will be defeated. As
they go, the King, Prince Tretaptus, and Halheid's
cousin, the King of Sverdin, are massing their
forces to defend themselves. The trail goes to the
wild port of Saltania, where they encounter the
thief trying to book passage up the Great Inlet to
the Northern Wastes—it's the High Lord of Sleiss's
brother Vagg! He has evil creatures at his command
and his brother has given Sleiss, Sverdin's neigh-
bour, over to Craxis. He attacks them and Gort the
dwarf is killed, taking Vagg's axe for Erik. Erik,
infuriated, takes him on but rather than fight, he
flees into the mountains, saying that Craxis will
rise and his brother will have Islaine, it has been
promised!

Fodder swore.

And then he swore again.

And then, just to be sure he'd done the job properly, he swore for a third time.

Crouched at his side in the conveniently positioned copse of trees in which they'd taken shelter, Flirt gave a fairly hefty sigh. "That's not going to help," she remarked blandly.

Fodder humphed loudly. "It makes me feel better," he retorted irritably. "Not much, but a little bit."

It was Shoulders who got straight to the point. "We're buggered, aren't we?"

Flirt pulled a face. "Fairly buggered, yeah."

Because, quite simply, they'd been about ten minutes too slow.

They'd known they had to catch up with the princess. It was as simple as that. In one respect, they had been lucky—with The Narrative snarled up in trying to clear up the mess it had encountered at the Grim Fortress, they'd managed to maintain their head start. And they'd also been fortunate in that the princess, obviously worn down by two whole days of rough living, had immediately headed for the comforts of the luxurious home she could see glistening on the horizon, rather than back up to the Grim Fortress, where The Narrative could have snared her more easily and instantly destroyed everything they'd been fighting to achieve.

But in spite of their faster pace as they'd hurried across the neat countryside between the edge of the Least Savage Mountains and the valley of the Vast River where the Magnificent City was usually located, they failed to capture her. Desperation had clearly driven Pleasance to greater feats of endurance than Fodder would have ever expected. And so it was that just as darkness had begun to fall, they had reached the small copse often used by the Merry Band to survey the Magnificent City for the first time just in time to see a battered and muddy princess throw herself against the Respectable Gate on the west side of the City and be hurriedly bundled inside.

That was when Fodder had decided to test the capabilities of his vocabulary. It had seemed appropriate.

If they could have caught her before she'd entered the City, whisked her off again before anyone knew she had gotten free… But now, word was probably already being passed to the Taskmaster, and she'd be guarded and cared for, and The Narrative was probably already on its way….

They didn't have much time.

Fodder stole a moment of it to lean back against a convenient tree, breathing hard. It had been a sod of a day all told. Shoulders's head wound had mostly healed up, but he still had an unfortunate habit of reeling off in the wrong direction if left unattended. Flirt and Shoulders had explained Grim's betrayal and Cringe's fence-balancing as they'd rushed along, sore and aching from their rough ride through the river. Fodder could see at once where it had gone wrong: Grim simply hadn't been able to believe their plan could work. Somewhere inside, he'd wanted to, had liked the idea of all that glory, but in the end his mind was unable to comprehend the idea that a rebellion perpetrated by someone who didn't look like a rebel could be destined to succeed. And so he'd gone running back to the safety of his preconceptions the moment they'd stupidly left him alone and dropped them in it from a great height in the process.

Why hadn't he realised what was going on in Grim's mind? Why hadn't he been able to see that even the Dark General's massive ego wasn't enough to outweigh a lifetime of the way things were?

Because he'd hoped. He'd wanted to believe Grim believed it. That someone believed it who wasn't him.

But now was not the time for recriminations or pointless musing. It was the time for action.

Because they had to get into the Magnificent City.

Fodder had only ever been to the Magnificent City a couple of times in his life. He didn't often need to. The City was more than well-furnished with Disposables and Ordinary folks of its own—which meant that, unlike in rural areas where Disposables were fewer and further between and often required to travel, the City rarely needed any extra numbers for Bulking Up.

There had been a notable siege that had drawn in just about every killable man in the land a while before, and he'd Bulked Up a pursuit there that had ended with him milling around and chatting to the Artisans, but Fodder had never spent what could be called quality time within its walls. But it probably wouldn't have mattered if he had. The Magnificent City, when it came to the specifics, was a very flexible place.

Although the streets, the layout, the locations and architecture of buildings, and indeed the gradient of the very ground on which it stood were subject to constant change, in general terms, Fodder knew where most important parts of it were kept. He knew that the City was divided by the confluence of three rivers: The Tumbling River from the Least Savage Mountains, the Shining River from the Noble Plains, and the Vast River from the Savage Mountains divided the City into four distinct quarters. He knew the Respectable Quarter the best, where the Interchangeables, Artisans, and respectable Ordinary folks tended to live. It generally hosted the Respectable Inn and the Bustling Market-place somewhere within it as well as an ever-changing mix of perfectly ordinary streets.

Across the Tumbling River to the south lay The Seedy Quarter. Although Fodder had never been there, he was aware that it was host to the ambush maze known as the Winding Alleys, not to mention various brothels, the Seedy Inn, and the Malodorous Waterfront. Away from the Narratively utilised parts, however, lay the pleasant homes of the Dark Family and the Thieves and Courtesans. Though the set piece of a stinking, narrow, foul urban area was required by the Taskmaster, it hardly meant that people had to live there.

It was across the Vast River to the east that the City became magnificent. South of the Shining River lay the Noble Quarter, admired by Fodder only from afar, home to the Mage and Noble families, location of the Knightly Barracks, the Tilt Yard, and the University. And, equally inaccessible to someone so Ordinary, to the north lay the Royal Quarter—steeped in rich magnificence, the sprawl of the Royal Palace and its gardens flanked by the off-duty homes of various current and retired Royal Family members, not to mention the small, neat cluster of buildings belonging to the Royal Servants and the Palace Guard. And though the Palace was rarely the same from one Quest to the next, the Artisans had been quick to insist it was always a sight to behold.

Even more so than the Grand Temple.

The Temple was, Fodder had to admit, a strange structure. Although the showy, ever-changing Narrative part of it was on occasion shifted to the mainland, the majority of the time it sat nestled on the island that lingered in the centre of the vast pool where the three great rivers of the land came and met. At the tail end of the island were the irrationally neat and orderly homes of the Officious Courtiers, Priests, and Scholars. But it was the small, grey building tucked to the Temple's rear that had always intrigued Fodder the most. For when he'd asked what it was for, one of the Artisans had told him that it never moved, never changed, never wandered at all. In a shifting world, it was the only piece of permanence.

Fodder had asked why. But the Artisan had simply shrugged and said it was hardly their concern.

Curious though he still was, it wasn't his concern right now either. His concern was how the heck to take what he knew of the City and use it to get inside and steal a princess again without getting caught.

"Well," he heard Shoulders mutter quietly. "Now what?"

As twilight gathered, Fodder squinted up at the stars that were slowly but surely phasing into view.

"We still have to get her back," he replied wearily. "And The Narrative is probably already on its way, so we'll have to be quick."

"We could dump our armour," Flirt suggested, although the look on her face implied that this was something she only offered out of desperation. "Swim in under the river gate."

But Shoulders was already shaking his head. "I've had enough of rivers," he stated emphatically. "More than bloody enough. But we're armoured up and nobody down there knows us. Why not just dump the Sleiss livery and walk up to the gate? If we tell them we're Bulking Up, they probably won't even blink."

"No, but they might pin us to the floor and keep us there until Strut arrives," Flirt pointed out grimly. "I can't imagine they haven't thrown around our descriptions."

Fodder was only half listening as he stared down into the gathering gloom at the city walls and the strange dark patch by the edge of the river gate that had caught his eye. Suddenly, he smiled.

"Or," he piped up, pointing carefully, "we could go in there."

Shoulders's expression dropped instantly. *"No."*

But Fodder was not to be deterred. He grinned. "Come on, Shoulders," he said with manic cheer. "You're the one who keeps saying that life is going down the drain. So why not climb back up the drain again?"

Shoulders fixed him with a pointed glare. "Because it will be disgusting. You seriously expect us to crawl into the city through the sewers?"

Flirt, however, was looking thoughtful. "It's an idea, isn't it? Most Narrative cities aren't even supposed to have them, so who goes there? We could get right across the Respectable Quarter, and no one would see us."

"If we can find our way," Shoulders retorted acerbically. "We'll be underground. How will we even know we're going in the right direction?"

"Well, we're heading for the classier end of the city," Fodder remarked with an outright grin. "So we look out for a better class of debris."

"Debris," Shoulders echoed sarcastically. "We all know what that's a polite word for, don't we?" He looked from Fodder to Flirt grimly but found little mercy in either face. His shoulders dropped wearily.

"You do realise we are going to regret this, don't you?" he muttered with profound resignation. "You will remember when we're knee deep in I-don't-want-to-think-about-what that I said this was a bad idea."

"Of course we will." Fodder had always found it easier to agree with Shoulders than try to persuade him.

"And if we get lost down there, I'll kill you. Repeatedly. With a stick."

"Understood." Fodder believed it. "From what Flirt's said about you decking Cringe, I've no intention of getting on your—"

"*Oh!*"

It was Fodder and Shoulders's turn to be bewildered as Flirt inexplicably and rather worryingly began to claw at the neck of her mail shirt.

"I forgot!" she exclaimed, her eyes finding Shoulders as she dragged a small velvety purse out of her front. "I never looked at what this thing was!"

Shoulders's eyes had also widened, but Fodder remained emphatically none the wiser. "What the heck is that?" he asked, moving closer as Shoulders did as Flirt groped at the drawstrings of the purse.

Flirt glanced up briefly. "Cringe gave it to us just before he told Shoulders to punch him," she declared. "He said if we didn't get the princess back, we'd still be able to mess up the story with it."

Shoulders was shaking his head as Flirt tipped the purse over her hand. "I think he was having us on," he exclaimed. "I don't see how anything so small could possibly..."

His voice tailed away as a shining object dropped into Flirt's palm.

Even by twilight, it glittered. The gold band was engraved with a tangled array of beautifully twisted mystic symbols. Two snake-like rivers of gold curled up to embrace the multi-faceted ruby that gleamed within its grasp, shifting shades of crimson and scarlet dancing beneath the crystal depths. It was a ring born to be lovingly described and gazed upon with awe.

Flirt was gaping appropriately. "This is the Ring of Anthiphion," she said softly. "The Ring of Destiny! This is the object of the Quest!"

Shoulders's eyes were huge. "Why did Cringe have it?"

Fodder actually laughed, fighting the bubble of euphoria that was threatening to break through. "Maybe you should have listened to Bard's *story so far* after all. He was supposed to have it. His character stole it, remember? The Merry Band have been chasing him down."

"But they *need* this." Flirt's smile was blossoming too. "They can't finish the Quest without it. It's vital to the Final Confrontation!"

Fodder didn't miss the hope that bloomed in Shoulders's eyes. "Wait a minute. Does this mean we don't need the princess back? We can ruin the story without her, can't we? There's no need to crawl into the City through the sewers!"

But as Fodder stared at the glistening prize that had dropped so unexpectedly into their laps, his mind was already running through what he knew of the Quest to come. The euphoria bubble burst with a weakly plop.

"We still need the princess," he said quietly. Both Flirt and Shoulders's grins froze on their faces as they stared at him in bewilderment.

It was Shoulders who voiced the mutual incredulity. "Why?"

Fodder sighed. "Because they don't need this until the end, and that's ages away. We can't sit around and wait the whole length of a Quest to sort this out. Do you really think we'll be able to stay out of sight for that long?" The looks he received in return were answer enough. "Besides, they have the Artisans. Who's to say they won't be able to make a new Ring of Destiny as soon as they find out this one's gone? We'll be okay as long as we keep it out of sight, but Cringe probably won't stay quiet about losing it forever."

Flirt grimaced. "He was protecting his own backside. If he holds true to that, he may have told them already. Otherwise, they'd be asking awkward questions about why he didn't tell them sooner that we'd *stolen* it."

Fodder stared at the Ring once more. "We'll keep it," he said firmly. "It's good to have a backup plan if this doesn't work out. But we still need to get the princess back."

Flirt nodded. "I'll look after this," she said, yanking awkwardly at the drawstrings as she reached down and started to unwind a strip of leather from the hilt of her sword. "I'll hang the purse around my neck." She grinned slightly. "Then if anyone wants it back, they'll have to fight me for it!"

"Heaven help them!" Shoulders exclaimed with sincerity. He glanced towards the City and sighed vehemently. "I suppose my saying anything else about this wouldn't be appreciated, would it?"

"Well, we'd appreciate it more if you didn't," Fodder admitted. "And with that, I think we'd better hurry up and get inside. The Narrative will probably be along in a day or so, which means we won't have much time to find her and get her out."

"Happy days." Shoulders was staring with distinct resignation at the distant grate that covered the large drain. "Crawling through waist-deep sewage into a city full of enemies to retrieve a princess who doesn't want to be retrieved any more than we want to retrieve her, and for what? The vague hope that we might get some attention? That people might like the idea of things being different?"

"That's pretty much it," Fodder conceded.

"Yeah, well," Shoulders muttered, staring at the slow drift of lights spreading through the windows of the streets below. "It'd be nice to think that there's some bugger down there who'd appreciate it. Because right now, it's the three of us against the world, and I can't see how the world's not going to win."

And at that moment, Fodder couldn't help but feel that listening to Shoulders might be a mistake, because unfortunately, he'd just made rather too much sense. Grim and Cringe had raised their hopes and let them down. But on the other hand, surely, somewhere there had to be someone who'd see the value of what they were doing. Once word was out, surely everyone would.

He hoped.

Well, now was not the time for this. They had a princess to retrieve.

Darkness had all but fallen. Sneaking to the drain via the cover of the reeds along the river probably wouldn't prove too challenging. It wasn't as though out-of-Narrative guards were actually doing any *guarding*.

He turned to his two friends and mustered a smile. "Come on," he said. "We've been in the metaphorical sewage for this long. Time to try out the real thing."

* * *

Prince Dullard of the Other Kingdom was, he was frank enough to admit, just a little bit bored.

Shifting his feet for the third time that minute, he gave a rather perfunctory glance to the character sheet he'd been presented with by Strut right back before this new Quest had begun. It was an unnecessary act, since he had committed it to memory on the day he had received it, but it passed as something to do, and Dullard couldn't bear pointless inactivity. Prince Tretaptus of Mond, he was to be called, a pompous, arrogant buffoon betrothed to the gracious and lovely Princess Islaine. His general instructions were to strut around being obnoxious until the princess fled at the prospect of marrying him, and then to show up again as a terrible commander who got his men killed before being saved by the princess in the Final Battle. As his Narrative roles went, it was fairly standard fare. And that was to be expected.

With his rather indulgent chin and slightly outsized overbite, not to mention a highly interesting if not particularly flattering nose, Dullard had never been destined for heroic greatness. The role of the Rejected Suitor—the less appealing but mostly harmless alternative to Evil Lords, Heroes, and Boys of Destiny—was the best he could have reasonably aspired to; and though it generally involved some degree of personal humiliation and shameful cowardice In Narrative, Dullard was very much aware that things could have been worse. After all, at least he had plenty of time to himself—and to Dullard, that was what really mattered.

For, like many characters whose Narrative time was reasonably limited, Dullard had developed a certain obsession with hobbies. He'd been a frequent visitor to the University library even before his elevation to Principal, and the leisure time provided by his new status as the Rejected Suitor allowed him the liberty of finally indulging himself in certain areas that had always held his interest. Although he was the first to admit that his dabbling in various areas of science, nature, and craftsmanship was of little distinction and valuable only in the sense that it kept him amused, he still took much pleasure from it. Even the simple satisfaction of recording what he learned filled him with the warm glow of achievement. That was why knowing that more than a dozen of the rock and ore samples he'd gathered on his most recent trip to the Savage Mountains were waiting on his desk to be catalogued made being forced to stand around pointlessly feel all the more frustrating.

But word had been received that The Narrative was finally likely to be heading in their direction, and the hive of preparations around the Palace and the City had left Dullard with minimal opportunity for privacy. One of Strut's priestly minions from the Grand Temple had rounded him up late that morning and shuffled him out into the Narrative-prepared areas of the Palace to await further instructions. Since said instructions had been less than forthcoming in all but generalities, the result was that Dullard and the entire cast of the Royal Palace had been left to cool their heels together for the whole of the afternoon and he was now, as mentioned, just a little bit bored.

Then again...observing the uncharacteristic twitchiness of the Priests who'd gathered them and the fact that nobody seemed quite sure what schedule they were supposed to be working to, Dullard couldn't help but feel that something or other seemed to be wrong.

In the absence of Strut, it was Quibble, the Officious Courtier who dealt with non-Merry Band nobility, who was directing events. Higgle, the Duty Pixie in charge of Landscape and Architecture, had been nothing more than a green blur as he'd hurtled around at the Courtier's direction and redressed the Palace as instructed. But there was a distinctly manic nervousness to Quibble's usually haughty demeanour. His little silver instruction book glowed gold with fresh instructions every other minute, and at every tinkle, he seemed to lose yet another precious iota of composure. Even as Dullard watched, Quibble's eyes widened almost comically at the latest words to fill the page, and without a word to his charges, he grabbed a Priest by the front of his robes and bolted from the room.

Dullard frowned to himself. Now, that really was most unusual.

A simple glance around told him that no one else seemed to have noticed the odd atmosphere pervading the Palace on this particular day. But that was hardly a surprise. Most of the other members of the Royal and Noble Families were simply wandering around the throne room, adjusting their bodices, strapping on their swords, and gossiping as they always did.

And although Dullard was always loath to speak ill of anyone, he was frank enough to admit in the silence of his mind that the only way to get an intelligent conversation in the Royal Palace these days was to talk to himself.

Because the trouble was that life in the Royal Palace was just so...vapid.

There was nothing to it. As was so often expected of their Narrative counterparts, certain areas of the Royal Family had raised idleness and pointless activity to a fine art. They drifted impressively through corridors. They gazed into mirrors. They practiced gracious smiles or swashbuckling, dancing and archaic pronouncement, gay laughter and soaring song. They never picked up so much as a goblet if a Servant could do it for them, and they fully expected that everything they should happen to need in order to wander through their lives should be provided without the slightest effort on their parts.

Dullard's loping, awkward stride was singularly unsuited for drifting. He rarely gazed in mirrors as no one, least of all himself, was much impressed by what stared back. And he'd never, ever understood the appeal of just sitting around and being waited on hand and foot. Where was the pleasure in that? Where was the stimulation? The other Royals lived for nothing but The Narrative, and all The Narrative did was guide them mindlessly in the direction chosen. They passed their entire lives without even once troubling to activate their brains. It was the most heinous waste of a life.

And no one else seemed able to see that.

He'd tried to explain it to some of them once, at the celebration ball for Vanity's marriage to the newly appointed Duke Valiant after the conclusion of *The Sword of Grul*. The husband of former Princess Sweetness, Count Bold—who happened to be a distant cousin of his on his father's side and for whom a slightly indulgent chin had worked out a great deal more beneficially—had taken to baiting him. Bold hadn't been happy since his Hero days had wrapped up after *The Vile Rose*, and had never settled well into the cast of supporting Nobles. Most of the more recent senior Royals had been present—Queen Eminence and King Paragon with their daughter Pleasance, Vanity and her clique, and a few others—when Bold had made a scathing comment about Dullard wandering off to visit the Artisans. So Dullard had decided to give them a chance to see how different things could be. He'd explained his point of view in intricately polite detail, being careful not to give offence and trying to ensure that they understood he really was trying to help them to lead richer and more fulfilling lives by stretching themselves and experimenting with their potential.

The mockery had lasted for days. It still hadn't fully died down.

Because they were Royalty, with the blood of generations of Narrative Kings and Queens, Heroes and Heroines flowing within their veins. They were honoured, unique, special. What need had they to prove anything?

Dullard's father had been a King, long ago, albeit a vain and foolish one beguiled by the Enchantress he'd later married. But Dullard had never really felt that that made him special. Until he'd taken up his hobbies, mostly what it had made him was bored.

Dullard had found the other Royals' treatment of his suggestions more than a little unreasonable. But he had founded his life on the idea of respecting common courtesy, and he always made the effort to be kind and polite to every person he met, no matter how obnoxious they might be in return. Kindness bred kindness, his mother always said, and he had stuck to the maxim vigorously, even in the face of the distinctly unkind behaviour of his peers. As a result, he was far too polite to turn back on his distant relatives and tell them he considered them to be a bunch of stuck-up, selfish prigs with as much human feeling as a dead squirrel and the collective mental capacity of a lobotomised goldfish. He was polite enough that he even felt guilty thinking it.

It didn't stop him, though.

It just didn't seem right that life was like this, that people so mindless and lazy got all the rewards both in and out of Narrative. But there wasn't exactly anything he could do about it, and no one around the Palace was likely to give him a sympathetic ear on the subject. They were far more likely to get the Servants to tar and feather him and hang him from the battlements.

And since he utterly refused to be drawn into the clusters of vapid gossip and preening around him, Prince Dullard's natural state in social situations was to be stood off to one side, twitching his feet and suffering intensely from boredom.

He gave a weary sigh. His musings had only killed a small amount of time. Botheration.

A flash of green distracted his attention. Above his head, Higgle, his tiny emerald wings working at blurring speed, was opening out the walls between the newly gleaming buttresses into long, elegant stained-glass windows. The darkness beyond the panes told Dullard that evening had snuck up whilst they had been hanging pointlessly around in the throne room. It was a shame really, as he was sure that with the sun behind them, those fine long windows would have flooded the room with lovely colourful patterns that would certainly dance nicely over the marble floor....

Dullard narrowed his eyes thoughtfully. *Glass.* That was something he'd never really considered before. It was superheated sand, essentially, and he knew plenty about sand from his rock studies. But what kind of sand would work best? What intensity of temperature would be sufficient to make it melt and be malleable? What manner of elements or chemicals other than pixie dust would create such vibrant colours? And glass could be blown, of course, into all manner of vessels and bottles and vials—he'd seen it done at a distance during his foray into the Artisans District, although it hadn't much troubled his mind until now. It would be fascinating to learn how it was done and see what he could make of it. Maybe between his rejection by the princess and the Final Battle, there would be time to...

"Pleasance! Oh, my baby, what on earth has happened to you?"

The mindless background hum of gossip died in an instant. Jerked out of his glassy reverie, Dullard followed the shocked gazes of his fellow Royals towards the door through which Quibble had vanished a few minutes earlier and found himself staring along with them.

It was Princess Pleasance. But not as he'd ever seen her before.

Her perfectly coiffured mass of blonde curls was a tangled wreckage, reminiscent of a bird's nest after the passage of a tornado. Her face was smeared with grime and greenish algae, and the evidence of several nasty cuts and bruises was fading against her usually alabaster skin. Her clothing was a ruin: ripped, torn and battered, and smeared with mud, dirt, and what looked like a species of river weed that, if he was not mistaken, mostly grew in the swirling pools of the upper reaches of the Tumbling River. It had always made good soup stock when mixed with cumin and a hint of—

"Mother!" The distressed wail that erupted from Pleasance's lips almost shattered Higgle's newly created windows. Queen Eminence had wafted elegantly down from the dais towards her daughter's side, but the sight of her filthy state stopped her cold in her tracks. Even as Pleasance threw off the blanket that the nervous Priest had wrapped around her shoulders and plunged into her mother's arms, Dullard could see the Queen struggling to keep her nose as far away from her daughter as she could. Pleasance had flung her arms around her torso as she burrowed her head against her mother's chest, but the Queen's hands snapped onto Pleasance's shoulders as she struggled at fingertip point to keep her traumatised child from messing up her clothes. She failed miserably.

"Oh, Mother!" Pleasance seemed to be utterly oblivious to Eminence's increasingly fervent efforts to pull out of the embrace. "It's been so horrible! It's all gone wrong, and I've had a terrible, terrible ordeal! I'm so happy to be home!"

"There, there, dear." Concluding that her outfit was now a lost cause, Eminence patted her daughter sparingly on the head as she turned her awkwardly and hurried her up the dais to the thrones with Paragon, Sweetness, Vanity, and a cluster of other intensely curious Royals and Nobles hard on her heels. "Come and sit down. You!" One finger snapped towards a gaping Servant whom Dullard recognised as Pleasance's Maid, Menial. "Run upstairs immediately and prepare my daughter a bath and a set of clean clothes. Tell the kitchen staff to bring food and wine immediately. Snap to it!"

With a startled nod, Menial bolted. Maintaining a careful arm's length, Eminence manoeuvred her daughter onto the King's throne before shooing back the curious crowd that had followed her up the steps.

"Give her some room, for pity's sake!" she snapped, absently brushing down the discoloured front of her bodice as she dropped into her own throne beside her. "Can't you see she's traumatised?" She turned to Pleasance, her eyes raking over her grimy form with shocked disgust. "My dearest, what's happened to you? Surely you should be safely In Narrative by now!"

Pleasance's lower lip was quivering like a grounded fish. "It's all gone wrong!" she repeated with a shrill, tremulous sob that drifted through a good couple of octaves. "They ruined everything! I was *kidnapped!"*

"Kidnapped?" Paragon boomed from the side of the dais as Dullard curiously drifted closer to the throng. "But the instructions said the kidnap attempt was thwarted!"

Pleasance gave another brief wail of distress. "I know! But they ignored the instructions! They kidnapped me! Kidnapped me and refused to give me back! They tied me up and gagged me! They dragged me up trees and down holes in the ground! They threw me into a river not once but twice! And they tried to *chop my head off!"*

Gasps of shock and disbelief shuddered through the horde of Nobles as hurried whispers broke out in the little clumps throughout the pack. Valiant and Bold, former Heroes both, exchanged a look of indignant fury as they grasped their swords and rushed forwards.

"Who did this?" Valiant proclaimed furiously. "Who perpetrated this indignity? I will track them down and rend the flesh from their bones for a thousand days! They will pray for the mercy of a death that will not claim them!"

"Disposables!" Pleasance spat out the word like a curse. "It was a pair of filthy Disposables and a shrewish Interchangeable Barmaid! They've disrupted my entire story! They dragged me off into the woods and made the Merry Band chase them; they married Islaine to Sleiss; and then they tried to kill me In Narrative! And do you know why?" She gave a histrionic laugh. "Because they think that *they* should be the Heroes! They want our jobs!"

Incredulous laughter punctuated the renewed surge of gasps. Sweetness was staring at her sister with her mouth hanging open.

"You can't be serious!" she exclaimed. "Two Disposables and a Barmaid want to be *Principals?"*

Pleasance was shaking her head wildly. "It's better than that! They want The Narrative to listen to them! They want the Taskmaster to do what they say! They think they can change the story! They actually think they can alter the plot!"

"It sounds to me like they've lost the plot," Vanity drawled dryly. "Are they completely insane? Who do they think they are? No one can change the story but the Taskmaster!"

"But...haven't they already? I mean, hasn't the story already changed?"

The long and deathly silence told Dullard that he should not have spoken that statement out loud. But he simply hadn't been able to help himself.

As those around him had ummed and ahhed in sympathy and repulsion at Pleasance's words, Dullard had been listening to the toll of a very different set of bells. At first he had wondered if Pleasance had somehow been mistaken, but the state of her and the very fact that she was here rather than riding into the city at the side of the Merry Band was enough to make him pause. Because, surely, no one could disobey the instructions. No one could defy The Narrative.

Could they?

But the story had changed. That was what no one else seemed to be grasping. No one was asking "How is this possible?" or "Why has it happened?" They were too busy revelling in the horror of Pleasance's ordeal. But Dullard's analytical mind had seized at once upon the big question, the matter of mechanics: "How could this be done?" And "What did it mean for them all that it could?"

Narrative word was law. The rules of the Taskmaster could only be obeyed. Except that two Disposables and a Barmaid had defied that. They had changed what was to be written. There was no kidnap in the instructions he'd skimmed through, no marriage to Sleiss for Princess Islaine or near miss with decapitation. But if Pleasance was telling the truth—and, aside from natural histrionic exaggeration, there was no reason to assume she wasn't—then the ultimate, inescapable lore of the land wasn't ultimately inescapable at all.

So surely the important matter in hand was not that Pleasance had had a nasty few days, but how she managed to have those few days in the first place.

Answers like that would do more than fill time. They'd change the world. Surely anyone could see that....

One glance at the faces of those around him, however, told Dullard that, as ever, anyone *couldn't*.

Bold fixed his distant cousin with a steely glare. "What's that got to do with anything?" he retorted crossly.

In spite of the fact that he could tell he was wading into a veritable quagmire of hostility, Dullard's common courtesy nevertheless required that he try and answer the question.

"Well," he managed, uncomfortably aware of the burn of eyes. "It's that it shouldn't work, should it? Those Disposables shouldn't be able to just change the direction of The Narrative. I'm very sorry for Pleasance and everything, but surely there's a bigger picture we need to consider."

"Bigger picture?" The words slithered from Pleasance's lips like venom. "I've been kidnapped, mistreated, hurled around, and humiliated! What exactly is *bigger* than that?"

Dullard pulled a face. "Well, if these Disposables have really got the power to change the course of The Narrative, that would make a fundamental change in both our thinking and our way of life. They've done something that shouldn't be able to happen, and that's significant. Your inconvenience may have uncovered—"

"Inconvenience?!" Pleasance's shriek could have cut through solid lead. *"Inconvenience?!* The only difference they've made to my way of life is to ruin it! They've delayed my entry into this story, and the sooner they are caught and locked away, the better! I have been brutally mistreated, and all you care about is whether they should have been able to do it? What does it matter if it should or shouldn't work when I've been treated like that?"

The cacophony arose then, soothing voices telling Pleasance that of course it didn't matter and that Dullard was an idiot who didn't know what he was talking about. Bold and Valiant fixed him with glares of doom. Then the Servant reappeared to usher Pleasance, her mother, and her sister away for a cleansing bath and a change of clothes. Quibble fussed around them like a hungry fly until the Queen chased him away. Grasping his book, he instead scampered back into the throne room.

"My Lords and Ladies," he declared, his high-pitched voice teetering slightly. "I've just received word that The Narrative will be here in the morning to collect the princess. As far as is possible, events will proceed from there as planned. You'll find your usual chambers prepared and your costumes hung out in your garderobes. Please check the fittings before tomorrow—we don't want anyone looking awkward!" He smiled fleetingly. "So bright and early here tomorrow morning. Thank you!"

In an elegant, gossipy hustle, the remaining Nobles and Royals headed *en masse* towards the door. As Dullard turned wearily to join them, he felt a heavy slam against his shoulder that sent him staggering.

Bold gave him a cold grin as he sauntered past, his own shoulder flexing from the intentional barge. "You think too much, Dullard," he told his distant cousin sourly. "You need to sort out your priorities. You don't seem to realise you're not the only unattractive buffoon this family has turned out. You wouldn't be hard to replace."

He was always polite. That was just who he was. In the face of all insults and all mockery, Prince Dullard always replied with a kind rebuff or graceful retreat. But for some reason, just this once, the smug look on Bold's blond goateed face as he turned away hit a previous untapped vein of spirit.

"Neither were you," he murmured under his breath.

Bold's head snapped back in Dullard's direction, his hearing worryingly better than anticipated. He scrutinised his cousin's immediately friendly smile for a moment, trying to establish in the tumult of the room if he *had* heard what he had heard; but then, with a final suspicious look, he swivelled on his heel and stalked out, sending several background Nobles flying as he barrelled through the door.

Dullard paused, considering the rather unexpected satisfaction that his retort had generated. That hadn't been as bad as he'd thought it might be.

But this place...

As he wandered off down the Palace corridors and up the winding stairs, watching as the herd peeled off around him to their chambers to primp and preen for a Narrative visit, his mind couldn't help but mull over the questions raised down in the throne room. If it was possible for an Ordinary Disposable to alter the course of The Narrative, did that mean that anyone could do it? But how would anyone possibly go about it? How would they resist the honey-like flow of the Narrative guidance in their minds? But if it could be done, if The Narrative could be defied and disrupted, then that might give the characters themselves the Narrative power. Why, almost anything might be possible....

Still ruminating, Dullard pushed open the door to his chambers. He glanced around at the scatter of half-catalogued rock samples piled on his desk, at the row of swords propped up in the rack near his bed and the cooking cauldron he'd borrowed from the kitchens and still needed to drop back some time propped next to the hanging cluster of herbs drying by the fire. Well, he'd better take a look at his costume, he supposed, left in the garderobe as usual to keep the moths away. The question was, would it be ridiculous lace this time or a ruff that made him look like he'd swallowed a plate?

With a gentle shove, he opened the door to the small side chamber that was home to both his wardrobe and his personal facilities and moved quickly down the narrow corridor into the garderobe chamber. There, as he had expected, hung his Prince Tretaptus costume: a green-and-blue clashing brocade doublet and hose with a huge, terrifying ruff and a quite embarrassingly snug-looking codpiece.

A little less expected, however, was the man's head sticking up from the open bowl of his privy chute and gazing at him with the kind of horror one usually reserved for the coming of a Dark Lord.

Dullard stared at the man. Open-mouthed, the man stared back.

"Fodder!" The female voice that rose from somewhere below was more than a little strained. "Why have you stopped?"

"I can't hold on!" The second, more distant voice belonged to another man. "I don't want to go back down into that stuff again! Hurry up!"

It seemed that three strangers were climbing up his garderobe chute. Well, it was a little unusual, Dullard had to admit. But, as ever, common courtesy won out.

"Hello there," he greeted in a friendly, if rather bemused, manner. "If you don't mind me asking…what are you and your friends doing in my toilet?"

* * *

He had walked through several miles of foul and stinking sewer under the weight of Shoulders's grumbling. With legs that were screaming at him in pain, he had taken the lead on a perilous climb up seven storeys of garderobe braced for the horror that could at any moment have dropped from above. But nothing could have prepared Fodder for what he found at the top of it.

He didn't know the man. That was something at least; if they'd never crossed paths, it meant there was a remote chance that they could bluff their way past him. And, in all fairness, the man standing before him had the look of someone who could definitely be bluffed past. He was slender, but awkwardly so, his limbs gangly, his hair a lank brown-black crowning a narrow face dominated by a highly distinctive nose and finished off with a not inconsiderable chin. Add in the impressive overbite and the vaguely bewildered air, and the distinct impression was of somebody who would probably take just about any hogwash offered at face value.

He hoped.

Fodder smiled back at the man, though with both his desperation and his pain, the expression was somewhat strained. *Need a story, need a story, need a...*

Inspiration struck like a bolt of lightning. "Cleaning it!" he exclaimed. "We're cleaning it! Me and my friends!"

The eyebrow continued its ascent. "Cleaning it? From...within?"

Fodder suspected his grin was a little manic, but he was clinging on for his life at the top of a seven-storey drop down into a world of misery, and it really was the best he could do. "Best way to do a thorough job!" he declared heartily. "How else would you make sure it's all cleaned out?"

The man tilted his head alarmingly thoughtfully. "Well, I'd use wet rags on a long stick," he informed Fodder, tapping one finger against his chin. "That way, you see, you could reach down without getting yourself dirty and scrub away to your heart's content!" His grin was absurdly helpful. "And if you used a nice springy wood like birch, you could probably even work it down those angled chutes they use in the garderobes on the lower floors and have a good go at those hard-to-reach places."

Oookay. "Brilliant!" Fodder exclaimed frantically. "Why didn't we think of that? I do feel silly now; don't we all feel silly?"

The chorus of "Yes!" that arose from below was distinctly half-hearted.

The man, however, was smiling self-effacingly. "I do like to think I have a knack for solutions," he said modestly. "I'm always keen to help out where I can. Oh and speaking of which..." His brow furrowed slightly. "You must be terribly sore and cramped up in there. Would you like me to help you get out?"

The grin was straining Fodder's cheeks. "That'd be nice!" he managed, his voice a thin, unflattering squeak. "Much appreciated!"

"Of course, of course!" The man hurried forward with an odd sort of lollop. He lifted the short wooden plank that covered all but the necessary round entry over the drop quickly and carefully away from Fodder's head. Fodder's hands lashed out at once to grasp the stone rim as the man's fingers dug into the back of his padded tunic and assisted him in his clambering. After a few awkward moments of joint effort, Fodder hauled his screaming legs safely over the parapet and staggered out onto the stone floor.

"Ow," he managed, his fingers drifting to the agonising mass of bone and tissue that he had once called his knees.

The man gave an odd little chuckle as he leaned down into the unappetising hole once more, grabbing hold of Flirt's arms and hauling her upwards too. "Sore knees?" he offered rather wryly. "I know the feeling! Back in my early caving days, there were times I had trouble walking in a straight line after squeezing my way through some tight chimneys up in the Savage Mountains. There was this one fault line I was following, trying to trace this particularly remarkable vein of feldspar—" He broke off as he and Fodder heaved together to haul the red-faced and shaky-looking Flirt out into the chamber, but the flow of inexplicable words was dammed only briefly. "And I ended up having to shimmy about fifty feet up a narrow chimney that really could only have been formed by some manner of water seepage, perhaps during a flood period, when the water table was raised slightly." Smiling and apparently oblivious to the bewildered expressions that Fodder and Flirt were now sharing, the man turned a final time and leaned down the hole once more to offer a hand to Shoulders.

"My goodness me, it was tricky! Water-smoothed rock offers less variety of grip and, of course, it narrowed significantly in the higher reaches. Why, by the time I reached the top, I was starting to think I might need to pay a visit to the Duty Pixies and get my knees replaced!" His eyes widened as he stared down the garderobe to where Shoulders was shuffling frantically upwards towards him. "Goodness me, it is quite a long way down there, isn't it?" He apparently took Shoulders's whimper as an affirmative. "I hadn't realised Higgle had made the Palace so high today! I'm sure there weren't all that many floors when I walked up here. It does put me in mind of that rock chimney I was just talking about...."

The babbling man caught Shoulders firmly by the armpits as Flirt and Fodder scrabbled for his hands. Leaning back with a grimace, the man heaved, hauling a distinctly bemused-looking Shoulders up to join them in the garderobe chamber. Shoulders's feet scrabbled for a moment against the stone, but he managed somehow to find purchase and a moment later was staggering sideways into Fodder. Dusting off his hands, the man then reached swiftly down and with one easy motion, deposited the toilet seat back in place.

"But it was all worth it, of course!" he declared cheerfully. "The rock climb, I mean! I happened across a series of pressure chambers brim full with a fascinating selection of igneous rocks. There was a wonderful vein of quartz running through the ceiling. It was quite a challenge to clamber up there and get my hands on it, especially after what I'd already put my knees through that morning, but I gathered some of my best samples that day!" There was something bizarrely endearing about the suddenly hopeful look that crossed his face. "You wouldn't happen to be interested in seeing them, would you?"

Fodder stared at him, this nameless stranger who, when faced with three persons unknown climbing up his privy, had not shoved them back down into the wasteland below or called the guard to thump them repeatedly at his behest but had offered friendly cleaning advice, helped them out of the aforementioned loo, and was apparently offering, quite sincerely, to show them his rock collection. He hadn't a clue what to say.

When he'd imagined meeting members of the Royal or Noble families, he'd assumed they'd all be Pleasance-like in their attitudes and personalities: obnoxious, self-obsessed and superior snobs, talking down to him, sneering and threatening him with multiple unpleasantness for the crime of being Ordinary. Nice, gullible, and completely barmy had never even entered the equation.

He'd been braced for disdain. He was used to it. But how the heck was he supposed to handle friendliness?

"Ummm..." he stammered.

The man's hopeful grin was spreading. "Honestly, it wouldn't take a minute! So few people ever take an interest in my hobbies! And besides..." His expression wavered slightly as he bit his lip carefully.

"While you're waiting, it might be a good idea for you and your friends to make use of my…facilities." With an awkward flick of one hand, he gestured to the pail of water and forlorn bar of soap resting next to the wooden basin by the narrow window. An immaculately folded towel rested beside them. "If you'll forgive me for saying so, the three of you do…pong, rather."

"Ummm…okay." Faced with such glittering sincerity, Fodder really didn't know what else to say. "Thanks."

The man beamed. "The pleasure's all mine, I assure you! Help yourselves to soap and water, and I'll go and see what geological delights I can find!"

In the same odd, lolloping gait with which he'd entered, the man turned on his heel and hurried away down the corridor, apparently oblivious to the moment of stunned silence left behind in his wake.

Three jaws gaped. Three sets of eyes blinked.

Shoulders was the first to recover enough wit to speak, and Fodder felt his words were spoken on behalf of them all:

"Who the ruddy hell is that nutter?" he exclaimed with feeling.

To Fodder's other side, Flirt had turned and lifted the label dangling from the hideous costume hung ready and waiting on the wall.

"This says his name is Prince Dullard," she told them. "He's playing Tretaptus of Mond."

"He's the Rejected Suitor?" Fodder raised an eyebrow. It was no wonder he'd never met him—Rejected Suitors rarely had much to do with rural guards. "A Principal?"

"Well, that nails it." Shoulders squared his shoulders as he cast his eyes hurriedly around the little room in which they had been left ensconced. "We have to clobber him!"

"What?" Fodder was surprised to find that the oddly aghast look on Flirt's face reflected his own feelings on the matter. "We can't do that!"

Shoulders gave an incredulous snort. "Why not? He's a Principal! One word to an Officious Courtier, and it's the torture chambers for us! We have to clobber him and tie him up before he has the chance to turn us in!"

"But we can't!" Flirt looked genuinely indignant. "You saw him, didn't you? He's harmless and nice and hasn't a clue who we are! If he heard us now, he'd probably offer to help us find a good stick to whack him with! It'd be like clobbering a happy puppy in a box!"

Shoulders huffed loudly. "Well, I for one don't want to risk your happy puppy peeing on my shoes. We need time to find the princess, and I don't want to leave some daft barmpot wandering around blathering to anyone who'll listen about the three folks he found down his loo. Because maybe he's too thick to twig that's dodgy, but one word to Strut or the princess herself..."

Reluctant though he was to admit it, Fodder had to concede that Shoulders had a point. It was not so much Dullard himself who was a danger but what he might inadvertently blurt out to anyone else.

"He's right," he admitted with a sigh. "Sorry, Flirt, but he is. Cruel as it sounds, we have to wallop him, tie him up, and hide him in here." He pulled a face. "It's a shame he's not more important. If he had a bigger role, we could take him instead of Her Royal Obnoxiousness, but a Rejected Suitor can be written out in a snap. We have to get him out of the way."

Arming themselves was tricky, given where they were, and Flirt and Fodder did not succeed. Preferring not to leave it in the sewer alcove where they'd concealed the rest of their kit, only Shoulders had kept his sword belt on for the climb up the garderobe. He therefore took the lead as they moved quickly down the narrow corridor towards the chamber beyond. As they approached, Fodder could hear Dullard's already-familiar voice still chattering away, apparently under the impression that they'd been listening to him.

"...so rare I really get the chance to talk to anyone about any of my interests. Most people here in the Palace don't really think that much of me having outside pursuits, you see. They think it's silly to want to know about anything that's not part of The Narrative and how to do this, that, or the other when all they have to do is click their fingers and have it done for them! I honestly don't know how they manage without getting bored out of their minds...."

As they stepped into the chamber, Fodder forced himself to blink. Beyond lay quite the most eclectic room he'd ever laid eyes on, immaculately tidy and yet filled to the brim with curiosities and contradictions. Immediately in front of them was a broad wooden desk piled high with scrupulously organised notebooks and papers, the row of neat quills slotted precisely in their pots to one side. A collection of small chips of rock had been laid out in tidy lines across the open patch of surface in the centre beside a small pile of blank labels. A strange diagram, layered like a crooked cake in different colours, was half inked beside them. Beyond, the near wall, half the far wall, and the corner were lined with a huge collection of leather-bound books, some professionally produced, others more loosely bound and apparently homemade, a repository of completed notes filed away for reference. On a slightly raised dais in the opposite corner, a gilt-edged harpsichord nestled by a large four-poster bed, and an incongruous rack of the finest collection of swords that Fodder had ever laid eyes on lined the wall below.

The underside of the vast bed appeared to be crammed with an assortment of sturdy wooden chests. It was here that Dullard was foraging, one chest dragged out and flung open as he crouched beside his sword rack, pawing through neatly labelled boxes of rocks with an intent expression on his face. A moment later, he shifted position as he delved ever deeper into his samples.

His back was turned towards them.

"And of course, they expect the Servants to do everything for them. I honestly don't see why. Aside from the fact they're perfectly capable of looking after themselves, it's not as though rank means much once we get out of Narrative. It's always seemed a little unfair to me...."

In deference to his companions' steely looks, Shoulders turned his sword carefully to angle the flat edge towards his oblivious victim. And then, on stealthy feet, he started forwards.

Dullard continued to root through the wooden chest, his eyes never lifting from his task as Shoulders moved quietly across the floor, gently, softly, step by step, edging closer and closer to the man he was about to clobber, his sword slowly raising in preparation for a knockout blow. Flirt and Fodder, in deference to their unarmed state, hung back, although Fodder did spot Flirt eyeing up the poker in the fireplace to their right.

"But I still can't quite believe what they had you three doing! The things they make the Servants in this Palace do these days!" Three steps away now. Almost there... "Honestly, it's quite absurd. They just don't think these things through properly!" Two steps away, the flat of the sword held high, both hands wrapped around the hilt. "I do tell them, but no one ever seems to pay much attention to me; they just look at me and see the same buffoon I have to turn into when I'm In Narrative!" One step, a shadow looming, muscles bunched, the distance almost closed... "Just once, it would be nice to have someone listen to what I'm saying and take me seriously...."

The sword whipped back. But in that instant, Dullard's nostrils flared. His head rose slightly, eyebrows bunched as he started to turn.

"Did you not find the soap—aah!"

The sword plunged down. But with an agility that Fodder, in spite of only a few minutes' acquaintance, would nevertheless have classed as uncharacteristic, Dullard dived out of the way, rolling off the side of the dais as he scrambled to his feet. Even as Shoulders wheeled, sword raised, for a second attempt, Dullard's hand whipped out, closing around the ornate handle of one of the swords glittering in the rack and dragging it smoothly free. He caught Shoulders's second blow easily against the blade, swirling it round with a casual grace that even Flirt would envy. The point plunged down, stinging Shoulders's fingers harshly and sending his blade flying away across the bed.

Eyes wide and utterly incredulous, Shoulders staggered back. His feet caught against the raised step of the dais and sent him sprawling to the ground. With a simple flourish, Dullard lunged in and pressed the tip of his sword gently but decisively against his throat.

Both Fodder and Flirt had half-started forwards, their moment of stunned astonishment finally shaken off, but Dullard had seen them too. With a quick lunge, he reached back, hauling a second sword out of the rack and whipping it in their direction. Fodder froze in his tracks a mere yard from the point; and Flirt, in spite of her acquisition of the poker, did the same.

There was a long moment of silence. Dullard's eyes were flitting frantically from one sword tip to the other, his expression a turbulent cocktail of anxiety, annoyance, and bewildered hurt as he raked his gaze over the three intruders in his chamber. His jaw visibly hardened.

"What did you have to go and do that for?" he snapped suddenly, although there was a plaintive note to his tone that almost overrode the irritation that was driving it. "I hadn't done anything to you! I helped you! I knew you were talking nonsense, all that cleaning business! Who cleans a toilet by climbing up it? But I was prepared to believe you because I like to think the best of people! But now, you see—now I'm going to have to go and call the guards! And you'll probably try to stop me, and I'll have to hurt you and chop you up and I really don't want to have to do that! I don't want to hurt anyone and I hate having to see people in bits!" His head was whipping back and forth, his chin trembling slightly as he worked himself up.

Flirt's cheery puppy, it seemed, had a little more bite than they'd thought. "You could have just gone, you know!" he wailed. "I wasn't going to stop you! I probably got a bit carried away with the rocks and everything, but you did seem sort of interested, and I get so few chances to talk about my hobbies without people sneering at me! I try so hard to be nice and polite and look for the good in everybody and all I get in return is sneers and put-downs and brush-offs! Everyone's like that with me! Everyone! Even you! Complete strangers and you just assumed…"

His two swords were shivering slightly, to the visible anxiety of Shoulders, who was in far greater proximity to his blade than Flirt and Fodder were to theirs. "You just assumed I'd be a pushover, didn't you? Some silly fool you could just clout over the head without any problems? Well, I am tired of it! I am not the useless idiot everyone seems to take me for! Maybe I'm not a great swashbuckler or a talented artisan, but at least I give things a try! At least I want to learn! I'm not content to sit around being my character and I don't see what's so bad about that!"

Fodder could feel discomfort prickling down his spine. Dullard was right. He had assumed he'd be nothing more than he'd appeared to be on a brisk, brushed-off first impression—naïve, a bit thick, and patently useless. But forced by an alarmingly proficiently held sword tip to stop and think, he realised just how little attention he'd been paying. Coldly and with shame, Fodder realised that he'd looked at Dullard in the same way that the rest of the world looked at him. He'd seen what he expected to see and dismissed him without even looking twice.

He'd watched the oddly fashioned face and the ambling walk and hadn't even tried to see past them. He'd seen odd and taken it for stupid, and that had been a big mistake. Dullard's stream of chatter flooded back into his head, and this time he actually acknowledged the words for what they truly were: This was a man who had apparently shinned up a fifty-foot rock chimney and was bright enough to figure out how it was made—not the act of either a weakling or an idiot. Every book in the room looked worn and well-thumbed—not the books of a man who kept a library to simply appear academic. The sword collection, with its variety of shape, edge, and form, was the mark of a connoisseur. And what were the odds that someone who knew enough to spot a damned good sword when he saw one wouldn't know how to use it too? Just because he looked like the kind of man to trip over his own scabbard didn't mean that he would do so.

And as for his words as they entered the room...

This was a man who had seen past the life that was laid out for him and was not happy that no one else could. A man who was tired of being treated like his Narrative role. *Just once*, he recalled he'd said, *it would be nice to have someone listen to what I'm saying and take me seriously....*

Fodder could have spoken those words himself. They certainly summed up his feelings. And yet, faced with an apparent kindred spirit, he'd ignored him, brushed him off, and gone along with a plan to bash him over the head.

His stomach felt like a solid ball of ice had lodged there. Had they just thrown away the chance of a new recruit?

"Nothing!" he said hurriedly, extending his hands before him in a placatory manner. "There's nothing bad about that! In fact, it's good!" He swallowed hard as Dullard's eyes switched sharply to his face, his grip on his sword hilt tightening, and fought the urge not to gabble. It wasn't easy. "We've obviously misjudged you very badly, and we're really sorry for that, but we've got kind of used to being ignored ourselves—and, well, I guess we weren't really paying the right kind of attention."

Dullard's eyes were narrowing slightly as he stared at him. Now he was looking at the Rejected Suitor through clearer eyes, Fodder could see that wheels were working inside his head.

"The thing is, you and us, we're kind of in the same boat," Fodder continued hurriedly. "Nobody ever listens to us either, and everyone expects us to take what we're given for Narrative use and be happy, regardless of what we're actually capable of. And that's why we're here. We're trying to make people see what we can do."

Fodder could feel the burn of Shoulders's glare from where he lay sprawled on the dais; he could almost hear his friend's voice chiming in his head and grumbling that this was not the time to go on a recruitment drive. But he was determined to plough on regardless. Dullard was clearly a clever man dissatisfied with his life, and if they couldn't make someone like him see their point of view, they might as well pack up and throw themselves into the dungeons right away, because the entire cause was hopeless.

But Dullard, it seemed, was already ahead of him. The prince's gaze flickered from Fodder to Flirt to Shoulders in one swift motion and then his mouth dropped into a wide O as his eyebrows rocketed up his forehead. Dawning realisation flooded into his eyes and, to Fodder's distinct surprise, his face lit up like a sunrise breaking through the clouds.

"Wait a minute," he breathed, his voice an inexplicable mixture of happy incredulity and excited joy. "I think I've just realised what's going on here! Are you the two Disposables and the Barmaid who kidnapped Pleasance?"

Fodder blinked. It was hard to know what to say. On the one hand, Dullard certainly did seem distinctly happy to see them, but admitting their culpability still didn't necessarily seem prudent with a sword blade levelled at their throats. Who was to say the prince wasn't considering the kudos he would get for bringing to justice the tormentors of his kinswoman?

Dullard, however, took their silence to be an affirmative. "You are, aren't you?" he exclaimed, all hint of the anger and frustration of moments before wiped from both his face and his voice in an instant. "Oh my goodness me! This is…this is just…*perfect!*"

It wasn't a word that Fodder would have chosen. But he found himself able to think much better of it when Dullard stepped back and abruptly plunged both his sword points into the floorboards with a grin that could have illuminated several dozen manuscripts.

"Oh my goodness me!" he repeated giddily. "This is just… You have no idea, I was just thinking about this before I came in and how much I'd like to…oh!" He extended his hands before him, palms outwards, half crouching as he stepped back. "Just...stay there! Hang on for a moment; I need to get a piece of paper!"

Fodder and Flirt exchanged a wide-eyed look as Dullard bolted abruptly for his desk, leaving Shoulders to unfurl and haul himself to his feet, staggering over to join his companions with lip curled and eyebrow raised. He rubbed his neck irritably.

"What the hell's he doing now?" he muttered under his breath, watching as Dullard rooted around his desk, apparently in search of an empty notebook to judge by his mutterings as he thumbed through several that were clearly already in use. "That man's more changeable than a ruddy weathervane!"

"Aha!" With a wild flourish, Dullard whipped a notebook out of his drawer. Grabbing a quill from the desktop, he turned sharply and rushed back across the room to where his three bewildered ex-prisoners were waiting.

"Now!" he exclaimed enthusiastically, his eyes shining as he juggled his notebook awkwardly and braced his pen against the parchment. "Tell me everything!"

Fodder tried to shake away his sudden bewilderment. He failed miserably.

"Everything?" he echoed weakly.

"Yes!" Dullard's grin, impossibly, stretched even wider as his eyes flicked excitedly from one face to another like an over-eager spaniel in search of a playmate. "Everything! About what you've done and how you did it! I want to know everything there is to know about how you've managed to do the impossible. I want to know how to defy The Narrative!"

The silence that followed his pronouncement was epic, vast, and highly impressive. It thundered. It deafened. It echoed and roared and rang and did everything a vast and epic silence tended to do when it was supposed to just stay silent. But it could not last forever in spite of its efforts, and Fodder eventually ventured in and pushed it carefully aside.

"You...know about that?" he managed tentatively. It was hard to believe, after their lonely few days of struggles, that in spite of the efforts of the Taskmaster to keep things in order, the truth had already leaked out. It was what they'd wanted, of course, but without the grand gesture, the big disruption they'd attempted, he hadn't believed it was possible. But was it happening anyway? Was word spreading? Were people actually beginning to see past the limitations and understand that things could change?

"Oh yes!" Dullard was nodding so vigorously that Fodder was worried for a moment that his head might fly off and roll into the corner. "Pleasance told us all about it! And, oh, they were all fussing about her terrible ordeal and not really listening to what she was saying, but I couldn't quite believe what they were overlooking! You people broke with The Narrative! That's unheard of! I didn't even think it was possible! I mean, the implications, characters dictating to the Task-master, the removal of the obligation to obey...the consequences on this world could be enormous! The potential of it!"

It was Fodder's turn to gape. "You can *see* that?" *Oh yes, oh yes, finally! Someone gets it! Just one person, maybe, but that's one more than before!*

"Of course I can see it!" Dullard brushed his statement aside with a flick of his quill. "I don't understand why everyone I tried to explain it to downstairs can't! It's amazing! You, what you've done, it's...amazing!" He laughed almost hysterically. "I really do want to know everything, everything about what you've done and how you've done it! I want to study it; try it; find the boundaries, if there are any; and see what can be done. I want to *understand* it, and you can help me do that."

Fodder had to admit that he hadn't really thought of it that way. His first rebellion had been almost an accident and now he was faced with an enthusiastic academic hunting for details, well... "I don't know how much I can tell you," he confessed, reeling rather from this sudden assault of interest. "It's not something I planned. It just sort of...happened."

Perhaps it was his imagination, but Dullard seemed to wilt slightly. But he bounced back again like a lively frog a moment later. "Well, some of the best discoveries turn out to be from accidents, you know!" he exclaimed, gesturing to the sword blades quivering slightly where they'd been buried in the floor. "Why, the metal compound I found works best in my swordsmithing came out of a small slip in measuring the ore quantities."

Flirt's eyes bulged as she stared at the swords. The nearest weapon had a long, indented blade decorated intricately with an engraved string of ivy leaves that spread onto the hilt wrapped up in gold leaf all the way to the pommel. The further one was bulkier and slightly recurved with a delicate, tapering spiral flying out from the hilt. "You made these?" she gasped.

Dullard's lips twisted slightly as his eyes ranged over the stunning selection nestling in the rack behind her: blades of every weight, shape, and calibre topped by delicate artistry, perfectly wrapped hilts, and shining pommels. "I know they aren't much." He shrugged with what seemed to Fodder to be highly inappropriate self-deprecation. "Nothing to what the Artisans down in the Respectable Quarter are capable of. But it's a hobby. Finding the right balance of metals for the blade and decoration, keeping the weight even but making it look splendid. It's such a fascinating way to pass the time. I picked up the basics of fencing from old Gallant the Knight in order to test out their properties, but I find the composition of the chemicals far more interesting than simply waving a sword about...."

Flirt was squinting at Dullard, and Fodder could sense that she was fighting to tell if the Rejected Suitor was in some manner taking the piddle. But, like Fodder, she found only sincerity in his face. Her eyes widened incredulously. One hand reached out, hauled the closer sword out of the wood, and hefted it thoughtfully. To judge by her expression, she didn't find it disagreeable.

"You really made these?" she repeated flatly. "Yourself? From scratch?"

"Oh yes." Dullard nodded cheerily. "In fact..." His lips pursed awkwardly and he shuffled his feet slightly. "I do feel ever so bad about shouting at you all earlier. I haven't had the nicest of days, you see, and I'm afraid you rather struck a nerve. So, I know they aren't much, but as an apology, if you'd like to keep one of them, you're more than welcome to help yourself."

Flirt's jaw dropped. "You're giving me a sword? A *proper* sword?"

"If you'd like it. As I said, I really do want to help." Dullard's fingers twitched anxiously around his quill, but his voice, when it came, was unexpectedly serious. "I really do believe that what you've uncovered here is so important. It's the ultimate discovery. It's how the world works. It's the meaning of our lives. If we know how to change the world, we can see how it works, the mechanics, the truth of it. You have done what no one in the history of our world has been able to do. You've destroyed the ineffable. You've slapped away the hand of God and said you're doing this *your* way!" He squared his shoulders. "That's why, whatever you're doing, I want you to keep doing it. I want to help you keep doing it. I want to come with you."

Shoulders was staring at Dullard with a low, level gaze. "Mate," he said with a snort. "You don't even know where we're going. *We* don't even know where we're going, and we barely know what we're doing. We've been chased, attacked, shouted at, and we'll probably end up spending the rest of our life dying of boredom in some dungeon. We're aiming to balls-up The Narrative so badly that no amount of floundering around with new instructions can fix it back up, and the Task-master and the Officious Courtiers are out to get us because they know it and they're terrified. This isn't some poncy experiment you can shrug off and write up afterwards. This is *bloody serious.*"

Fodder stared at his friend for a moment, surprised that he had been the one to lay the truth of it on the line. But then, he supposed, of all of them, Shoulders was the most aware of the consequences and what happened to those who ignored them.

But Dullard, it seemed, was not to be dissuaded: He locked his jaw and thrust out his substantial chin in response. "I don't care. I want to help. I want to *learn.*"

Shoulders's eyes narrowed. "We've had offers of help before," he said bluntly. "And the bastards tried to turn us in. How do we know you aren't the same?"

It was a reasonable question, although, as far as Fodder was concerned, the difference in sincerity between Grim and Dullard was so glaringly huge it was chasm-like. Dullard's expression was suddenly solemn. He regarded them, each one in turn, with a look so steely it could have been forged into armour.

"Anything you want me to do," he repeated stubbornly. "To prove myself. I'll do it."

It was Flirt who grinned first, the light of an idea flickering behind her eyes.

"Actually," she said cheerfully, "there might be something. How well, exactly, do you know Princess Pleasance?"

* * *

With a deep and languorous sigh, Princess Pleasance eased herself out of the warm and soothing bathtub and, with tangible pleasure, wrapped herself in the vast, fluffy towel that had been provided for her. Her pale skin almost seemed to sparkle by the dancing lantern light, her wet hair smooth and clean once more as the travails of the last few horrid days were shed from her skin along with their filthy legacy.

It was so good to be home.

Already, her ordeal was fading from her like a terrible dream. The ropes that had bound her, the horrible gag that had tasted of chain mail, the indignities and coarse rudeness that she'd suffered and borne like a saint—all dwindled into insignificance before the roar of a glowing fire; the hot, soapy water that stroked the skin; and the tray laden with wine, sweetmeats, and fresh fruit for her delectation. A fresh costume had been provided, laundered carefully and smelling faintly of rosewater.

An hour before, Quibble, on behalf of Strut, had delivered a crisp new set of instructions detailing how Princess Islaine was recovered from the river by a passing patrol of her father's men, half-drowned and terribly traumatised by her ordeal at the hands of Sleiss and claiming to be unable to face the prospect of marriage to anyone, let alone to the insensitive and foolish Tretaptus. Desperate to escape her wedding and eager to avenge herself on the allies of her tormentor, she was to stow away with the Merry Band, and the story would proceed as before, only with the added angst that Bumpkin-as-Erik would now have to ease past her emotional barriers and work his way around her defences in order to win her love. It would be a far more complex relationship than the adolescent griping that had been planned and, loath as she was to admit it, Pleasance had to concede that in that lone respect, those rotten, interfering Disposables had done her a favour. It would be an emotional, grown-up type of romance, difficult and angst-riddled and ultimately more rewarding. It might have been nice to be swept off her feet by some swashbuckling adventurer, but she'd take a bit of depth over the childish conflict originally scripted any day. No one would make fun of Islaine now.

If only it wasn't with Bumpkin.

The thought put a damp blot onto her otherwise contented musings. If only she'd had some kind of choice as to her partner in this endeavour. If only it didn't have to be a gawky, blond teenager who slobbered all over her whenever his lips touched hers—and stared mostly at her cleavage when they didn't—then she could truly look forward to her big Narrative moment. True, most Boys of Destiny started out this way and bloomed into full-blooded Heroes by the Quest's conclusion. Perhaps as their Quest progressed, he would grow on her—and *not* like a fungus, as her mind had treacherously supplied.

But it was just so hard to picture that they'd ever really get along. He was so petulant and self-obsessed, unsubtle and lacking in any kind of poise or charm or depth. She had always wanted a Hero who would excite her, who could handle danger with bravery and panache and yet still find time to pick her an exquisite bloom or write a few stanzas of poetry about the infinite depths of her eyes. And she knew that, unless he had a full personality transplant during the course of the Quest, that wasn't going to be Bumpkin. She had heard Bumpkin's parents boasting proudly that the post-Quest name he had chosen for himself was to be *Regal*, and it was all she could do not to laugh out loud—for that name was simply everything he was not.

But it was more than likely that this would be her only Quest as Heroine—luck like Vanity's was rare, for unlike so many Narrative roles, Heroes and Heroines were not often recycled. Both In Narrative and beyond, it seemed very likely that she'd be stuck with Bumpkin, and so all Pleasance could do was grit her teeth and resolve to make the best of it. Perhaps the Quest would help him to change for the better. And if *it* didn't, *she* would.

But she wasn't about to let such thoughts ruin her good mood. The Narrative would arrive first thing in the morning, and she needed to make sure she was prepared.

Thoroughly dry in all but hair, Pleasance abandoned her towel and pulled on her silk dressing gown and soft satin slippers. She briefly regarded the tray of treats the Servants had placed beside her bath for her to enjoy, but decided it would be undignified to carry them through to her dressing chamber personally, and proceeded out of her bath chamber unencumbered. Menial the Maid was waiting for her quietly by her dressing table, her head lowered in her usual respectful manner.

Pleasance gave the mousey Servant a dark look. After the unexpected mercy she had received at the hands of those blasted Disposables, Menial had been rounded up by gallant Sir Roderick into The Narrative and had spent a whole day with the Merry Band before being left in a friendly village to be escorted back to the Palace by Nyolesse soldiers. As a result, Princess Islaine's Maid had spent more time In Narrative than the princess herself; and, faced with such a grievous injustice, Pleasance did not feel inclined to be kindly.

"Where are my mother and sister?" she snapped curtly as she settled herself onto her cushioned stool with an elegant sweep of her dressing gown and gazed at her much-improved reflection in the mirror. "I thought they were going to wait here until I was done."

Menial bobbed a chastened curtsey. "If you please, Your Highness," she murmured awkwardly, "Her Majesty and Her Highness went to try on their Narrative outfits. Her Majesty suggested you might like to join them in her solar when your bath was done."

"What?" Menial jerked sharply at her mistress's violent eruption. "After all I've been through, they couldn't sit and wait for me for one hour? They expect me to go traipsing all the way down the corridor just to convenience them?"

"I couldn't say, ma'am." Menial bobbed again. "I only know what they said, ma'am."

"Of course you do." Lifting her chin, Pleasance carefully examined her reflection, running her finger over her cheek and the line of her jaw to check that the vile gag hadn't left any kind of mark or blemish that The Narrative might pick up on. "Brush my hair. Gently."

Obedient as ever, Menial quickly scooped up the gilt hairbrush resting on the dressing table and took a gentle hold of a lock of her mistress's hair. Pleasance settled elegantly into place, her hands resting delicately on her knee as the brush began its passage through the damp mass of royal hair. Soothed by the action, Pleasance allowed herself a hint of a smile as she began a precise, inch-by-inch assessment of her features.

"Did anyone else call by while I was bathing?" she asked absently, distracted rather by the fine outline of her cheekbones in the shadowy lantern light. "Did they bring gifts, flowers, good wishes?"

Menial bobbed once more, awkwardly given that she was

attempting to smooth out her mistress's hair without causing an incident. "If you please, Your Highness," she offered again, somewhat tremulously, "there were no gifts. But Prince Dullard was here."

"Dullard?" The sound of the name caused Pleasance to jerk out of the pleasant reverie she had been enjoying as she considered the fine curve of her eyebrows. The Rejected Suitor's irritating intervention in the throne room came flooding back in a rush; the sheer insensitivity he had shown towards her terrible plight had been infuriating. "That useless buffoon? What did he want?"

The smoothing stroke of the brush shivered down her back once more. "He said he wanted to apologise, ma'am. He asked me to say he was terribly sorry he'd been so insensitive in the throne room and he was hoping, if you'd forgive him, that you might be able to spare him a few minutes later tonight."

"A few minutes?" Pleasance wrinkled her nose in what she had to admit was a quite charming manner. "A few minutes for what?"

"To work on your scenes together, ma'am." Brush, brush, gently went the brush. It really was most relaxing. "He said he wanted to make sure that he behaved in just the right obnoxious way to drive Islaine away and he was hoping you might be able to coach him as to how you want him to do it. He wants to be sure he makes himself look as foolish as possible next to your grace. He very much needs your help, ma'am. He said he'd even be willing to grovel for it."

"Grovel?" Pleasance rather liked the sound of that.

"On his knees, ma'am. He was ever so contrite."

"On his knees, you say?" It was so satisfying to have a face upon which even smug satisfaction sat like a beautifully crafted statue. "Well, perhaps I might be able to spare him a moment or two on the way to join my mother. I want you to run and take my Narrative outfits down to my mother's solar. On your way back to help me dress, stop and tell him I'll spare him a few minutes of grovelling time. But only a few minutes. I don't want to have to look at that joke of a face for long. Is my hair done?"

"Yes, ma'am." And indeed it was, the snarls brushed free from the drying locks as they eased back into their naturally curly state with magnificent elegance.

"Good." Carefully, Pleasance raked her emerging curls into place with her tapering fingernails. "Then get on with it."

"Yes, ma'am." With yet another curtsey, Menial turned and scurried away, collecting the range of beautifully stitched outfits arranged on the bed before awkwardly bundling both them and herself out of the door.

Pleasance paid little attention to her Maid's plight, lost as she was in the contemplation of her face. For it was a face well worthy of Narrative attention. And soon, it would have its chance to shine.

It was so nice to know all the horrors of the past few days were behind her. Her Quest would be hers at last. The Narrative would be here in the morning, and those obnoxious Disposables would certainly be rounded up very quickly now they no longer had a prisoner as bargaining power. They'd soon see how foolish they'd been and go back to their rightful place as nothing-whatsoever-that-mattered.

It was her turn now. What could possibly go wrong?

* * *

Despite the long and anxious wait for the knock on the door, Fodder still jumped a good foot when it finally came.

He wasn't the only one. Flirt, who had been flourishing her new and impressive sword with an alarming glint in her eyes, swivelled sharply at the sound, blade held low. Shoulders, who had taken advantage of the lull to steal a fitful doze on the bed, woke from his snore with a start. And Dullard, who had been busily packing what looked to be a significant proportion of the contents of his chambers into a pack for the road, dropped his coil of rope and climbing axe abruptly as he jerked quickly to his feet.

"Into the garderobe!" he hissed sharply. "Hurry!"

Fodder didn't need to be told twice. With Flirt and Shoulders hot on his heels, he ducked into the narrow corridor, pushing the door quickly closed until only the narrowest of cracks remained. Ignoring Shoulders's brief protest at being pushed aside, he placed one eyeball carefully against the crack as Dullard straightened his doublet and reached for the door handle. With a last, assuring nod at the garderobe entrance, he pulled open the door.

"Oh hello there!" he greeted the unseen figure in the corridor in his usual jovial manner. "Menial, isn't it? Tell me, have you been able to pass my message to the princess at all?"

"Yes, Your Highness." The voice that drifted up in response was soft and timid. "Princess Pleasance sent me to say she'll be along to see you once she's dressed."

"Excellent! And please, there's no need to curtsey to me!" Dullard's hand waved dismissively. "And there's no need to call me *Your Highness* either! But thank you. Do you have any idea how long the princess is likely to devote to getting dressed?"

"She usually takes about a quarter of an hour, Your Hi...sir."

Fodder was fairly certain that Dullard was stifling a sigh, but he did not correct the unseen girl again. "Very well. Please tell her I will be waiting in avid anticipation. I take it she liked the prospect of my grovelling?"

"She did seem quite keen, sir."

There was a slightly weary edge to this statement; Dullard smiled at this first hint of personality. "Well, thank you for pleading my case. I'm sure you did an admirable job."

"I repeated everything you said, sir. It's just a shame..." Fodder heard the girl—Menial—stifle herself sharply, but too much of the sentence had already escaped.

Dullard's smile was kind and encouraging. "No, please do go on. I won't say anything to the princess, if that's what you're worried about. It's not as though she'd listen to me anyway."

Fodder could hear a light pair of feet shifting nervously back and forth but, with the sentence half spoken, Menial obviously felt it was probably too late to avoid taking the plunge.

"It's just it's a shame that you have to grovel, sir." The sentence tumbled out headlong. "If you'll forgive the impertinence, we all like you, sir, down in the Servants' quarters. You don't shout and you don't boss us about and you chat and treat us nicely, sir, and we're happy to do things when you ask us because you do *ask* instead of yelling." There was a gusty sigh. "But they boss you around just like they do us, sir. We're Servants, sir; we have to expect it. But it doesn't seem fair to do it to *you.*"

"Not to anyone, I would say." Fodder caught a glimpse of a thoughtful flash crossing Dullard's face as he shrugged slightly. "Such is the way of the world, I suppose," he declared rather dramatically. "But still…" His face took on a conspiratorial cast. "Given everything that's been happening lately, I'm not sure the way of the world is quite what it was. What with the instructions…changing…" He pursed his lips. "The whole Palace is talking about what happened to poor Pleasance. And you were there, weren't you? When it all started?"

Fodder risked a quick glance at Flirt and saw the same brief flash of alarm on her features that he could feel rising across his. *Oh blimey. He's supposed to be getting rid of her! What is he doing?*

"Oh yes, sir!" The timid shyness of the voice was slipping away into still deferent but rather more animated engagement. "I was supposed to be killed, sir; it said so right there in the instructions but that Disposable…he didn't do it, sir! I was relieved, sir, because I hadn't much liked the idea of being killed—but it was supposed to happen, and it didn't. And he took the princess away, sir! He wasn't supposed to do that either!"

"I know!" Dullard's voice rose in incredulous agreement. "Against the Taskmaster's instructions too! Who'd have thought such a thing could even be done? And yet you saw it happen! I mean, it does make you think, doesn't it? If a simple Disposable can shrug off The Narrative like that, well… It's almost as though the old rules needn't apply anymore. Why, it might just be that anyone could do it!" He chewed on his lip for a moment. "I mean, can you imagine if a Servant tried it? Or even all the Servants? Can you picture the looks on the faces of my relatives if they woke up one morning and found they had to get their own breakfast? And how foolish they would look swooping around In Narrative trying to look austere and powerful if nobody was doing what they said?"

The oddly distant and vaguely wistful sigh that drifted from the corridor suggested to Fodder that Menial clearly could. Fodder found himself battling to fight suddenly rising laughter as his brain finally caught up with what his new ally was up to. *Oh, Dullard, I think I'm going to like you.…*

"But, anyway…" Dullard smacked his hands together cheerfully, rubbing his palms against each other vigorously. "I mustn't keep you from your mistress with this chatter! I'm sure you and the other Servants will have plenty of time for such talk whilst your masters and mistresses are making the most of all that Narrative time they get!

Lovely talking to you, Menial."

"Yes, sir. Thank you, sir." There was a distinctly thoughtful note to this final send-off. With a gentle patter of footsteps, the Maid retreated down the corridor.

Gently but firmly, Dullard closed the door. "It's safe," he called cheerfully. "You can come out."

"Yeah, after listening to you blathering on with someone you were supposed to get rid of." Shoulders, it seemed, had not quite caught the point. "What was all that mateyness about?"

Dullard smiled with distinct satisfaction as he ambled back over to finish cramming his numerous notebooks into his pack. "Oh, just planting an idea," he said airily. "Just because we agreed it wouldn't be safe for us to stay in the Palace once you've recaptured the princess doesn't mean we can't do a little groundwork here before we go."

"Oh, gawd." Shoulders rolled his eyes towards the ceiling. "Don't tell me you're a gardener too."

"Well, as it happens, I have dabbled in the study of naturally occurring flora, though I've yet to cultivate—"

"I thought it was very clever." Fodder intervened before the conversation could veer off at a wild tangent. "You were trying to get her thinking about it, weren't you? And maybe talking about it with her friends? You were trying to make her realise what was in it for them."

Dullard beamed at this observation. "Precisely! I thought it astute to seize upon the natural dissatisfaction she expressed and show her the possible benefits your way of thinking might have for her and her compatriots. I do think that a lot of the Servants here would be quite receptive to your ideas, so I thought perhaps if I left the idea behind for them to discuss amongst themselves, let them draw their own conclusions…?" He waved one hand in a wild but thoughtful gesture. "I have observed in the past that people don't like to be lectured. They do seem to respond better when they think something is their own idea—a strange fact in our society, but nonetheless a true one! And, of course, the more they then hear about a group of brave souls out there, disrupting The Narrative, the more they'll start to see it's not just an idea anymore—it's something that could work for them. And word will spread out from them and keep spreading until it's unstoppable. Or that's the theory, anyway." He gave a hopeful smile. "It's worth a try, don't you think?"

"Definitely." Fodder couldn't help but smile back. "And quick thinking there, too. It's good to have you on board, Dullard."

Dullard's face lit up like a true Narrative sunset. "Oh, it was nothing, really," he muttered awkwardly, sliding the words around the edges of the smile he was trying to restrain. "I just want to help! And speaking of which...I've been thinking about what you said about getting Pleasance killed In Narrative."

"Me too." Shoulders offered dreamily. "Fun, isn't it?"

The look Dullard gave Shoulders held the most diffident hint of reproach that Fodder had ever come across. "I wouldn't say *fun*," he said, uncomfortably. "Though Pleasance and I have never been bosom companions, I do feel rather bad about tricking her. But I can see the practicality of it as a way to disrupt the story, and I did think—have you considered approaching Poniard?"

Fodder racked his memory for a moment until it finally provided an answer. "The Assassin?"

Dullard nodded as he placed the last of his never-ending supply of notebooks into his pack and folded it carefully shut. "That's right. Do you know him?"

Fodder shook his head. "Assassins don't tend to work out at Humble Village. I've heard his name mentioned once or twice, though."

"He's very fine at his Narrative role," Dullard asserted with a nod. "If he took Pleasance—or rather Islaine—into Narrative, she certainly wouldn't come out in any fit state to continue the Quest, and it would be nice and quick for her too. And Smelter, the chief weaponsmith down in the Artisans Quarter, did mention to me that he has recently started to express a certain...dissatisfaction with his position." He pursed his lips awkwardly. "I'm not sure if it's *quite* the kind of dissatisfaction we're looking for, but it might mean he's open to suggestion. We might have to tread carefully, though. He's an odd sort of stick."

Flirt, after a few practice attempts, finally sheathed her new sword in one fluid motion. "Odd? Odd how?" she asked.

Dullard's mouth underwent a series of bizarre contortions. "I'll explain later," he hedged. "Pleasance will be here in fifteen minutes or so. We need to be ready to go as soon as she's caught."

Fodder caught Flirt's eye. He could see she didn't like the sound of *odd sort of stick* any more than he did, but Dullard was right about the time. Shrugging off his misgivings for the time being, Fodder turned back to the task in hand.

"Right," he said firmly. "Who wants to do the sack?"

* * *

Ah, velvet. I do love velvet.

Velvet had substance. Velvet had class. Velvet was heavy enough that it gave the motion of her walk a sweeping elegance without bouncing all over the place and swishing madly about in the wind the way a lighter material might. Velvet didn't swish. Velvet *undulated.*

Wriggling herself in satisfaction, Pleasance swirled first one way and then the other as she admired the sky blue velvet dress that Menial had helped her don. The intricate silver and gold embroidery of the bodice gathered the material in a flattering way; the hanging sleeves trailed behind her in a suitably ethereal manner; and the skirt, of course, undulated nicely as she turned. Oh, yes. This was more like it. This was what being a princess was all about.

Sweeping her hair with delicate care to one side, Menial carefully placed the sapphire-studded golden necklace around her neck. The look was complete.

Pleasance permitted herself a smug little smile. Just because she was going to have to settle for Bumpkin didn't mean that she wasn't going to make it abundantly clear how much she outclassed him. If he didn't have to scrape his jaw off the floor the first time he laid eyes on her, she simply hadn't done her job properly.

"Menial, go on ahead to my mother's solar and prepare my clothes," she ordered the Maid as she turned, slipping her feet into a dainty pair of embroidered heeled shoes. "I'll be along shortly."

"After you've seen Prince Dullard, ma'am?"

"Dullard?" Pleasance frowned for a moment. In her haze of velvet pleasure, her decision to stop off and watch that irritating buffoon grovel had entirely slipped her mind. But making him crawl on his hands and knees and kiss the hem of her skirt whilst begging her forgiveness remained an appealing image. "Oh, yes. After I've seen him, I'll be right there. Now run along!"

"Yes, Your Highness." With a bobbed curtsey, Menial scurried quickly out of the door.

Pleasance permitted herself a final, lingering look at the vision of Royal perfection arranged in the mirror before her. She sighed happily.

The princess to end all princesses. That was what she was going to be.

And then, with a precisely orchestrated sweep of her skirts, Pleasance turned and glided out into the corridor.

Abused but still dignified. Tormented but elegant. That was Islaine. A vision of beauty made nearly unobtainable by her emotional distress. Perfection with a troubled soul.

She almost squealed to herself. Even with Bumpkin, it was going to be wonderful! Who would ever forget a princess like this?

Dullard's door loomed ahead. Beaming to herself, Pleasance reached out and delicately rapped on the wood.

"Coming!"

Pleasance fought a brief surge of irritation. Coming? Why wasn't he waiting at the door for her arrival with bated breath, anxious apologies on his lips? Why wasn't he poised at the handle awaiting her arrival with a bunch of flowers or a necklace and perhaps some tasty sweetmeats to present to her with a contrite flourish?

Honestly, didn't the man know anything? He was so useless!

The door half opened. Dullard, with his overgrown chin and stupid nose, peered round it and flashed her an uneven smile as his eyes, unbelievably, focussed not on the vision of perfection arranged before him but almost furtively along the corridor behind her.

"Hello!" he greeted her with frankly uncouth levels of cheeriness. "So glad you could make it! Why don't you come on in?"

Pleasance felt her eyes narrow. He was holding no jewellery. She could smell neither flowers nor sweetmeats, and he was most emphatically not on his knees. He hadn't even fully opened the door for her! What kind of grovelling did he call this?

Couldn't he do anything right?

"I understand you have something to say to me," she declared, her tone clipped and terse. "An apology for your abominable behaviour earlier?"

"Yes. Indeed." Dullard's smile dropped away into a more serious nod. "If you'll just let me show you inside…"

Suddenly Pleasance was infuriated. Infuriated that she was wasting her time with a man who didn't even know how to apologise to a princess properly, infuriated by his stupid face and that gabbling voice. He'd deflected so much of her sympathy down in the throne room, stolen her moment, her thunder, just like those blasted Disposables, and now he wouldn't even grovel for her properly. Why should she go into his stupid chambers? He should be apologising in front of everyone! She should make him do it in *public*.

"I don't think so." She did take a distinct satisfaction from the look of alarm that flashed across Dullard's features. "Because I don't think a simple, private apology is going to be enough! I don't want a summons from you for a quick *I'm sorry* behind closed doors! I suffered a terrible ordeal, and all you could do was make light of it! So I want you to come with me. We'll gather the whole family together in the throne room and you can apologise to me in front of everyone. I expect you on your knees, begging my forgiveness! I expect you to kiss my shoes and the hem of my dress! I expect flowers and sweetmeats and compliments, and I expect you to renounce every foolish word you said about my suffering being unimportant! And that, you see, is a *proper* apology to a princess! That is the apology I *deserve!*"

The look of profound alarm on Dullard's face really was immensely gratifying. "What you deserve…" he stammered awkwardly. "Yes, of course. You must get what you deserve." He swallowed carefully, his eyes thoughtful. "But…well," he said suddenly. "I must admit, I'm a bit of an amateur at this whole apology business and since I have wronged you so very much, I want to make sure I do the thing absolutely right. So perhaps, before we go downstairs, we could hold a little…rehearsal? If you want to just step inside for a few minutes, you can talk me through exactly how much dress kissing you'll need, what kind of flowers you want. You can even pick my outfit, to make sure that we don't clash!" He smiled tentatively. "I want to do everything in my power to make sure you're happy with the apology you get. So…"

He gestured over his shoulder into the room. Galling as it was to concede anything to him, Pleasance had to admit that she liked the sound of what he proposed. Spontaneity was one thing, but a beautifully prepared and choreographed apology did hold a definite appeal.

"Oh...very well," she conceded with feigned reluctance. "But you must memorise the instructions I give you to the letter, is that understood?"

"Of course!" Dullard nodded as he stepped back, pulling the door open wide at last and gesturing into the strangely dim room beyond with a sweep of one arm. "Please, after you!"

"Hmph!" Pleasance glided regally past him, making sure to undulate her skirts in just the right manner. "But I insist you light some candles! I can hardly see a thing in—"

The sharp slam of the door behind her killed her sentence dead. Even as she wheeled, a shadow hurled itself out of nowhere and then sackcloth, coarse and rough, was yanked over her head, crushing her precisely ringletted hair with savage inconsiderateness. She managed a single squeak of horror before something heavy walloped against the top of her head and sent her tumbling into darkness.

* * *

"Did you have to be so...abrupt about it?"

Fodder glanced up from where he was securing the bonds of the unconscious princess. Dullard was still standing by the door, one hand pressed against his lips, his mouth twisted and his expression one of the utmost discomfort.

"Well, yeah," he responded frankly. "We said we were going to down her quickly. The girl's got a scream on her that could melt stone, and the last thing we want is attention."

"But just hitting her over the head like that..." Dullard rubbed his hands together awkwardly, his eyes drifting over to where Shoulders was replacing the fireplace poker with a thoroughly satisfied grin. "You couldn't have reasoned with her first? Attempted a little gentle persuasion?"

Shoulders gave a hefty snort. "Persuasion? With her? As if that would work!"

"But have you...well...*tried?*" Dullard's eyes remained fixed on the trussed-up bundle of sackcloth and velvet slumped on the floor before them. "I mean...I'll admit she can be difficult and fairly unpleasant at times." Shoulders's second snort was even louder than the first. "But I like to think there's some reasonableness in everyone, and my mother always said that kindness breeds kindness. Bashing Pleasance over the head, tying her up, and gagging her is never going to make anyone amenable to your point of view, let alone someone as proud as a princess. But perhaps if you sat her down and explained to her why you're doing this..."

"She knows, doesn't she?" Flirt wandered back from the garderobe, where she had been securing the rope they were to use in their escape. "She's heard us explain it enough times."

"But have you ever explained it specifically to her?" Dullard opened his palms with a wide shrug. "There's a world of difference between overhearing what your captors are up to and having someone sit down and respectfully explain it."

Though he could intellectually see Dullard's point, Fodder's mind refused to reconcile the kicking, screeching ball of threats and insults they'd been hauling around with a calm and reasonable young lady who'd listen to their ideas and give the matter some thought.

"You're more than welcome to try it, if you like," he told Dullard with a wave of one hand. "Just expect screaming."

"My eardrums are sturdy enough." Dullard's reply was crowned by a hint of a smile. "But honestly, I think after all she's been put through in the name of your cause, it's only fair to at least give her a chance to understand why, don't you think?"

Shoulders shrugged as he bent down to scoop up the supine princess, ready for transport down the privy bowl. "It's your funeral. Or your hearing's funeral anyway. Just don't expect us to learn sign language for you."

Dullard winced as Shoulders flung the limp form of Pleasance heavily over one shoulder, her head missing the sturdy stone of the fireplace by the narrowest of margins and the force sending her showy necklace flying across the room to ricochet off a bookcase.

"Why don't you let me carry her?" he intervened anxiously. "I know it must be a terrible burden to you, and I'd be quite happy to..."

"She's all yours, mate!" Shoulders's expression was that of a man whose characters had all come at once. With unseemly speed, he tossed the velvet bundle towards Dullard's hurriedly extended arms. "In fact, you can keep her! My back's more sick of her than the rest of me!"

Only the Rejected Suitor's quick reactions saved Pleasance from a heavy tumble. Juggling her limp form awkwardly for a moment, Dullard hoisted Pleasance rather more gently into the cradle of his arms.

"Perhaps," he offered delicately, "if someone were to take the sack off...?"

Looking unconvinced but nonetheless opting to play along, Flirt reached out and pulled the sack away. With a firm look, she grabbed one of Dullard's handkerchiefs from a nearby bureau and fixed it sturdily over the much-ruffled curls as a gag. She sighed at Dullard's look.

"She'll scream the place down if she wakes up before we're out of the city," she reiterated firmly. "And then we'll be done for, won't we? Sorry, Dullard, but the nicely-nicely approach is going to have to wait until we're out in the sticks. Now come on. We need to get moving or we'll run out of night!"

Dullard frowned, but he conceded the point. "Very well. But speaking of sticks, before we go, did you want to try your luck with Poniard the Assassin? He has lodgings over the river in the Respectable Quarter. And at this time of night, so Smelter told me, he's usually to be found in the Rowdy Tavern. It isn't far from the bridge." He pulled a face. "I understand he spends a lot of time there these days. It has to do with his...issues...."

By now, the four of them had moved into the narrow corridor that led into Dullard's garderobe. With a great deal more care than Shoulders had ever mustered, the prince laid the princess down and secured her to the rope, ignoring with considerable grace Shoulders's muttered suggestion that she just be dropped.

"We could do," Fodder said. With The Narrative on its way to the city, the idea of dealing with the princess problem right there and then held a certain appeal. But *odd sort of stick* was ringing in Fodder's ears almost as loudly as *issues.* "What sort of issues are we talking about here? Is he going to be a problem?"

Dullard's face as he clambered to the edge of the garderobe could best be described as cagey. "Well...that rather depends. You see, the problem with Poniard is that what he wants more than anything simply isn't something anyone is in a position to offer him...."

* * *

The Rowdy Tavern, currently perched on the waterfront of the

Respectable Quarter between the present locations of the district of the Artisans and of the Merchants, was exactly what any good Narrative would expect of such an establishment. The sign depicting a hanging bunch of grapes was crude and badly drawn, creaking in the gentle breeze that rose up off the nearby river. There was a manky water trough full of green, algae-riddled water suitable for drunkards to have their heads dunked in mere moments after they muttered the immortal line "You and whose army?" to appropriately irritated Merry Band members. The battered wooden door creaked suitably and, after numerous of its patrons had been ejected through it the hard way, had the look of something nominally held together by nailed boards and frayed lengths of cord.

In spite of the absence of The Narrative, the tavern keeper apparently felt obliged to maintain a familiar ambience: the low-roofed, heavy-beamed room was smoky and close; the dirt floor was strewn with straw; and the tankards were bent and rusty. The furniture consisted of rough, splintering wood hammered together with bent nails that looked on the verge of collapse—the beautifully crafted shoddiness was probably some Artisan's pride and joy. The counter was filthy, the barrels leaky, and the fireplace solidly black. If it wasn't for the fact that all but one of the patrons were neatly dressed, cheerful, and only marginally tipsy Artisans, the place could have been lifted straight from The Narrative itself.

The one exception, unfortunately, turned out to be the man they'd come to see.

Dullard led the way. In spite of his assurances that the Rowdy Tavern was a perfectly respectable establishment most of the time and that the patrons were generally of a sensible and sober disposition, Fodder had seen far too much potential for bum pinching and use of the word *wench* behind that sign. He had therefore opted to leave Flirt and Shoulders outside to guard the still thankfully unconscious princess in a nearby alley. Dullard, much to Fodder's surprise, had hailed the barman and several of the patrons with familiar ease; under his breath, he admitted to Fodder that he had spent several happy evenings here, discussing the art of swordsmithing with some of the more experienced smiths.

"I did show them a few of my pieces, of course," the Rejected

Suitor had added softly. "But they went ever so quiet and then Smelter suggested strongly that I shouldn't tout them around to anyone who might be in a position to compare my work to theirs. I thought that was very kind of them, really, to consider my feelings like that. After all, I'd hate for my meagre efforts to look foolish by comparison to experts."

Fodder, who had spotted the tight, nervous looks a couple of the leather-aproned smiths had tossed in Dullard's direction when he'd greeted them, privately suspected that Dullard's feelings had been the last thing on their minds when they'd laid eyes on his workmanship. Fodder had seen a goodly number of swords in his time and been cut down by most of them, and he knew that the *meagre efforts* of the prince were nothing to be sneezed at.

But Artisan politics were not the reason they had come. The reason was the unshaven man plonked down at the rough table before them, grasping a slopping tankard of finest tavern swill in one hand and, rather alarmingly, a very sharp dagger in the other. His eyes were bleary; his dark hair a scruffy, tangled mess; his dark leather clothes stained liberally with food and spilled beer. His gaze, such as it was—for in his present state of partial inebriation, he seemed unable to focus more than one eyeball at the same time—was currently swirling somewhere in the region of the ceiling beams.

He wasn't massively drunk, as far as Fodder could tell, just erring on the distant side of tipsy. He was more accurately, as Dullard had stated, an odd sort of stick.

"The thing is, right, the thing, the thing that matters, is that nobody, no, nobody respects what I do!" Poniard punctuated his statement with a violent stab of the inoffensive air with his vicious dagger. "I mean, other people, right, when they do something, it stays done, doesn't it? They can show it off to friends and neighbours, can't they? But I can't do that! No one ever cares what a fine job I do, oh no, not when it never stays done long enough for people to admire!" He paused long enough to allow himself a hearty swig out of his tankard. "All that panache and craftsmanship wasted! It's enough to drive a man to bloody drink, let me tell you."

"It's as we've explained, you see, Poniard." Fodder had to admire Dullard's persistence. He'd handled the Assassin's half-cut, depressed ramblings without so much as faltering from his smile. "I think the problem is that you've never really had the right target. I don't know, perhaps if you were to kill someone that The Narrative needed? Someone whose death everyone would take note of? I mean, it would be there in The Narrative for all to see, your workmanship set down forever, and no one would ever forget."

"But what's the use?" Poniard's intervention was morose. "What's the use of it? Hmm?"

"Well, if you want people to respect what you do…" Fodder tried, but it was immediately obvious that the Assassin wasn't listening.

"I know six hundred and seventy-three ways to kill a man," Poniard cut in wildly. "Six hundred and seventy-three! But there's no point! No point to any of it! Because what's the point of being a highly trained and sophisticated killing professional in a world where no bugger *ever stays dead?"*

On a personal level, Fodder couldn't help but feel that living in a world where a sword through the belly was nothing more than a minor setback was a definite perk of the job. But in a grim kind of way, he could sort of see Poniard's point. It was like carving a statue only to turn around and find someone had glued all the spare bits back on and left you with the rock you'd started with.

"Old age. That's all anyone ever dies of. Old bloody age." The Assassin downed another hearty swig of ale. "And it's those bloody pixies…" His fist clenched so tightly around the tankard that Fodder could have sworn the metal bent. "Every piece of fine work that I do, every stab, every slice, every dagger in the forehead, cut throat, poisoned chalice, sword through the heart, every single drop of blood I spill, they swan in and put right. They fix up every slash and plug every hole with that sparkly, happy dust of theirs! Squick, that *smug little bastard…"* With a violent gesture, he hurled his dagger into the table top, leaving it quivering. Dullard prudently and rather nervously yanked his fingers away and tucked them safely onto his lap. "It reflects badly on me, that's all I'm saying! What kind of a reflection is it on me, hmm, what reflection, when I can never ever do the job *properly?"*

Although he had to admit that this was one matter of choice that he hoped would never get granted, Fodder nonetheless thought it worth taking one more pass. "But surely the Narrative death is what matters?" he suggested tentatively. "I mean, a character's death In Narrative is dead forever, isn't it?"

Poniard fixed him with as much of a bleary glare as he could manage. "But they aren't dead, are they?" he muttered angrily. "They *get up* afterwards."

"The person does," Dullard offered helpfully. "But their character doesn't."

Poniard pulled a harsh face. "What's the bleeding difference?"

"A great deal." Dullard seemed to be hitting his stride again. "A person and their character are two very different things. And while one lives on, you've completely done away with the other."

Poniard was frowning. "But that's not real."

"It's real in The Narrative."

"But not once it's gone."

"Only once it's left you. The death goes on within the Quest."

Poniard looked very much as though this conversation had stepped several levels beyond his inebriation threshold. "But they *aren't dead,*" he repeated doggedly.

"To us they aren't. But to The Narrative, they're lost. And since The Narrative is what makes this world what it is, then surely that's all that matters. The person who portrays the character is irrelevant as far as the Taskmaster is concerned. It's character that matters."

Poniard squinted at Dullard crookedly. "Are you saying that when killing someone, it only matters if the Taskmaster sees it? And as long as they stay In Narrative, the buggers stay dead?"

For a brief, euphoric instant, Fodder thought the Assassin had finally caught on. *This could soon be over! One quick stab of the princess when The Narrative arrives in the morning...*

Dullard shared his moment of misplaced optimism. "Yes! That's it exactly! So if you were to kill someone of great significance to The Narrative—I don't know, Princess Islaine, say—then that death would certainly catch the Taskmaster's attention. Everyone would recognise and admire your work for Quests to come. Why, the whole world would talk about it."

But Poniard's gaze was already several dozen yards further down a distant tangent. "So you're saying," he muttered absently, "that if I want to off those bloody pixies properly, I'd have to do it in The Narrative?"

Dullard's mouth closed with an audible snap as Fodder's dropped wide open.

"That's *it*, isn't it?" The light of maddened fire ignited behind Poniard's eyes was more powerful than a joint conflagration of Shoulders's expression when confronted with Clank and Flirt's when the dreaded *wench* word was pulled out. "That's what I'd have to do; that's the answer! I need to grab hold of that bloody Squick, kill him off In Narrative, and make sure he stayed there! That'd put a stop to magic dust and all that fixing!"

"Oh lord." The quiet exclamation dropped off Dullard's lips into the gap that most persons, including Fodder himself, would have filled with something fruitier. "Poniard, that really wasn't what we meant."

"I mean, all I'd have to do is strap his little corpse to my belt and then stay on In Narrative." There was a distant, dreamy quality to Poniard's voice. "I could off as many people as I liked, and there would be no one to fix them! My work would be advertised everywhere! The world would be my oyster!"

We've created a monster. The thought was inescapable as Fodder met Dullard's eyes and found within them many variations of *oops.* For once, Fodder found himself heartily hoping that Poniard would be unable to resist The Narrative's honey-like commands.

"I really don't think it would work like that…" he tried, but it was immediately obvious that Poniard was well past listening.

"Hacked limbs staying hacked, cut throats staying cut, stab wounds that stay wounded…" he rambled on in his psychotic haze. "No more pixies. No more *bloody pixies*…"

Dullard leaned carefully towards Fodder's ear. "I think it might be time to go," he suggested awkwardly. "I have a feeling we aren't going to get anywhere."

"I think the pixie fixation gave it away," Fodder agreed, his eyes still watching the Assassin's distant, carnage-filled gaze. "What worries me is what he might do when we're gone."

Dullard glanced across the room. "I think I may have a way to mitigate some of the damage." Carefully, he stood up. "Umm, Poniard, we're going to go now. It was…errr…*nice* talking to you."

Poniard made no reply, his mind apparently lost in a blissful land of slaughter. Dullard nodded to him awkwardly all the same and then, with Fodder following a half step behind, he turned and headed over to a cluster of red-faced, leather-aproned men gathered around a table by the fire.

Fodder ducked his head sharply into the depths of his hood, hanging back as Dullard approached them. It had been a long time ago, and the odds of his unremarkable face sticking in anyone's memory were slim, but he did recognise several of those Artisans, and there was no point in taking chances.

"Hello, Smelter." Dullard smiled at the largest and reddest-faced of the gathering—a balding, heavily paunched man with arms the size of tree trunks. "Could I have a quick word?"

Fodder didn't miss the look of mild panic that flitted briefly across the Artisan's face, but nonetheless the man nodded. "Aye. What kin we be doin' fer ye, Yer Highness?"

Dullard flapped one hand. "Oh, there's no need to waste dialect on me, honestly. I know some of the Nobles expect it, but there's no need to put yourself out. I just wanted a word about Poniard."

"Oh, Poniard. Yeah, I saw you were chatting to him." The folksy dialect vanished in a split second. "Raving about wanting to kill the world again, is he?"

"To say the least." Dullard's brow furrowed in brief thoughtfulness. "I just wanted his opinion on the balance of a blade I've been working on." The alarm flashed back over Smelter's face like an igniting lantern. "But he was far too drunk to listen." The Rejected Suitor bit one lip in artful concern. "I think all this business with the princess might have wound him up a little. He was asking me about this changing The Narrative business that's been swirling around in the Palace, but then suddenly he was talking about harming Squick the Duty Pixie In Narrative. He seems to think that people will stay dead if he does." He glanced nervously over his shoulder. "I don't know where he got the idea from, but I think someone needs to keep an eye on him. If he remembers this when he's sober, we don't want this pixie vendetta to get out of hand. I'd hate to see anyone get hurt."

Smelter and the other Artisans exchanged long, weary looks. "It's not the first time he's threatened Squick," Smelter replied with a sigh and a puff of his pipe. "Don't worry your head, Your Highness. We'll sort him out come morning. A few cups of old Hubble's best herbal hangover remedy will clean him up. He only gets these violent urges when he's tipsy. Once he's sober, he'll just be morose."

"I hope so." Dullard smiled again, wanly. "I would hate to think I'd accidentally stirred up any trouble. Well, thank you, gentlemen. A pleasure as always."

Heads nodded with polite relief as Dullard moved away. While Dullard's peers might regard him as an idiot, it was clear the Artisans saw him as a friendly but potent threat.

Dullard stepped back politely, allowing Fodder to move through the battered door before him and out into the street.

"Well, hopefully the Artisans will sort Poniard out," he said thoughtfully. "And I don't think they suspected we might have dropped the idea there by accident. But oh dear me..." He shook his head softly. "What an awful man he can be. I know how frustrating it must be not to be able to share one's skills, but *really...*"

"He's a nutter." Fodder opted not to beat around the bush.

Dullard's lips twisted awkwardly as he and Fodder moved away from the well-lit tavern front towards the alley where they'd left the others. "I do hope we haven't brought down trouble on that poor pixie."

"Squick can handle himself." Of that much Fodder was certain. "He's canny. A drunken Assassin is nothing."

Dullard sighed. "If he can't, it's not just him; we've brought a great deal of trouble down on everyone."

Fodder gave a dark laugh. "We're doing that anyway. Even if it is for their own good."

The prince's face was serious, bathed in half-shadows and the pale, reflected light from the nearby windows. "But the good of one person isn't necessarily the good of another," he offered quietly. "I think talking to Poniard has proved that. I know the overriding objective in all this is a matter of choice, but the choices of some will always negate the choices of others, and balancing one against the other is never going to be easy. There has to be some kind of order. Who's going to make those decisions if the Taskmaster doesn't?" The pause that followed was just long enough to make Fodder profoundly uncomfortable. "You?"

Fodder shook his head emphatically, trying to ignore the uncomfortable feeling that Dullard's words had lodged in his chest. "I'm no leader. And..." He hesitated a moment as he tried to clarify his feelings on the matter into some kind of order. "I'm not out to overthrow the

Taskmaster. This is still the Taskmaster's world when all's said and done, and we need it to be. I just want it run a bit more fairly."

The slight smile Dullard offered in return was reassuring. "I'm glad about that. I was a little concerned you hadn't thought it through."

Fodder laughed outright. "I haven't thought any of this through!" he exclaimed. "I'm making it up as I go along and hoping for the best. I've got Flirt to boss me and Shoulders to find every downside and now you to do the serious thinking. I'll stick with the muddling through."

It was Dullard's turn to laugh, an odd hopping, hiccupping sound. "Well, you're doing a decent job of it, as far as I can tell. Your muddling has certainly got the Officious Courtiers rattled."

"Good. I can't think of anyone I'd rather see rattled."

Dullard huffed mildly. "My uncle is an Officious Courtier, you know. I almost became one myself."

"Oh." Fodder allowed himself an appropriate moment to squirm. "Sorry, I…"

"Oh, don't worry." The dismissal was cheerful. "For the most part, I agree with you. But Uncle Primp is a nice enough old stick, and he runs the AFCs, who are such a charming, easy group to work with. I was their prisoner for a while a couple of Quests back, and, let me tell you, I don't think I've ever had such an enjoyable time. That Gibber is a chap of many talents. Do you know he taught me to play the harpsichord in less than a week?"

Fodder, whose principle memory of Gibber the AFC was a spindly, saw-toothed creature who had swooped out of a tree and eaten his innards before patting him on the back and challenging him to a game of chess in the pub afterwards, didn't find it as hard to believe as most would.

"I suppose it wouldn't have been too bad being Officious Courtier to them," Dullard mused as they continued to amble down the quay-side. "But to anyone else…"

Fodder frowned suddenly as a thought occurred. "How come you ended up with an Officious Courtier for an uncle anyway? I mean, being Royal, I wouldn't have thought…"

"My father was a Weak King and my mother a beguiling Enchant-ress," Dullard answered the tailed-off question. "But her mother was a Priestess, which is why my uncle went to the Temple." He gave a lopsided half-smile. "I'm a little bit of everything, really. It's no wonder they never knew what to do with me. When I was a child, you see, I was technically half-Royal and half-Mage, but I was gauche and awkward and, well, I've never really had the kind of panache that one needs for those sorts of positions. But Uncle Primp offered to show me round the Temple and explain how it worked. It was extremely interesting, seeing the Golden Tome and The Narrative library and the Outer Sanctum and everything, but I was never cut out for that life." He made an awkward hand gesture. "I just can't abide bossing people around, you see. And since that's rather the essence of the job description..." He shrugged. "I ended up as the Rejected Suitor almost by default. I was the only person of Royal blood who was unattractive enough."

There wasn't much Fodder could say to that. "Why the Temple, though?" He gestured out over the dark river to where glittering torches illuminated the shining Narrative face of the city's religious centre. Its obscure grey companion building was lost in shadow and night. "I always thought it was a façade. I can understand the Priests hanging about there, but why the Courtiers?"

Dullard fixed him with a puzzled look. "It's nothing to do with the Temple," he replied, his tone surprised. "That's nothing more than Narrative window dressing. It's the Sanctum that matters to them. After all, without the Sanctum and the Golden Tome, how would they get their instructions?"

Fodder stopped cold, his eyes locked on the distant, glimmering lights of the island and the unseen building that lurked in its shadow. Inside his head, several things dropped into place with a loud and echoing click.

"What do you mean by that?" he said softly.

Dullard had continued several strides oblivious to his halt and had to backtrack hurriedly, his expression one of confusion.

"I'm sorry but...what do you mean what do I mean?" he answered with outright bewilderment.

Fodder met his gaze firmly. "I mean this Sanctum—that's the grey building, right? The one that never moves?"

Dullard nodded cautiously. "Well, of course."

"And it's important somehow? To the Taskmaster?"

Dullard's mouth dropped open almost comically. "Wait a minute—

you don't know about the Sanctum? Or the Golden Tome?"

Fodder's expression was frank. "Would I be asking if I did?"

"But I thought…surely *everyone* knows…"

"I don't." Fodder pulled a face. "The Artisans I asked about it once don't either. It sounds to me like your *everyone* is more like a privileged few."

Dullard seemed to be genuinely off balance. "But that doesn't make any sense," he muttered almost to himself. "Didn't you ever wonder where your instructions came from?"

"They came from Preen."

"And where did he get them from?"

"That stupid little book of his. Or Strut."

Dullard's look was almost relieved. "You know about the books? Good. That's something. The books are the important part of this. The critical part, you might say. And the Golden Tome, which is kept in the Outer Sanctum, is the most important book of all."

Fodder was staring at him, at the reverent tone in his voice. "Why?" he asked.

Dullard's voice was hushed. "Because the Golden Tome holds the thoughts and wishes of the Taskmaster. Raw. Written down as they come. It's the origin of every instruction we receive."

Something was buzzing deep inside Fodder's brain, an idea congealing, but he kept it down and out of sight for now.

"Instructions appear in the book," Dullard continued quietly. "Writing that writes itself—I've watched it. Then the scribes of the Sanctum take over. The Priests translate the thoughts into instructions and write them into their versions of the books. That information will then appear in the Courtiers' books as well, and they become responsible for carrying those instructions out. The Scholars are responsible for the library. Every instruction we've ever had for every Quest there's ever been is shelved in their library somewhere. The Outer Sanctum is the origin of everything we do."

Fodder's racing mind latched on to the discrepancy at once. "The way you're saying 'Outer Sanctum' implies that there's an Inner Sanctum," he pointed out. "And even I know that Inner Sanctums are the ones that matter."

Dullard pursed his lips. "There is an Inner Sanctum," he confessed.

"Although almost no one is allowed inside. Strut, the Head Priest, and the Chief Scholar are the only ones who can enter, and only then at certain times. Everyone else is repelled."

"What, it smells?"

Dullard's look was politely exasperated. "By magic of some kind," he corrected deliberately. "There's a force that keeps everyone out. It can only be accessed between Quests. It's never open when The Narrative is running."

"But what's in there?"

Dullard shook his head. "Only three people know for certain, and none of them is saying. The rest of us can only speculate."

"But this Golden Tome." Fodder's mind had returned to the idea he'd temporarily put aside. "It's the source of all the instructions, right?"

"Yes, that's right."

"So without it, this Quest would be a bit buggered, wouldn't they?"

Dullard's eyes narrowed. "Well, they'd have their old instructions but I should tell you…"

"But old instructions wouldn't be any good." Fodder ignored the impending proviso as he tumbled on. "Not if we were changing things. If we had that Tome, the Taskmaster could instruct us forever and a day, but no one but us would know what was said! If we could steal it…"

"Which I'm afraid we can't, as I was trying to tell you. Aside from the fact it's six foot across and sealed to the pedestal by magic that only releases it when a Quest is complete…"

"Well, if we can't carry it, maybe we could rip the pages out…"

"And made of a parchment that cannot tear…"

"Or chuck water over it…"

"Or smudge…"

"Or even set fire to it if we have to…"

"Or burn…"

"Or…"

"Or be damaged, harmed, or destroyed *in any way*," Dullard finished pointedly. "The moment one Tome is removed, another will instantly appear and the writing will begin anew. It doesn't work like the books of the Courtiers—it's being on the pedestal that matters.

Away from that, every Golden Tome is just another book for a Scholar to shelve in the Sanctum library. I'm sorry," he added on seeing Fodder's downcast expression. "It was a good idea. But I'm afraid it's not practical."

Fodder sighed. "I should have known it'd be too good to be true," he said wearily. "I really thought I'd cracked it for a moment there, that your Sanctum and that Tome were the key. The idea was there, and it felt right...." He pulled a face. "Not to mention I'm buggered if I know what we're going to do next."

"Actually," Dullard offered diffidently, as they turned the corner and headed into the mouth of the narrow alley where they'd left the others with their retrieved armour. "I have had one idea about that."

Fodder smiled sincerely. "You have a lot of ideas, don't you?"

Dullard's answering smile was almost shy. "Well, I do my best. And this makes a wonderful academic exercise. There are so many different corners to think my way around, so many avenues to explore—I've never had a study like it. True, unencumbered thought." He nodded enthusiastically. "Honestly, it's really quite liberating."

Fodder grinned. "Well, stay liberated. Like I said, I need someone to help out at times of serious thinking. Come on then, let's hear it."

Dullard nodded gratefully. "You're aware, of course, that every Quest has a map?"

"Yep. Why?"

"Well, I was wondering. What would happen, do you suppose, if we took the princess and sailed off the edge of it?"

* * *

Princess Pleasance was enraged. The emotion had started off as simple anger, had pushed up through the borders of fury, and was now erupting out onto the shining mountaintop of incandescence. There were berserkers in the Barbarian fortress who'd devoted their lives to mindless, drooling, raging bloodlust who would have gazed upon the glow in the petite blonde's eyes with scarcely muffled jealousy. That was, if they'd been able to hold her gaze long enough without turning and running for their lives.

And at that particular moment, the victim of this blazing lightning strike of a gaze was the inoffensive-looking figure who was ambling awkwardly beside the nearby fire as he pottered around a bubbling cauldron in a woodland clearing by the light of a fading sunset.

"Honestly," she heard him declare to the two scruffy Disposables and the common wench of a Barmaid who were gathered around the fireplace beside him, watching his antics with no small amount of bemusement. "It does work. I had quite a bit of spare time during *The Tide of Crimson,* and I passed it enjoyably studying various kinds of native flora and their applications and combinations when used in the culinary arts. The cooks in the Palace kitchens were ever so helpful—I mean, I owe what basic skills I have in cookery to them—but you'd be surprised how delicious the most unexpected things can taste when they're garnished with the right herbs and spices." Pleasance watched as, with surprising delicacy given the awkward oaf he was, the *hideous, treacherous turncoat* Dullard dipped his ladle into the cheerfully bubbling cauldron and extended it towards his vile new friends with an oddly pleading expression.

"Here," he said with an unappealing smile. "Give these a try."

The ratty Disposable with the dirty blond hair who'd spent the days prior to her escape flinging her about like a sack of potatoes was regarding the ladle with a distinct edge of mistrust.

"They're tree roots, Dullard," he said flatly. "From a tree. That tree. I watched you dig them up."

The traitor's smile widened with highly inappropriate joviality. "Yes, but with a sprig of rosemary and a pinch of those mushrooms, they really can be quite tasty. Not to mention that they have a surprisingly high nutritional value."

His peasant friends remained unconvinced. The ratty blond was glaring disbelievingly. "But tree roots?" he exclaimed incredulously. "It'll be like chewing old boots!"

"No, honestly!" The lying, deceitful blackguard was shaking his head. "They soften ever so well if you boil them up properly. Just give it a go. Please?"

"Of course," the frizzy-haired harridan injected suddenly, "we wouldn't be having to eat tree roots if *somebody* hadn't dropped my pack into a deep, damp, stinking river of sewer ooze, now would we?"

At her pointed look, the ratty whining weasel replied with a glare as filthy as the aforementioned route. "I got it back again, didn't I?" he retorted sharply.

"Yeah," the brown, bland, former axe-wielder chipped in. "But did *you* want to eat that bread afterwards?"

Those sewers. Pleasance felt herself shudder at the memory. It had been bad enough waking in that heinous dump of an alley to find the harridan and ratty boy gurning down at her and telling her that she was their prisoner again and, by the way, they'd lowered her down a garderobe chute in order to escape the Palace. And then to find herself faced with the awful truth that *Prince Dullard*, a member of the Royal Family, a (thankfully very, *very*) distant relative, was the one who had betrayed her back into their clutches and had the temerity, the utter gall, to lay hands on her and carry her down into that dreadful, stinking pit under the city! Over an hour they'd spent down there, edging along beside the utter filth, not to mention the time it had taken to retrieve first the fumbled pack and then the fumbling Disposable who'd gone in after it. Once clear of the city, they'd dunked him in the river repeatedly—although, alas, it had made little difference—and then ruthlessly stolen a small boat, which they had punted downstream along the edge of the Vast River for the entire of the following day. At sunset, they'd moored their looted craft in a small bay alongside the other edge of those same tatty woods they'd hauled her through on that dreadful first night. They had dragged her off to this foul, uncultured clearing, dumping her against a filthy oak tree and lashing her to it whilst Prince Dullard proceeded to root around like some truffle-hunting pig.

Dragged down a toilet, hauled through a sewer, dumped in a stolen boat, and expected to sleep in filthy woodlands. It was no way to treat a princess! And these people wanted to be Heroes? How could they even presume it? No Hero would ever do something so...so...uncouth!

They'd taken her moment. *Again.*

It had been better. *Islaine* had been better. If before she had been her ambition, Islaine had turned into the princess of her *dreams*. A complicated, memorable, emotive character with the chance to grow and change had been dangled before her and then cruelly taken away. She'd lost it all. It had been snatched away for a second time through no fault of her own. She'd done nothing to deserve such treatment!

And it was because of *him.*

The lightning-strike glare fixed back upon Dullard once more.

Cooking. He was even cooking. For them! For Ordinary peasants! Standing there with his ladle outstretched, pleading for their approval! Had the man no style at all? Had he no dignity or grace? Had he no *pride?*

It was no way for a prince to behave when not instructed to by Narrative. She was ashamed that she had ever given the deceitful, filthy traitor the time of day! How dare he drag her back into this hell? What kind of a cruel, heartless, evil excuse for a human being was he?

"Go on, honestly! You shouldn't be afraid to try new things, you know!" The backstabbing swine shuffled one foot slightly. "Is that not what all this is about?"

The harridan and the bland one exchanged a long, slow look. And then carefully they extended the plates that they had earlier spent more than fifteen minutes scrubbing clean in the nearby brook.

Heaped, steaming tree root was piled onto their plates. The ratty blond still looked wary, but at a sharp nudge from his bland friend, he too accepted a dollop of the traitor's swill without complaint. Tentatively, the harridan reached down and speared a tree root with her fork.

"It doesn't smell too bad," she offered. "In fact, it smells…good."

The fork rose towards her lips. Pleasance glared. *I hope you choke on it! I hope it burns your tongue and rips out your tonsils! I hope it…*

The frizzy-haired wench gave a thoughtful chew. Her expression changed instantly from one of wariness to…

"Mmmm!" she exclaimed, swallowing hard as her fork dived down towards the plate once more. "That is *fantastic!*"

The bland one followed her lead at once. The ratty one was examining his plate with disbelief, as though trying to ascertain if she was eating the same meal that he was. Reluctantly and with resignation, he too dug in.

"Ga'e'weawy goog!" The bland one, now mentally renamed the uncouth one, didn't even have the courtesy to finish chewing before he spoke, shovelling down the food like a pig in swill. "Wewl gwne Guwarg!"

"It doesn't taste like tree, I'll give you that," the ratty one conceded. "Given that it is tree, that's an achievement."

To Pleasance's disgust, Prince Dullard actually blushed, his expression modest as he smiled and spooned another helping onto a fresh plate. To seek approval from Ordinary common Disposables was bad enough, but to be flattered by it! Why, she doubted they'd know good food if it was pelted at them in the stocks! Given the hogs' food they probably ate on a regular basis, the sewer-drenched bread would probably have been a step up!

"You enjoy!" he said with sickening cheerfulness. "I'll go and feed Pleasance."

As he came to his feet, the ratty one gave an unpleasantly stewy snort. "Do us all a favour," he chimed up chirpily. "Leave the gag on and pour it down her nose instead. After what happened at breakfast, it's probably the only way you'll come back alive."

If Pleasance hadn't known better, she would have classed Dullard's returning look as reproachful. Huh! As if he cared!

"Don't be silly," he simply chided as he moved past the three pigs filling their faces by the fire and over to the tree against which she had unceremoniously been secured.

"Hello!" he greeted her with that infuriating, awkward smile as he settled himself down on the ground beside her, placing the plate and spoon carefully out of kicking range. It was a lesson she'd taught him the hard way at breakfast time.

"Now," he said quietly, his anxious expression most likely fuelled by the venom she was spitting at him from her eyes. "I know you aren't happy with me." He paused a moment, allowing the vicious swipe of one foot she aimed in his direction to be completed. "You did make that abundantly clear this morning when I gave you breakfast. And I'll say it again because I'm not sure you heard me this morning over your screaming: I am truly sorry I got you into this, and if there had been another way, I really would have taken it. But, you see, the thing is, shouting at people like that… Well, what good is it going to do? It's not going to make us let you go, and it doesn't exactly make anyone inclined to help you, now does it? Really, Pleasance, the best thing you can do for all of us, including yourself, is just calm down and try to be a little more reasonable about this. I know the others have threatened you, and I'll be honest—I don't really agree with that. But maybe if you'll let me try and explain to you what this is all about, those threats won't be necessary, and you'll even understand a little better why it is I did what I did. All right?"

The ratty blond snorted into his stew again. "You're wasting your breath!" he called out in a mocking, singsong voice.

Dullard, however, ignored him. "Now, I'm going to take the gag off. Please hold still. And…I'd appreciate you not biting me again. Thank you."

Spindly fingers reached around behind her head to where the knotted handkerchief had been secured. Gently, he teased it free and pulled the gag away.

"TRAITOR!!!!" To Pleasance's fury, Dullard just managed to get his hand clear before her snapping teeth could close upon it. "You treacherous, ungrateful, *miserable* excuse for a *bastard worm!* You've betrayed your *heritage*, you've betrayed your *family*, you've betrayed the *Taskmaster* and the *Quest!* You are going to *rot* in the *deepest, dankest, foulest* dungeon the world has to offer, and I will visit you there and I will spit in your face and laugh! *Laugh! Laugh, I tell you!*"

She paused, breathing heavily from the effort of expelling her words with so much venomous force. She glared daggers at Dullard and waited for him to wilt into a puddle of contrite shame.

But instead he simply lifted the plate and smiled. "Stew?" he said.

Pleasance rallied her rage admirably as she wound back up to speed. "You are a *canker!*" she hissed. "A *filthy, lying, deceitful, deceiving pustule* on the Royal Family tree! If it were possible to drown someone at birth outside of Narrative, then they would have *done it to you!*"

"It's really very nice, apparently. Even Shoulders thought so."

"You are a *weasel!* You are a *snake!* You are a *mongrel cur*, a *cowardly, pathetic animal!* You are a *swine* and a *maggot* and a *cockroach* and a…a…*goat!* You are the *bloodsucking tick* supping on a *flea* that lives on a *plague-riddled rat* that's been eaten by a *rabid dog!* You are *scum!*"

"Only, it probably won't be so tasty if you let it get cold.…"

"When we get back to the Palace, I will take *great pleasure* in watching them kill you *over and over again!* I will *personally* tie you to four wild horses and watch them *rip you apart!* I will hold you facedown in that *foul, disgusting sewer* that you dragged me through last night! I will tear out your innards and *hang you from the walls* with them! You will rue the day you ever tried to *ruin my Quest!*"

"And though I'll happily make you some more—waste not, want not, I always say…"

"WILL YOU STOP TALKING ABOUT STEW WHEN I'M THREATENING YOU???"

Dullard looked genuinely taken aback. "Well, there isn't much else to say, really," he replied with a lopsided shrug. "All those things are just words. They aren't going to change anything. And if you're honest with yourself, I doubt they're making you feel better any more than they're bothering me." He actually had the gall to keep smiling at her. "As my mother always used to say, sticks and stones may break my bones, but names will never hurt me."

Pleasance gritted her teeth. "Then *get me a stick*," she growled.

Dullard shook his head gently as he heaped a stack of tree root stew onto the fork he was holding. "As I've already explained to the others, there is no need to be uncivilised about this. Kindness breeds kindness, and common courtesy is never out of place. I really do believe that. So you can shout and scream and threaten me and call me as many names as you like, but the thing is…"

He leaned forward carefully, the quiet smile never leaving his face. "You aren't going to stop me being nice to you."

Pleasance stared at him thoughtfully for a moment: the jutting chin, the distinctive nose, the ridiculous expression, and the sincerity in his eyes. And then she bit his nose.

The inconsiderate bastard still fed her the stew.

And it was nice too. That was just *rude*.

* * *

"You know, there's optimistic and there's stupid."

As he mopped up the last of his delicious stew, Fodder glanced over at the sound of Shoulders's voice. His fellow Disposable was watching the relentless prince feeding the recalcitrant princess her supper with a cynical expression on his face.

"I don't know." Flirt grinned over her plate. "Maybe he's getting through. She didn't draw blood this time, did she?"

"Not through lack of trying. Did you see those teeth strike? For a cow, she lunged like a snake!" Shoulders shuddered. "I'm bloody glad he was so keen to take her on, but I think he's an idiot for trying to talk to her. We should have glued that ruddy gag on!"

Flirt shrugged slightly as she dropped her cleaned plate down beside the fire and licked the last of the stew from her spoon and fingertips. "Let him try. He's not doing any harm, is he?"

"Except to himself," Fodder pointed out as he deposited his plate next to Flirt's. "Putting a stop to it might be for his own good. Or at least, the good of his extremities."

"And it's hopeless," Shoulders added archly. "There's nothing between those perfectly formed Royal ears but rancid fluff. And banging on about *laughing* again. She can't even think of an original threat!"

Fodder glanced over to where Dullard, his nose looking distinctly tender, was still crouched, with a smile on his face, as he offered another heaped forkful to the pouting lips of the grimly glowering princess. Her expression could have skinned bark from the trees in white-hot strips.

"I get the feeling Dullard just wants to think the best of people," he remarked fairly.

Shoulders gave a snort. "You think her best is much better than her worst?"

"Not really." Flirt agreed, shifting awkwardly as she began the nightly struggle to extract herself from her chain mail shirt. "But like I said, there's no harm in letting him try, is there?" With a grunt and a heave, she tipped herself out of the shirt with an ungainly, metallic slump, revealing the stained padded under-tunic and Cringe's velvety purse dangling on a leather strip around her neck. She breathed a sigh of relief. "Blimey, that's better. It's nice to be armoured-up, but that thing doesn't half chafe."

Fodder could smell a dangerous sentence when he heard it, and his tongue almost tripped over itself in its haste to change the subject.

"Whose turn is it to do the washing up?" he exclaimed in a rush.

Flirt's long, slow look only made it worse. But thanks be to whomever was in charge of such things, she let the dodge pass. "I'm not sure," she replied. "We haven't really had a rota, have we? Volunteers?"

The profound silence that followed this statement made it clear she was not onto a winner.

"Okay then," she rallied. "Anyone got a coin? We'll have to toss for it."

A brief search of all available pockets turned up nothing. Fodder hadn't really expected that it would, since coins were a Narrative tool rather than something they needed, and if they happened to cross into Narrative in the near future, having spending money would be the last thing on their minds. But Flirt was not to be thwarted.

"I know!" she exclaimed, grasping at the velvet purse and emptying it swiftly onto her palm. "We can use this."

The facets of the ruby glittered against the curling tendrils of gold that folded it against the Ring. Mystical symbols glinted mysteriously.

"The Ring of Anthiphion." Shoulders's tone was flat. "You want to use the mysterious, all-powerful Ring of Destiny to toss for the washing up?"

Flirt shrugged. "We aren't In Narrative. Out here it's just a shiny piece of costume jewellery. Mystical symbols upside down or right way up?"

"They're *mystical symbols,*" Shoulders pointed out. "How can you tell what way up they are?"

"We'll use this swirly one here by the ruby." Flirt grinned. "Weird knotty flowery bit up or down?"

Shoulders gave in. "Down," he said with resignation, though his eyes remained incredulous. "Though it'll probably blow a crater a mile wide when it lands."

"It's *just* a ring," Flirt repeated deliberately. "Mystic doesn't work outside The Narrative, does it Fodder? Oh, and up or down?"

Fodder had to admit he'd never thought much about it. But Flirt's assertion rang an immediate bell in his head. Oh, the pixies had the power to change whatever they saw fit to change of their non-Narrative world, but mystical, magical objects of awe and terror were of little use but for decoration once The Narrative had passed. Magic was a Narrative domain.

And for the first time, Fodder found himself wondering why.

"Yeah," he agreed absently. "And up, please."

"And I'll say up too," Flirt exclaimed. "Here we go."

And with one jerk of her hand, she tossed the Ring into the air.

By all rights, it probably should have exploded or blown a hole in the ground or hovered, glowing mysteriously in midair. But the little spinning shape of red and gold simply arced briefly into the darkness before tumbling down into the leaf litter at Flirt's feet with an utterly unremarkable clink.

Fodder had fought to conceal a wince as it had tumbled back to earth. Shoulders failed entirely not to shy away.

Flirt stared at them both and shook her head but thankfully did not remark upon their wussiness. She simply stared down at the Ring.

"And the weird knotty flowery bit is...down!" she declared. "All yours, Shoulders."

Shoulders's shoulders slumped noticeably, brief primal terror at being blown to smithereens replaced instantly by mundane irritation.

"Oh, that's bloody typical, isn't it?" he grouched immediately, peering round the fire to squint at the Ring and then groaning again at confirmation that the Barmaid was indeed telling the truth. With a moody snatch, he gathered up their plates and utensils. "Who needs mystical when you're ruddy unlucky?"

Still in a huff with his mucky cargo clattering, the Disposable turned and marched off towards the river. Fodder considered pointing out the brook was closer but suspected it wouldn't be well received.

Flirt flashed a grin at Fodder as she gathered the Ring up from the leaf litter once more and tossed it gently in the palm of her hand. "You didn't really think it was going to explode, did you?" she asked him.

Fodder stared at the glittering ruby once more, his mind circling awkwardly around the words that had pushed it into action. Awareness had fired into life in his mind; there was something there, something important in what had just been said, he was sure of it.

"I don't know," he replied, trying to limit his words to simplicity so as not to disturb the ponderings of his brain. "It's just..."

He felt Flirt's gaze intensify, the grin fading as her eyes fixed upon him from beneath the shadow of her curly hair. The Ring stilled in her grasp.

"What?" she asked softly.

Fodder shook his head. "I don't know," he repeated quietly. "There was something about what you were saying. It felt...important. But I'm not sure why!"

"We can try and talk it through." All levity had vanished from Flirt's tone. "Maybe that'll help."

"I don't know," Fodder said again. "It's the Ring. It's something about…" He shook his head once more. "It's just odd, you know? That it can be the all-powerful saviour of worlds in one place and just a piece of costume jewellery in another. What makes the difference? What makes the magic work?"

Leaves crinkled as Flirt shuffled closer, peering at Fodder's down-turned face curiously. "Well, The Narrative does," she offered with a half-shrug. "Everyone knows it's The Narrative that makes the magic work. Magus and Bumpkin don't go around casting spells except when they're up to their ears in The Narrative. I saw Magus try to summon a tankard once when he was really drunk but he couldn't do diddly with it and everyone knew he couldn't because the power doesn't come from him, does it? It's The Narrative's."

Fodder gritted his teeth. There was something, something to be known here, and it was hovering right there on the edge of his thoughts.…

"But how does The Narrative make it work?" he muttered almost to himself.

Flirt gave him an incredulous look. "How does The Narrative make anything work? It works because it's The Narrative."

"But it's not The Narrative that does the magic." It was so close, so tantalisingly close. "It's the objects or the people. But the objects and the people don't have the magic when The Narrative's gone."

Flirt was frowning. "Because The Narrative puts it there, doesn't it?"

Fodder puffed out a sigh. "But…it's not just The Narrative that does that. We aren't puppets when The Narrative takes us—it pushes us and directs us and makes it much easier to obey than not, but it only gives ideas and lets us shape the characters ourselves. I mean, if you think about it, the best characters In Narrative are the ones we get to help make. The ones that are only Narrative tools are always so… *wooden*. It's like…like…like The Narrative *needs* us to help bring things to life somehow. And to work properly, it needs us to do it willingly.…"

He stared up at Flirt. She was watching him with no little confusion.

"Are you saying…you think that *we* have something to do with making the magic?" she asked finally.

"Yes!" Fodder stabbed the air with a finger.

"But how?"

"No idea." Fodder deflated almost immediately. The tantalising scrap of idea fled abruptly from his mind. "But it might be worth bearing in mind. Especially since we've got that thing."

He gestured to the Ring. Flirt raised an eyebrow with a small smile. "I'd better keep this safe then," she declared, depositing the Ring firmly back into the velvet purse around her neck. "Maybe you'll find some way to make it leap into life and spirit us to safety!"

Fodder met her playful gaze with a mock frown. "Now that's just silly."

"I must say, that was an absolutely fascinating discussion."

Fodder jumped in spite of himself as Prince Dullard, his nose red and sore, wandered back into the circle of firelight grasping the princess's cleaned plate.

"I hope you don't think I was rude for eavesdropping," he added hurriedly at the surprised looks on their faces. "But I could hear you, and it was such an interesting idea you've both come up with…" He beamed at Fodder. "I have to say, the idea of trying to deconstruct the ways and means of The Narrative is one that intrigues me. But since I've never participated in it as anything other than a character, I don't feel yet as though I'm ready to join in your debate. But when I have had that experience, perhaps I could discuss these ideas with you?" He beamed hopefully. "I so rarely get the chance for a good, academic conversation, especially on such a fundamental subject…."

"Ummm…" Fodder didn't consider himself to be up to much in the way of academic discussion, but to say no to that face would have been like stealing sweetmeats from a starving child. "Well, yeah. If you want," he managed.

"Thank you!" Dullard glanced around, suddenly curious. "Where's Shoulders?"

Flirt gestured towards the river. "Doing the washing up."

Dullard glanced guiltily at the plate in his hand. "I'd better go and give him a hand then. Back soon!"

Fodder watched Dullard lope off. He allowed himself a moment to rummage through his mind once more, to see if he could grasp the trailing edges of the elusive idea, but it had slunk away into the shadows.

But he knew that the thought had been important. And if it mattered, he could only hope he'd have better luck in trapping it.

* * *

Delicious the stew might have been, but it was clinging to the edges of the plates like innards up an oak tree. With a mighty huff, Shoulders threw a smidgen more frustrated force into the task, glaring down at the dark waters swirling sluggishly before him. The muddy bank beneath his feet shifted slightly as he adjusted his crouch. Swearing fluently, he fumbled the plates for a moment before regaining his balance with the aid of some sharp river reed. His hand stung at the contact, he could feel damp mud coating his backside, and it'd be the perfect end to a perfect few days if he went headfirst into the river. And would he get an ounce of sympathy from those so-called friends of his?

Would he bollocks.

Typical, wasn't it? Always the way. If there was a situation to come out worst from, a matter of luck to win or lose, it would home in on him like a bee to nectar! Stuck between a probably mad mate and a dungeon cell for a lifetime and why? Because he'd been standing in the wrong place at the wrong time! Because Fodder, bloody Fodder, had grabbed his arm and hauled him off into his grand cause without so much as asking! He'd lost a life he'd had no real objection to, aside from Clank's headhunting, and exchanged it for one in which he'd been chased, kicked by an obnoxious brat of a princess, thrown into rivers, dragged through sewers, and now, now he had to do the sodding washing up!

The scrubbing intensified as Shoulders's brows knotted fiercely. He hadn't asked for this! He hadn't had a say! He'd been tarred with Fodder's brush, and now he had no choice but to stagger along in the wake of his daft, pointless scheme because it was the only chance he had to come out of this mess with a future! What had he done to deserve this? Why did the weird knotty flowery bits always seem to land down for him?

Oh and as for Flirt... Bloody hell! Gone was the cheery Barmaid who'd provided many an understanding pint and the woman who'd taken her place was a terror! Like back at the fire, for goodness' sake! What had she been playing at back there? Handed a mystical object of great import, most people would have secreted it away in some safe place and clung to it fiercely and with the cautious respect it deserved. But oh no, not Flirt! No, she decided to use it to toss for the washing up! Toss for it! Oh it was fine for her to sit there all breezy and confident, but had she known it wouldn't blow them all to kingdom come? No! Had she gone ahead and thrown it anyway without the slightest consideration for any of them? Of course she had! There had been a glint in her eye ever since they'd snuck out of the Archetypal Inn that night, and it was a glint that Shoulders was not loath to admit he didn't like one bloody bit.

Because he was starting to wonder if she hadn't gone and bloody done it on purpose. She liked her fights! She liked it when things got dangerous! Was that what this was for her? Some big thrill-seeking, danger-teasing adventure? It wasn't as though she couldn't have found some other, less risky, more respectful way to pick a washing-up-doer, was it? But no, she'd dived straight in with the mystical Ring of Anthiphon and in spite of what she'd said, she hadn't known really what was going to happen, and he'd bet that was exactly why she'd done it. *Maybe I'll blow up*, she'd be thinking, and *maybe I'll take my friends with me, how exciting will that be?* No finding some other way to choose, oh no, let's find the most unpredictable, unconventional thing we have and *chuck it!* It was probably a game to her, an addiction to unnecessary risk. And for Shoulders, who was addicted to necessary safety, it was an appalling prospect.

What a week he was having! What a turn for his life to take! His oldest friend had gone doolally and decided to take him down for the ride. The cheery Barmaid at his local had turned into a thrill-seeking nutter. He'd been saddled with dragging around the most horrific, banshee-like creature ever to don blonde curls and velvet. And as for that relentlessly, overbearingly cheerful excuse for a prince they'd got lumbered with…

"Goodness me! If you scrub that plate much harder, you'll wear right through it!"

At the sudden voice, Shoulders started violently, his tentative, muddy footing skidding as he jerked with shock. It was only the hurried, securing grab of a hand against his arm that prevented the anticipated undignified tumble into the dark waters below.

"Bloody hell!" Furiously, Shoulders jerked his head around to find Prince Dullard watching him with the pursed-lipped, oddly nervous stare that the Disposable personally found so infuriating. It was like staring at a weirdly deformed rabbit.

"What are you doing sneaking up on a man like that?" he snapped angrily, shaking his arm free of Dullard's rescuing grasp. "I almost went in the river!"

"Oh gosh, I am sorry." There it was; even in the shadows of the dark riverbank, Shoulders knew that rabbit expression was glowing away. "I didn't mean to startle you. I thought you would have heard me coming."

"Well, I didn't." Shoulders gave a lusty sigh. "What are you doing here anyway? I thought you'd still be feeding Princess Chomp pieces of your nose."

Dullard's prominent features underwent several contortions, but apparently he chose not to rise to the matter. "I've finished feeding her, as it happens. I was just bringing her plate down to—"

"Oh, fine!" Shoulders interrupted harshly as he chucked the mostly clean wooden plates back up to a grassier part of the bank. They landed with a noisy clatter. "Brought me more work, have you? Slaving after Royalty, so much for Fodder's grand revolution! All right, hand the bloody thing over and piss off, will you?"

There was a moment of silence. Dullard's lanky outline was a still silhouette in the pale moonlight.

"Actually," he ventured quietly, "I was just going to do it myself. If you don't mind."

Shoulders could feel the wind sucking out of his sails. He gritted his teeth. Oh, that was just lovely, wasn't it? Now the Royal pillock was making him feel bad!

And hang on...

"If I don't mind?" he repeated acerbically. "Why would I mind you doing your own dirty work? What, you think we common folk worship the chance to bow and scrape and do your work for you?"

"No." There it was again, bloody rabbit face! And there was that soft, tentative rabbit tone that went with it! And this man called himself Royalty? "I just didn't want to get in your way."

"Well, you're not." Shoulders swept his arm towards the river in an expansive gesture. "All yours."

But Dullard hadn't moved. His expression hadn't changed. In fact, his eyes seemed to be searching the shadow-riddled contours of Shoulders's face.

"Are you quite all right?" he ventured gently. "I don't mean to impose, especially on such a short acquaintance, but…you do seem to be awfully out of sorts. Most of the time, as it happens, and…well, I thought perhaps if there was something wrong…"

Shoulders could feel his eyes narrowing. Pity. He could smell it on the breeze. There was going to be pity.

"My sorts are all in and accounted for, thank you," he retorted sharply. "If they were out and about, you'd know about it."

"I rather feel like I do." Dullard winced under the weight of Shoulders's glare but, annoyingly, he didn't back down. "I just thought there must be something in particular on your mind. After all, here we are in the midst of this great endeavour and—"

"Great endeavour?" The two coldly thrust-out words killed the rest of Dullard's sentence dead. "Great endeavour?"

Dullard bit his lip. "Well, isn't it?"

Shoulders shook his head in disbelief. Of all the witless, naïve…

"Let me see," he exclaimed in mock thoughtfulness. "I've been dragged away from my home by my mad mate and a psychotic Barmaid. I've been chased, drowned, chucked in several rivers, thrown off castles, walked through a sewer, and climbed up a toilet. I've had to escort the brat from hell, and there's a better-than-reasonable chance I'm going to end up spending the rest of my life in a dungeon! You call it a great endeavour, mate! I call it a bloody disaster!"

Rabbit, rabbit, rabbit… "But the possibilities! The improvement we could make, to our lives and everyone's…" Dullard broke off as a manic chuckle escaped Shoulders's lips.

"I do not get you," Shoulders exclaimed flatly. "I really don't. You had such a cushy number going up at that Palace. You had good food, good clothes, a good bed, regular character work In Narrative—and you've chucked it away for root stew and being bitten on the nose. And you're so *bloody cheerful* about it!"

The prince gave a slight smile. "Well, I do like to look on the bright side."

Shoulders snorted. "What bright side? We're being pursued by the all-powerful master of our land! We've lost everything we had for an unlikely shot at a future that probably won't be much better anyway! How can anyone find a bright side when there's so much to be down about?"

For a moment, Dullard's slender silhouette made no movement. And then slowly, gently, he turned and crouched down by the dark water, swilling the plate he had brought in the cold water. Shoulders was irritated to note just how much more easily the stew residue seemed to come away from it for him.

"We have the chance to make a difference." When it came, the prince's voice was soft. "A chance to use our own brains and skills for our own benefit and that of others. A chance to ask questions that no one has ever asked before. We have the chance to do what no one has ever done before." He glanced up at Shoulders, his face half-hidden in shadow, half-washed by pale moonlight. His smile gleamed. "How can anyone find a downside when there's so much to be bright about?"

Shoulders stared at Dullard. Something uncomfortable prickled at the back of his mind, that irritating little corner that whispered sometimes that maybe he was protesting a bit too much and might be happier if he just went along with Fodder's madness. No more ditches, no more head-chopping, no more Clank...

Or more likely, no more freedom.

It was a stupid corner. He didn't like it and wasn't having it. Firmly, he told it to sod off.

He just wished he could be sure it was listening.

"I don't get your attitude," he repeated, though the lack of conviction in his own voice was annoying. "I don't get anyone who enjoys being stupid."

Dullard rose, shaking his plate dry carefully as he moved with an oddly effortless lope back up the muddy bank. "I don't get yours either," he replied with a shrug. "I'm afraid we shall just have to agree to disagree." He nodded respectfully in Shoulders's direction. And then, he turned and headed back towards the nearby glow of the camp.

Shoulders stared after him for a moment.

What a *bloody pillock*.

He turned to collect his plates and his boot came down firmly on a patch of mud. Skidding and with arms flailing, his inevitable splash followed moments later.

* * *

Fodder had to admit, if there was one thing he admired about his new friend Dullard, it was his perseverance. He'd never seen anything quite like it.

There he sat in the bow of their liberated boat, his clothes still bearing the faint stains of his numerous, fractious attempts to feed the princess, the bite marks on his hand and nose fading but visible—and yet he was still smiling, still calm, still reasonable to the point of infuriation as he patiently continued to try and win Pleasance around. As far as Fodder was concerned, it was a cause so lost as to be laughable, but Dullard seemed absolutely determined that before they reached the coastal town of Salty Port and attempted to hire a seaworthy ship for the purposes of sailing off of the Taskmaster's map, he would persuade the most self-obsessed, irritating, stuck-up brat Fodder had ever met that everyone in the world deserved an equal chance. Against the protests of the others, he'd even removed her gag so that she could argue back. If Dullard actually succeeded in doing anything but making her bellow high-handed insults, the flocks of flying pigs would probably be circling for days.

"How do you even have the gall to talk this way? You are a Royal by blood, and you should know how absurd this is! You can't have some common, ache-riddled peasant leading a story! It would be an absurdity!"

"But why? In most Quests, the Hero and even occasionally the Heroine are of humble origin."

"Oh, *origin!* Origin is nothing! It's *blood,* and blood will out! They may start as peasants but they end as Kings for they have the blood of Kings, however well-diluted! That isn't something some Ordinary layabout can conjure! Whoever heard of a genuine peasant being anything but background noise?"

"But that's the point, you see. We haven't heard of it because it's never been tried. And if it's never been tried, how can we possibly know if it would work out or not?"

"Of course it wouldn't work! They don't have the breeding! And anyway, who would want to hear about a Quest about some common-place Ordinary people? A Quest is about aspiration, about losing yourself in the lives of people that everyone would secretly like to be! Who could ever want to live in some smelly village shovelling dung? Who would want to be plain-faced and homely? Who would want to be anything but *me?*"

"I wouldn't." Shoulders intervened firmly from his position on the left-hand oar. "Too much ruddy screaming."

"You haven't got the figure for it either," Flirt offered with a grin from the oar on the right. "But I wouldn't want to any more than you. The dress isn't my colour, is it? Not to mention if I can't swing a sword, I'm not playing."

"Precisely." Pleasance's voice swung shut like a steel trap. "Aspiration. Everyone wants to be us."

Dullard's smile was gentle. "Then why not let them?"

Pleasance's expression was one of affronted confusion. "I beg your pardon?"

The prince shrugged slightly. "I'm not saying that Heroes shouldn't be noble and save the world. But why are they always from the same families? In terms of Quest plots, The Narrative can continue much as it chooses, if it comes to it. All we want is for everyone to have an equal chance to shine."

"But why should they?" Pleasance snapped back. "They have their place. They were born to it, bred for it, raised to it, just as we were bred to ours! They should be happy to be what they are! Why should they want anything else?"

Dullard pursed his lips, his expression pleasantly reasonable. "Aspiration. Everyone wants to be you."

Pleasance's eyes could have flayed a man alive. But Dullard didn't even flinch. His sincere smile never wavered. He was a gentle, friendly soul, but Fodder was learning quickly that that didn't mean he couldn't use his niceness like a ballistic trebuchet loaded with red-hot boulders when the situation called for it.

In spite of the fiery gaze he was subject to, Dullard ploughed bravely on. "It's a matter of opportunity, really. It's knowing that there's a choice. People will be much happier to be hacked to pieces or totter around in the background if they know that they'll have the chance to do the hacking in the foreground next time around. It's spreading the opportunities more widely. It's giving everyone the chance to be a Principal."

Pleasance growled. "But they're Ordinary. They don't have the looks! The talents! The glamour!"

"They may have the talents. Who knows? Why, as you must have seen last night, Flirt here is a fine, natural swordswoman; but because she was born into an Ordinary family, the talent she has is wasted on serving drinks in a country inn." Flirt glanced up and grinned at the compliment. After his bout with Pleasance over supper the night before, Dullard had taken the time to show Flirt a few of the fencing rules he'd picked up from old Gallant. As a result, Flirt's natural proficiency had already developed an alarmingly dangerous edge.

Fodder, however, had also noted the look of outright shock on Princess Pleasance's face as Dullard had demonstrated a particularly complicated parry. It seemed his gift for swordsmanship had come as much of a surprise to her as it had done to Shoulders back at the Palace, and she had spent most of the rest of that evening watching him with bewildered incredulity. In that respect at least, Dullard had certainly opened her eyes.

At this particular moment, however, Pleasance's eyes were narrowed as her lips twisted into an unladylike sneer. "Perhaps by freak chance, she's picked up some basic ability," the princess drawled, her nose so far in the air that Fodder was privately surprised that no one had pulled out a pickaxe and attempted to scale its north face. "But what you seem to be forgetting is the matter of breeding. Royalty is bred to be Royal. We have the looks and the talent for it, and we mix very carefully to insure that talent is not diluted." The superior look that she cast at Dullard implied that she considered his unusual origins to be a considerable watering down. The mild look that Dullard returned with was a very quiet and reasonable assertion that he didn't care.

Although unsettled by the gentle, unspoken retort, the princess nonetheless ploughed on. "The point I am trying to make is that everyone in this Realm is born to be what they are. Generations have bred every one of us to fit the needed niche. Too much interbreeding amongst the wrong people could turn out all sorts of strange, pointless combinations." She paused a moment, gauging herself, the smirk that poked at the corners of her lips implying that she was gearing herself up for an insult. Her lips parted—

"As with me?" Dullard suggested mildly.

Pleasance's lips smacked shut. She glared the glare that can only be glared by someone whose thunder has just been stolen.

Dullard shrugged again. He was still smiling. Fodder honestly didn't know how he did it. "That's one way of looking at it, I suppose," he offered up thoughtfully. "But you could also say that how do we know what better possibilities we might be missing without mingling more?"

"Or the generations of carefully planned heritage we might be losing!"

"It's possible." Dullard gazed absently off into the middle distance. "But wouldn't it be good to shake away those dusty expectations? Take the leading families, all so constrained by their conventions. To use a random example, how about the fact that the Heroine must always marry her Narrative Hero, regardless of how they get along? A marriage is for life, not just for The Narrative. Don't you think it would be much fairer to give everyone a choice in the matter?"

Hunched at the tiller, Fodder waited for the retort. It didn't come.

Instead, there was silence.

Rowlocks creaked. Oars splashed gently. Somewhere along the bank, a blackbird gave a noisy chatter.

Pleasance's mouth opened. It closed. Her eyes hardened harshly.

But Fodder hadn't missed the look that had lingered briefly on her face. Impossible as it seemed, Dullard had struck a nerve.

Aha. Someone's not that keen on Bumpkin, then....

"It is a duty." The words that eventually escaped from Pleasance's lips were a vicious hiss. "In the name of the bloodline! Not that you would know anything about either of those things. You're a traitor to the half of you that shares my noble heritage! You're nothing more than a mixed-up, ill-bred, ugly, treacherous *freak!*"

Ah. Insults. Any minute now, the screaming would begin again, and they'd have to put back the gag. It had already happened twice since they'd set out that morning.

"I'm sorry you feel that way." Dullard's expression was sincerely contrite. "But never mind. Are you hungry? I think we have some berries left from breakfast."

He leaned forwards, rummaging in Flirt's pack as Pleasance stared at him open-mouthed, the wind sucked from her abusive sails once more.

"Why do you keep doing that?" she exclaimed with genuine perplexity. "I insulted you! I called you a freak! And then you offer me *berries?*"

Dullard settled back again, a small pouch cradled in his palm. "I *am* a freak," he stated with cheerful frankness. "There's no point in denying it. And I already told you, it's all sticks and stones to me. But you got pulled into this through no fault of your own, so I'm certainly not going to do anything to make things more unpleasant for you. Besides"—the look that crossed his face for an instant was distinctly on the shrewd side—"call me presumptuous if you like, but...I don't think many people have ever been that nice to you before, have they? Polite perhaps, deferent and of equal condescension, but not, I'd venture, nice in the sense of *nice*. That's not how life in the Palace works. So I thought, well, if I show you what it's all about, you might just come to like it." He rummaged in the pouch before extending one hand carefully towards her. "Blackberry? It's a little lopsided, but I doubt that'll damage the taste...."

Pleasance was staring at him. Her mouth was open once more, and her expression was one of such frank, daunted bewilderment that, for a brief, passing instant, Fodder almost felt sorry for her. There were many things, he was sure, that life as a princess prepared a girl for, but an assault of raw, unfiltered kindness was apparently not one of them.

Her stare flickered to the lopsided blackberry. She eyed it as though it were a live snake. "No, thank you," she said stiffly. "In fact...I think I'd like my gag back, please."

The gentle splash of the oars came to an abrupt halt. As one, Flirt and Shoulders exchanged an astonished glance with Fodder before swivelling to stare over their respective shoulders.

Dullard's expression was one of genuine regret. "Are you sure? Don't let the way it looks fool you. Honestly, I'm sure it will be delicious if you give it a chance."

"No!" The retort was sharp but surprisingly, the princess's voice winnowed down from snappishness to a more moderate, if strained, tone. "No...thank you. Just...put the gag back, please. I don't want to talk to you anymore."

"Very well." Dullard looked sincerely disappointed by this turn of events, a stark contrast to Fodder's usual sense of relief when the time came for the replacing of the gag. "Please hold still, then."

With gentle fingers, Dullard eased the handkerchief gag back into place. Pleasance stared at him blankly as he did so. She didn't even take a snap at him. It was really quite disconcerting.

He smiled at her, quiet and friendly as she settled back into the bow of the boat. She turned sharply away. Her eyes fixed determinedly on the rippling waters of the river and did not rise again.

Dullard frowned briefly at her hunched shoulders for a moment. And then he shook himself and turned back to meet the stares of his new friends.

"Are you two all right?" he said suddenly, glancing to the unmoving oars of Flirt and Shoulders. "Are your arms tired? Fodder and I can swap with you if—"

"Nah, I'm still good." Flirt snapped immediately back to business. "I just got distracted, didn't I? Shoulders?"

"I can keep going for a bit." Shoulders shrugged his namesakes awkwardly as he turned and settled back to his oar. "Just so long as you aren't expecting us to row this little thing all the way out into the ocean. I have no desire to try and get reconstituted from a sea monster's doings, thank you very much!"

"Nah." Fodder settled back against the tiller once more. "Actually, I was thinking more along the lines of...Flirt?"

The Barmaid eyed him slightly. "You're not floating out to sea on me, mate. Do I look that buoyant to you?"

Fodder grinned. "Is there any way to answer that safely?"

"Nope." Flirt grinned back.

"Then I won't try it. But I was thinking... Doesn't your uncle live in Salty Port?"

Flirt nodded. "Uncle Reel. He's a professional Grizzled Seadog."

"Would he be able to get us a boat?"

Flirt tilted one hand as best she could whilst heaving on an oar. "No idea. I haven't seen him for five or six Quests. But even if he could—do you know how to sail one?"

And there was the sticking point. Fodder was a rural boy, born and bred. He'd never been near a seagoing ship in his life. But he was hoping…

"No, but…Dullard?" he queried, more in expectation than hope. But he was in for a disappointment. The prince was already shaking his head.

"I'm afraid I've never had cause to learn," he admitted. "I know it was my idea, but I've never had any reason to come down to this ocean before, let alone learn how to sail. I've always thought it would be a fascinating pursuit, though, and it would of course enable me to investigate all manner of plant and animal life residing within our waters, but…"

"You haven't done it yet." Fodder cursed himself in the silence of his mind. Why had he assumed that Dullard would know? Admittedly, in the few days they'd known him, Dullard had managed to pop up with all sorts of useful and unexpected talents, but relying on him to automatically bail them out was a dangerous path indeed. "So we'll need to persuade some sailors to help us."

Shoulders gave a snort as he heaved on his oar. "Well, that'll be nice and easy," he drawled with a distinct degree of sarcasm. "Given that our converts this far number one and a half. An entire ship's crew will be a breeze."

"A half?" Fodder queried tentatively.

"Cringe," Shoulders retorted. "Though 'a half' is generous. More like a third of a conversion, really."

"I think you may have made more of a difference than you realise," Dullard dropped in with, in Fodder's view, unwarranted optimism. "After all, I was converted before I even met you. How many other converts are waiting out there to be found?"

"Maybe," Fodder conceded with reluctance. "But it'd be a seriously unlikely piece of luck if…"

"Fodder."

"…those hidden converts turned out to be the crew of a ship…"

"Fodder."

"…just waiting for us in Salty Port…"

"Fodder!"

The boat gave an ungainly lurch as Shoulders's oar dipped into the water and pulled without the aid of its compatriot. For Flirt had frozen halfway through the motion, her eyes fixed with sudden alarm on the horizon behind Fodder's head.

"Look!" she exclaimed. "There!"

Fodder turned. And his heart sank.

For, glowing with unreal brightness against the horizon perhaps a couple of miles upstream, was the too-familiar light of The Narrative.

"Oh, my." Dullard sat up straighter as he stared back at the ominous gleam. "I should have thought of that."

"Thought of what?" Shoulders snapped, his face pale as he stared alongside his friends.

"That the Merry Band would have to follow the road on the other side of the river." Dullard looked slightly embarrassed. "It's in the instructions, you see. They must be on their way to the big fight at Salty Port. And if they are looking for us and someone reported this boat going missing..."

"We could drown the princess." Flirt's lips were tight as Pleasance's head shot up sharply. "Here and now, when it sees us. Get it over with."

But Fodder was shaking his head. "The conditions are too unpredictable. There are too many things The Narrative could use against us. We aren't ready."

"Then we have to get ashore and out of sight." Dullard was leaning forwards, his expression unusually intense. "Now."

Flirt grabbed her oar at once. But Shoulders was still staring at the glowing horizon.

"Wait!" he exclaimed. "What's *that?*"

It was there and then gone in a second, a vivid streak of emerald green that rocketed over their heads along the course of the Vast River. Even as they swivelled as one, hypnotised by its progress, a curtain of sparkling green enveloped the river perhaps one hundred yards in front of them. Something echoed with a terrible crack, the water frothed and surged, and then came a deafening roar and a surge of spray that rose to tumble tumultuously towards the heavens. The boat tossed and weaved and then, with a sudden jerk, almost like a rope had been yanked, it swirled and, unaided by human hand, began to travel far too hurriedly downstream.

And ahead, in a cloud of rainbows, the horizon vanished.

"Higgle," Dullard breathed, staring at the bright speck of the Duty Pixie in charge of Landscape and Architecture as he turned and vanished in a flash. "He's made a *waterfall.*"

Shoulders gaped at the mass of spray as their boat began to accelerate. "But that's cheating!"

"That's the Taskmaster!" Flirt grabbed her oar frantically. "Stop moaning and row!"

Fodder jammed the tiller desperately over as two oars floundered awkwardly in the suddenly turbulent river, his eyes fixed upon the imposing mass of dancing water that rocketed into the sky ahead of them. It would be an impossibly long drop, he knew that. There would be sharp rocks at the bottom and a suitably placed pebble beach for the washing up of the bedraggled but lucky survivor. Some truths were simply self-evident.

And if they went over under Narrative control, he knew just who the lone survivor would be.

"Dullard!" he bellowed over the swelling crescendo of tumbling water. "Whatever you do, keep hold of the princess! If we go over, keep her out of The Narrative!"

Dullard, who had been rummaging frantically in his pack, glanced up and nodded. He caught the trailing end of Pleasance's restraints and curled it around his belt, knotting it securely before diving back into the pack to continue his search for who-knew-what. There were fifty yards to go now, maybe less, and the current was accelerating far more intensely than the shore was nearing.

"Not more water!" Shoulders groaned. "I'm sick of bloody water!"

"If it's too bloody, we'll be in trouble when The Narrative comes!" Flirt continued to yank at her oar, although the quick glance she exchanged with Fodder was enough to tell him that she could see as well as he could that they weren't going to make it. "Try not to get hurt, will you?"

"Tell the bloody waterfall that!"

Behind them, The Narrative was closing fast, a threatening glow of vividness outlining the last lumps and bumps of the landscape behind them. Just one more outcrop and curl of the river and the Merry Band would see them. And the moment they did, Fodder knew their fate would no longer be in their own hands. Defying The Narrative on dry land was one thing. Defying it whilst at the complete mercy of natural elements was another.

The Taskmaster was very clever.

They were perhaps ten yards from the shore. Twenty yards in front of them, a wall of spray roared, an irresistible force drawing them closer and closer to the long plunge down. Flirt was rowing frantically, loath to give up even in the face of such hopelessness, her cheeks flushed with effort as she dragged at her oar. Shoulders was matching her blindly, his eyes fixed with a vague hint of horror on the approaching glow just over Fodder's shoulder. The princess's eyes were more concerned with what lay ahead, staring with a blank, resigned horror at the vanishing water, her porcelain cheeks white. And Dullard...

"Aha!"

The exclamation was so unexpected that four sets of eyes snapped in his direction. With an air of spray-sodden triumph, Dullard was dragging a strangely angled metal spike out of his pack. Grabbing it firmly by the shaft, he shook it sharply; with a clunk, three curled metal protrusions unfurled themselves and jolted into place.

A grappling hook. It was a grappling hook....

Of course. Dullard's a climber.

"The rope! Quickly!"

Shoulders could not shove the curl of rope into the prince's hands quickly enough. Dullard snatched up the end, threading it with disconcerting deftness through the round loop in the butt of the hook and knotting it tightly. Hurriedly, he thrust it into the air, bracing his legs under the seat as he gritted his teeth.

"Heads down!" he cried out over the deafening roar.

Fodder obeyed instantly. The black hook whirled overhead in a rapid rotation—one, two, three, gathering speed until it was nothing more than a spinning blur. Ahead, the horizon vanished beyond the prow of their boat, the drag of the rushing water all the more frantic now that rowing had been abandoned. Five yards, four, three, two...

The boat was tipping....

With a whistling whoosh, Dullard let go.

There was a violent jerk as, with a woody thunk, the grappling hook buried itself into the twisted mass of a distinctly unsturdy-looking willow tree that jutted out from the bank. Fodder saw Dullard's knees lurch as he tried to take the strain, saw his backside leave the planking as the inexorable pull conquered his leg strength and sought to catapult him out of the boat...

And then, to his utter astonishment, he saw Princess Pleasance hurl herself forwards and land with the full force of her weight into his lap.

Dullard's eyes crossed. Pleasance had landed elbows first.

Fodder had to admire his fortitude, though. He kept hold of the rope. And, forced down by the weight of a whole princess, his backside returned to the planking with a thud.

But the Disposable could still feel the boat slipping sideways, teetering along the spray-riddled drop as the current and the angle of the rope began to drag them inevitably shorewards and downwards....

"Grab it!" Flirt's sodden curls plastered her face as she dived forwards. Fingers grasping the rope, she helped to take the strain. Fodder's hands whipped out to join hers, scrabbling at the slippery hemp, and Shoulders quickly followed their lead.

The boat swung and danced along the brink of the abyss for several agonising, hour-long seconds before it thudded against the side of a jutting and highly clingable rock. Fodder could feel his fingers screaming as he dug them into the damp rope, hooking one leg under the wooden plank that formed his seat to prevent being rocketed out into the water just as Dullard had almost been. He doubted the princess would come to his rescue.

He caught a glimpse of Shoulders, his legs locked around his seat as he clung on. Flirt had rammed herself against her oar, her arms wrapped around the rope in an almost fervent embrace. Dullard's lower lip was jammed between his teeth, and there was a distinctly misty quality to his eyes, but the princess's weight in his lap was keeping him in place for now. His arms were thrust out before him, straining under the pull.

Beyond him, beyond the prow, the world fell away. There was a haze of white water and rolling clouds of spray, punctuated, inevitably, with a beautifully crafted selection of sharp rocks down at the bottom. They were carefully positioned to ensure it would be very difficult to escape their grasp without a severe battering.

Fodder risked a glance over his shoulder. Against the nearest horizon, The Narrative gleamed.

The moment it reached them, the hook would give or the rope would snap. It was unavoidable. The labyrinth of rocks would knock them senseless and before they had time to come round and get out of its way, The Narrative would pounce. Resisting it whilst intact was one thing. But Fodder wasn't certain that even his determination would be enough to keep him going against The Narrative whilst burdened with fatal wounds. If he was injured In Narrative, then he was injured. That was simply natural law.

Well, we can't stay here....

"Heave!" he bellowed over the ear-numbing roar of falling water. "We have to heave to shore!"

He could feel the incredulity of several gazes whose owners were struggling to simply manage with holding on. But this was no time for debate.

"On three!" he roared in a voice that brooked no argument even from Shoulders. "Left arm first! One! Two! *Heave!*"

His right arm screamed as it momentarily was forced to take the pressure alone. But then his left hand found slippery purchase. The boat jerked forwards, a reluctant but definite motion.

Yes!

"And again! Right arm! Heave! Left! Heave! Right! Heave!"

Slowly, painfully, they began to make progress, abandoning their helpful rock with a violent jerk as they swung back into the current and back towards the brink. But Fodder's sharp instructions kept them moving as the riverbank edged closer and closer and closer....

"Jump for it!" There was a definite strained quality to Dullard's voice, although whether it was from the effort or the elbow effect, Fodder couldn't be sure. "We're close enough! Take the packs and jump!"

Shoulders barely even hesitated. Grabbing both packs from the bottom of the boat, he hurled them one after the other onto the riverbank. They landed with a noisy but safe clatter on the grass. A moment later, with only a brief and awkward scrambling against the damp and muddy river's edge, he'd followed them.

Flirt, however, had hesitated. She glanced from Fodder to Dullard and back again and Fodder could see the truth that had just dawned in her eyes.

"Flirt!" he yelled. "Go!"

"But…"

"We'll sort it out! Go!"

Flirt's brow creased. But nonetheless, she slackened her grasp, turned, and made the leap. The treacherous mud almost sent her sliding back into the turbulent waters, but luckily Shoulders's quick reactions saved her from a tumble. He hauled her quickly up and dragged both her and the packs into the dense shelter of the weeping willow where the hook was lodged a dozen yards upstream.

Fodder glanced towards the shining horizon. Good old Shoulders; it was smart of him to get out of sight.

"Fodder! You too!"

Fodder shook himself as his fingers screamed. Now it was his turn for a futile protest. "But…"

"The princess can't jump tied up, and I can't jump and hold on!" Dullard's face was set. "But if you hurry up, maybe the three of you can pull us to shore before The Narrative has time to break the rope. But you have to go!"

He was right. Fodder knew he was right, though it still felt like a desertion. But what choice did he have?

Abandoning the rope, Fodder turned, pushed off, and leapt. It was an ungainly landing that involved mud and a great deal of slip-sliding, but he found his footing quickly and hit sprint from a standing start as he scrambled upstream to join his friends. Ahead, vivid light was advancing at a roll down the river. The Merry Band were almost at the crest of the outcrop.

He snatched the rope. "Help me!" he cried, and Flirt and Shoulders were at his side in a moment, hauling frantically as the beleaguered Dullard and his Royal paperweight were hauled closer and closer and closer…

But it was already too late.

"Here it comes!" he heard Flirt scream.

The Merry Band crested the rise.

Vivid light swept like a torrent downstream. Fodder saw Dullard's eyes widen, saw him glance at the rope and sigh.

"Oh dear," Fodder heard him say.

And then, mere seconds before The Narrative light could sweep in and seal his fate, he simply let go.

"Dullard!" Fodder half started forwards, but Flirt and Shoulders had already grabbed his arms and hauled him bodily under the thick branches of the willow. They were only just in time, as vivid light engulfed the riverbank, the surging waters, and the waterfall's brink, rolling around their place of concealment like a storm battering a beleaguered isle. Fodder caught an impossible, Narratively intense glimpse of the little boat tipping like a seesaw, saw Dullard wrap his arms around the white-faced and silently screaming princess as he closed his eyes and gritted his teeth. And then, in a rush of spray, they vanished over the horizon and were gone.

The Narrative had seen them fall. He could not have seen them so clearly if it hadn't.

He let go on purpose. He let go so that The Narrative would see only them and not us.

It didn't change one simple fact, though. With The Narrative all around them, they were trapped.

* * *

Erik rode like a boy possessed. Behind him, he could hear the frantic bellows of Elder to wait, to pull his reins and pause in his frantic flight long enough for Sir Roderick or Zahora to catch up with him, but he could not, dared not hesitate. How could Elder even ask it of him?

Princess Islaine.

He had seen her only for a moment, a brief, fleeting second before the inevitable drag of the terrible current had hauled her vessel over the brim of the waterfall and plunged her out of sight. But it had been enough to see the terror in her poor eyes, the horror on her face as yet again, her ruthless kidnappers subjected her to infamy beyond reason.

He had to find her. He had to save her.

He could only pray with all his soul that he was not already too late.

* * *

The Vast River was vast. That was kind of the point.

But nonetheless, bathed in the unreal—or was it over-real?—light of The Narrative, Fodder could see the distant far bank quite clearly as he peered out through a tiny gap in the willow's thick branches. The Merry Band were faraway outlines as they clamoured and shouted and it didn't take long for Fodder to see why: a lone figure on horseback had streaked away, dragging the brightest focus of the light behind him as he pelted towards the waterfall at frantic speed.

Ah, so that's how they're playing it....

"They've sent Bumpkin off in quick pursuit," he whispered softly, his eye pressed gently against the curtain of wood. Long, woody fingers of willow branch itched at his back but he manfully ignored them. "They're scared. They want to get the princess into Narrative as soon as possible."

"Just be careful, will you?" Shoulders's voice was distinctly nervous as he rested with his back against the tree trunk as far from the ring of Narrative light as could be managed. He had already dragged back on the chain mail shirt he had earlier abandoned whilst rowing and was fingering his sword impatiently. "If you let that sodding light get in, we're buggered and you know it."

"I think we're okay here." Fodder wasn't sure if the words were to convince Shoulders or himself—the sea of vivid light that washed around their fragile island of self-control was hardly reassuring, but surely from so far away, they'd be safe enough under cover. He squinted once more at the hurtling figure on horseback heroically charging to the rescue. "Bumpkin's focussed on the waterfall, and we're a long way away. Too far for even someone with mysterious powers to spot an eyeball, I reckon." He pulled a face. "I think it's Dullard and the princess we've got to worry about. They're about to hit a big chunk of Narrative."

"Dullard can take Bumpkin, though, can't he?" There was deliberately placed confidence in Flirt's voice in spite of her usual qualification. Having retrieved the rope and hook, she too was in the process of rearming herself and strapped the elegant sword the prince had given her to her waist with a pointed flourish. "Especially if it's one on one."

"Without this?" Shoulders hefted Dullard's sword, a plainer example from his own collection, which was still strapped to his pack. "And he's never been In Narrative like that before. How do we know he's up to it?"

"How do we know he's conscious?" Fodder added. "Not to mention that Bumpkin has mysterious powers to fall back on. The Narrative is Bumpkin's story. It can cheat him out of any trouble anytime it wants to."

Flirt's hand was on her sword hilt in an instant. "We need to get down there. Dullard will need help and we can't lose the princess now, can we? Not after all this!"

"The minute we go out, The Narrative will see us!" Shoulders retorted. "And then it's us in trouble!"

But Fodder had noticed something. "Maybe not. Grab the packs."

Shoulders's expression flashed with incredulous disbelief. "You can't be…"

"The Narrative's running with Bumpkin!" Abandoning his lookout post, Fodder rushed forwards and, following the lead of his friends, pulled the chafing, heavy metallic mass of his chain mail coat over his head. "And Bumpkin's about to ride down the side of that waterfall! And as soon as he's below the horizon…"

"We'll be out of Narrative sight!" Flirt flung her pack emphatically over her shoulder as Shoulders more reluctantly followed suit with Dullard's. "We can make a run for it!"

"But the rest of the Merry Band are still out there!" Shoulders jabbed one angry finger in the direction of the willow curtain. "They'll see us!"

"But not Narratively! And I'm betting the Taskmaster will care much more about getting the princess back in The Narrative's clutches than turning around to try and catch up with us."

"They'll chase us!"

Flirt snorted. "Then we'll have to run fast, won't we?"

Shoulders's eyebrows were knitted together in one anxious line. "But…"

The vivid light that had encased the willow faded, flickered, and dimmed. A moment later, it vanished.

And Fodder screamed out, "Go!"

* * *

The brink of the cliff sheered out before him, the wide road transformed all at once from a broad, safe track into a narrow, perilous decline. But Erik barely slowed, confident in the sure footing of his loyal mount as he hurled himself down the winding trail, his eyes already scanning the turbulent waters below for some hint that the mysterious young woman who had tugged at his heart from the moment he'd set eyes on her had not perished on the jagged rocks below. His search was frantic, fervent, desperate, for she could not be dead, she was not dead, he knew it, he could feel it...

And then, glory be, he saw her.

Shattered wood, the remains of the boat, lay scattered in broken chunks across a narrow, pebbled inlet on the river's far shore. A bedraggled shape wrapped in vivid sky-blue velvet lay slumped and motionless in its midst.

Islaine!

Until the day he died, Erik had no idea how he managed to cross the river. One moment he was galloping towards the nearest bank, and the next, his horse was skidding to a bemused and bewildered halt amongst the pebbles of the previously distant beach. Aware as he was that something strange had just happened, Erik nevertheless dared not pause to ponder it—leaping from his saddle, he stumbled and staggered his way through the wreckage, hurling himself to his knees beside the tumbled, sodden mass of beautiful blonde curls.

She was so still! Carefully, almost reverently, he stroked back the soaking hair to expose one perfect, porcelain cheek and the soft curve of her throat. Gently, beside the tattered remains of what looked like a handkerchief, he rested his fingers against her swan-like neck and prayed for a miracle.

A dull thudding greeted his touch just as a soft exhalation escaped from her lips. She lived! She lived!

He leaned closer, his mouth just inches from the delicate shell of her ear.

"Princess Islaine?" he whispered softly. "Princess, can you hear me?"

She sighed gently. Her eyelids fluttered....

She was waking! Erik leaned closer, unable to keep the smile from his face.

"Princess," he whispered. "Princess, you're safe now. I'll look after you, I—"

The crunch of a foot against pebbles was startlingly close. The young man started to turn...

* * *

There was no doubt that Shoulders hesitated. But Flirt had seen it coming, and her fingers wrapped with abrupt firmness around his arm. Ignoring his screech of protest, she all but flung him through the scratchy screen of branches before plunging through herself.

Fodder had already darted forwards to slap against their protective curtain, his mailed arms raised to shield his face as he shoved his way through the hanging twigs and out into the open. He heard the yells rising at once from the far side of the river, but he did not dare stop and look to see who'd seen them—his legs pumping, his arms swinging as he bolted up the slippery, grassy slope of the riverbank, fingers scrabbling for purchase as he dragged himself over spray-dampened roots and protruding rocks and hurled himself into the cover of the trees.

This lower reach of the Rambling Woods was thicker than the woods around his home, and three steps in, his progress was seriously impeded by a bramble patch. Luckily, his mail was protective enough to prevent a serious scratching. Powered by sheer momentum, he gritted his teeth and piled on through the undergrowth, staggering as his boots trampled the thorny stems beneath him. A muddy hole sucked at his foot and sent him reeling to bounce with bruising force against an ivy-covered tree—sticky leaves clung to his armour as he flailed his way free of their grasp. Rolling spray from the roaring waterfall off to their left had sneaked its way between the trees, filling the air with splattering, half-blinding dampness. Fodder could hear the squelch of Flirt and Shoulders's footsteps off to one side as they encountered a patch of ground this rolling wall of fresh water had quickly made its own. A moment later, mud-splattered and battered, just as he was, they broke out of the trees behind him.

Fodder barely hesitated. "This way!" he roared over the waterfall's rumble, sweeping one arm round in a beckoning gesture that gained him a handful of spider's web and a very disgruntled eight-legged passenger. Yes, they had to keep going, and keep the waterfall to their left, because that way they would still be heading down to the bottom, to where Dullard fell, to where they needed to go and—

Fell. Down. Even as Fodder swept aside a hanging branch and hurtled mindlessly on through the spray-riddled undergrowth, the thought dropped into his head with a clang. If Higgle had dropped the landscape where the river was, basic natural law would mean he'd have to drop it on either side as well. And that would mean a...

Slope.

Big slope.

A fold of sky opened out before him. Treetops glimmered damply at eye level.

Oops.

Only his reactions saved him. Even as the woodland floor disappeared from beneath his feet, tumbling away down a drop that teetered on the brink of sheer and was littered with rather bewildered trees that had started the day on far more level ground, his hands lashed out, smacking around an overhanging branch. His feet pawed for an instant over empty air but, fingernails digging into bark, he desperately clung on, scrabbling his heels against the muddy drop-off as he tried to find his footing.

But it was too late for that.

"Look out!"

He heard Flirt's screech, caught a glimpse of her flailing arms as she struggled to stop, but momentum and wet leaves left her with little option but to hurtle into Fodder with a solid crash. Impossibly, for a moment, his grasp held them both, but Shoulders's whoop of horror told him that the respite was only brief. A moment later, his fellow Disposable barrelled into them both with an echoing thud.

Fodder's fingers parted. Scrambling desperately for something, anything to hold on to, his hand lashed out and grasped around the first solid item it encountered.

Unfortunately, this was Shoulders's belt.

It proved a bad move for all concerned.

The ground vanished. A moment later, however, it made its presence felt rather more solidly. Tangled impossibly in a cluster of metal-clad limbs, Fodder could only gasp as every ounce of breath was driven from his body by their first bruising bounce. A hard elbow drove into his chin, a leg whacked against his chest, and roots drove into his back as he tumbled over and over. Clinging trees got in their way, but the pull of gravity was stronger. He bounced off bark, ricocheted off rocks, leaves, ground, sky, leaves, ground, sky flashing dizzyingly before his eyes. He could hear Shoulders wailing in sore horror, could hear Flirt's grunts at every battering blow as he rolled himself up as tightly as he dared and prayed for the mercy of geography.

And then, abruptly, he got it.

The flash of leaves parted. Muddy ground slipped into a softer gradient, and then suddenly they were rolling over grass, out into a small but blessedly flat clearing as the terrible slope finally ran out of steam. Their momentum pushed them on for several more yards, a silver ball of bruises, but slowly, hesitantly, they rumbled to a halt, unfolding with a metallic sigh into a heap of battered limbs and lolling heads. For a moment, Fodder could only lie gasping, face against the cool grass, with what looked like Shoulders's leg hanging over his chest and Flirt's arm slumped and twitching by his face. He couldn't be certain, though. For all the feeling he had left in his limbs, they could have just as easily been his own.

His head was swimming. The world was a blur of green and blue, interspersed with odd grey smudges. Dizzily, he struggled to bring his eyes back into focus but they bluntly refused to co-operate. The smudges danced before his eyes, rippling, moving, coming closer...

"Well," he heard Shoulders groan from somewhere behind him. "That's one way to make a getaway!"

Fuzzily, determinedly, Fodder forced his eyes into some shadow of reluctant obedience. The nearest smudge swam woozily into focus, solidifying into scaly grey skin, vicious curved claws, and four long toes that impatiently tapped the grassy ground. From somewhere overhead came a leathery rustle.

"'Fraid not, mate," said a gravelly voice. "Nice try, though."

And then suddenly the ground was shaking, or at least that was how it felt as a pair of legs clad in thick, hide-bound fur pounded into Fodder's line of sight, scattering the cluster of grey-scaled feet from its path with violent abruptness. A meaty fist thrust itself across the dazed line of his vision, closing around the front of his mail shirt and hauling him upwards with a vicious jerk.

A vast face filled his world, wild bloodshot eyes glowering with almost enough force to be physically painful as they peered out over the top of a truly epic bush of a beard that smelled like a badger's backside.

Thud the slain Barbarian grinned. It was not a pretty sight.

"Gotcha!" he snarled.

* * *

Erik had time only to catch a glimpse of the curved outline of an oar before he flung himself to the ground, solid wood missing the side of his head by mere inches. Even as he scrambled to his feet, scrabbling for the hilt of his sword, the oar swung again with deadly force, knocking his feet from under him and hurling him to the ground. A hand lashed out, ripping his sword from his grasp as the point swung round and came to rest against his throat.

Bewildered, battered, and astonished, Erik stared up into the bloodied and drawn face of Prince Tretaptus of Mond.

There was no mistaking him. Although Erik had only ever seen his picture on the wedding notices that they had passed on the roads of Nyolesse what felt like years before, the profile was not one to be forgotten easily.

"Prince Tretaptus?"

The distinctive nose of the prince screwed up quizzically. "How did you...oh blast, the wedding notices." He pulled a face. "I'd forgotten about those but, of course, it just said." His hand gave an odd sort of tremor and he frowned with reluctant irritation. "And that's quite enough of trying to make me stumble and drop my sword, if you don't mind." He addressed his obscure remarks to the general air around him, glaring with an odd pointedness up towards the empty sky. "I'm better than that, thank you very much. I will not be made into a clumsy oaf again!" He smiled, quick and fleeting, as his odd gaze shifted back to Erik once more.

"You know, this is easier than I expected it to be!" he remarked, conversationally. "Possibly it's because I'm only having to work against a single point of view. But, you know, I think what really matters is going into it in the full and certain knowledge that you are exactly who you are." He nodded, his lips twisting thoughtfully. "Yes," he added absently. "I do think that might be it...."

He's completely insane. The thought dropped unbidden into Erik's head. *The man is a raving, nonsense-spewing lunatic...*

With a sword.

Elder and the others couldn't be far behind him. If he could just keep him talking...

"You kidnapped the princess, didn't you?"

The prince cocked an eyebrow. "Well, I helped," he said rather diffidently. "But I wouldn't want to take all the credit."

"But why? She's your betrothed. You were going to marry her and—"

Tretaptus's long sigh killed off the remainder of Erik's sentence. "Look," he said almost sympathetically. "We both know you're just trying to keep me talking, and I do need to get to the point. And I want you to know that I really am terribly sorry about this. But I hope you'll understand that what I'm about to do is for the good of everybody, because this quest, you see...well, it has to be stopped. And since this quest is all about you, well..." He shrugged apologetically. "Now just hold still." The sword teased sharply against the skin of Erik's neck. "Honestly, I promise you. Having your head chopped off really isn't so bad."

The sword pulled back and then descended, the blade slicing through the air—

And then with shocking violence, Prince Tretaptus was hurled backwards. The sword flew out of his hand and clattered away to splash into the water as he tumbled to the ground with a gasp of pain.

"Mysterious powers!" Erik heard him rasp. "Forgot the mysterious powers!"

But Erik had no time for any more of the prince's mad ravings. Scrambling to his feet, he hurled himself over to where the princess lay, her fingers twitching and her eyelids continuing to flutter. He had to get her out of here before—

The impact of the oar drove all the breath from Erik's body. Tretaptus was already half on his feet, moving with shocking speed as he brought his original weapon back to bear.

"I'm sorry!" he gasped. "I really am, but I have to do this!"

The oar swung ruthlessly round once more, the force a harsh contrast to Tretaptus's apologetic expression. The second blow lifted Erik clean off his feet and sent him tumbling with a splash into the river. For a moment, he scrambled desperately as the weight of his clothes dragged him down, but suddenly he was gasping on the beach once more, the water abandoned by means beyond his understanding. And then, from atop the waterfall, he heard a gloriously familiar call.

"Erik? Erik!"

Elder! It was Elder! He was...

"Oh, blow! That's torn it!" The oar descended onto Erik's head with a sickening crunch. The world swam in a haze of blood and darkness and hollow agony...

But then there was light, soft and gentle and calling him back again....

"Erik! What happened?" Elder's bearded face was leaning down over him through a mist of colours and painful sound, the glow around his fingers shining brightly as it leached away the head wound that might have otherwise taken his life. But Erik had no time for his near miss; he shook away his mentor's concerned hands and dragged himself to his knees.

"The princess!" he gasped out. But one glance across the little beach was enough to tell him that both mad Tretaptus and poor Princess Islaine had gone.

"It's Prince Tretaptus!" he gasped. "He's turned traitor! He hit me over the head and tried to chop my head off! And he's taken the princess again!"

"Tretaptus?" Erik hadn't seen Sir Roderick arrive—he could only assume that Elder had propelled him here using whatever magic he had used to cross the river himself. "But the man is nothing! A sniveller and a coward who never deserved our noble lady's hand! Why would he take her when she was already so unworthily his?"

"I know not." Elder had come to his feet, pulling Erik up behind him as he glared into the nest of trees that lined the riverbank with eyes so filled with fire that it seemed impossible that the very leaves themselves did not shudder under the force of them and burst into angry flames.

"But when we find him, I will make him sorry for it." His terrible eyes snapped to Roderick. "Gather the others and bring them here quickly. We will pursue this foul turncoat and rip these woods into splinters if needs be in order to bring him to justice. This will end by sundown!"

Erik sighed as he stared into the dark trees with grim determination. He could only pray that the beautiful lost soul he had touched so briefly would soon be safe once more. For how much longer could this absurd pursuit drag on?

* * *

"Bugger."

Shoulders's summation from over his right shoulder pretty accurately summed up Fodder's feelings on the matter. He was tempted to echo it himself.

"Yep," he replied.

"Well put," Flirt added from behind and to his left. "So. Now what?"

Fodder shook his limbs tenderly. The chains around his wrists and ankles chafed tightly, though he could hardly blame Thud for that piece of ruthlessness, given the trouble they'd been causing.

"The chains feel pretty secure," he remarked, struggling to maintain a straight and level tone as his mind screamed at him. "It's kind of flattering that they're that worried about us." He worked his wrists again as the metal bit uncomfortably into his skin, feeling the shoulders of his friends as they pressed together in their back-to-back huddle. "Bit inconvenient, though…"

"Inconvenient?" There was a low, dangerous note to Shoulders's tone. "We're chained up in a huddle waiting to be dragged off to spend the rest of our natural lives strapped to a rack in a deep, dank dungeon, and you call it *inconvenient?*"

"What would you prefer I called it?" Fodder tried and failed to keep the frustration that he had been desperately suppressing out of his tone. "You think I'm not every inch as frustrated as you? We were doing so well; we were getting the hang of it! We were so close!"

"Calm down, both of you," Flirt's voice snapped from behind them. "This isn't over yet, is it? Not until they've got the princess."

The chains rattled as Shoulders jerked. "For all we know, they've got her already!"

Fodder felt his eyes drift towards the tree line, to the vivid glow of Narrative light hovering away towards the riverbank. Had Dullard managed to stay conscious? Had he kept hold of the princess? Had he been able to enter The Narrative and keep control of his wits?

They could only hope.

It was all they had left.

But even if Dullard was free, it didn't mean much to the three in chains. For them, the Quest was over. Surely not even Dullard would be so foolish an optimist as to try and free them. Only a Narrative Hero would be able to pull off such a feat against such odds, and Dullard, talented as he was, had no such advantage, especially with a bitchy and recalcitrant prisoner like Pleasance in tow.

It was always so easy for the Merry Band when they got into these kinds of scrapes. If this was The Narrative, he was sure, one of them would have found a magically secreted lock pick somewhere up his sleeve and would be working to unlock their padlocked wrists in the concealment of the back-to-back huddle that Thud, in his Narrative-minded way, had indeed placed them after the chains had been secured. On a whispered signal, they would have broken their bonds, grabbed their weapons from a convenient heap nearby, and taken out a goodly number of their opponents in their brave rush for the safety of the trees. He had been the victim of such charges on several occasions.

Fodder knew they should be plotting their getaway. They should be talking in codes and whispers, planning their audacious flight to escape the dungeons they had so battled to avoid. But the truth of the matter was that they were chained in a heap with no way to break their bonds and no reasonable expectation of getting free unaided. Without a fresh idea or outside intervention…succinctly put, they were buggered.

"I don't suppose either of you have a lock pick secreted up your sleeves, do you?" he inquired hopelessly.

"Lock pick?" Shoulders gave a snort. "Why would I have a lock pick? I don't know how to pick locks!"

"Just a thought," Fodder muttered gloomily. "Mind you, the state of us, it's not like we'd get far in a fight if we could get free." He sighed wearily. "How's your elbow, Flirt?"

His sigh was echoed. "Sore, but healing. It's not a bad break, and it's my left one so it could be worse. I reckon it'll be good as new in a couple of days or so."

"Just in time for the dungeons," Shoulders added acerbically. "That'll be handy. And my ribs are still killing me, since you didn't ask. I reckon I've broken at least four."

Fodder gritted his teeth, resisting the urge to point out that Shoulders's ribs would have been his next enquiry. The last thing they needed now was to bicker.

Fortunately Flirt headed off any further remarks on the subject. "What about your neck, Fodder?"

Fodder tried an experimental turn of his head but the lolling wobble immediately suggested that this wasn't a good idea. At least his head was back on straight....

"I reckon I've done a couple of vertebrae," he said, wincing at the shooting pain the movement had sent scurrying down his back. "My head's a bit loose and my neck's ruddy sore, but I've had worse. It's not unbearable. If I tilt my head sideways, my helmet's there to keep it steady."

"They could have asked if we were hurt," Shoulders groused, and Fodder could sense his glare as he stared out at the ring of captors that encircled them so casually. "They must have been able to tell we were damaged."

"It's not their fault." Flirt's voice was low, but Fodder was nonetheless sure that he could see several bat-like ears swivelling in their direction. "With Thud howling at them like that, what else were they supposed to do?"

"I've never had any problems with them," Fodder added with equal quietness. "In fact, when I've chatted to Gibber, Fang, and Frenzy, we've always got on quite well."

Flirt leaned closer, her curly hair escaping the grasp of her helmet to tickle against his sore neck. "Are any of those three here?" she asked softly.

And therein lay the problem. Fodder had absolutely no idea.

For in his pursuit of them, Thud, it seemed, had tired of relying on Preen's Disposables in his effort to gain revenge and had decided to call in the big boys. Looped around them in a firm, if rather reluctant-looking circle, were just over a dozen claw-fingered, heavy-toothed

Assorted Freakish Creatures.

Fodder had always liked working with the AFCs. He had spent an enjoyable half hour a couple of Quests back discussing tactics with Fang and Frenzy before a pitched battle and, of course, he'd played chess with Gibber after the latter had eaten his innards in an ambush. But the trouble he'd always had in trying to strike up any kind of permanent friendship was that, more than any other person in the land, it was impossible to know what an AFC would look like from one Quest or even one scene to the next. When he'd chatted to Fang and Frenzy, they'd been altered into orcs with heavy jaws, boar-like faces, and leathery green skin. The Gibber who'd eaten his innards had been a vicious goblin with saw-like teeth and spindly limbs. He'd met them stretched and stout, broad and bandy, scaled and furred, reptilian, insect, and beast alike. Fodder had the utmost respect for their work, but their ever-shifting features made it very difficult to have any idea whom he was talking to.

The AFCs of this Quest had no specific name; they were simply *the creatures*. Their appearance was basically monkey-like, excepting the fact that few monkeys were known to have huge bat-like ears, grey-scaled skin, vast leathery wings that protruded from their backs, and mouths overrun by an unnecessary number of teeth. In Narrative, they were a terrifying force designed to strike fear into the hearts of all unfortunate enough to cross their paths. Out of it, however...

As best he could, Fodder glanced around at the professional monsters holding them captive. One of the nearby AFCs was sharpening his claws thoughtfully with what looked like a nail file. Another was peering into his friend's mouth as he helped him to adjust his teeth into a more pleasingly crooked arrangement. Yet another was consuming an apple in a messy hail of peel as he mulled over what looked like a sheet of fresh instructions. And as for the rest—well, most were slouching around or lingering with their arms crossed and looking, in spite of their frightening appearance, not remotely threatening at all. What they mostly looked was bored.

Bored and irritated. And to judge by the huffy half-glances they were slipping in a certain direction, the source of their irritation was something they and Fodder shared.

"I don't care what it's doing over there! This is more important!"

Thud's rising holler was enough of a distraction to pull Fodder away from his own internal conversation in time to hear the far more reasonable retort.

"Forgive me, but it is not up to you or me to tell The Narrative what is important, Thud. The Narrative decides for itself."

"But it's decided *wrong!*" Like a toddler having a tantrum, the huge, bearded brute actually stamped his foot in fury. "We've got them, right here and now! We have to wipe them out."

"But we don't have the princess! And that, I think you'll agree, is more important!" The Officious Courtier whom Thud was haranguing was a tall, prim, white-haired man with loping limbs like a fastidious scarecrow and a nose that was both highly distinctive and very familiar. Fodder could see that it was from his Uncle Primp's side of the family that Dullard had gotten both his most distinguishing facial feature and his infinite well of patience.

"But I want to kill him back!" Thud's roar almost shook the nearby treetops. "Why can't that be Torsheid's big entrance? Why can't he stride in, having wreaked glorious vengeance for his brother's death on the two bastards and the stupid wench that stole the princess in the first place?"

"Wench?" Fodder felt their shared chains jerk as Flirt's head whipped round furiously. Her shoulder dug harshly into his arm as she yanked at her bonds. *"Wench?* Why that..."

"Ow! Flirt!" Shoulders's exclamation implied that Fodder was not the only one getting a battering. "Bloody hell! *We* didn't say it!"

But the chains continued to twist painfully at the Barmaid's struggles. "I'll give him *wench*, the stupid, smelly, weak-blooded, ham-fisted, bottom-slapping git! I'm not taking this, not from him, not anymore! Not after I've had to put up with his groping, dirty hands and his slobbery, beardy lips, having to smile as he gave me bruised thighs and a pinched arse! Just unchain me and get me my sword, and I'll give that bastard *wench!* I'll—"

The tirade stopped in its tracks, halted by the firm but gentle placing of a grey-scaled, many-clawed hand over her face. The monkey-faced reptilian AFC who had silenced her shrugged his winged shoulders with a smile that was almost apologetic.

"Look, pipe down, yeah?" he said, his voice both reasonable and unexpectedly normal given that it was emerging from a mouth with more teeth than was good for it. "'Cos Beardy over there ain't going to give a monkey's what you think, but if you keep on yelling, he might just ask us to shut you up and we don't want to do that any more than you'd want us to. We don't want to be here any more than you either, but it doesn't look like any of us'll be getting a choice about it. So just pipe down. Okay?"

The look on the horrific face was almost pleading. Flirt's eyebrows remained knitted together in a furious line, but she nonetheless gave a grudging but distinct nod. Gently, the AFC withdrew his hand and, when the reluctant silence held, he nodded with a toothy smile and stepped back again.

"Ta," he thanked her softly.

Fodder took note of the quiet looks the scaly creatures were exchanging as they glanced back towards where their Officious Courtier and the Barbarian continued to wrangle. As Flirt's intervener had stated, it could not have been any plainer that they had no desire to be here. The AFCs were an elite force of monstrous predators In Narrative, and it was as such, Fodder suspected, that Thud had recruited them. But what the Barbarian had failed to account for was the fact that out of Narrative, they were simply a bunch of folks doing their jobs.

Fortunately, perhaps, Flirt's rant had not distracted Thud from his own raving.

"...need to be killed and seen to be killed! I want Narrative justice! I want them taken down and you, you stupid idiot, you're getting in my way! Why wouldn't you want them to pay after kidnapping the princess..."

"But they don't have her now!" As his voice rose in angry retort, it was apparent Primp's reservoir of patience was rapidly draining away. Clearly, he lacked his nephew's stamina for enduring abuse. "And the princess is what matters here! Weren't you paying attention when I showed you what my instructions said?" He shook a little green-grey book in Thud's direction. "As far as The Narrative is concerned, they no longer have the princess! They no longer matter! They can be sent off to the dungeons without The Narrative being involved!" He took a short gulp of breath, his face wavering slightly but remaining set. "It's Prince Tretaptus they're after now. He's the only kidnapper they care about, and he is still at large."

Fodder's head darted up quickly—too quickly, as it turned out; it lolled forwards onto his chest with irritating looseness. It took several sharp jerks of his body to fling it back into place.

But the distraction did not deflect from what he had just heard.

Dullard! Dullard is free!

He'd clearly had a run-in with The Narrative, since they'd identified him by his character. But the fact that he was free afterwards was a bloody good hint that he had defied it successfully and gotten away with the princess to boot. And as long as he remained at large, there was still hope for all of them. Even if they locked them away, as long as Dullard could keep fighting for them, there was a chance of being heard, a chance of release....

But as he settled his head back into place, Fodder realised he had not been the only one to take note of Dullard's Narrative name. The ears of every single AFC had pricked up.

Of course! Fodder had almost forgotten the rest of that conversation back in the Magnificent City what felt like forever ago. Dullard had said he'd been an AFC prisoner once, that he'd enjoyed his time in their captivity, which implied that they'd gotten along. Yes, he'd even mentioned that one of them had taught him the harpsichord....

The sudden interest of the AFCs certainly seemed to imply that they'd been friends. Maybe they could use that to persuade them to let them go....

"We can't just let them get away with this!" The one person who didn't seem interested in the Rejected Suitor's involvement was Thud. "I want every man in this kingdom to see me give them what's coming to them! I want to speak to Strut about this! Go get him!"

Primp drew himself up. "He is in the middle of co-ordinating a vital pursuit!" he retorted, the slight tremble to his prim voice the only hint that the person being pursued was his nephew. "The prince is lost in the forest, wandering without direction—they think he may be looking for your prisoners. Strut has to organise the efforts to corner him and get the princess back. He's not going to come running because you're in a mood."

"Fine!" Thud snapped back. "Then you take me to him! Go on! Lead the way!"

Primp shot a glance at his freakish charges and the prisoners they encircled. "But…"

"You watch the prisoners!" Thud's voice was harsh as he glared at the suddenly less indolent AFCs. "Take these but don't get too close to them in case they try anything, and don't leave this clearing either! And if you see anything suspicious, you come and get me. Right?"

The nearest winged figure—Fodder thought it might have been the one who'd silenced Flirt, although the AFCs all looked so alike, it was hard to be sure—stepped forward and nodded as he caught the keys that Thud had thrown. He fixed them carefully to the rough leather belt straps he wore looped around his scaled body. "You've got it. If we see anything, we'll come right to you."

"You'd better!" Snarling, Thud took a firm hold on Primp's narrow arm and hauled him, protesting, off into the trees. "Right! Where is he? I'm going to let him know exactly what I…"

The angry, echoing voice was swallowed a moment later by the trees. Both captors and prisoners gave visible sags of relief.

"Bloody great oaf," Fodder heard one toothy figure mutter. "Who does he think he is?"

"Power's gone to his head," the first AFC replied as he turned back from the trees. "He's Merry Band, isn't he? Answers to the Hero. He's not used to being in charge of things."

"He's treating us like we're still In Narrative." The nail-filer had abandoned his task to join in. "There's no call for it."

"Nor for pushing Primp 'round either," one of the tooth-fiddlers added. "Ain't his place."

Fodder knew an encouraging start to his kind of conversation when he heard it. "Thud shouldn't have the right to push you around just because he's a Principal, you know. As a matter of fact, that's why we…"

But the first AFC had already raised one clawed hand. "Mate, I wouldn't waste your breath," he advised in a firm but friendly manner. "We know what you and your friends are about. We've got damned good ears in this shape, and we've been listening to Thud, Primp, and Strut hissing on about you lot for a couple of days now. And whilst we have plenty of respect for your nerve and sympathy for the spot you're in, your crusade ain't for the likes of us." He grinned widely. "'Cos we like what we do. We got no problems with our life apart from Thud, and he's only around 'cos of you lot anyway. We hate to be self-centred, like, but there's nothing but trouble in all this for us. So sorry but no thanks, okay?"

Fodder opened his mouth, his brain forming half a dozen fresh retorts, but there was something about the set of the leathery winged shoulders around him that told him that this was a battle he was very unlikely to win.

"You've made your minds up already, haven't you?" he said softly.

The lead AFC nodded. "Yep. Sorry."

"And there's nothing I can say to change your mind?"

"'Fraid not, Fodder."

The use of his name startled him slightly, although he wasn't sure why it should. He took a gamble. "Gibber?"

The AFC grinned again, almost wryly. "Nah, it's Fang, mate. That's Gibber." He gestured to the nail-filer stood beside him, who waved with a clack of his teeth. "Good on you for taking a pot, though. Most folk don't even try."

Fodder joined in the round of wry smiles although his remained deeply unimpressive compared to his captors'. "I'm sorry. You all change so much, it's so hard to tell…"

"No problem, mate." Fang gave a hissing chuckle. "Most humans can't." Out of nowhere, his crooked smile turned oddly nostalgic. "Only ever met one who could, and even I'm damned if I know how." His expression was fond. "How was it he said he did it, Frenzy?"

"Something about our bone structure, he reckoned." The AFC who had called Thud an oaf was the one who answered. "Whatever fiddling they did on the outside, the shape underneath was the same, he said. You just had to know what to look for." He laughed out loud, an odd, whooping noise that bounced harshly off the trees. "Said he wanted to do a study on it! Bless him! He wanted to do a study on everything!"

"Bloody good singer too," Gibber added, to the thoughtful nods of his companions. "Best Ophelion we ever had. That rendition of 'The Maid of Mercy' he did—well, I'm not ashamed to admit he damned near made me cry."

"That last line," Frenzy agreed. "The final note—that was a thing of *beauty*. Our Dramatic Society was never the same after we had to give him back." He shook his head. "Poor bugger. He's wasted at that Palace."

Only an idiot would have failed to twig whom they were talking about or miss the opportunity implicit in their words. Fodder opened his mouth, anxious to explain that they knew Dullard too, that he was helping them, and that they agreed that he was wasted and surely, if he was their friend, they'd want to help him help them…

"*Mind you.*" There was something so very pointed about Fang's interruption that Fodder's mouth snapped shut almost of its own accord. "He *did* used to have some funny old ideas. And though he'd never dream of complaining, you could tell he never did much like that he couldn't use his talents In Narrative. Don't you reckon, Chomp?"

"Yeah," one of the tooth-fiddlers, apparently Chomp, agreed with highly deliberate thoughtfulness as he tapped one clawed finger with faux casualness against his chin. "Even though we came along on this gig 'cos we got told by Primp he was in trouble, like, and they'd kidnapped him along with the princess, I can't help but think, you know, if he wouldn't be more inclined to *help them out.*"

"I mean, maybe these ears of mine are playing me up, but it did sound awful like Primp said they was out chasing him." Frenzy waded in firmly, emphasizing every word before he expelled it into the air. "And I can't see why he'd be on the run if he was a prisoner. You'd think he'd just give that princess right back, wouldn't you?" He shook his head, his lips pursued with highly suspect sincerity. "Mind you, knowing him, it could just be one of those funny ideas. He does get them and he never means any harm. I can't imagine he'd cause *real trouble*, not our mate Dullard. Can you, boys?"

There was a very deliberate chorus of agreement.

"Good thing this is all *speculation,* though." Yet again it was Fang's pointed enunciation that overrode Fodder's attempt to speak. "I mean, 'cos if it weren't speculation and some stupid bugger opened up his fat gob and told us it were true, we'd be *obliged* to turn our mate in, being as how we *definitely ain't* on their side at all. But we know nothing. Ain't our business if no one's *actually* told us."

Fodder closed his mouth again, but it was an effort to keep himself from smiling as sudden hope welled up inside him.

Aha…so that's how it's going to go.…

"And though we wouldn't *dream* of helping our prisoners escape in *any* way," Gibber enjoined speculatively, "if they *were* out chasing good old Dullard in the woods, for whatever reason, and he happened to stumble across us here and, well, we happened to get distracted or something by…I don't know, a pretty bird, say?"

"Maybe an interesting tree?" Fang added with a nod.

"Yes, interesting trees are *very* distracting," Gibber agreed. "And, well, for some reason, if he took it on himself to nick the keys off Fang's leather belt and free them to run off while our backs were turned, well, I don't see how it could possibly be *our* fault."

"'Course, it is just *speculation*," Chomp exclaimed with a sigh. "'Cos maybe if I'd been listening, I'd have heard someone say he's lost out there and doesn't know where these people he might take it on himself to free are."

"I know," Fang agreed with a slow, carefully formed grimace. "And, I mean, if—*not* that we ever would do it, of course—we felt inclined to draw him here, it's not like we can go off and find him or call out for him seeing as we don't know what he's doing out there and can't possibly dream of leaving our prisoners anyway. So, as I said, if—*not* that we would ever do it, of course—we were going to try and draw him here, I wonder how we'd do it."

"Speculatively?" Frenzy asked.

"Oh, *completely*."

"I think this is a bit of a dodgy subject, you know." It was Gibber who intervened, tapping his clawed fingers carefully against one scaled leg. "But all this talk of the old days when Dullard was in the Barren Wastelands Dramatic Society with us and him performing 'The Maid of Mercy' has got me all *nostalgic*." He glanced around with a smile that was both beatific and utterly crammed with teeth. "So, what do you reckon, lads? Is anyone else up for a nice *loud* singsong?"

* * *

There was no doubt about it. He had definitely passed that particular gnarled oak once already.

Breathing hard and bathed in sweat, Dullard stumbled to a weary halt. The weight of the princess over his shoulders was not overwhelming, but it was hardly a boon either. He could only be thankful that, to judge by the lack of kicking he had received, she had not fully woken. Behind him, through the trees, he could see the vivid glow of The Narrative raking its way along beneath the leafy canopy, could hear the strident voices of the Merry Band as they plunged through the undergrowth aided by weapons and magic alike. Mysterious powers had been hauled emphatically out of the bag. They *really* wanted the princess back this time.

And he alone could stop them. Everything Fodder and the others had fought for depended on his ability to keep Pleasance from their grasp.

And what was he doing? Running in lost and hopeless circles in the woods.

He gave serious consideration to muttering a curse word. How had things all gone so quickly wrong?

The worst of it was that he felt so silly. He'd been amazed when he'd stepped into Narrative and found how easily he had kept hold of his personality and purpose. The confidence that had filled him had been glorious. He'd seen the opportunity to end the Quest by ending Bumpkin, and he'd stepped in quickly to take it in spite of his personal misgivings. But he knew now that it hadn't been *his* confidence at all, that The Narrative had shown far greater cunning than he had given it credit for. For it was that confidence that had got him into place and kept him talking, compelled him to apologise instead of simply striking off Bumpkin's head and having done with it. Such violence was against his nature, and The Narrative had known he'd hesitate. It had let him be too much himself. It had used his own personality against him!

But he would be ready for it next time. He would be stronger. If he got the chance.

He *hoped.*

The Narrative was getting cleverer, it was true. But they also had it worried. Why else would it have been forced to resort so much to its emergency standby, manifesting Bumpkin's mysterious powers? They'd left it no option but to start cheating in order to stop them. And that, it had to be said, was a very hopeful sign.

But all the hope in the world would prove no use if he were to be captured....

He glanced around at the surrounding wall of trees once more. He could hear voices, closing in from all directions. To his right, The Narrative light was growing brighter.

If only he knew which way the others had gone. If he could just find some direction, some purpose, some sign…

And then, he heard it.

"…as the wind blows *through* her corn-silk *hair!*"

"Oh the *maid!*"

"Oh the *maid!*"

"Oh the *fair, fair maid!*"

Dullard blinked. For a moment, he wondered if his brain had somehow imploded and was spitting out random pieces of his past into his ears…

But no. It was real. He could hear it. He could hear voices. And they were singing…

His song.

"As she *dances* with a *grace* so pure and *rare!*"

"Oh the *maid!*"

"Oh the *maid!*"

"Oh the *fair, fair maid!*"

His mind flashed back to his time in the Barren Wastelands, to the cheerful, friendly souls that had lain beneath a range of deliberately grotesque exteriors—not to mention a surprisingly fine range of singing voices. He'd been so flattered when they'd allowed him, a rank amateur, to join in with the latest project Doom the Dark Lord had come up with for their little Dramatic Society, a charming musical romance called 'The Maid of Mercy', although performing this touching story of forlorn love opposite a female AFC called Mania, whose blonde wig had fitted most snugly over her tall, sharp antennae, had added an interesting new dimension to his acting. And there had been one song in particular that he had loved to perform, and that several of the most hard-bitten AFCs had insisted that his performance of the last line in particular always made them melt to hear. He had known they were simply being polite to a guest, of course, but it had been a nice thing to be told all the same….

And he was in no doubt who the singers were. Nobody else could harmonise quite like the chorus of the Barren Wastelands Dramatic Society.

But why would they be here? Why would they be singing it now unless…

Unless they knew he was out here. Unless they were trying to find him.

"Over *rock*, over *hill*, down the *meadow* and the *dale!*"

"She will *dance*, she will *dance*, through the *forest* and the *vale!*"

A more suspicious mind than Dullard's might have suspected a trap. He was very much aware of that. But he was also aware that the singing voices belonged to his friends, and he was going to trust them.

He glanced at The Narrative light, its gleam growing ever closer. He didn't have much choice.

Balancing the still silent princess carefully over his shoulders, Dullard steeled himself and moved quickly in the direction of the song.

* * *

Over the course of his career as a Disposable, Fodder had been witness from the sidelines to many an awe-inspiring sight. He had seen volcanoes explode and castles crumble. He had seen dragons roar and magic burn. He had seen epic battles and heroic last stands. But he had never in all of his days seen a sight to match a dozen grey-scaled, leathery winged beasties clustered together in a variety of heroic poses with their clawed hands clasped as they raised their tooth-filled maws in beautifully harmonised song.

"…as the *wind* blows *through* her corn-silk *hair!*"

"Oh the *maid!*"

"Oh the *maid!*"

"Oh the *fair, fair maid!*"

"As she *dances* with a *grace* so pure and *rare!*"

"Oh the *maid!*"

"Oh the *maid!*"

"Oh the *fair, fair maid!*"

Gibber—at least Fodder was fairly sure that it was Gibber—was leading the vocals, with a fey and wistful expression on his face as he raised his scaly palms towards the sky as though in prayer. It was a posture that Bard would have envied. His companions, no less misty-eyed, had also turned their gazes skywards, although Fodder did note that their bat-like ears were swivelling in a variety of directions as though raking the trees for some sign of approach.

"Over *rock*, over *hill*, down the *meadow* and the *dale!*"

"She will *dance*, she will *dance*, through the *forest* and the *vale!*"

"And I *pray* that when she *comes*, she will *dance* before me *too!*"

"For, oh *fair* and *beauteous* maid, *I love you!*"

There was a massed gasp of indrawn breath. And then with barely a hesitation, the AFCs launched *en masse* into their next verse.

"Oh my *fine and bonnie* lass, will you *come* with *me?*"

"Oh my *maid!*"

"Oh my *maid!*"

"Oh my *fair, fair maid!*"

"For 'tis *only* in your *arms* I feel I am *free!*"

"Oh my *maid!*"

"Oh my *maid!*"

"Oh my *fair, fair maid!*"

But something was changing. Although not one single voice missed a beat, a mass of ears swivelled as one towards the trees just off to Fodder's right. Unable to turn his head without embarrassingly lolling, Fodder was unable to squint in the appropriate direction; but out of the corner of his eye, he did spot a dark shape lurking in the shadow of the leafy boughs.

Please be Dullard, please be Dullard, please, please be Dullard....

"Down to *sea*, up to *sky*, I will *follow* where you *go!*"

"For my *life* is not mine, on your *mercy* I must *throw!*"

"And I *beg of you some sign* that you *hear my plea!*"

And then, with a unity that was both abrupt and shocking, the AFCs clamped their mouths shut and, as one, flung their left arms out almost in supplication towards the shadow in the trees.

And from behind the trunk of a knotty old oak, a lone voice rose and in a soaring tenor, stepped in to complete the song.

"For *without you, all means naught to meeeeeee!*"

The powerful note echoed against the tree trunks for a moment, bouncing and dancing as though it intended to live on forever. But slowly, inevitably, the roar of the waterfall and the rustle of the leaves subdued it into gentle silence.

Several of the AFCs were snuffling their noses and nodding with profound approval. Fodder could have sworn he saw Chomp wiping his eyes as he muttered "Bloody beautiful projection…" into his fingers.

It was the sound of Fang's hands clapping together that brought the brief, wistful moment of musical appreciation to an end. Rubbing his scales together thoughtfully, he did not offer so much as a glance in the direction of the trees as he turned to face his compatriots.

"Well, I don't know about you lads," he exclaimed with vast and hearty enthusiasm. "But I feel much better for that *merry singsong!*" He leaned forwards then, extending one clawed finger before him and waggling it in emphasis at every word he spoke. "But we'd best be *careful*. It'd be *easy* for a bunch of prisoners to *escape* if we all turned our backs at once, like, and got *distracted* by something like an *interesting tree* or a *pretty bird.*"

"He's bang on right!" Gibber strolled over to his side. "We have to be on our guard, just like Thud told us. We have to report *everything* we happen to *see!* So we must make sure that what we *see* is what matters! We can't let ourselves get…" He trailed off with a distinctly over-dramatic gasp of indrawn breath. "Oh *look! A pretty bird!*"

Frenzy mirrored Gibber's epic gasp. "Where?"

"In that *interesting tree!*" One clawed hand shot out, pointing with melodramatic fervour in the direction of the slope down which Fodder and his companions had tumbled. "Hey, everyone! Turn this way and look at the pretty bird in an interesting tree!"

As one, a dozen leathery winged shapes turned away from Fodder and his companions to stare with a deliberate intensity in the opposite direction. And in the shadows, Fodder could see a figure was moving, coming closer, sneaking at a crouch into the light.…

It was Dullard. His clothes looked battered and his face was bloody, but he grinned dryly at his friends before shooting a fond glance in the direction of the cluster of AFCs in the middle of the clearing. A blue velvet bundle was slung over his shoulders; carefully, he laid Pleasance down on the edge of the grass. As far as Fodder could tell from the lack of kicking and struggling as Dullard had carried her, the princess had yet to rouse from her trip over the waterfall.

"It's *very* pretty!" Fang's voice rang out once more. "And the tree is *very* interesting! I *do* hope that no old mate of ours comes sneaking out of the woods and steals the keys to the chains from off my belt while I'm looking at them!"

"Yes!" Gibber added. "It would be *terrible* if our prisoners were being set free while our backs are turned!"

With an unseen nod of acknowledgement for the hint, Dullard set off across the clearing at a soft-footed scurry, half-crouched as though he expected a hidden blow to fall. As far as Fodder could tell, his quiet caution was unnecessary—he suspected that Dullard could have crossed the clearing doing back-flips with bells tied to his wrists and ankles whilst yodelling and playing the drums for all the attention the AFCs would have paid him. But it seemed to make him comfortable and it was hardly the time to start critiquing his rescue.

Dullard had reached the wall of leathery wings. Gingerly, he moved up behind Fang and gently began to peel one of the bat-like protuberances out of the way as he slipped one hand towards the leather straps wrapped around the creature's body.

"Do you know," Fang remarked loudly as his companions continued to umm and ahh about what a fine combination of bird and tree they'd happened to stumble across, "I'm so intrigued by this pretty bird that I probably wouldn't even notice if someone was looking for my keys on the *wrong side* of my belt!"

"Oops!" Dullard let the wing drop back as he scurried, still bent over, to Fang's other side. "Sorry!" he whispered hurriedly.

"Gosh!" Chomp remarked as Dullard set to work teasing back the other wing. "Ain't the world full of surprises today? That gust of wind moving through the interesting tree sounded just like someone apologising! Did anyone else hear it?"

"Mmmm! Yep! A surprising gust of wind!"

"It's the kind of thing you'd expect from such an interesting tree, though."

"Yeah, 'specially one such a pretty bird would choose to sit in!"

There was a metallic rattle and a grunt as Dullard yanked the ring of keys free of Fang's belt. Carefully, he drew them clear of the hanging wing and delicately released his hold on it.

"Thank you!" he hissed softly as he turned and moved swiftly across the grass in the direction of his chained-up companions.

"You know," Gibber declared as Dullard arrived at Fodder's side, flashing the three of them a quick smile as he wiggled down between Fodder and Flirt and set to work on the padlock of their mutual chains,

"I think that pretty bird must be the rare and famous *Gratitude Bird.* You know, the one whose call sounds like someone saying *thank you?*"

"A Gratitude Bird. Ain't we lucky?"

"What a wonderful, if terribly distracting, thing to see!"

There was a loud clunk. With a rattle, Fodder felt his chains slump. Hurriedly, he snatched his hands free of the restraints, just managing to catch his loose head and push it back as his momentum almost toppled it. He saw Flirt stagger to her feet, gripping her left elbow as she turned and darted in the direction of the packs. Shoulders was slower to rise, grasping his torso with a wince, but Dullard was rapidly at his side, helping him upright with solicitous hands. Fodder was quick to join him.

"Are you all right?" he hissed, gesturing to the knot of blood tangling the prince's dark hair and streaking down his cheek.

Dullard nodded. "It's superficial. I bounced off a few rocks but no serious damage. How about you?"

"Broken neck. It'll heal but it's a nuisance." Fodder pushed his wobbly head back into place once more. "We fell down that ruddy slope over there and rolled straight up to Thud. Flirt's done her elbow in and Shoulders has cracked some ribs, but it's nothing we can't work through. The princess?"

Dullard moved quickly to where he'd abandoned Pleasance's slumped form. He paused to check her eyelids before hoisting her with thoughtful care back over his shoulders.

"She hasn't woken," he murmured as he hurried back to join them. Flirt returned a moment later, wordlessly tossing one pack to Shoulders as she lifted the other and handed back their swords. "I thought she wasn't that badly hurt, but I haven't had a peep out of her. She must have hit her head harder than I thought."

Shoulders gave an indelicate snort as he strapped his sword back to his waist with a distinct air of relief. "If she was awake, you'd know about it, especially with the gag off," he muttered. "Count your blessings!"

"So now what?" Flirt exclaimed. "Where do we go from here?"

"As far away from The Narrative as we can get." Fodder gestured to the vivid light patrolling the nearby woods. It was unmistakably angling in their direction. "We need to take a few days and get healed before we're ready to try anything."

"Salty Port still?" Shoulders hissed.

Flirt shook her head. "Bad idea. The Narrative's heading there next, isn't it? What about the Wild Forest?"

Fodder pursed his lips. "Well..."

"You know, interesting as this tree is and pretty as I find this bird, there's only so long a chap can hang around hoping his prisoners aren't *bloody well hurrying up and escaping!*"

Fang's voice carried a slightly irritable edge. Gibber's tone was an unmistakable echo of the sentiment: "Yes! It would be terrible if instead of standing around jabbering, they *sodding ran for it* right now!"

"Mmmm!" Frenzy assented. "Especially since, besides the wind in the trees and the song of the Gratitude Bird, I'm sure I can hear *Primp* heading *back this way!*"

"Bugger!" Shoulders was moving towards the trees in an instant. "Come on, we have to go!"

"Wait!" Flirt cried. "We owe them a Gratitude Bird! *Thank you!*"

"Thanks!" Fodder echoed.

"Thank you so much, everyone!" Dullard added, swinging round so hurriedly that a mass of blonde curls only narrowly missed Fodder's face. "I hope we can catch up soon! Oh, and lovely harmonies on the second verse!"

"Ah, the Gratitude Bird!" Fodder heard Gibber exclaim. "Such a nice song!"

Dullard was already turning back, and this time Fodder had time to duck as blonde hair swirled above his lolling head. He blinked. Wait a minute... Had Pleasance's eyes been open?

He hurried past Dullard as he followed Flirt and Shoulders rapidly towards the far side of the clearing and peered as best he could into her supine face. But no, the Royal eyelids were firmly sealed shut....

He shook himself. She couldn't be awake or she'd be kicking up a fuss, trying to get back to Bumpkin and The Narrative. He must have imagined it.

The edge of the woods loomed before them. Following Flirt's back as best he could with his joggling head, he darted into their embrace, caught his foot on a jutting root, stumbled sideways, and fell straight into Primp.

It was hard to tell who was the most surprised. The Officious Courtier had clearly been scurrying along in something of a hurry as he darted out from behind the unintentional concealment of the tree over which Fodder had tripped, his prissy tunic sweat-soaked, his momentum halted by the impact of Fodder's body. His eyes bulged as the Disposable staggered back, scrabbling at the bark of the tree to regain his balance and straightening his head as Flirt and Shoulders wheeled in horror beside him. And then his gaze skipped past Fodder and fixed upon the dishevelled, princess-laden form of his nephew.

Dullard's eyes were wide. He bit his lip.

"Uncle..." he started anxiously.

Primp closed his eyes, one thrust palm whipping out to cut off the sentence. "Don't!" he exclaimed, his voice taut and pained. "Just don't say a word, Dullard; I don't want to hear it." His eyes still closed, he grimaced and shook his head. "I thought your mother raised you better than this. What's she going to say when she finds out, hmmm?"

Dullard gave a nervous little smile. "She always used to tell me that I could do whatever I liked as long as I had a good reason for it."

Primp opened his eyes again simply for the pleasure of rolling them. "Oh, she would, wouldn't she?" He shook his head once more as he glared around at the four still frozen, still horrified statues before him, settling once more upon his nephew. "I must be mad," he muttered caustically. "Right. This is for your mother's sake and hers alone. You've got twenty seconds and then I yell for Thud. Don't waste them." He glared as he drew in a deep breath. "Twenty!" he snapped out. "Nineteen! Eighteen!"

"Run!" Fodder didn't need Dullard's exclamation to set his legs pumping again; both Shoulders and Flirt were already on the move. These woods were less heavily thicketed than those atop the impromptu waterfall, but as Primp's countdown echoed in his ears, he knew that thinner undergrowth would be of no advantage when their flight might be more easily spotted. Through the trees away to their left, The Narrative gleamed between the trunks, a predator waiting to pounce. If they were forced into a Narrative fight with the injuries they were carrying...

Trees whipped past on either side as Fodder stumbled over the uneven ground, his madly wobbling head making it almost impossible for him to tell where he was going. He could catch only glimpses of the silvery shapes that were Flirt and Shoulders as they plunged through the trees ahead of him, of the pale outline of Dullard with his blue-and-yellow burden as he huffed and puffed at his side. And behind, fading but not far enough, he could hear the final faint whisper of Primp's countdown.

"Two! One! *Thud! Over here!* They've escaped and they're *over here!*"

Bugger.

The whack of a branch against his face knocked his head to an irritating angle. Pursuit or not, he couldn't go on like this.

Flirt and Shoulders didn't notice as he staggered to a halt, too caught up in their own flight, but Dullard skidded to a stop a few yards in front of him, Pleasance bobbing loosely as he wheeled sharply, his lips parted with questions. But Fodder had no time for them.

"Keep going!" he snapped. "I've got to strap my neck!"

Dullard's head swivelled towards the Narrative light gleaming through the trees. It was undoubtedly getting brighter and the distant sounds of hoofbeats echoed against the trunks. "But..."

"Go!" With a hearty tear, Fodder ripped a vast strip off his battered surcoat and began to wrap it hurriedly around his loose spine. Dullard dithered a moment longer, but at Fodder's fierce expression, he screwed up his nose and, with obvious reluctance, turned and bolted in pursuit of the others.

It was the work of seconds to wind the thick material into place and knot it firmly. It was no neck brace, but it would keep him looking in one direction until...

Light...

The arrow missed the Sleiss soldier's head by inches. Zahora hissed and ground her teeth as the tattered rascal gaped at her for an instant before turning and bolting for the cover of a nearby stand of oak. As he plunged into the leaves...

...lost

Damn, damn, damn! Fodder cursed fluently as he staggered, struggling to shake off the weight of the sudden burst of Narrative as he hurled himself as fast as he dared in the opposite direction. Where the bloody hell had *that* come from? The Narrative had been close but not that—

A burst of light erupted in the trees ahead of him. He caught the barest glimpse of shining metal plates and a horse's flank before he dived headfirst into a nearby stand of hawthorn, crouching and struggling to suppress the sound of his breathing as the brightness skimmed past him in the flurry of hooves and creaking metal that signified Clank.

Realisation dawned. Oh, the Taskmaster was clever; he gave the blighter that. The Merry Band must have split up amongst the trees, and now The Narrative was bouncing from point of view to point of view, ready to pounce at the first sign of them.

The glow of light vanished as abruptly as it had appeared. Slowly, Fodder backed his way out of the hawthorn bushes, drawing his sword in an awkward, steely shiver. Why did he have the feeling this was not going to end well?

"Diiiieeee!!!!"

The swing of the axe blade missed Fodder's face by less than an inch. As he stumbled back with a cry of shock, Thud's vast, bearded face leered down at him in manic fury.

"You won't get away this time!" he roared madly, spittle flying from his lips to splatter across Fodder's cheeks with unpleasant dampness as one beefy hand lashed out to slam him against the branches. "I'm going to hack you to bits, you little bastard! I'm going to rip off your limbs and wear them as trophies! I'm going..."

Light...

"...to see you rue the day you slaughtered my poor brother!"

Gort the dwarf reined in his mule in sharp, violent shock. His jaw dropped as he drank in the scene before him: the daunted figure of the battered Sleiss soldier, his back pressed against a spiky stand of hawthorn as the towering bulk of a shockingly familiar figure loomed over him with his awesome axe raised high.

"Halheid?" he exclaimed in disbelief. "But you're dead!"

But as the bearded figure's gaze snapped towards him in shock, Gort realised all at once that he was mistaken. For although the likeness to his poor, dead companion was striking, there was something in the set of this man's nose and the shape of his eyes that spoke of subtle yet profound differences.

But then, who was he?

"What differences?" the Sleiss soldier snapped with sudden and inexplicable fervour. "He's exactly the same!"

A meaty knuckle slapped across the soldier's face, driving him to the ground with a visage stained in scarlet. He started to rise, grasping at the strange bandage of ripped material that fluttered at his throat, but the so-familiar stranger's boot slammed ruthlessly three times into the side of his head and dropped him into stillness.

For an instant, it seemed to Gort that this bearded newcomer's hands were shaking as though against some invisible foe. He seemed to struggle, apparently attempting to raise his axe for a killing blow; but after a moment, the strange effort was abandoned. He grimaced as he turned to Gort.

"I am not Halheid," he declared gruffly. "I am his brother. I am Torsheid. I came here from the mountains to take revenge upon those foul animals who slaughtered my kin." His bearded jaw tightened truculently as he jerked his head in the direction of his unconscious captive. "And I will not be denied it!"

"And we would not deny you." The echoing voice caused Gort to jump but it was too accustomed to otherwise distress him. With a flurry of hooves and a glint of metal, Sir Roderick emerged from the shadows of the trees to join them. The knight came to a halt a few yards down the path from the barbarian and his prisoner, lifting his visor with a respectful nod. "It is your right, brother of my friend. His life is forfeit to you, and we would not challenge you. But first, there are things we must know of this miscreant. We must take him to our sorcerer, who has, by means of rude enchantments, the ability to extract from him what needs to be known. But afterwards..." The knight smiled grimly. "We shall watch you dispatch the fiend with pleasure."

The enormous, hulking man's lips split into a cold, deliberate smile. Turning, he hoisted his axe high above the soldier's head and, with all the force he could muster, dragged the trouble-making soldier into a vindictive headlock. And then, with Roderick leading the way, the little party moved off into the woods.

~~~~~~~~~~~~~~~~~~

In the shadow of the trees not far from her companions, Zahora had barely finished cursing her own ill timing over losing sight of the first Sleiss soldier when the bushes before her burst apart and spat another mailed figure in tatty Sleiss livery directly into the small clearing in her horse's path.

It was hard to tell who was more surprised. But the soldier's shock seemed so profound as to almost unman him, for he was staring around with a kind of mute horror, wobbling on his feet as though drunken as he clutched at his head. His hand jerked towards his sword hilt, battling as though against some invisible bond as he struggled to grasp his weapon.

"Oh no!" she heard him keen shrilly. "Oh no, no, no! Leave me alone!"

Bewildered as she was by the man's odd behaviour, Zahora had trained as a warrior from birth, and her bow swept up almost of its own volition. She sighed as she took aim directly between the man's rolling eyes. At least one enemy would trouble them no more....

The blow to her stomach came as a staggering shock. Even as she wheeled, pitching in the saddle, her bow raised, the flat of a sword hurtled round a second time to smash across her helmet and hurled her into the air. Her bow tumbled from her fingers, lost, as she slammed into the ground with a bruising thud. The wind left her lungs in a rush, but nonetheless she groped desperately for her sword hilts as she tried to stagger to her feet. A smaller mailed figure, whose dark curly hair protruded in an unmanly fashion from beneath his helmet, darted round the back of her horse, a bewilderingly beautiful sword grasped in a competent if amateurish fashion. But this time Zahora was ready for the blow, rolling beneath the swing of the blade as she dragged one of her own weapons free. The soldier's fine sword returned again with shocking speed— where had a common Sleiss soldier obtained such a magnificent piece of work? Stolen; it could only be stolen—and the warrior woman barely managed to bring up her own slender blade in response. She whipped her sword around in a complex arc, but her enemy parried the move with irritating ease, ducking under the retaliatory swing and replying with a vicious lunge that only quick reflexes saved her from being skewered on.

She caught a glimpse of the soldier's face. He was grinning with elation.

And then suddenly, her sword went flying. The soldier barrelled into her and smacked her fisted hands aside as his weight descended onto her supine figure and pinned her ruthlessly in place. The hilt of the stolen sword slammed with harsh force into the side of her helmeted head. Zahora blinked, her eyes spinning with stars as she felt the strength abandon her limbs. Dazed and drifting, she looked up.

A confusingly contrite-looking face peered back down at her, with a frown knitting eyebrows that, at such close quarters and even through her daze, looked distinctly, almost impossibly feminine. But how could that be? No woman would be permitted in the army of Sleiss. And no other woman could defeat her in combat! It was rare to even find a man who could.

Through a haze of shifting colours, the soldier bit his/her lip. "I want you to know," she said, and it had to be a she, for the high-pitched voice left very little doubt in the matter, "I have the utmost respect for you." With a yank, Zahora felt her dented helmet being pulled away. "I'm really sorry to do this. But, hey..." The soldier woman's lips quirked slightly. "At least I'm sparing you the badger beard, aren't I?"

Once more the hilt descended and this time, there was no beaten metal to protect her. Pain seared through Zahora's head as everything went...

...dark

Breathing heavily, Flirt heaved one last non-Narrative blow onto her opponent to insure she stayed down out of the light. And then she stared down at the unconscious Harridan, barely able to believe what she'd just done. She'd defeated her heroine. She'd knocked out the Taskmaster's official Warrior Woman. In spite of her guilt, she couldn't help but allow the small, just slightly smug smile that crept across her face. She'd always known she was better than serving tankards of ale and now, to have bested the character she'd always wanted to be...

She shook herself. This was no time for self-congratulation, was it? They had to get out of here!

Besides, she respected Harridan. It was Thud she really wanted to see skewered....

The light of The Narrative had fled the instant her blow had fallen, driven to find new eyes by the loss of its point of view, but The Narrative would know they were here. It would not be long before backup arrived.

She turned towards Zahora's horse, briefly considering the option. But she was no fan of four-legged transport, and a horse was too easily lost to The Narrative's control. She smacked her hands at it, ignoring the pain in her elbow that resulted, and with a whinny, it turned and bolted.

And that just left the two of them.

They should have taken more care in their frantic flight; she could see that now. They should have bothered to pause and check that Dullard and Fodder were still behind them, rather than turning too late to find that both had somehow disappeared. They should have tried harder to stick together. But what was done was done.

Critically, she examined the gaping double wound she'd just gouged in Harridan's head as she clambered to her feet again. It looked fatal enough but was probably fixable if a magic user happened along. Perhaps she ought to cut her head off, just to make sure. After all, this was not a death The Narrative would have wanted. And Shoulders would probably quite enjoy seeing someone else get—

A heavy thud against the grass drew her gaze away from Harridan's staved-in head. A moment later, wide-eyed, the Barmaid was running.

For Shoulders lay in a heap on the ground, gasping and holding his ribs. As she reached him, sheathing her sword, he gritted his teeth and stared up at her with desperate horror.

"I can't do it, Flirt!" he stammered between rasping breaths. "I tried, I really tried, but I can't do it! I can't fight The Narrative!"

"You can!" Struggling to conceal her dismay, Flirt knelt swiftly at her friend's side, grasping his shoulders with determination. "Shoulders, you can, you just need to believe in yourself! You just need to—"

"No! No I can't!" There was desperation in the Disposable's eyes.

"If I go back in there, it'll get me! You have to keep it away from me, Flirt! Keep it away or I'll…"

Hoofbeats tore out of the shadow of the trees just to their left. Branches snapped as a heavy figure on horseback forced his way through. Light flickered through the canopy and then erupted at its edge.

Shoulders stared at the breaking branches with hopeless despair.

"Oh bugg—"

Light…

"—er!"

Sir Roderick reined in with sharp shock as his eyes fell upon the two figures in chain mail crouched upon the forest floor in the small clearing before him. He could feel the fearful burn of their eyes as Gort on his mule and Torsheid, still dragging his unconscious prisoner, came to an equally surprised halt just behind him.

"Not him!" One of the figures emitted a hopeless, desperate whine. "Anyone but him!"

But the smaller figure's eyes had alighted on the motionless figure clamped in Torsheid's grasp. His eyes widened with shock.

"No!" he proclaimed, his voice a shocking high-pitch. "No!" He rocketed to his feet and, with a warrior's instinct, his hand whipped down to haul his impossibly ornate sword from his scabbard in a swift if somewhat ungainly manner. His companion remained slumped on the ground, one hand pressed against his forehead as he gasped and moaned.

"Let him go!" the high-voiced soldier ordered shrilly. "Let him go right now or I'll make you sorry! Just like I made her!"

Roderick felt himself frown. Her? What did he mean by…?

And then, he saw her, slumped in a heap on the ground, blood pouring from a gaping wound in the side of her skull. Only the faintest rise and fall of her chest implied that she had managed to keep clinging to life.

Zahora!

The soldier grimaced. "I knew I should have cut her head off!" Roderick heard him mutter.

But rage was coursing through Sir Roderick's body, white-hot like blacksmith's iron and vicious as the blades it forged. They had a prisoner now, the means to find the Princess Islaine safe and sound. He need show no mercy to these others who had reaped such violence upon a woman he had come to consider as his kin.

"Black dogs!" he bellowed, his heavy broadsword yanked from its sheath with a deathly shiver. "I will make you pay for this infamy! Yah!"

With a jab of his spurs, his heavy war horse thundered into motion. In a few brief strides, it closed the gap between them. The avenging knight rose in his stirrups, raising his blade over his head to deliver a crushing blow. With unexpected bravery, however, the smaller soldier held his ground, gritting his teeth as he raised his finely crafted sword in a pointless effort to parry...

"No!"

With a crash of undergrowth, a slender figure came hurtling out into the clearing just yards in front of Roderick's epic charge. His sword grasped and his face grimly determined, Prince Tretaptus of Mond wheeled on the thundering knight, ducking beneath the swing of his blade with unexpected agility. His own sword darted out, slashing towards Roderick and his mount, but the almost delicate blow struck neither the horse nor its rider.

Instead, it sliced neatly and cleanly through the girth strap of his saddle.

There was no stopping the charge. It was far too late and carried far too much momentum. The soldier grasped his apparently dazed companion and dived for it, leaping aside with inches to spare as the war horse pounded past them. Roderick struggled desperately to keep his balance, but the weight of his swing was already carrying him over, over, down...

With a massive crash of metal and a frantic, wavering screech, the pride of Nyolesse plunged heavily into the leafy mulch of the forest floor.

"Quick, dullard!" The high-pitched soldier seemed to have hurled this remark at Prince Tretaptus, although the half-stunned knight could see no cause for him to insult the man who had just saved him. "You take clank and I'll get thud!"

Roderick shook his head sharply. Either he'd taken a harder whack than he'd believed or the man was talking utter nonsense....

As he shook his dizzy, furious head and grabbed for his broadsword, the knight heard Torsheid gasp with shock.

"By the Lords of Sky and Earth!" he heard the man thunder. "It's a wench!"

Even over the clanking of his armour, Roderick felt the strange, deathly silence that seemed to fall across the narrow glade. And indeed, as he raised his head, he could see that the high-voiced soldier had lost his helmet in his dive, leaving dark, curly hair to flow out and expose the truth beneath.

And the truth beneath was a furious-looking woman, whose fist was clenching her sword hilt so viciously that it seemed impossible not to draw blood as she stared at the barbarian with a hatred so fierce it seemed to burn holes through the air.

"I'll give you *wench*, you groping, bearded git!" she screamed fervently. "You've pinched my arse for the last time!"

And then with the force of a raging bull, she raised her sword and charged.

But Roderick had no time to watch as the angry little woman dived at the brother of his dead friend. For Prince Tretaptus was advancing on him rapidly, sword held professionally low. The silly man's jaw, with its jutting chin, was set firmly. And though his face was tremulous, his eyes were like steel.

"I'm sorry!" he exclaimed, his words a rapid tumble. "But I really do need to kill you now. It's terribly important!"

Roderick shook his head as he finally regained his feet. The stupid man was a buffoon! Surely he would not be so foolish as to try and defeat the greatest knight of Nyolesse!

"I think not!" he hissed through his visor. "Have at you, cur!"

Heaving his enormous broadsword, he swung at the unarmoured man with a tremendous overhand heave but the prince caught his blow upon his own, much smaller blade and, with a gasp of desperate effort, turned it aside. Roderick was quick to reverse the blade but again Tretaptus saw the blow coming, leaping over the swing with an agility unanticipated in so awkward a man and darting forward in a rapid lunge that scored along the side of Roderick's heavy armour-plating with a screech that set his teeth on edge. Grimacing, the knight pounded in once more with a series of vast, damaging blows but Tretaptus was quicker than he appeared, catching each one with a ringing clash on his surprisingly enduring blade. It was all the knight could do to stop himself gritting his teeth in frustration. What was this sword that held so well? Any other weapon would have shattered to pieces against such an onslaught! Why did this one not?

He heard a grunt of profound pain. Glancing up, he saw Torsheid drop to his knees, barely fending off a flurry of sword blows with his axe hilt as he grasped with his free hand the apparently now tender part of his anatomy his female attacker had just kicked. But the attack was unrelenting as chips of woods flew in a hail from the beleaguered weapon.

"Torsheid!" The cry came from Gort. Grabbing his hammer, the bold dwarf hurled himself from his mule and rushed forwards. But he was no warrior, just an engineer, and this woman whose blade spun with such vicious, desperate speed was already turning, weapon held high and braced to strike a deadly blow....

And then, impossibly, at the last instant, the soldier woman twisted her blade out of Gort's path. The dwarf stumbled past her, carried by his momentum as he tripped over her motionless companion and sprawled helplessly onto the floor. For a moment, it seemed as though the dwarf's reprieve had been but temporary, but with an angry stamp, the woman wheeled away and turned back on the rising Torsheid.

"Don't kill the dwarf!" she cried out echoingly. "It wants us to; I can feel it! So don't kill him!"

Torsheid was roaring as he staggered back to his feet. "Stupid wench!" he screamed out. "I'm going to—"

But he got no further. For in that instant, the woman's eyes flared anew. Wheeling on the barbarian, she lunged forwards with shocking speed, her elegant sword lancing smoothly forwards as it plunged straight through Torsheid's heart.

The barbarian gaped for a moment as bloody froth bubbled through his lips. He stared at the sudden, victorious laughter that danced from the lips of his killer.

"I'm nobody's wench!" she declared fiercely. "And there'll be no battle glories for you!"

The gasping barbarian glared at her through desperate eyes. "Not for me!" he choked out, spitting blood from his crimson-stained lips. "But I have...another brother...to avenge me!"

And then, with a final cough, his eyes rolled and he slumped backwards off her blade and lay still.

The woman stared down at the barbarian's corpse with something akin to chagrin on her face.

"Oh, you cheating bastard!" Roderick heard her hiss.

"Ummm...excuse me?"

At the deferent exclamation, Roderick turned sharply to find Prince Tretaptus staring up at him with his head cocked to one side and an eyebrow raised. His sword was raised but not in motion, as though frozen halfway through a thrust.

"Hello!" he greeted with an awkward little smile. "Me again! Sorry to intrude on your point of view and all but...weren't we having a fight?"

"Why didn't you just clobber him, you idiot?" The gasping shout came from the other soldier, who was still slumped in a heap on the far side of the glade. He had drawn his sword at some point and seemed to be having some manner of battle with himself about what he was supposed to do with it. "He wasn't even looking!"

Tretaptus looked genuinely affronted. "That would hardly be gentlemanly, now would...ah!"

The prince managed to raise his sword just in time to deflect Roderick's attack, but it was a close-run thing. He ducked under the swing, back flexing as the blade missed his nose by less than half an inch. Roderick could hear pounding footsteps as the woman soldier hurtled to her ally's aid, but yet again, Gort flew at her with fury, hammer raised in a hopeless charge. Almost delicately, however, the woman sidestepped his advance and, rather than cutting him savagely down as might have been expected, she simply lashed out with a hearty kick on the rump that sent him reeling.

"I'm not going to kill you!" Roderick heard her cry. "So just push off!"

"Still fighting!" Tretaptus's voice cut through as his sword blade bounced off the knight's shoulder plates, denting the metal harshly. "Please do pay attention! It's almost rude!"

But in spite of the fight, it was still Gort's reeling figure that captured Roderick's eye. The dwarf seemed unable to catch his balance as he staggered in an ungainly lurch across the narrow glade to where the other soldier had just stumbled to his feet, his eyes tight shut and body tense and shaking as he battled against some unseen foe.

"I won't!" Roderick heard him stammer. "I won't, I won't, I..."

His arm lashed out, puppet-like, almost of its own accord. The sword blade gleamed.

And Gort, lost and without control, had no chance to avoid the blade.

With one harsh sweep, the dwarf fell in a flash of blood and dropped into horrible stillness.

"Oh bugger!" The exclamation came from the woman. "Shoulders, just sit down!"

"I can't!" The other soldier's cry was almost a wail in response to the nonsense statement as he jerked in an ungainly circle, limbs flailing. "I can't, I can't, it won't let me!"

Suddenly, a tremendous blow crashed down onto the top of Roderick's helmet, driving him to his knees as his ears rang and lights danced before his eyes. He looked up into the distinctly miffed-looking face of Prince Tretaptus.

"Now, really, look what you made me do!" The admonishment was supposed to be stern, but it was about as forceful as being spanked by a puppy. "I've tried to be patient and polite about this, but it's not on! If we're going to have a fight, the least you could do is pay attention!"

His blade lashed out, catching Roderick's sword and knocking it fluidly to the ground just out of reach. "I've tried to be courteous, I really have!" he declared as the woman, after a brief anxious look in the other soldier's direction, rushed over to join him. "I was trying for a fair fight! But I can see your mind isn't on this, so I'm sorry, but I'm just going to have to finish it now!"

"Kill him!" the woman demanded as she closed the last few yards between them. "Stop being so damned nice and do it, dullard! This is an emergency!"

"I know!" The prince pulled a reluctant face. "I just didn't see the need to be rude about it....”

Roderick's gauntleted fist lashed out, driving into Tretaptus's stomach. The prince staggered back gasping, but the woman was already there, her sword raised and her expression grim as she swung around in a killer blow...

“No!”

The bushes erupted and, with a hearty crack, spat out Erik and his steed.

Tretaptus's face dropped. “Oh no, not aga—ah!”

With a cry of frustration, both the woman and the prince were hurled off their feet by some invisible sledgehammer blow, tumbling backwards to land in an ungainly heap beside the unconscious form of their companion. Both battled at once to rise, but even as Erik yearned that they should not, it seemed as though unseen bonds enfolded them and pinned them in place.

Erik's eyes raked over the horror-filled glade. What was happening here? He could see his friend Roderick staggering to his feet as he snatched up his fallen broadsword from the leaf litter where both Gort and Zahora were slumped with agonising stillness. And there was another figure too, an impossible figure, for how could Halheid's body come to be lying here and not in its high mountain grave?

He could see that three enemies had fallen. Treacherous Prince Tretaptus and the woman dressed in chain mail and the livery of Sleiss still lay pinned and struggling next to the foul Sleiss soldier who had tried so hard to part Princess Islaine's head from her shoulders in the fortress of his lord. Thankfully someone had made a fine job of staving in his head and he showed no sign of waking. And as for the fourth...

But Sir Roderick had seen him too, for that last chain-mailed figure continued to reel and stagger as though drunken, swinging his sword randomly through the air as he muttered and struggled against some vicious, unseen foe.

“I don't want to surrender!” Erik heard him stammer. “I'm not throwing down my sword! Get off me! Get off!”

Roderick was moving swiftly now, sword lifted, expression set and cold. Relieved now from the traitor Tretaptus's assault, the knight gathered speed as he charged at this enemy and spun upon his heel, the great blade lifting, singing, soaring as he heaved it in a mighty arc towards the staggering soldier's throat.

"Shoulders!" Tretaptus screamed inexplicably, struggling desperately against his invisible bonds. "Look out!"

But it was too late. With one awesome slice of the dreaded broadsword, the soldier's head was sent flying.

For a moment, the body seemed to continue to stagger, almost as if it were unaware that its most important appendage had just hurtled away into the bushes. But then, with an almost audible sigh, the chainmailed torso folded and slumped to the floor.

And then, from the bushes into which the head had vanished, came a long and echoing scream.

Erik gasped as his heart pounded at the sound of a cry he would know anywhere.

Islaine!

Distantly, he heard Tretaptus gasp too. "But she was out cold!" he exclaimed, even as the bushes erupted once more, this time gloriously expelling a mass of blonde hair and a slender, beautiful figure cloaked in sodden blue velvet. Islaine's hands and ankles were bound but had not, it seemed, stopped her from rolling down the slight incline from her hiding place into the glade, her pale face flushed and her dress splattered with fresh blood. A moment later, the loose head of the beheaded soldier rolled gently down the slight slope and spun to a halt beside her.

"He landed in my lap!" Erik heard her cry in desperate distress. "Right in my lap! He blinked at me!"

He could restrain himself no longer. He had to cry out.

"Princess Islaine!" he exclaimed.

Her eyes flashed up. She stared at him.

And for a brief, inexplicable instant, it seemed to him as though her eyes had filled with horror.

Erik fought down a surge of distress. Well, she did not know him. She had no reason to...

"Don't move!"

The voice echoed from the far side of the glade. Erik's head shot up. He stared.

The Sleiss soldier, the brute from the execution whom Erik had earlier discounted, was on his feet. In spite of the throbbing head wound that should have negated any hint of consciousness for some considerable time to come, he showed no sign of distress or disorientation. In one hand, he was holding a small velvety pouch that he had just lifted from the restrained form of the woman soldier. His expression was one of raw, grim determination.

"No one move!" he repeated, throwing the admonishment at Sir Roderick, who had half-started towards the princess. Behind Erik, the bushes parted a final time to reveal the breathless forms of Elder and Slynder. Their party was at last complete.

"Why should we listen to you?" Elder's hand was extended; Erik could only assume it was he who held Tretaptus and the woman pinned in place. "My magic can crush you in an instant, dog!"

"But I have magic too!" With a jerk of one hand, the soldier emptied the little pouch onto the palm of his hand to expose a small, glistening object that seemed almost to set the light around it dancing...

A ring. It was a ring.

"The Ring of Anthiphion!" Slynder breathed the words in shock, his hands grasping his dagger hilt. "You have it!"

"Surrender the Ring and we will consider letting you live!" Elder's voice was a tower of thunder. "It is of no use to you!"

"But it's magic, right?" The soldier's hand was shaking but his face remained stubborn. "And everyone here knows and believes it's magic. That's how magic works."

"Your nonsense talk will not spare you." Whole armies would have fled from the look in Elder's eyes. "Give me the Ring!"

The soldier pinched the Ring between two fingers as he lifted it into the air. "Everyone knows it's magic," he repeated softly. "That's it. I believe it too. And I believe that if I want, I can use the magic in this Ring to pick up me, my friends, and the princess and drop us in the wild forest, far away from all of you."

"You cannot wield the Ring!" Elder snapped, but Erik could hear the slight tremble of uncertainty beneath his tone. The soldier heard it too.

"You're worried!" he exclaimed. "You're not sure! You think I might be able to do it! And do you know what?" He grinned, impulsive, triumphant. "I think that's all I need. Because I, my friends, and the princess are going to the wild forest! Right now!"

Light blazed like fire across the clearing as the Ring burst alive with scarlet flames. Erik caught one last glimpse of the soldier's face as he whooped with triumph and then the light was...

...gone

For a brief, everlasting moment, all Fodder could do was stare at the sky. Not that there was much sky to be seen, brief cloudy glimpses between twisting, gnarled limbs and finger-like shattered branches that clawed at the air above him. But he stared at it nonetheless, his breath rising and falling, his head itching and tickling from the Narrative damage done by the impact of Thud's boot, his neck still disconcertingly loosened. But none of that mattered.

Because the Narrative light was gone.

And he knew these trees. He was in the Wild Forest. And the soft breathing he could hear nearby told him that he wasn't there alone.

He'd done it.

He'd done it.

He wasn't entirely sure how he'd managed to wake. Such a severe Narrative wound should have left him unconscious for hours as long as the light lingered. But he'd been able to hear his friends struggling, battling without him, losing, and he'd been so desperate to help them that somehow he'd fought his way back through the demand he stay unconscious, back to a wakefulness he shouldn't have been able to achieve. And then...

He'd *done magic.*

Magic was a Narrative conceit. He knew that. His thoughts from the night before had surged back into his head, and he'd finally grasped the idea he'd groped towards before. It worked because the characters *believed* it worked, and The Narrative made anything they believed possible. And even though he'd wondered, even though he'd doubted, those around him had doubted too and with the Ring in his hands, that had just been enough....

"Did that just...*work?*" Flirt's voice drifted in, bewildered, from somewhere to his right.

"He used Narrative belief." Dullard's response from over to Fodder's left sounded awestruck. "He turned The Narrative against itself. That's *genius.*"

"Could…" The high-pitched, faltered sentence came from somewhere beyond Fodder's feet. Pleasance's voice sounded both harrowed and flustered. "Could someone please…be so good…as to get this…*thing*…out of my lap?"

That didn't sound promising. Slowly, carefully, Fodder pushed himself up to a sit. Curly-haired and dishevelled and grasping her sword, Flirt appeared to one side. Dullard gently pulled himself to his feet and loped the couple of yards past the headless and twitching chain-mailed body to where Princess Pleasance sat, bound and staring down at the blond and bloody head of Shoulders the Disposable, which lay nestled in her velvet skirts. Her lip was quivering with a mixture of distress and fury.

As Fodder and Flirt approached, Dullard carefully lifted the detached head away from the whimpering princess, cradling it cautiously beneath the ears.

Fodder bent down and stared into the unshaven face.

"Shoulders?" he said softly.

Shoulders's eyes snapped open. He stared straight back.

"You okay, mate?" Fodder queried softly. "How are you feeling?"

Shoulders stared at Fodder for a brief moment longer. His eyes darted across to where Flirt was watching with her lips twisted, to Dullard's long fingers grasping his cheeks, and to Pleasance's horrified expression. And then finally, inevitably, his eyes alighted on the stumbling form of his body as it staggered and wheeled, without the aid of attached direction, to its feet.

He blinked.

"Naaarrrrghhhhh!!!!" he said.

TO BE CONTINUED IN … *The Merry Band*

www.ThinklingsBooks.com
Facebook.com/ThinklingsBooks
@ThinklingsBooks

Thinklings Books started out when three speculative-fiction-loving professional editors—Jeannie Ingraham, Deborah Natelson, and Sarah Awa—got together and formed a writing group. We called ourselves the Thinklings, in honor of C.S. Lewis and J.R.R. Tolkien's group, the Inklings.

Over time, we found ourselves agonizing more and more about how messed up the publishing industry had become. Why couldn't good books get published? Why were so many bad books published just because their authors had big Twitter followings? We wished there were something we could do about the problem . . . and then we realized there was.

As a developmental editor, a substantive/line editor, and a proofreader, the three of us knew good writing when we saw it—and we knew how to make it even better. We had a lot of experience walking our clients through the publishing process—both traditional and self-publish—and we had contacts with marketing and design experts. We had some amazing unpublished books lined up and ready for production. We had, in fact, everything we needed to make a great publishing company. All that was left was to actually do it.

So we're doing it.

Spectacular Reads. Every Time.

I will win. I have to.

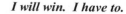

My plan was to keep my head down, do my job, bring endless rounds of coffee to my genius boss. But see, I have this thing about bullies. Doesn't matter who they are—evil fairies, ravenous demons, powerful traitors, or my own family. The moment they try to enslave my brothers, murder my king, and fold up my boss like a literal hand towel, they're my enemies.

I don't have magic. I don't have power. I don't even have much money. But as long as I have a brain and a will, there's nothing I won't do to save the people and the country I love.

So bring it on.

Bargaining Power by Deborah J. Natelson

One bite on her hand…a million problems slipping through her fingers.

After a wild animal attack, Melanie Caldwell thinks she just needs to go to the doctor. Then she's kidnapped on the day of the next full moon, and discovers in the worst way that monsters are real…and that she has become one of them.

All Melanie wanted was to get a boyfriend and graduate college. Now she has to deal with agonizing monthly transformations, a secret organization stalking her, friends and enemies trying to discover her secret, and hunters looming on the horizon.

Hunter's Moon by Sarah M. Awa

Immeasurable imagination. Unmitigated magic.
Spectacular style.

The clockwork man is crafted, to begin with—commissioned by that terrible tyrant Time to serve as her slave for all eternity. His brain boasts balance wheels and torsion springs; he can wind himself up with a key in his side; and, most importantly, his gyroscopic tourbillon heart glimmers with pure diamond.

He is a living being and he is art, and he refuses to remain a slave forever. He therefore slips through Time's fingers as the Sands of Time slip through the cracks of reality (at least, when the time cats aren't using them as a litter box).

Among astounding adventures, despite harrowing hardships, and in between escaping interfering enchanters, the clockwork man seeks his imagination, his purpose, and his name.

The Land of the Purple Ring by **Deborah J. Natelson**

Beware of Spilling Ink

Skate is a thief, trained and owned by the local crime syndicate, the Ink. When she tries to burgle a shut-in's home, she gets caught by the owner—a powerful undead wizard. He makes a deal with her: "borrow" books from other wizards in return for a place to stay.

Caught between her growing fondness for the wizard and her past with the crime syndicate, Skate doesn't know where her loyalties lie. But she'd better figure it out, because there's a new player in town, one whose magical hypnotism puts them all at risk.

Skate the Thief by **Jeff Ayers**

Technology Hates Janet

After she accidentally smashes a floatcar through City Hall, the bureautopia sentences Janet to captaining the starship S.S. *Turkey* and its misfit crew. Her mission: to boldly rescue a prisoner from the one corner of the universe colder than her ex-boyfriend's heart—Pluto. Which, aside from not even being a real planet, is the one place in the universe where chocolate is illegal.

In between studying The Space-Faring Moron's Guide to Common Science Fiction Plot Devices, falling for a rival captain's boyfriend, and avoiding unnecessary time travel, Janet has a chance to save two worlds . . . or doom them to permanent chocolatelessness.

The Cosmic Turkey by **Laura Ruth Loomis**

True Love vs. Ancient Curses

When the Egyptology department needs funds to offset a recent spate of museum thefts, Theodora Speer grudgingly trades her painting smock for an evening gown. Charming donors isn't usually her idea of a good time—but then, she doesn't usually get to meet handsome and mysterious men like Seth Adler.

Seth Adler is desperate to get close to a very specific Egyptian mummy, and attending a fundraising gala seems just the ticket. He doesn't expect to meet Theo, refreshing in her honesty and intriguing him against his will . . . and he definitely doesn't expect her to interfere with his plans.

Frantic to escape before the police catch up, Seth kills himself in front of Theo. Except it turns out he's not so dead after all, and it's up to Theo to keep him that way. Even if it means fleeing the police, practicing ancient Egyptian magic, and confronting the real thief.

Painter of the Dead by **Catherine Butzen**

About the Author

Katherine Vick was born in the middle bit of England longer ago than she'd care to admit (1979, if you must know. Aren't you nosy?). She studied geography at the University of Wales, Aberystwyth, writing her dissertation on the role of landscape and culture in fantasy novels. She then moved on to a master's degree in literary studies and creative writing at the University of Central England, where she wrote the dissertation that inspired the creation of Fodder, so she hopes you'll feel she put her education to good use. She flirted briefly with fast food and retail work before settling down as a college administrator. She spends occasional weekends on historic battlefields in her capacity as a rather clumsy late-medieval reenactor. She (mis)spent a part of her youth writing stories based around other people's literary and media creations. She likes to read and watch fantasy, history, and science fiction—frankly, anything that gets her away from the real world, which is far too much trouble. Occasionally she even gets around to writing stuff.

You can visit Katherine at
https://realmofkatherinevick.blogspot.com/

Made in the USA
Monee, IL
08 November 2021